Praise for

The Silent Girls

"*The Silent Girls* is Vermont's own *True Detective*. Eric Rickstad masterfully renders Frank Rath, a PI and single father who's been beat up and beat down but never backs off. Three-dimensional characters, a moody rural-noir vibe, and a compulsively readable story make this a stunner of a crime novel!"

Steve Ulfelder, Edgar®-finalist author of *Wolverine Bros.*
Freight & Storage

"Eric Rickstad's *The Silent Girls* is a bone-chilling mystery set in one of New England's darkest corners, the kind of place travelers are well-advised to avoid after nightfall. This well-crafted book will have you staying up late, turning pages and afraid to turn off the light."

Paul Doiron, author of *The Poacher's Son*

"Finely drawn characters, a narrative that beguiles and surprises, and stark, poetic writing make for a novel as dark and brooding as its rural Vermont setting. *The Silent Girls* is both an exceptional detective story and a terrifying meditation on good and evil."

Roger Smith, international best-selling author of
Wake Up Dead, *Dust Devils*, *Mixed Blood*, and *Sacrifices*

"*The Silent Girls* is a thrilling ride to very dark places. I kept turning pages, scared of what I'd find but compelled to look. It'll keep you reading all the way up to its shattering conclusion."

Jake Hinkson, author of *Hell On Church Street* and *The Big Ugly*

A beautifully written literary thriller. A dark, page-turning, up-all-night story by a great novelist.

Tyler McMahon , author of *Kilometer 99*

Instantly elevates the rural noir genre. Every bit the novel of *Winter's Bone* (a favorite). You will be hard pressed to set it aside until you reach the shocking final page.

Drew Yanno, author of *In the Matter of Michael Vogel*

Lie in Wait

A brilliantly crafted crime novel. *Lie in Wait*'s whiplash pacing and disturbing psychological profiles will grip readers until its startling conclusion.

Lisa Turner, Edgar®-nominated author of *The Gone Dead Train*

Another gem. Rickstad has invented his own genre, and *Lie in Wait* ups the game. Gripping. Deft. Unexpected. Surprising. Readers will be glad he took them on this ride.

Drew Yanno, author of *In the Matter of Michael Vogel*

A flawless mystery, brilliantly told, with a twisted, spiraling plot that gets under your skin and sends your nerves into overdrive.

Classic Book Reader

Also by Eric Rickstad

Reap
The Silent Girls

Lie in Wait

A Novel

ERIC RICKSTAD

WITNESS

An Imprint of HarperCollins*Publishers*

Excerpt from *The Silent Girls* copyright © 2014 by Eric Rickstad.

LIE IN WAIT. Copyright © 2015 by Eric Rickstad. All rights reserved. Printed in the United States of America. No part of this book may be used or reproduced in any manner whatsoever without written permission except in the case of brief quotations embodied in critical articles and reviews. For information, address Harper-Collins Publishers, 195 Broadway, New York, NY 10007.

HarperCollins books may be purchased for educational, business, or sales promotional use. For information, please e-mail the Special Markets Department at SPSales@harpercollins.com.

FIRST EDITION

ISBN 978-0-06-242477-8

16 17 18 19 20 ID/RRD 10 9 8 7 6 5 4 3 2 1

For my lovely wife, Meridith

Lie in Wait

PART I

Chapter 1

VICTOR JENKINS STARED into the fire outside Jed King's sugar shack, praying for strength.

Lester Graves, a local, and Daryn Banks, from New Hampshire, stood across from him, both men praying silently as well. Good people. Godly people, Jenkins thought.

Each man wore a plaid shirt and blue jeans and steel-toed work boots. Victor had bought his boots earlier that day at Payless. Though he'd rubbed the boots with dirt to dull the virgin leather's sheen, they remained too tight and gave him blisters. The other two men's boots were well trod with beaten leather toes through which a hard steel shone.

"Them toes'll put a hurt on you," Jed King barked as he powered over to the men from out of the darkness. He clapped a big hand on Victor's shoulder, squeezed too hard, until it ached.

King polished off his can of beer, belched, crumpled the can, and lobbed it into the fire heaped with dead soldiers. He grabbed a fresh beer from a cooler, cracked it, blew foam from the top, and swigged it. Licked his handlebar mustache.

"Follow me," he ordered.

The three men followed, Victor trailing behind.

King stalked around the back of the shack to an old woodshed. A motion-sensor light flicked on to illuminate the side of the shed with the brightness of daytime. Victor started at the sudden, accusatory light. King took the term "king of my castle" to heart and protected his homestead with the latest technology. The motion-sensor lights were just one example. He also had game-trail cameras hidden along his drive and at the boundaries of his tightly posted property. The cameras took video and still pics of anyone who trespassed. Victor knew this because Victor had put the cameras out at King's behest.

At times, Victor thought King's thoroughness bordered on paranoia; but he understood it. In this day and age a man could never be too careful when performing God's work. Tonight was such a night. Jenkins was impressed with King and his commitment to an unpopular but noble cause. Jenkins prayed silently for the strength he knew was required.

King fished a mess of keys from his Dickies and unlocked the padlock on the woodshed door.

Inside the shed, propped against the back wall, lay a pile of signs stapled to tomato stakes. King grabbed a sign, picked up a hammer, and took them outside, where he pounded the stake deep into the ground, as if driving it into the heart of a vampire.

He straightened the sign and stepped back to read it:

TAKE BACK VERMONT

"Nice," Graves said.

King crossed his arms over his chest as though studying a work of art. His animal biceps stretched his T-shirt, and his *18:22* tattoo bulged on his forearm.

"Load 'em up," he commanded.

Victor loaded his signs and a hammer into the backseat of his wife's rusted Cavalier, the trunk too full of sports equipment to fit the signs. Done, he loaded King's signs and hammer into the back of King's brand-new Chevy Extended Cab. King did all right for himself; Victor had to admire it. King would never know what it was like when mothers wagged fingers and threatened you whenever you told them their boys weren't good enough to make the football or baseball team. King didn't know the words *career* or *salary*. He worked for himself. Took orders from nobody, save God, whom he feared and obeyed. He had a crude way about him, surely, which led to his being a widely misunderstood man by secularists and those whose interpretation of the Bible was lax.

"King'd never kowtow to those mothers," Victor often said to Fran when faced with a mother's inevitable vitriol each sport season.

"And Jed King's twice divorced," Fran'd say. "How is that a man of God? And not even his kids can stand him, I hear. You're more a man than he'll ever be."

Dear, sweet Fran. Vic's true ballast. Long ago she, and the Lord, had saved him. She'd never know just how much. Bless her.

"*Vic*," King barked from inside the shed. "Quit daydreaming and get in here."

Victor hurried inside.

King stood at a card table, on which a large map of the town of Canaan was laid out before him.

"The end of the abominations of this state starts tonight. We can no longer permit this to stand," King announced. He glanced at Vic. "The only thing my ex-wives and I agree on. This erosion of morality. My first ex and I try to teach our boy what's right and he's *bullied*. Not just by students. By teachers, the principal, forcing their agenda."

"Jesus," Graves said, softly, with reverence.

"Jesus has got nothing to do with their devil's handiwork," King said. "My boy brings in a book on deer hunting for show-and-tell and the teachers scream 'cruelty to animals!' But they push *their* books about two dads down my son's throat, and I can't say squat. I have to *tolerate* it. You wanna sin in your bedroom, you wanna warp your own kid at home? I can't stop you. But don't go making it part of the school I help fund, then take away the stuff's that's been there forever, like celebrating Christmas."

"It's the same in New Hampshire," Banks said.

Victor nodded. "My son got scolded for *getting* Valentines, because other kids' feelings got hurt. Being popular isn't allowed these days. Kids can't pass Valentines out anymore."

"How is your boy?" Graves asked.

"Blessed," Victor beamed. "But he works hard for that blessing. Home alone now, nose buried in his playbook so—"

"We all know all about your golden boy," King said. He jabbed a finger on the map, chugged beer and tossed the can in the trash. "Let's get this done."

"I'd like to pray first," Victor said and bowed his head and prayed again, openly this time, for the resolve needed to carry each man through the test before him.

Chapter 2

THE BABY WAS finally asleep and Jessica Cumber, forever restless and in need of busying herself, decided to wash a load of laundry before the Merryfields returned home. They wouldn't be long. Mr. Merryfield had been sick with the bug going around, and tonight was his first night out in a week.

Jessica worshipped Mr. Merryfield. Secretly, of course. He was so mature. Jessica found maturity very attractive. Plus, Mr. Merryfield was a *star*. He was on TV practically all the time because of The Case.

Kids at school, *teachers even*, pressed Jessica every day for info on the Merryfields and The Case. Jessica didn't know thing one about it and, would never ever betray Mr. Merryfield even if she did. Though sometimes, she had to admit, she enjoyed the attention and would give the impression she had some insight into The Case.

As she climbed the creamery's elegant staircase, her stomach bubbled. She hoped she wasn't getting the bug. In a town as small as Canaan, sickness spread swiftly.

Jessica stood atop the stairs, clutched the mahogany post to steady herself and peer over the banister. She was positively mad about the wooden staircase, its graceful curvature stretching toward the palatial foyer below. Light from the full moon outside lit the entrance door's windows and pooled on the marble floor, the marble quarried by young local men now a hundred years dead. Iron radiators clanked and hissed. Jessica shivered. She imagined the plumbing as the creamery's circulatory system, the coursing water its hot foaming blood.

Jessica slipped off her sneakers and padded shoeless down the hallway, trailing her arms out to the side, fingernails rattling on the wainscoting.

At the master bedroom's doorway, she drummed her fingernails on the doorjamb, then, with a dramatic flourish, flipped the light switch. Ta-da! Each time she did this, she couldn't help but marvel at the *enormity* of the room. Her mother's entire trailer would fit inside this one bedroom. The ceiling, which rose so high you'd need a ladder just to change a lightbulb, still had its original pressed ornamental tin and was trimmed with a white crown molding so glossy you'd think the paint was still wet. Decades' worth of paint had been stripped from the wainscoting to reveal mahogany beneath. Jessica knew these details because Mrs. Merryfield had made Jessica privy to them the first time she'd given Jessica the tour and interviewed her for the job; the whole time Jessica had been praying and praying she'd get the chance to babysit in *this* house. For this man and his family.

Now, here she was.

A dream come true.

When Jessica had told her mother about the grand old home, her mother had said, "I wouldn't know how to live in such a place."

"I'd *learn*," Jessica had proclaimed.

Jessica tiptoed over to the sleigh bed, the carpet's lush pile squashing beneath her bare toes, cool and cushiony as a fresh bed of moss. The edge of the mattress rose to her rib cage. The frame was carved from the same wood as the wainscoting— manly, though the bedding, the duvet, was fluffy and flowery: *trés feminine*. Recently, Jessica had become taken with all things provincial. One day she would go to Provence. She was saving her babysitting money for it, and for college, of course. And veterinary school after that.

Jessica had lain on the sumptuous duvet just once. Briefly, and against her better judgment, with her beau.

Beau.

Oh. She liked the sound of that! So refined. So mature. Even if her beau, in reality, wasn't either of those things.

When she'd lain in the bed that one time she'd felt like Goldilocks who'd found the bed that was *just right*. She hadn't wanted to ever get up.

Jessica started across the room to retrieve the Merryfields' laundry in the master bath. As she paused to view herself in the dressing mirror, she heard what sounded like the entrance door opening and clicking shut in the foyer.

Hot water gurgled in the radiators.

Jessica cocked her head.

Silence throbbed in her ears.

She stepped into the hallway and looked over the rail.

The radiators clanked.

The front door was unlocked, as was every front door in Canaan. This was Vermont after all.

The radiators quieted. The old creamery fell as still as a monastery.

"Hello," Jessica said, her voice echoing in the marble foyer.

The house did not answer.

The *baby*, Jessica suddenly thought, panicked. Something's wrong. Jessica felt it, queasiness rising from her belly to burst acidic in her throat.

She raced down the hall to the baby's room and stood at the doorway, breathless. Her heart fluttered behind her tiny ribs.

Not a peep came from the room.

Jessica tiptoed to the crib, frightened, not bothering with the light switch.

At the crib, she drew a deep breath and looked down.

The crib lay empty. The baby was gone. She knew it. As her eyes adjusted to the blackness, she saw, there in the low light, in the crib, beneath a mobile of prancing antelope, baby Jon, perfectly still, and breathing. Sleeping.

"Oh," Jessica said and sagged with relief against the crib. "Oh. Thank you. God." Jessica kissed her fingertips and touched them to baby Jon's hot forehead. She returned to the top of the stairs and stared at the unlocked front door.

"No one's here," she whispered to the empty house. She remembered her mother saying, "You can't make an old place like that new again. No matter how you pretty it up. It's always going to be drafty. Moaning all night. Haunted."

Jessica returned to the master bedroom.

A cold draft edged along the floor. Jessica shivered, wishing now for her shoes. With the new coldness, the duvet seemed all the more inviting. She could take a nice doze and neaten it afterward, she reasoned. Who would know? She sank her hand into the duvet and hoisted herself onto the bed. As she lay down, something dug into her side. She felt around the comforter and pulled out a hard plastic object. A woman's aid. She dropped it as if stung by a wasp, and sat up.

A month ago, her beau had shown her a Web site on Mr. Merryfield's laptop. The site sold all shapes and sizes of women's aids. When Jessica had used this term and told her beau to get out of the site, he'd called her a prude. "You're naïve," he'd said. "But I'll corrupt you yet. I bet the Merryfields have sex toys stashed all over the place."

"I hate that term 'toy,' " she'd said. "And the Merryfields aren't like that."

"We're all like that," he'd said.

She'd wanted to protest, but he was more versed in these things. That was part of his draw, wasn't it? His age? His experience? And the secrecy because of it.

For a moment, Jessica wondered if the noise she'd heard earlier had been him, slipping in the house. Had he waited for her to check the baby, then planted the aid in the bed and sneaked out, just to prove a point? He was always pulling pranks like that. He *always* had to be *right*. It was like a sickness with him. And he liked to scare people. Jessica, especially. He had a weird side to him that way. He got a real kick from it. Scaring her. Who did stuff like that? No one liked to be scared. But, the more scared she was, the harder he laughed. Sometimes, she realized, age did not equate to maturity; especially when it came to the male gender. Still, she loved him.

How she loved him.

Jessica had pushed him away that night, though, made him shut down Mr. Merryfield's laptop. She wasn't supposed to use it.

And soon he'd been kissing her. Whenever there was any silence between them, any downtime, he swooped in and kissed her, as if her silence were permission.

He'd ended up on top of her, then taken her downstairs to the couch. Again. His weight pressing. Her scent rising. She'd opened to him. Afterward, she'd felt guilty, as usual, like she'd let herself down, risked her whole future, veterinary school, a career working in equine breeding, her vacation home in *Provence*, all for a stupid selfish moment.

When the Merryfields' Land Rover had pulled up outside that night, the headlights swooping through the parlor, her beau had escaped out the side door just in time, the sensation of him still pulsing inside her when Mr. Merryfield strolled in the front door and asked, "Any trouble tonight?"

Jessica sighed now and extracted herself from the bed.

In the bathroom, she scrubbed her hands. She grabbed a load of laundry from the hamper and dumped it into a basket and lugged it out of the room.

As a precaution, hamper in tow, she called out over the stairway: "I'm coming down to do laundry! If you're down there and jump out at me, I swear to God, I *will* kill you."

Downstairs, she ducked low to avoid knocking her head on the beam above her as she managed the cellar steps, each stair creaking as if the nails would pull free and the treads collapse below her.

The old door behind her started to close, as it always did.

At the bottom, she had to stoop beneath beams and hurry to the corner before she lost light from above. She pulled a string that lit a lone ceiling bulb. The bulb oozed a sick yellow light that was quickly swallowed by the dark, windowless cellar. The stone foundation sweated and seemed to pulse in the dimness. The air was close and greasy and smelled of mold. The stone and dirt floor was slimy and cold on her bare feet. She saw a mouse, dead in a trap, bloated, its neck broken, eyes popped out of its skull. Jessica's mother was right: There was no way to make a place like this new again. Jessica ducked beneath support beams. Cobwebs caught in her hair. The Merryfields had had plans to turn the kitchen pantry into the laundry room, until plumbing problems had arisen.

It was no wonder the Merryfields preferred Jessica not bother with laundry down here, where you could see the crumbling stone foundation, cramped and damp as a grave, on which the glamorous house stood.

The washing machine and dryer sat at the center of the light-bulb's pathetic yellow stain. On the crooked wooden shelf above them sat an old radio. Jessica turned it on, cranking the knob to find an upbeat pop tune from a Montreal station.

A heap of dirty men's clothing sat on the dryer. She picked up a pair of Mr. Merryfield's dress pants from the pile, checked the pockets for change and pens. With care, she sprayed stain remover on chocolate smeared on the front of the pants until it was saturated properly, according to the directions on the can. She liked doing Mr. Merryfield's laundry. She liked to defeat stubborn stains. The more stubborn the stain, the sweeter the victory. She picked up one of Mr. Merryfield's shirts and brought it to her nose, closing her eyes as she inhaled.

The shirt smelled of his aftershave and of his cigar smoke, yes. But of him, too.

His body.

"Jon," she whispered.

She loved the sound of his name on her tongue.

Jon.

Her spine tingled to say it.

Jon.

She stuffed his pants and shirt into the machine, dumped in a precisely measured cup of detergent, shut the lid and started the machine on COLD.

She checked the dryer. The load in it was damp. She turned the dryer on to finish the load.

As she folded a shirt on the machine, she thought she heard a stair creak. Thought she saw a slice of light from above, as if the door to the upstairs had been opened. But it was hard to tell. She could see so little beyond her weak cone of light. The washing machine thumped. She returned to folding the shirt.

The noise came again. Jessica squinted into the darkness. Her blood felt hot. "Hello?" No reply came. "If that's you, say something. Don't scare me like this!"

Another noise came. The clearing of a throat?

Then. Nothing.

Her heart seized.

She needed to get out. Now.

Some animal instinct told her this: Get out of the house. Now. Run.

But to where? There was no escape up the stairs.

The bulkhead, her mind screamed.

As she moved swiftly toward the darkness where the bulkhead was, she smashed her forehead against a timber joist. A shattering of stars bloomed in her head. A hand grabbed her. She shrieked. She was spun around. A bright light shone in her eyes. She could not see beyond it. She looked down and tried to catch her breath as she saw the hammer held in the hand.

Chapter 3

"DAMN," JONATHAN MERRYFIELD groaned.

He removed his eyeglasses and pinched the bridge of his nose, set his glasses back on and shifted in the passenger's seat of the Land Rover as its headlights raked across the brick-and-ivy façade of the creamery.

"What is it?" Bethany said.

Jon shook his head, as if to rid a bad memory. "That kid." He sighed. "That *boyfriend*. Whoever he is. We're going to have to let her go." He moaned and hugged his stomach. Bethany killed the Rover's engine and headlights. The creamery windows fell black. She rested a palm on her husband's shoulder. "Feeling any better?"

"If by better you mean I don't feel like I am about to vomit all of my insides. No."

"Sorry I insisted we go," Bethany said and pulled her hand from the shoulder of her husband, who'd spent the end of their evening in the restaurant restroom. Suffering. She felt poorly for insisting they go out to dinner just because that's what they always did on Wednesday nights. Insisting was her nature: insisting on things that seemed imperative at their inception, vital and necessary—an urgency created out of the anxiety of wanting perfection, and afterward seemed so trivial. Often her demands involved events that even she did not want to attend, but felt she *should* attend. Jon always obliged, predictably. It infuriated her, his predictability. Why, for once, couldn't he stand up for himself and say, *No. We're not going out. I'm still sick.* They both could have stayed home and rested. Instead, he'd caved. How was a man who was so aggressive, commanding, manipulative, and steadfast in his thorny and taxing professional life so dithering in his personal life? It was as though he were two completely different men. And, by the way: When had she come to disdain the consistency and stability, the predictability, she'd worked most her adult life to obtain and had once claimed she'd wanted and even admired in a spouse?

"I'll talk to the girl," Bethany said. She had spotted the boy herself once, sliding off in the darkness a few weeks earlier. She'd spoken with Jessica about him. "You can have girlfriends over. But no more boys." Oh, how the poor girl's cheeks had reddened, as flush as if she'd been slapped across the face. "It won't happen again," Jessica had blurted, then crossed, actually crossed, her heart and hoped to die.

Bethany understood Jessica better than Jessica knew. Jessica would be shocked out of her panties to learn just how many boys Bethany had *entertained* in high school when she'd babysat, or while her parents had been out at yet another of their lousy, obligatory soirees, from which they inevitably returned pickled and bickering. One such Sunday, when Bethany's parents were off to get soused in Seer Sucker, her father's business partner, one for whom Bethany babysat, Mr. Alcott, had dropped by to find Bethany home alone basking bikini-clad beside the pool, her brain fuzzed from the beating sun and a half pitcher of her mother's gin and tonics already slipping around inside her. She'd turned seventeen, just the day before. "Why, Little Beth," Mr. Alcott had said and sat beside her on the edge of her chaise longue. "I see the cat's away." Bethany had adjusted her top, which was unstrung, and cupped her hand to her brow, eyeing him and glancing at his Carmen Ghia, parked in the driveway. She had felt the sweat bead on her upper lip. "Apparently," she'd said, rolling her tongue inside her mouth to taste the tart bite of lemon, the juniper of gin. Mr. Alcott had set his smooth, manicured hand on her tanned calf. "Care to go for a ride?"

The *ride* had lasted all summer.

She'd never told a soul. Not even Jon. If ever she prided herself on anything, it was her ability to keep secrets. It had served her well.

Bethany stepped out of the Land Rover and hurried around to assist Jon. His tie was slack around his neck. His shirt rumpled and untucked. His face shiny with perspiration.

Bethany escorted him up the front walk. Their motion activated the walkway lights. Bethany opened the front door and ushered her husband inside.

The baby was crying.

Bethany's heart registered the sound before her ears heard it.

No. Not crying.

Wailing.

The house was a riot of wailing. It reverberated throughout the creamery, *from* it. The terrible plaint of a baby abandoned.

Bethany envisioned Jessica servicing some pimply, groping boy while baby Jon shrieked. The little bitch. "Jessica!" Bethany hollered from the bottom of the staircase. She kicked off her Ferragamos and slung herself up the stairs two at a time, leaving Jon slumped on the edge of the deacon's bench, head in his hands. "Jessica!" Bethany cried again.

Baby Jon yowled so it seemed his tonsils would rupture in a mist of blood. The sound leeched the marrow from Bethany's bones.

Atop the stairs, Bethany ran down the hallway, bawling: "Jessica!"

Bethany burst into the baby's room. She threw on the light and raced to the crib. Little Jon. His scrunched and purple face was swollen and sopped. Bethany scooped him up, a feverish churn of legs and arms. She pressed him to her breast, stroked his head. "Shhhhh. It's all right. Mama's here. Shhh."

His screams diminished. Bethany took him downstairs, her pulse throbbing in her wrists. She hurried over to her husband. "Jon. Something's wrong."

Jon lifted his head from his hands, looking as though he might vomit; but he stood at the word *wrong*.

"Wrong?" he said. He touched the baby's shoulder, rubbed it with his fingertips.

"Jessica," Bethany said. "She isn't *here*."

"She has to be here," Jon said.

"I've been *shouting* for her. I checked the baby's room. She's not allowed to be in any of the other rooms upstairs, except the bathroom."

"She's not allowed to fuck boys on our couch either."

"You need to pull yourself together and do something."

Jon stepped past Bethany and began to climb the stairs, using the rail for support.

With baby Jon clutched to her breast, Bethany searched the kitchen, the study, the library, the dining room, the parlor, and the guest bedroom, where Jon slept of late; his deluge of work and his stomach bug keeping him sleepless. The bedroom was off-limits to Jessica, though who knew what anyone got up to in private? Bethany had certainly snooped around as a babysitter. As she strode across the living room, she stopped. The cellar door was open, just a hair. But it was normally shut tight unless someone was downstairs.

Baby Jon stirred in Bethany's arms. She balanced him and opened the cellar door. The sad yellow light of the cellar's single bulb died at the bottom of the stairs. Bethany felt an icy blade of guilt slice between her ribs. The radio was playing. Jessica was doing laundry. Since being caught with the boy—and despite Bethany insisting she need not bother—Jessica had taken to doing chores after Little Jon was in bed and Jessica's homework was finished. Jessica was downstairs now and had not heard Bethany and Jon come home over the sounds of the radio. The old stone foundation, the beams and trusses, the thick floors, they cut you off from the world. Bethany's one stipulation was Jessica take the baby monitor down there. But Bethany had forgotten it herself on plenty of occasions. Once, she'd come from the cellar to find baby Jon crying as if he were being held to a hot stove. How quickly she'd leapt to crucify the girl.

"Jessica," Bethany said, her voice bare of anger. "Jessica."

She descended the stairs.

With each step she called the girl's name.

With each step her voice pitched louder. "*Jessica.*"

JON MERRYFIELD WAS upstairs in the master bedroom, noting that the bedsheets were amiss, when he heard his wife howl.

Chapter 4

DETECTIVE SONJA TEST yanked her rattling Peugeot into the Merryfields' driveway and brought it to a lurching stop behind two cruisers.

Damn it.

The Vermont State Police were already on the scene, the cruisers parked at odd angles, doors left flung open as the police radios squawked, blue lights strobing in the black November night, turning the facade of the old creamery into a madman's funhouse.

Damn it.

She'd hoped she'd be first on the scene. She was last, apparently. Which meant she'd have to rely on others to fill her in on the details instead of seeing them firsthand and arriving at her own conclusions and theories. She did not like relying on others. Especially regarding crime scenes. Not that she'd been to a murder scene in her young career. And if her superior in the Canaan Police Department, Senior Detective Harland Grout, had not been in the hospital for an appendectomy, she'd not have been to this one either.

Test had still been in her old Dartmouth sweats when the call had come in. She'd just finished her daily 10k on her treadmill, the country roads of Canaan too dark and treacherous with blind curves to run at night. She didn't need to get struck by a car and left in a ditch like Stephen King. Besides, George and Elizabeth had been in bed, and Claude had not yet come home. What had been keeping him, she'd had no clue. It wasn't like him to be late and not to call. She'd phoned him several times and finally got him, to find the roads over the mountains from St. Johnsbury, where he'd been preparing for his exhibit, were perilous with black ice. There'd been no time to get her babysitter, who wasn't the most reliable anyway.

Test cranked the heater—if a fan that stirred cool air could be called a heater—then leaned back over her seat to hand her iPad to George. "You and Elizabeth can watch *Peppa Pig* or *Caillou*. Or play games your little sister likes. But no scary games to upset her. Got it?"

"Don't leave, Mama," Elizabeth whimpered from her car seat, her emotions ragged from being hauled out of a deep sleep and tossed into the car in a flurry of activity to get to the scene.

Test reached back to pinch Elizabeth's tiny chin between her thumb and finger. "Georgie will take care of you till Daddy comes. I'll be right up there." She pointed to the old creamery.

"When's Daddy coming?" Elizabeth whined. "I don't wanna be alone."

"Soon," Test said, not knowing if that was true or not. "And you're not alone. You have Georgie," she said, thinking, *What kind of mother leaves her kids in front of a murder scene on a cold Vermont night in a car with a crap heater?* But the only way she could be more irresponsible and heap more guilt upon herself would be to leave her kids sleeping alone in the house to possibly awaken without her there, or bring them inside the creamery to witness whatever gruesome scene awaited. "Georgie, take care of your little sister. And *no* scary games. *Peppa*, *Caillou*, or games your sister likes. That's it."

"They're boring," George said.

"You heard me."

Test hastily dusted her cheeks and nose with foundation that hid her freckles. She was partial to her freckles, but in a professional setting they projected a girlish image she believed undermined her authority in a mostly male world. She'd not bothered to change out of her sweats, or to shower, wanting to get here straightaway. She'd thrown on her coat and strapped on her sidearm, bundled up the kids and buckled them into the car. She wished now she'd taken the two minutes to change out of her sweats. If she was going to be late anyway, it would have been good to be dressed accordingly. Now, she'd have to keep on her long parka while in the house. She probably smelled ripe with sweat, too. It was less than professional, but arriving at a murder scene posthaste had trumped decorum. All that, and she was still last to the party. As much as she had felt she'd been breaking a land speed record while leaving, getting the kids out of the house always took exponentially longer than she imagined.

"Keep the doors locked," she said to George as she shut the door behind her and strode toward the house.

CRIME-SCENE TAPE, STRUNG across the boundaries of the yard, snapped in the November gust.

From the few houses down the dark street a ways from the old creamery, residents came out to stand on their porches and dead lawns. They gawked at the blue lights that splashed across the darkness, and stared at each other's shadowed faces as if to seek permission from one another to proceed.

Then, they advanced, in bathrobes and unzipped parkas tossed on over pajamas, slippers and barn boots—the attire of a weekday evening that stripped them of any hint of the varied standings or tastes that divided them by daylight.

Those who lagged began to hurry. They swung their arms with the exaggerated restraint of speed walkers, not wanting to appear as eager as they really were to discover whatever horror waited at the old creamery. They formed a line behind the yellow police tape as if waiting behind the velvet rope of a swank nightclub.

Test noticed a sign staked in the lawn: TAKE BACK VERMONT.

The sign made Test cringe. It was an insult to human rights, as she saw it. Others saw it as gospel. The original signs had been the ugly brainchild of opponents to the 2001 civil union passage, the historic and incendiary law that had ignited bigotry and a seething, divisive hatred in people across the state and across the country. Test had been at Dartmouth at the time, and some students whom she'd counted among her friends had reacted in ways that had frightened and disillusioned her. The law had also brought out a compassionate nature in folks from whom Test had least expected it. With the actual gay marriage bill now being hammered out, the Take Back Vermont signs had cropped up again, like poisonous weeds never fully eradicated.

For some people, the ashes of that time were being stoked into flames again by Jon Merryfield and his work on The Case.

As Test approached Officer Larkin at the door, she wondered how he had managed to get here so soon and be so put together in his patrol uniform on a night she knew he had off from duty. It made her look bad. Then again, Larkin, with his boyish face and lank body, lived in the village, and not a half hour away in the hills as Test did. And he was single, with no sleepy kids or absentee husband.

As Bethany nodded at Larkin, the Canaan County ambulance pulled into the drive. Its lights were off, which meant one thing: The victim, Jessica Cumber, whose name Test knew from the updates on the police radio in her Peugeot, was dead.

Seeing the ambulance, those neighbors who had not yet reached the creamery raced toward it. They elbowed to join the crowd. A father perched his young daughter atop his shoulders as if they were watching a circus act. Behind them, two TV crew vans had set up, their harsh lights invading the darkness.

"Do me a favor?" Test said to Larkin, wishing she could retract what she'd just said. She was not used to being in command; however, with Grout MIA she needed to be assertive. She was not asking for an optional favor, she was giving a mandatory directive.

"Name it," Larkin said, shaking his head with disdain at the crowd.

"Bag and tag that sign in the yard," Test said.

"On it."

"And. Keep an eye on my car, the Peugeot," she said, trying not so appear as embarrassed as she felt.

"Of course, Detective."

"My two kids are in there. Make sure it stays that way?"

If he was taken aback by this revelation he concealed it expertly. "Yes ma'am, Detective Test."

TEST STEPPED INSIDE the home, even the soft soles of her Asics echoing in the vast marble entry. In the fireplace room off the foyer, Richard North, senior detective for the Vermont State Police, stood between John and Bethany Merryfield, both of whom looked like they'd just been washed ashore after a shipwreck.

North spotted Test and grimaced, then looked back to Jon Merryfield.

In her brief interaction with North, Test knew the state police detective as affable. But that interaction had been at a softball tournament fund-raiser, not a murder scene. She couldn't expect the same congenial man tonight. Especially since state police detectives defended their turf ardently. Even if Test had not been late, the investigation would still belong to the state police, with her in a subordinate and supportive role. Being late only made it more difficult for Test to gain entry into the inner fold of the investigation.

Test made room for two forensics technicians, both wearing surgical gloves, white paper booties, and hairnets, to pass by her with lighting equipment. One of them, a woman, barked at her: "If you plan to go any farther into the house, put the garb on." The woman nodded at a plastic tub containing booties, masks, and hairnets and strode away.

Test peered into the plastic tub. She glanced at North. He wore no hairnet, though he likely didn't require one. His hair was shorn severely tight. A mask hung backward behind his neck from its elastic band. She could not see from her vantage if he wore booties; but his hands, big hands, were gloved.

Test took a moment to put on the garb, letting the mask hang around the front of her neck, so she could speak to North.

Done, she waited for North to come over and brief her. When after several minutes he didn't extend the professional consideration, Test went to him.

As Test approached, North averted his eyes to the cellar stairs. Test could tell from the creases carved in his face by his scowl that whatever was down in that cellar was nasty. She'd not worked a murder scene. They were few and far between in Canaan.

She prepared herself by taking a slow deep breath through her nose; a technique she employed when running half marathons.

Her first homicide and she would work it—or support it, rather—alone.

"It's not pretty," North said to Test without saying hello or shaking her hand. Had he thought she'd think it would be pretty? Was he patronizing her? She was uncertain.

She disliked being uncertain even more than she disliked relying on others.

Under the circumstances, she was willing to give North the benefit of the doubt. For now.

"I don't expect it to be pretty," Test couldn't help saying, realizing too late that it may have come off as defensive. "I'd like to see."

"We've already seen it," North said. "I have. And the ME. Cause of death was a blow to the cranium. A hammer or pipe, likely. No weapon found." He tapped his forehead, between his eyes, with two fingers. "Right here."

"Ironic," Test said.

"What?" North dug a thumb between his belt and chinos, and Test noticed he'd hand-tooled a rough, extra hole in the black leather belt to accommodate his narrow waist. The time she'd seen him before, last summer, he hadn't had the build of the typical state police detective: that compact, bulldog's build that imposed a physical dominance on a subject and came in handy when approaching a car pulled over on a dark, lonely stretch of Vermont highway. No. North was tall but lean. In the several months since, he'd lost tremendous weight, and not in a good way. Test wondered if he was ill.

"What's ironic?" North repeated.

"The frontal lobe," Test said, touching her forehead. "It's the part of the brain that helps us decide between bad and good behavior."

"Hmm," North said, unimpressed or perhaps just confused.

"It allows us to imagine the future repercussions that might come from our present actions, so we can overcome our base urges," Test continued. "Something the doer obviously lacked."

"Hmm," North said. No mistake now. He was clearly unimpressed.

Test wished she hadn't said anything. Her own sticky, flypaper brain had a knack for snatching bits of factual flotsam out of the air as much as her tongue had a habit of then spouting those facts. At Dartmouth, she'd spewed inane and arcane facts with all the certitude and desire to astound that was shared by insecure undergrads everywhere. She still harbored a nostalgic embarrassment at the earnest girl she'd been, so desperate to be taken seriously that she'd mistaken reciting numbing facts as intelligence and subverted her own native intellect in the process.

These days she brought forth such facts only when useful to her police work, or when she was nervous or excited.

"I'd like to see the victim," Test pressed.

"As I said—"

"I recognize this is your case, Detective," Test said. "The state police's case. I respect and appreciate that. Still, this *is* my jurisdiction. My town. I live with these people. They're my neighbors. It's my duty to them to be involved and to help in whatever capacity I am able."

"In whatever capacity you are allowed," North corrected. "It is not your duty to be involved. It is at my discretion. Not that I don't welcome your assistance. I do. Ready?"

Test nodded, her fingers shaking.

North noticed. "Nervous? We all get that way our first few murders. Especially ones like this. It's normal."

Test wondered how normal North would think she was if she told him the truth: She wasn't nervous. She was excited. Senior Detective Grout's misfortune of being in the hospital was her good fortune.

"Be careful," North said, "follow closely."

As Test followed North toward the cellar stairs, she attempted to peer out a window to her car. But the glare on the windows from the lights inside returned a warped reflection of herself. She hoped Claude would be here soon to take the kids home. She had her cell phone on vibrate in her coat's pocket for when he called or texted, which she had expected him to do by now.

North shone his flashlight down the cellar stairway. A soft thumping came from the darkness, like the muted beat of a heart hidden beneath floorboards.

Thud. Thud thud.

North ducked his head and started down the stairs. Test placed her foot on the step gingerly, her heart knocking. As a young girl, she'd had an irrational fear of cellars. When her father would send her to their basement at night to retrieve a bottle of wine, she'd descend the stairs with a sense that someone, or something, was down there, lurking in the dark recesses, waiting to snatch her. She'd hurry down, search wildly for the bottle lying in its rack, then race back, certain she'd be grabbed before she got to the top stair. She'd outgrown the fear, of course. Now, however, it did not seem so irrational after all.

Thud. Thud thud.

At the bottom of the steps, North paused. From the cellar rose a bodily stench that polluted the nostrils and caught in the back of Sonja's throat. She felt overheated even as her skin felt clammy. Her excitement fled in a rush.

She placed a palm flat to an old beam, steadying herself. "Breathe," she whispered quietly, so North would not hear. "Breathe."

North turned as though he'd heard her. Rumor had it North was astute at sensing mood, could peg a person's true nature quickly. A quality trait in a detective, and one Test hoped to hone for herself.

North shone his flashlight at the floor and crouched. The ME's klieg lights were off, the skeletal metal legs of the several tripods looking alien. Why was North using just a flashlight? Test could barely see her own hands.

Thud.

North pointed. "See that?"

Test leaned over his shoulder, got a whiff of aftershave that reminded her of the hunk of cedar wood Claude put in his drawer. "No," she said.

"There." He pointed again.

"Yes," she said. She saw: The ghost of a boot print in the dirt on the stone floor. An evidence card marked #1 sat beside the print.

"Could be our man," North said.

Thud.

"What is that noise?" Test said.

North ignored her and trained the flashlight just ahead of the boot print.

"There," he said.

"Where?" Test said.

He pointed.

The delicate impression of a small bare foot. It, too, was marked with an evidence card: #2. A score of such cards pocked the way to the darkened corner.

North stepped off the bottom stair, avoiding the marked footprints. Slowly, he made his way past numerous cards, past the washer and dryer, until he almost disappeared in the darkness.

Thud.

The sound was coming from the dryer. Something thudding in it as it went around and around. What on earth was in there? Why had the detective left the dryer running?

Test picked her way toward North, squatted beside him.

The beam of his flashlight jabbed into the corner's crowding darkness.

"Why aren't the klieg lights on?" Test asked. She'd kept quiet as long as she had because she feared there was some obvious answer she could not comprehend and she'd look the fool for asking.

"This is how it was when I arrived," North said. "Just the light of that weak bulb."

Of course. He wanted to see it as it had been at the time of the murder.

Test's eyes followed the beam that cut through the darkness.

"No sign of a struggle," Test said.

North did not reply.

"What the hell is thudding in the dryer?" Test asked, unable to hold back.

"A pair of running shoes. Among men's clothes. Jon Merryfield says they're his shoes. He said it was like the girl to go overboard with chores, even though she was told not to concern herself with things other than child care. The machine has about ten minutes left. We found it with sixty-two minutes left, when we arrived at seven thirty. So, unless the killer decided to do laundry, if the dryer was set at the maximum ninety minutes, the victim was killed no earlier than six fifty."

The victim. Jessica Cumber. North's cold use of the term "the victim" unnerved her.

"See that," North said. "There."

She saw.

A foot. The pale soft foot of Jessica Cumber, the heel grimy with dirt.

A child's foot.

The other foot was not visible.

North worked the flashlight up, following a leg clad in jeans.

The other leg was bent beneath the body at a peculiar angle.

As North stood, his back cracked audibly.

He inched closer to Jessica Cumber. Test followed.

Jessica Cumber lay with her face against the grimy stone floor. An arm, like her leg, torqued beneath her body, so the shoulder looked dislocated. Test felt her own shoulder twitch.

"This is how we found her," North said. "Or close to it. We tried to put her back as she'd been when her photos were taken, and before the ME and I looked her and the surroundings over."

Jessica's hair was a pale strawberry blonde, cut at the nape of her neck. In her tiny earlobes were stuck simple silver stud earrings in the shapes of stars. The kind of earrings one found on assortment placards on turnstiles at every Rite Aid and Walmart.

North held the flashlight out to Test. "Keep it on her."

The flashlight was heavy. Its hatch-marked steel handle cold.

Test held it so the light shone on the back of Jessica's head.

North touched Jessica's shoulder gently, as if he intended to wake the child. Then, he took firm hold of the shoulder and turned Jessica over with a great show of courtesy and humility. Jessica rolled over like a log in water.

Test's throat clenched. She thought she'd prepared herself. But no one could be prepared for this. Test's world swam. At the academy five years prior, it had been pounded home for cadets to keep emotions in check, go numb to the violence. But they never told her *how* to go numb.

"Keep the light on her face," North said, curt. Test lifted the flashlight. She'd let it fall in her shock. Her mouth tasted metallic. Her throat burned. Dots of silver light glimmered in her vision.

"Sorry," she managed to whisper.

"It's OK."

Test had not been speaking to North. She'd been speaking to Jessica. She was sorry for her. Sorry that sorry changed nothing.

Jessica's forehead was obliterated. A gaping wreck of skull from which brain and a swamp of blood soaked the floor, turning it oily. Her face was no longer a girl's face but a bloated macabre caricature. Her eyes stared out at oblivion, fogged with death.

One blow. A heap of rage.

"Whoever did this despised Jessica," Test said.

"That's a leap." North grabbed the flashlight from Test, startling her. "There's no damned murder weapon," he said, swinging the flashlight to light dark crevices. He stood.

Test remained crouched. She touched Jessica's blood-splattered cheek, the girl's flesh like cold clay.

Not a girl anymore.

A body.

A corpse.

"Come on," North said. "Let's get the fuck out of this hellhole."

Chapter 5

"YOU SAY YOU saw a boy as you were pulling up?" North said. He stood in the Merryfields' kitchen leaning against the slate countertop, the edge pressed against the small of his back as if he were trying to relieve pain. Test noted his belt dug into his bony waist, and wondered again if he was ill. He poised a pencil above his notebook.

Test pulled out her recorder, checking her iPhone quickly as she did to see if she'd missed a text or call from Claude. She had not. She worried about the icy roads.

"Yes. A boy. Sneaking out," Jon Merryfield said and wiped his face. Sweat glistened on his broad forehead below his thick, dark hairline. The man looked washed out. Test did not feel so flush herself. Her fingertips still thrummed from the jolt of seeing Jessica. Jon Merryfield's wife stood a few feet from Jon, cuddling her swaddled sleeping baby against her chest. Her cheeks were muddied with runny mascara, her eyes foamed pink and swollen from crying.

"Could it have been a man?" Test said.

Jon looked taken aback, but gave it thought. "I suppose," he said.

"Or a girl?" Test said.

North cut her a look. Hers was not to ask, but to observe, listen. Follow.

"It was a male," Jon said. His eyes flashed at Test. "I assumed it was the boy Bethany had seen previously."

"What time did you get home?" North said.

"Seven fifteen, seven twenty," Bethany said. "Somewhere in there."

"Can you be any more precise?" Test asked.

"No," Bethany said, curtly. "We left early. About halfway through. Jon's been sick and the food was too rich. After he used the bathroom, we left. While I waited, I glanced at my cell phone to check messages and saw it was just after seven. It struck me because we'd told the sitter—" She paused and took a breath. "We'd told Jessica we'd be out till at least eight."

"What—" Test began, but North cut her off.

"Tell me about this boy you saw," North said, asking what Test had been about to ask.

"I'd seen him about a month back," Bethany said. "He left out the same door Jon saw him—the person—leave from tonight. I had spoken to Jessica about him."

"Who was he?"

"She wouldn't say."

"But you saw him clearly that time, to know for certain it was a boy?" Test said.

Bethany Merryfield smoothed a hand along the back of her neck. "Not exactly. I saw someone leave with a hoodie on, you know, like kids wear, so—"

"You assumed," Test said.

"So, you can't say for absolute certain?" North said.

"I guess not but—" Bethany began.

"I—" Test started, and again was stymied.

"Did the girl admit to having someone here that first time?" North said.

"Yes," Bethany said.

"But she gave no name?" North said.

"No. And I didn't ask."

"So this boy, or this man. Tonight. What was he wearing?" Test asked and caught a disapproving shake of the head by North.

"Tonight?" Jon said. "A dark jacket."

"So. Not a hoodie," Test said.

"Not that I saw. And jeans, maybe. Darker pants anyway. I guess jeans. A ball cap. I told this to Detective North already. He's asked these things."

"Color?" Test said.

"Black, maybe blue."

"Which?" Test said.

"I don't know. Dark."

Merryfield, Test noted, was vague when pressed for clarity.

"You see his face?" Test said.

"No. As I said earlier."

"So you don't really know what color it was, his ball cap?" Test said.

"Dark," Jon said.

"Do you have any idea at all who this male might be?" Test asked.

Jon shook his head.

"I wish I'd asked her his name," Bethany said. She closed her eyes as if to shut the light off on a memory and leave it in the dark, unseen, less dangerous; then cooed in her baby's ear, shifting from foot to foot to rock her child.

"Why would someone kill a girl in your house?" Test said. It came out sounding accusatory. She'd not intended it to be. The Merryfields trained their eyes on her. North watched her too. "I mean. If someone had it in for her, this mysterious boyfriend, say, why would he do it here?" Test said.

"How could we possibly know that?" Bethany snapped.

"Do you lock your door?" Test said.

"This is Vermont. Do *you*?" Bethany said, challenging.

There it was again, the defensive attitude. "Actually, yes," Test said, though it wasn't true and she had no idea why she said so. To be contrary. To keep Bethany under pressure.

"Well. You're a police officer." Bethany shifted her baby to her shoulder. "Of course you keep your house locked."

"Detective," Test corrected. "I'm a detective." She felt a bit like a PhD insisting she be called *Doctor*, but being called an officer felt like a Green Beret being called a Cub Scout. "Your husband is the most controversial man in the state. He's—"

Bethany tossed her head back sharply to flip the bangs out of her eyes and fixed Test with a heartless gaze. "So we're supposed to know our babysitter is going to be—"

"Your husband is *hated*," Test said.

"That's enough, Officer, thank you," North said and held up a palm to warn her. He addressed Bethany Merryfield. "We don't even know if who you saw leaving did anything."

"Of course he did," Bethany sniped.

"Perhaps he fled because he was in danger himself," North said. "Or he'd come to visit her and not found her. Or found her and got scared."

"We're not blaming you," Test said.

North shot her a look: *Zip it. Or else.*

"I should hope not," Bethany said.

"Did you get threats?" North said, asking what Test would have asked next.

"It comes with the territory," Jon said.

"I warned Jon that we would." Bethany's face pinched as she switched her baby from one shoulder to the other.

Test tried to see out the window behind Bethany, to her car. She couldn't. What had she been thinking, bringing her kids here, leaving them alone in the car? If another mother had left kids George and Elizabeth's ages in a car this long in a store lot, the mother would be charged with neglect. Test wondered if Larkin was even out there anymore. Certainly he wouldn't leave without telling Test, if he were relieved of his post. Would he? And why had Claude not called?

"Did you take the threats seriously?" North said.

"Of course," Bethany said.

"Not this seriously." Jon worked his jaw, not in the manner of someone angered, but someone trying to relieve the pressure of a heinous headache. His pallor was that of left-over oatmeal, and Test was worried he might vomit.

"Why didn't the threats concern you?" Test said. She would not be muzzled. North had no official authority over her. She would ask those questions she believed pertinent. And she would get answers. Let North go to Barrons, her chief, if he took issue.

"You get so many threats, you become immune. It becomes

white noise," Jon said, authority coming into his voice as he squared his broad shoulders.

"Maybe *you* do," Bethany said icily, her stare lacerating.

"A threat against me," Jon said. "I can handle. Myself. But, this. You think this has to do with the case?"

"What do you think?" Test said.

"We don't *know* what to think," Bethany said. "You make it sound like—"

"I'm not making it sound like anything, ma'am. I need to ask uncomfortable questions. I won't apologize. Now. What's your best *educated* guess? Because it either has to do with the case or it has to do with something else. Is there anything else in your lives, your marriage, that—"

"He killed the *girl*," Bethany said. "What can she have to do with our marriage?" She stared, tight-lipped, eyes slits, and Test caught the whiff of the privileged class; not of a person who had married into it, but a person born to it, oblivious lifelong to her innate condescension.

Test suddenly felt exhausted and wanted dearly to check on her kids and get them home. Whichever way she sliced it, her kids' well-being was her priority, whether it was convenient to her profession or not. But she couldn't tend to them now. Just. Couldn't. It would undermine all her standing. If North even suspected her kids were out in her car and she was distracted by that choice . . . she hated to think of his reaction. She hoped George and Elizabeth had fallen asleep. She hoped they were not terrified. She had no clue how long she'd been in the house or how much longer she would be in here. Claude had not shown up yet, otherwise a text would have come. Her face had the pasty feel that meant her makeup was melting, revealing her freckles.

"These threats," North said. "Were they e-mails, phone messages, in the mail?"

"Mostly phone," Jon said. "Ninety-nine percent of it you disregard as crackpots."

"And the other one percent?" Test said.

"You worry," Bethany said. "I worry. I worry about most of them."

"Do you save the messages?" Test said.

"Some," Jon said. "I delete them after a while."

"I told you, you should have saved them all," Bethany said. "I told him to report them. He wouldn't listen. Some of the messages, they were so vile and—"

"Enough," Jon said.

The baby mewled and Bethany slung him gently over her shoulder and rubbed his back. "Shhh. Shhh." The baby was as calm as any Test had seen; certainly calmer than George and Elizabeth had ever been at that age, the two fussbudgets. *Calm* was not a word Test associated with colicky George and motor-baby Elizabeth.

"We'll need to listen to any messages you have," Test said. "Don't erase them."

"Right," Jon said. "I'll leave what's there."

"What about the boy?" Bethany said, addressing North and ignoring Test. "He must—"

"We'll find him," North said. "You two take a load off. Your house is going to be crawling with forensics geeks for a spell yet. Don't touch anything and try to think of anything you can about the boy, and about Jessica. Rest."

"We'll have to take your fingerprints," Test said.

"Fingerprints?" Bethany protested. "Why on earth?"

"To compare our prints against ones foreign to the house," Jon said.

"It can wait," North said and jerked a thumb at Test. "Let's go."

Jon and Bethany left the kitchen, Jon slipping his hand around his wife's torso, his wife, Test noted, slipping out of it as if by second nature.

North cocked an eyebrow at Test. "You certainly keep the pressure on. What do you think?"

His question surprised her. She'd expected a drubbing. "There's a few possibilities," Test said. "One: The boy, if it is a boy, and if it is the same boy, or man, who was here before, killed Jessica out of jealousy or rage for a reason that has nothing to do with the case." Test knew a sick mind concocted reasons the general populous could never understand, but that were entirely rational and logical to the perp. "The blow to her forehead means she either knew the attacker or she did not have time to realize the danger, simply turned around and . . . Two: The boy did it for someone, to send a warning to Jon about his involvement in the gay marriage case."

"A local kid hired to do a hit with a hammer or a pipe?"

"If it was a boy. And if he was local."

"I don't buy number two."

"Third . . . maybe the boy—"

"—or man."

"Or man. Did it as his own warning to Merryfield being involved in the case."

"Kill the babysitter? Why?"

Test said, mockingly, "How could I possibly know that?"

"Watch it, Officer."

"Detective," Test said.

"If it was planned in advance, whoever planned it knew somehow the Merryfields would be out tonight." He tapped his pencil against his chin. "I've got to get with forensics."

Test wanted to go with him to get apprised, but she couldn't bear not knowing what state her kids were in and needed to try to reach Claude.

"I'd like to get crime-scene photos sent to my e-mail, and whatever notes you have from before I arrived here," Test said. She handed North her card and he walked off toward a state police forensics expert without a reply.

Peeling off her surgical gloves, and tearing off her hairnet and the mask hanging about her neck, Test hurried out of the house past the two forensics personnel now lifting prints from the stair railings leading up to the second floor.

Officer Larkin was not on the porch.

Test could not see her car; a news van had pulled in and blocked it from view. Test yanked off her booties and jogged toward the van, where reporters camped.

A reporter tried to shove a microphone at her, but an officer who wasn't Larkin strode between Test and the reporter. "Keep back, back behind the tape. You know the drill," he said.

Test came around the other side of the van and stopped dead.

Her car was gone.

She looked around madly, trying to see over and around the crowd milling about her. What did these fools want to see? What did they think this was, a sporting event? Test shoved a man to get by and broke out onto the road. She spun around, taking in the scene, the people and cars and lights and cameras jammed at every odd angle along the street.

Then, she saw it.

The car was parked farther down the street, under a street

lamp. Officer Larkin was leaning against the front fender, arms folded across his chest as he ate a licorice whip. He spotted Test walking over to him and must have sensed her panic and realized his error.

He trotted over to her and said, "Sorry. I moved the car. There was so much commotion around it. I was worried the kids were scared. I've been here the whole time. I didn't think—"

Test exhaled a long breath of relief and looked up at the full moon. The air was crisp and cold. She could see her breath. "It's OK."

"They're fast asleep," Larkin said.

"No sign of my husband?"

Larkin glanced over Test's shoulder as headlight beams flooded his face.

Claude was just pulling up in his old Bronco II.

He got out and trotted over, hands tucked in his peacoat pockets, eyes darting as he tried to take in the scene outside the home, to understand it.

"Sorry," he said. "Done?" He peeked inside the car at the kids.

"I was," Test said. "But if you take them home in my car, I'd like to go back in."

Claude ran his hands through his dark hair. "See you at the house then," he said. "Sorry to be late. The roads . . ."

Chapter 6

Jon Merryfield dreamt.

He was a boy, cowering in a corner. He did not dare look up. He could hear breathing. Close. Feel breath on his neck. Too close. He screamed. "Look at me," a man's voice said. Jon looked. It was himself, older. "No," Boy Jon said and shrank from his older self. "No."

Jon awoke, someone shaking him. His skin was feverish. Vision blurred. He lay on the sofa, curled in a ball. The room was dark, the cops gone.

"You had another dream," Bethany said.

"Nightmare," Jon said and took her hand and gave it a squeeze. She took her hand away.

"You should never have taken up this case," Bethany said. "You put our family at risk over nothing. Damn you."

Chapter 7

IT WAS LATE when Test tried to enter the house quietly, but Charlie, the beloved Labrador–retriever-and-German-shepherd mutt Test had rescued years earlier, before Claude and the kids, came waddling up to her anyway, working a squeaky toy in his jaws and swishing his tail in greeting as he wove between Test's legs. He whined and wedged his snoot between her knees. His muzzle had gone white. His eyes runny. Time was catching up with him.

"Hi boy," Test said, her voice strained. Charlie nuzzled. Test nudged him away. She was too burned out to give him her usual love of getting on the floor to rub his belly. He was such a needy galoot.

Charlie pressed, tried to plant his paws on Test's chest, but his rear legs were too lame to get him up that high anymore. It was a habit Test wished she'd quashed in the early days. But back then, single and living alone in her studio apartment in Lebanon, New Hampshire, freshly graduated from the Vermont Police Academy on this side of the river, she'd found it endearing; and knowing the abuse the poor dog had endured at the hands of his previous owner, she had permitted it. Hell. She'd encouraged it; spoiled him and let him have his way. But now, when she was wiped, she had no patience for it.

Charlie whined and gave her his best forsaken look.

She wasn't buying it.

He tried once more to get his paws on her, and Test snipped, "Enough, Charlie," and shoved her knee hard into his chest. Charlie limped off into the living room, where he plopped down with a harrumph and began sulking.

As Test made her way upstairs, she promised herself to love him up doubly first chance she got.

SKIPPING HER NIGHTLY regimen of cleansers and lotions, Test washed her face briefly with hand soap, gave her teeth a quick once-over, fished the mouth guard she wore for grinding teeth from a plastic Solo cup of Scope and wedged it in her mouth. She shed her clothes and left them where they fell, replacing them with flannel pajama bottoms.

In the bedroom, she set the preliminary case file on the nightstand. Before she'd left the station, she'd downloaded and printed photos and the notes that North had sent her via an encrypted e-mail. She'd expected the detective to hold out on her; but he'd come through after she'd sent two texts requesting the information.

She slid into bed beside Claude, who had fallen asleep with his latest Ivan Doig novel resting on his chest beside the pint of nearly melted Chubby Hubby ice cream.

He came to, pretending he'd only been out a moment, though judging by the state of the ice cream it had been at least a half hour.

Both of them sat topless in their matching blue drawstring flannel pajama bottoms, their backs cushioned by twin husband pillows. She said nothing for a long spell. Test liked that they could sit in comfortable silence together.

Test watched the bedside clock change from 1:11 to 1:12 A.M.

Claude slipped a spoon into the pint, mined a hunk of dark chocolate from the soft ice cream.

From her room down the hall, Elizabeth cried out in a dream, "Mommy!" then fell abruptly silent, though not before sending a chill through Test.

Claude spooned another chocolate chunk into his mouth. "Ah," he said and slid his tongue around his mouth lecherously. He licked a smear of melted ice cream off the back of his hand.

"Attractive," Test said, noting the irony as she adjusted her mouth guard to speak. "How can you eat ice cream with so much junk in it? You can barely find the ice cream. Give me vanilla. Chocolate. Strawberry. Real ice cream."

"But look at all the treats left even with the ice cream half melted."

Test used to love ice cream, but since training for marathons, limited herself to eating it on Saturday, her off day. She seldom had the appetite for sweets now, anyway. She preferred dates and jumbo raisins and other naturally sweet snacks that had at least some nominal nutrients. Ice cream seemed to coat the inside of her stomach like an oil slick.

"Vanilla and chocolate are for amateurs," Claude said and kissed her cheek.

Test opened the folder and placed her finger on a photo of Jessica's face.

Claude grimaced, set his ice cream on the nightstand. "God," he said.

"Whoever did it was either very lucky with the blow. Or practiced."

Claude sat up against the headboard. "Practiced? You saying he's done this before?"

"I'm not saying anything. Just. Maybe the perp chose Jessica as a smokescreen, to make it look like it had to do with something else. The case, or whatever. But it didn't. I don't know what I'm saying. I made an ass of myself most of the night."

"You're too hard on yourself."

"I'm realistic. I should have listened more, talked less. Noted how Detective North handled witnesses, and himself—"

Sonja flicked her finger against a photo.

"He whacks her once. Out of anger," Test said. "Or passion. Or revenge. One of the trio. Then he freaks and flees."

"He knows her?"

"Statistically. Absolutely. At least saw her around. But I think he *knows* her. I think it was the boy Jon saw. A boyfriend. Or a kid she rejected as a prom date or something."

"Why not some old perv?"

"I'd be up for that scenario more if Bethany hadn't seen a boy previously," she said. "But, there's no outward sign Jessica was molested. No sign of struggle. All her clothes were on her. Lloyd, the ME, might conclude differently. But usually, a stranger, it's sexual violence."

"So if it is a jilted kid . . ." Claude sat up farther against the headboard, yawning. The Doig novel slid off his lap and thunked on the floor.

"Could explain why he doesn't have it in him to keep pounding away," Test said. "Anger gets the best of him. But when he sees her on the cellar floor like that, he can't bring himself to hit her again, to make sure. I mean, for all he knew, she could have been just knocked out, and woken up. Though the damage that was done—" She tried not to think of it.

"He got seen at least."

"Not enough for a positive ID."

"If it's a kid that was hung up on her, other kids will know about him," Claude said.

"I plan to hit the school tomorrow morning, after I go back to the house."

"Are you allowed to do that? If the school is even open after this, the kids will be a mess. And. Don't the state police handle—"

She cut him a sidewise glance. *Allowed* was not part of her vocabulary.

"They lead the investigation. Everything I learn that's important, I need to pass on to them. But all I've got going now through the department is a domestic violence case that's open and shut. The wife's talking, for once."

"Why do you need to go back to the house?"

"I want to ask a few questions I didn't get a chance to ask the wife last night. I got a sense there was a rift there between her and her husband."

"You think—"

"I don't know what I think."

She sighed and closed the folder, placed it on the nightstand.

"So you won't be able to get Elizabeth to her annual checkup at one tomorrow?" Claude said.

"Shit. I forgot."

"I'll do it." Claude kissed her forehead and settled in under his blankets.

Test sat in bed for a long time, playing the evening over and over in her head. She was exhausted, but wired; jacked on adrenaline.

She picked up the folder and started going through it again.

Chapter 8

DAWN'S PALE LIGHT edged through the Venetian blinds. Jon peered at Bethany across the room, asleep on the sofa. He went and stood over her. She looked so peaceful as her chest rose and fell, and air whistled from her nose. Their baby son lay asleep in the portable crib in the corner of the room. Jon lay a palm on him. So warm. So unaware. He stooped and kissed his son's forehead.

In the kitchen, Jon listened to his voice mail. The state police were due to come and listen to all the messages today. Three messages Jon listened to now were from attorneys working with him on the case. A dozen were from reporters regarding the previous night. Another dozen or so were from strangers, as far as he knew, who left messages along the lines of him being in league with Satan and a faggot lover and a fucking cocksucker.

Jon went through the messages until he found the one he was seeking.

He listened as revulsion washed through him.

The same voice he'd heard from for the past week or so. The first message had been just eight words that left him feeling drained of blood. There were five messages total. Each more demanding and threatening.

Jon had erased the most recent message. Then he erased the other messages left by the same voice. In a spontaneous, reflexive panic, he erased all his messages and the caller ID history.

He called his work phone and erased all the messages from the same voice.

Then he slipped out of the house to get to the office and think about what it was he was going to do to try to keep his life from blowing apart.

Chapter 9

BETHANY LOOKED AROUND the room, blinking back sleep. Jon was gone. From where she lay on the couch, she could see the open doorway to the cellar stairs. A phosphorescent glow pulsed from below, as if from a laboratory where bizarre experiments were being conducted. You'd think they'd turn off the equipment, she thought.

She wanted to close the door but did not want to get closer to it. She wanted to flee. Now. Leave her dream house. She felt filthy and afraid in it. She wanted to scour herself, let hot water rinse her flesh if not her mind of last night. She wanted to dress in new clothes, cut her hair, transform herself into a woman who knew nothing of this world. Take her son out in the fresh air. Breathe. She feared whoever had killed Jessica would be back. That this was not the end of things; but just the beginning.

She admired Jon for his work. He'd made a career of taking cases for underprivileged victims of violence. Especially juveniles. Boys. But this case. It was trouble from its inception. Dangerous no matter how you looked at it. The couple he was representing had had their civil rights violated, and Bethany believed in their cause; but they were not victims of the sort Jon normally took. He did not take civil cases. He prosecuted. Yet, he had taken this case, against Bethany's wishes. They'd quarreled. Bethany had warned him the case would bring out radicals. They'd blame Jon. Target him. Target his family. Jon had called her paranoid.

It could have been me in the cellar, Bethany thought. *Me.*

Bethany lifted baby Jon from his crib. She stroked his head as she saw the detective from the night before, the woman, out on the back lawn.

Chapter 10

THE MORNING AIR was biting cold. The sky was gray and glary in a way that pained Test's eyes and made her squint. She felt listless from her pittance of sleep and from a brain that had refused to shut down even in her scant two hours of restless sleep.

She snapped on a pair of surgical gloves, tight as a second skin, and stepped across the dead, November grass of the backyard, which edged up to the woods. She walked with the deliberate, mindful motion of one navigating a minefield. After each step, she paused, sometimes for so long she had the sensation of turning into a painting of herself. She'd first experienced this phenomenon when she'd sat for Claude so he could paint her portrait to hang in his studio. She'd resisted at first. Could there be anything more preposterously vain or archaic than getting your portrait painted? *It's not for you, it's for me*, Claude had said. So, of course, she'd granted it.

She scrutinized the patch of earth where she was about to step. She stooped to poke at the lawn with an extendable pointer that reminded her of her old high-school geography teacher.

She poked at something now. Something stuck in the semi-frozen ground at the edge of the woods behind the house; woods anyone could have slipped out of and back into and hardly be seen, even in daylight. Except that these woods, even with aid of a flashlight, were so dense and tangled, one would never be able to find one's way deftly at night.

Test could not see clearly the object she poked at now. She knelt over her find, feeling like a girl with a magnifying glass. With the camera around her neck, she took two photographs, one photo up close, another from a standing position. Then, with a precise movement, she plucked a metal pincers from her shirt pocket and extracted the artifact from the grass and held it before her eyes. It was a simple thumbtack. She fished an evidence bag from her jacket pocket anyway and dropped the tack inside. Sealed the bag. Marked the time and date and location on the outside of the bag, in each appropriate field, with permanent marker.

"Can I help you?" a voice calcified with contempt said from behind her.

"No," Test said without acknowledging the voice in any other way.

"What are you doing here?" the voice said.

Clearly, Test was not going to be left alone, so she stood and turned, planted her hands on her hips.

Bethany Merryfield stared at her, the fuzzy pink slippers she wore on her feet tapping on the dead grass. Except for the slippers, she remained dressed in the clothes she'd worn the previous evening, her makeup smeared and face puffy. She had the baby done up in a front-riding baby sling. She seemed unsteady. Her color was no good, her eyes hidden behind the enormous sunglasses that were all the rage, with a certain type.

"You okay?" Test said with an empathy she'd lacked the previous night. She came and stood at Bethany's elbow.

"Fine," Bethany said.

"You're doing better than I am," Test said. "Your baby is adorable."

Normally, a mother would have melted with pride at such a comment. Test sure had, and still did. She couldn't help it.

"Thanks," Bethany managed.

"I have two," said Test. "Not babies. A boy and a girl. Just turned four and seven a week ago, born on the same day, three years apart."

The melting frost was seeping through Bethany's slippers. "Do you want to go back inside?" Test said.

"What have you got in that bag?" Bethany said. She seemed almost in a trance.

"Nothing," Test said and held up the bag. "You need anything? You want a doctor?" The trauma of the night before might just now have been seeping into the woman, just dawning on her the magnitude of what had happened. Test worried she was in shock.

"No," Bethany said and gave a pained grin. "Yes, actually. I need help back inside. I feel I might collapse. I seem to be stuck in place and feel like I was struck in the head."

Test took her by the elbow and led her back into the house through a screen door.

Inside, Bethany sat on the couch with Test's help.

"What are you doing here?" Bethany said.

"I've come by to ask a few more questions and have a look around in daylight."

"I thought the state police were in charge."

"I'm helping in whatever capacity I can."

"I don't want to have to tell ten people the same thing over and over."

"I appreciate that. I just have a few questions. They may spur something new. Your husband and you were out last night at the Village Fare?"

"We went over that already."

"What time?"

"Six until about seven. I told you all this."

"I just want to reconfirm. It was an emotional evening. I want to make sure none of us missed anything. And now with daylight and your head a bit clearer—"

"I'm not so sure about that."

"What time did you get home?"

She sighed heavily. "Maybe seven fifteen. Why aren't you writing this down? Why are you bothering me if it's not important enough to write down?"

"Because it's what you told me last night."

"Which is why I just wish to be left alone and not have to repeat these boring questions."

"A child was murdered in your home. Sorry if you find it boring. It's not to me."

Bethany gave her chin a tiny petulant shake and hugged her baby closer to her chest.

"So you drove to the restaurant?" Test said.

"Right."

"Why?"

"I don't understand."

"It's a fifteen-minute walk or so. It was a beautiful if crisp night."

"My husband's been sick, for one. Two: We were running late.

Three: It was actually cold last night. With that wind. Not *crisp*. I don't see how any of this is germane."

The prickly demeanor bothered Test. Had from the start. Why the abrasiveness? Why the disdain? Did this woman think somehow that she was the one most victimized in all of this? Or was there something else at work? Test scribbled nonsense in the pad to buy herself time.

"About the voice-mail messages you received," Test said. "The threats. I'd like to listen to them if I may." She nodded at the cordless phone sitting on the coffee table. "If you could dial your voice mail and bring it up for me."

The baby started to wriggle awake, stretching; he uttered a short, sharp cry so abrupt it startled Test.

"I'll give you the number and password," Bethany said, standing, rocking in place to try to lull the baby. Test picked up the phone and punched in the numbers as Bethany Merryfield recited them to her.

Test listened. Stared at the phone in her hand. "I thought you and Jon said you'd leave any threatening messages on the voice mail. There's not a single message, that makes a threat or otherwise."

"Maybe you did something wrong."

Test handed the phone to Bethany. "Check for yourself."

"I'm busy with the baby," Bethany said.

"Check later. But there are no messages on your phone."

"Did you accidentally erase them?"

"I don't accidentally do anything."

Test did not mention what she found even more odd: that the caller ID history had been erased completely.

"May I speak with your husband?" Test asked.

"Why would Jon erase the messages?"

"I'm not saying he did. On purpose. He mentioned perhaps there weren't any threatening ones saved. It happens. As I said, last night everyone was in a state. I'd like to speak to him, however."

"He's not here. You can see his Rover's not out front."

"I thought perhaps it was in the garage."

"We hardly ever use the garage. I hate that it's not attached. What's the point? You can check for yourself for the Rover."

"That won't be necessary. Do you know where he is?"

"He was gone when I awoke."

Test wondered what could possibly have been so pressing that a husband would abandon his wife and his child the morning after such a heinous night? Why would he erase those messages? He, or someone else, had done so. If not, someone had certainly deleted the caller ID history.

"I'll show myself out," Test said. "I may be in your yard a while yet."

BETHANY WATCHED THE detective from the kitchen-sink window.

She knew for certain messages had been on there as of the day before because she'd had to skip over more recent ones to get to one left by her Pilates instructor about the change of time for a weekly class.

Bethany turned on the faucet and splashed cold water on her face.

In the hallway, she inspected her image in the mirror. Ghastly. She plucked an eyelash from her cheek. As a girl, she would have made a wish and blown the eyelash off her fingertip. She flicked the eyelash away, not so naïve as to believe a wish could help her now.

Chapter 11

TEST'S PEUGEOT NUDGED a speed bump as Test pulled the car into the Lamoille Valley High School parking lot, coffee sloshing from her cup into her lap. "Damn it," she shouted, wiping at herself. The coffee was cold so it didn't burn her, but it left her pants wet in the crotch. She eased over another speed bump. More coffee spilled. "For fuck sake!" she barked. With the car's old heater now stuck on high and now blowing volcanic heat instead of cool air, she had her window rolled down. A boy on a skateboard alongside her car laughed and kicked off on his board to make use of the speed bump for a trick.

Duly humiliated, Test parked and fished tissues from the console to dab her crotch. She hoped no one drove by her. The only thing worse than entering the school with a wet crotch was to be caught fiddling with her crotch in the parking lot. She grabbed her backpack and got out.

The school was an ugly, pedestrian one-story mid-century brick affair, the sort of uninspired and unimaginative box that always made Test wonder what the fuck they were thinking back then.

She pushed through double doors, leaving the bright sunlight for industrial fluorescent lights.

Three girls sauntered by, each dressed in low-rise jeans and scant tops to reveal belly-button rings and cleavage. Tattoos peeked above their waistbands, flirtatious etchings on the small of their backs and across hip bones.

A girl bent over to get her books. The waist of her jeans pulled away and her shirt rode up. Her Celtic tattoo stretched and Test could clearly see the crack of the poor thing's naked butt.

The girl forced a pained smiled as she passed Sonja, revealing the type of braces you weren't supposed to notice. Her eyes were bloodshot and she looked traumatized. The school superintendent had been notified of the crime too late to cancel school entirely, and the students would have just learned of the crime in an early morning assembly. Grief counselors would arrive soon, if they were not here now. Most of the students Test would speak to would be in shock and grieving. It would be painful to interview them in this state, but it might also be useful: genuine shock and grief were difficult to fake.

The halls were empty now. Sonja's crotch was still damp, so she ducked into a girls' restroom to tend to it.

Inside the restroom, she pressed paper towels to her pants. A dark damp circle stained her shirt, too. She untucked it and placed her 9mm on the sink beside her. She unspooled more paper towels. Taped to the towel dispenser was a pink sheet of paper.

LGBT MEETING TONITE!
If you're Lesbian Gay Bi or Transgender
or a friend

*come share your concerns about LGBT issues
and GAY MARRIAGE.
Tonight at 7 pm
at the Brew Ha Ha coffee house
See you there!*

Principal Maude Gardiner greeted Test with a hearty hand-shake and welcomed her into her office. Gardiner had a commanding voice and short, spiked hair.

According to her dossier Gardiner had started at Lamoille Valley High as a softball coach in 1987, then moved into a full-time slot as physical education teacher when the former phys-ed teacher was felled by a heart attack while showering, against the rules, in the boys' locker room. Vic Jenkins had found him. Gardiner had worked alongside Vic Jenkins for four years, until she'd risen to guidance counselor for LVHS in 1996. By 2002, she was vice principal. She'd been Principal Gardiner for two years now.

"Sit," Gardiner said, all business behind a broad wooden desk devoid of papers and photos. "We'd have preferred to have can-celled school altogether, of course, and will be sending students home early; but consider my office yours. I believe it evokes a sense of authority. It's been used more than once for interrogative purposes."

"I'm not here to interrogate anyone. I just want to talk to Jessica Cumber's friends," Test said.

"There were few with whom she was close." Gardiner pushed a folder across the desk. "But I've taken upon myself, as a civic duty, to list each and every friend *or* acquaintance who I, her teachers and her counselor know of. Kids lead very secretive lives. I sug-

gest you fish around for other acquaintances during your inter-
rogations. Follow leads. As they say." She smiled. She wore braces
too, Test noted. The same translucent kind that reminded Test of
her mouth guard. Gardiner seemed to have a speck of dark food
trapped in the front brace. "I've arranged for each student to show
up every fifteen minutes starting in"—she glanced at her wristwatch "—eight minutes. There are nine students in all. They will
appear in alphabetical order, as you will find on your master list."

"Thank you."

"I put them in alphabetical order because I did not want to
prejudice the process by having you think I believe one way or another about any student's involvement. If I had suspicions I would
tell you. There are three boys and six girls on that list. I know
each very well. I've mulled it over and believe none is connected,
directly, consciously, to Jessica's . . . end."

"I see," Test said, and had to restrain herself from saying she
guessed she didn't need to waste her time any further, if the high-
school principal had said there was no connection. Gardiner's de-
duction and bold claim might have been insulting if it weren't so
preposterous.

"I'm not a professional detective, obviously," Gardiner said. "I
do, however, read detective novels, a lot of them, and I have a feel
for the procedure." She glanced at her bookshelf. Two rows of pa-
perback detective novels lined the top shelves, each spine flush
with its neighbor, arranged in alphabetical order by author's last
name. Softball trophies served as bookends.

Gardiner sat straighter and adjusted her long wool skirt.

"That does not preclude the idea that they *may* know something." She stood. "Please. Take my seat. You'll find the students
focus on you much better when you're behind the desk. I'll send

the first student in"—she glanced at her watch—"four minutes and twenty seconds."

TEST STARED AT the spines of Gardiner's paperbacks: *Murder 1-2-3*, *Murder After Dark*, *Murder at First Light*, *Murder by Number*. What pleasure did Gardiner take from them? Test wondered. Was it the mystery? Test had lost interest in mysteries in junior high, when she'd read *Story of O* and abandoned the mysteries of Nancy Drew for the dark and ecstatic mystery of sexuality that bloomed in her. Pulp mysteries were written to make the reader feel clever, as if no one else could be cagey enough to see the clues sprinkled throughout the early chapters as obviously as blood splattered on a white bed sheet.

And the killers. The vogue seemed to require killers be cold and monstrous but also somehow forever charming. Ingenious and coy, enigmatic, worldly and dashing. *Empathetic.* Someone by whom you might not mind being murdered, if you had to be, of course. The cops were drunks with failed marriages and in possession of preternatural criminal minds that linked them mystically to their quarry, a telepathic contrivance to forward an improbable plot. The hunter and the hunted, two sides of the same brain. Twins of darkness.

What shit. Detective work took diligent, thankless, tedious effort and focus.

The victims in most books were for mere body count.

Test wished she could take Gardiner down into the creamery's cellar and put her face to Jessica Cumber's face. *Smell that?* she'd ask. Why does that odor want to make you vomit? Because it's the smell of what's *supposed* to be inside the girl leaking out of her ruined skull. And why's the cellar stink of shit and piss?

Because when one puts into a single furious swing of a hammer all the rage one can no longer contain, and blasts your skull with it, your bowels and bladder let go. You soil yourself like the baby your mother once held when you needed her for your very survival and she knew it, and she was afraid of it. So she rocked you, knowing she could not rock you forever; knowing one day the world would get its seedy paws on you, and only by the grace of God and by luck and by fate, even in the *best* of worlds, would you be spared. And in the worst of worlds? Deep in her mind, under a trapdoor where a mother's nightmares lurk, she feared most that before her daughter reached Sweet Sixteen, she would wind up on that dirt floor, head ruined like an egg splattered against a brick wall. Her dreams. Her future. Her life. Spilled by someone who decided she would die here. Die now. And now she's gone. And everyone she ever touched—part of them is gone with her too.

How did Gardiner like her mysteries now?

Test stared at the paperbacks. She thought of George and Elizabeth. As a mother, her role was not to protect her children from the world, but to prepare them for it. It was all she could do.

"Excuse me." Gardiner stood in the doorway. She'd caught Test studying her books. "If you want to borrow one," she nodded to her shelf, "the *Murder My Love* series is the best."

"I have my fill just now," Test said.

"Well." Gardiner turned from Test to summon a girl from out in the hallway.

The girl chewed her bottom lip. Her eye makeup had bled and been swiped at but not cleaned from her cheeks, so what remained looked like faded bruises. Just behind her stood a man and a woman, distraught and fidgeting, clearly unsure what to make of this new world into which they'd all been thrust, and from which they would never fully depart.

"Olivia," Gardiner said, her voice unexpectedly warm. "This is Detective Test. Just answer her questions as best you can." She looked at the parents. "If you wish to wait in the counselor office next door," she said.

"If Olivia needs you for anything at all, I'll get you immediately," Test said to the parents.

"Is she in trouble?" the mother asked, her voice breaking.

"I only hope she might be able to help answer a few questions. If you prefer to stay—"

"I'll be OK," Olivia said.

The mother kissed her daughter on the forehead, then Gardiner shut the door as she turned to lead the parents to the office next door.

Olivia sat with her knees together and her hands in the lap of her long denim skirt, twirling a turquoise ring around her pinkie finger. The laces of her left sneaker were undone.

Test opened the folder Principal Gardiner had given her and glanced at the list. Olivia Grable, Age: 14, GRADE AVG: 3.4, PARENTS: MARRIED, SIBLINGS: none

"I'm just going to ask you a few questions," Test said.

Olivia nodded. She wore no earrings, no makeup. Her hair was straight and brown and parted in the middle and fell to her shoulders. She wore cat's-eye-style glasses Sonja's mother had worn long ago, a style that Test had not known was back in fashion. Perhaps it wasn't. They begged for a neck chain. Olivia's lips and tongue were free of piercings. But, maybe beneath her clothing her flesh was riddled with piercings, solid blue with tattoo ink. Maybe she'd learned of her friend's death before school and had come to be among her friends and not bothered to wear what she'd normally wear. Perhaps she had dressed plainly on purpose, suspecting she might be asked questions by someone in authority and wanted to portray a dowdy, simple look. Or perhaps this was her real look, regardless. Who knew? Test considered Olivia for a moment and decided the clothes were her usual. The glasses. It was the glasses that made her think this.

Test retrieved a pair of eyeglasses from her backpack and put them on. They were not prescription and had no function other than to lend her an air of seriousness. She had first bought a pair of glasses like this when Olivia's age, to make herself look smarter. She had a drawer full of them. Claude found it amusing and disconcerting. "You *are* smart," he said.

"They're just an accessory," Sonja had said.

"To what crime?" he'd ask.

Test adjusted the glasses and hit the red circle on her recorder.

"How did you know Jessica?" she said.

Staring at her hands, Olivia said, "She was my best friend."

"I'm sorry," Test said.

Olivia shrugged.

"How long had you been best friends?" Test asked.

"Forever." Olivia scuffed her sneakers back and forth.

"Do you know if she had a boyfriend?"

"No."

"No, you don't know? Or no, she didn't have a boyfriend?"

"No. She didn't."

"Are you sure?"

"I'm her best friend."

"How about a boy she liked, then? Not a boyfriend. But a crush."

"No one special."

"Anyone though? Any boy at all you can think of that she even talked about?"

"She never talks about boys. I mean, she does. Just not lately. She likes them. Boys. She's not lez or anything."

"How long had it been since she talked about a boy?"

Olivia worried her ring. "I don't know. Maybe, like, a few months. Maybe longer. No one that, you know, sticks out in my mind."

"What about before? Did she ever have a boyfriend before?"

"Before what?"

"Before she stopped talking about boys. Did she ever have a boyfriend? Or a guy friend that she liked a lot or that liked her a lot, maybe more than she liked him?"

"Jessica never had a boyfriend. I mean, we're fourteen. I am. She just turned fifteen a month ago. We didn't really get into boys much till like the past year, you know?"

Test knew.

"So never anything serious?" Test said.

"Uh-uh."

"What about things that weren't serious?"

Rachel hesitated. "Maybe one kid. Jeremy Lang. She liked him. But he didn't even know she existed. "

"How do you know she liked him?"

"She could barely even look at him let alone say hi. He moved away though. Like to Florida or something. Last year."

"Anyone else?"

"She and this one kid." Rachel took off her glasses and rubbed a lens on her shirt, then set the glasses back on her nose. "We used to go to the movies and stuff. Our parents would drive us.

She didn't make out with him or anything. She's not like that. I mean she's kind of serious. She likes to get good grades and likes to work hard. I hardly even saw her myself that much the last few months."

"Why's that?"

"She got a couple Bs on tests in September. She said she had to knuckle down. She doesn't want to end up like her mom, you know? She wants to go to college. Be a veterinarian. We're going to apply to the same schools together. Dorm together. And when we—" She stopped speaking as if she'd been slapped hard across the face.

She stared at Test then shut her eyes.

She sat stock-still. Then, slowly, she began to moan. It was a moan that came from some well deep within her, sad and tortured. She leaned forward and wrapped her arms over the back of her head as if to protect herself from a blow as the moan morphed into a howl too terrific and too ancient to come from such youth.

"Do you want me to get your parents?" Test said.

Olivia waved a hand. "No, no," she said, her voice hitching. "Please. No."

Finally, her sobbing diminished to gasps and she wiped at her tears and her runny nose with the back of her blouse sleeve. She tried to smile but it would not come.

"I haven't been much help," she said, hiccupping.

"Yes you have. You've been wonderful."

She closed her eyes again, and squeezed her small hands into tight fists. "She was my best friend."

Test put a hand on the girl's knee.

"What am I supposed to do now?" Olivia sobbed.

ALL AFTERNOON IT was the same conversation with the students, at times with parents present, though most students preferred their parents not be in the room.

"Did Jessica have a boyfriend?"

"No."

"Had she made any guys mad or jealous?"

"No."

"Did she have a crush on anyone?"

"No."

Tears were shed.

A boy named Eugene Franks had begun to weep before he'd even sat down. At first, Test had thought she might have a lead, as the young boy, through his hitching breath confessed, "I loved her."

Test had pressed. "Did you ever tell her this?"

"Yes."

"And what was her response?"

"She loved me too."

"Did she?"

"Sure."

"She told you this?"

"Yeah."

"Did other friends—did they know?"

"Why wouldn't they?"

"No one's mentioned you."

"Oh," Eugene said.

When she asked the next student, a girl, about Eugene, the girl said, "Eugene. He's harmless. He's gay. They were like, pals. Sister and brother."

Test asked each of the boys if he had feelings for Jessica. Two had. Secret little crushes. Not one of the students knew of a boyfriend. Why would Jessica keep a boyfriend a secret? Or maybe that wasn't it. Maybe Jessica had lied to Bethany that night Bethany had seen a boy leave the house. Or made it seem the boy was a boyfriend when he wasn't. But if he wasn't a boyfriend, who else could he be?

Chapter 12

THE BEEHIVE DINER buzzed.

Below a hornet nest suspended in tree branches, Victor, who'd just come from the morning mass that consisted, unfortunately, of just five of its total forty-six souls, sat at a counter stool, loosing bits of bacon gristle from between his teeth with a toothpick. His gums bled as he swigged at his cup of black coffee and swished. Swallowed.

Larry Branch sat next to him. Victor had known Branch all his life: a small-engine repairman, Branch had owned the Two-Stroke Shop in town for thirty years. Now semi-retired, he fixed Black and Decker engines for Sears in St. Johnsbury. He claimed to love it; said he could still get his fingers dirty, listen to the farm report on AM 640, and call it quits by 4 P.M. without having once to deal with a single customer. An old independent Yankee finding peace at Sears.

God works in mysterious ways, Victor thought as he opened the *Lamoille Register* to the sports page.

The waitress ambled over and rested a bowl of oatmeal and a

small pewter pitcher of maple syrup in front of Victor. "Boy must make you proud," she said, nodding at a photo of Victor's son on the front of the sports page, the boy's arms thrown up, face jubilant yet nearly savage in victory.

Pride bloomed in Victor, and crossed himself, secretly admonishing himself and reminding himself to keep his pride in check.

"He needs to work on his mechanics if he wants Division One teams looking at him," Victor said. "He throws off his back foot too much, and across his body when he should just throw the ball away. Andrew Luck, he's not." Victor always compared Brad to more talented QBs in conversation. Partly to practice humility. Partly not to jinx his son, who *was* blessed with talent. Victor was thankful each day of his life for this blessing. The kid was everything Victor had almost been. Should have been. Victor did not deserve such a son.

Victor removed the toothpick from his mouth. "He's got interest from a couple Ivy schools. Scholarships from plenty of Division Three programs. I'd like to see a bigger program redshirt and develop him. But from this state it's a tough slog just to get any Division Three to look at you. Let alone Division One. He wins a fourth state championship this year, he may get a glance. He set every state record there is to set, a year ago." There he was again, unable to help himself from the seamy vortex of vanity. Much as he tried, he couldn't be humble for long. Could not resist the temptation. There were worse transgressions than vanity, he knew. "He could use some help from the Lord."

He held up his mug. "Hit me again, Gwynne."

Gwynne topped him and stood with a hand on her cocked hip. She glanced at the front page of Victor's newspaper. "Awful 'bout that poor girl."

Victor looked at the headline: LOCAL GIRL SLAIN IN ATTORNEY'S HOME. He had avoided the story, and just seeing the headline now caused a trickle of sweat to leak from under his arms down along his sides. Last night had been a long and arduous one, and had not gone as planned in some respects. "Merryfield should know you can't do certain things in this world and expect not to have trouble," he said. Even as he said it, he felt the spike of hypocrisy stab him in the ribs.

"That's a terrible thing to say, especially from a deacon," Gwynne said. "I'm sure he didn't expect a child to be killed."

"Of course not." Victor was sweating profusely now. "But you can't just have men marrying men and—"

"Why's that?" Branch spun to face Victor. His faded canvas ball cap bore the logo of his son-in-law's company: Cut-the-Crap Plumbing. "All these folks yak 'bout marriage like it's the greatest damned thing since the microwave when half of us have been divorced. Been married twice myself. Divorced twice. Let the homos have their insurance and let half of 'em get divorced just like the rest of us."

"You can't make it legitimate," Victor said. "Where's it end? Brother marrying sister?"

"Half a what you probably do with your wife ain't *legitimate* according to the blue laws still on the books. Who knows what all any of us get up to?" Branch winked at Gwynne.

"I don't do anything of the kind with my wife," Victor said.

"Missing out," Branch said.

People thought it was easy, living up to the Lord's standards. But the Lord sometimes asked that hard tasks be done by his flock. Just ask Abraham. "They certainly don't need to be teaching it in our schools," he said.

"Jesus," Branch said. "If a kid's bent that way, he's bent that way. You can't *teach* a kid to be homo. You can teach respect though. School ain't gonna turn 'em the other way any more than you would have turned me off girls." Branch took off his cap and scratched at his bald crown. "What the hell you so afraid of anyway? What do you care what two men do with their dicks? Long as they aren't molesting kids."

Victor bristled as Branch handed Gwynne a ten-dollar bill. He didn't care at all for this kind of talk.

"Keep the change, darlin'," Branch said and headed toward the door.

Victor watched Branch go. The man was as full of crap as an outhouse at a chili contest. He acted as if he knew something. Maybe he did. But not about God.

Chapter 13

THOUGH DETECTIVE NORTH parked his cruiser a block behind the back of Greg and Scott's place, two reporters still hustled toward him as he got out of it.

North waved a hand at them. "No comment," he grunted and picked up his pace, entered the backyard through a small wooden gate.

"Are you close to making an arrest?" a reporter shouted.

North ignored him.

The backyard grew wild with autumn flowers and ancient apple trees. The air here smelled of rotted leaves and turned loam.

Near the back steps, North paused beneath an apple tree whose few stunted apples lay on the ground, gone soft in the dead grass. Yellow jackets clung to the rotted fruit, wings quivering drunkenly.

North heard a moan like that of an old man awakening and looked to see, in the shadows beneath the tree, a yellow Labrador retriever, its muzzle grizzled, cataract eyes. The dog whined and North gave it a good scratch behind the ears.

In the flower bed, a clutch of purple asters had somehow survived October. They were Loretta's favorite fall flower and she had just tossed out a bouquet of them that had wilted in the vase on the formal dining room table they never used. She got fresh flowers every Friday, often wild ones she picked herself. Fresh Flower Friday. North's granddaughter would abbreviate it to FFF. Loretta's mother had brought fresh flowers into the home every Friday when Loretta had been a child. Loretta had picked the practice back up now that her mother was living—dying—in the mother-in-law apartment they had built above the garage, outfitted with a wheelchair lift.

As North reached to pluck a handful of asters, a yellow jacket stung him on the back of his hand.

"Bastard," he said and sucked at the sting on his hand.

The back door of the house opened and Gregory Sergeant stood there, barefoot in frayed cords and a yellow V-neck sweater that may have been cashmere. He was a slight, compact man with alert savvy green eyes, ginger hair cut close, and a goatee.

"Practicing your kissing?" Gregory said, nodding at North sucking at his hand.

"If I don't have it down by now, I never will," North said.

"You're the detective that phoned?" Gregory said.

Over Sergeant's head, a rainbow flag and a Vermont state flag hung from rods sticking out from the small back porch. Sergeant looked over North's shoulder at the reporters gawking from the edge of the yard.

"We've been ever so popular today," Sergeant said as he escorted North into the house through a dining room to a kitchen straight out of Ozzie and Harriet.

The 1860s eyebrow cape had a funk of cigarette smoke about it. Liquor, beer, and champagne bottles stood about, many tipped over to sit in pools of their spilled drink. Bowls of coagulated dip sat on platters beside dried hanks of smoked meats.

"Please sit," Gregory said. His partner, Scott Goodale, sat at a kitchen table that had a baby-blue Formica top speckled with silver stars and trimmed with chrome, its tubular legs curved like swan necks. A refrigerator of the same baby blue and chrome sat beside a bomb-shelter-era gas stove. Either the two men had intentionally made a retro art installation of their home, an ironic slap in the face to McCarthy's TV-dinner-era of Closet Queens and homo bashing, or they actually liked this stuff. Whatever the case, North half expected to be served some pineapple upside-down cake and a cup of Sanka.

North knew both men from news coverage and from public meetings. Scott appeared different this morning. His eyes were bloodshot and he wore a ratty Billabong T-shirt, Emerson College sweatpants, and purple Converse All-Stars. North had never seen him in anything but a suit and tie, groomed impeccably. He was good-looking, with silvery eyes that shimmered like hot solder and the slight roundness of face found in men in their thirties who still maintain the suggestion of the strong jaw they once had but will soon lose forever. A smudge of a cleft that marked his chin was obscured by black stubble that grew in contrast to the blond hair atop his head, which while still in enviable abundance was a wayward thicket this morning.

The chair's vinyl cushion wheezed under North as he sat.

"Get you anything?" Gregory asked from where he remained standing.

"Ovaltine?" North quipped.

"How's that?" Scott said sliding a mug back and forth on the table between cupped hands.

"Nothing," North said, "water's good."

Gregory snatched an old jelly jar from the cupboard and opened the refrigerator. The bottled water, tofu, organic milk and yogurt inside the refrigerator disappointed North. He'd envisioned casseroles and Jell-O molds and Hi-C to go with the decor.

Gregory plucked a bottle of Evian from the refrigerator and handed both bottle and glass to North. He lay a hand on Scott's shoulder from behind, tapped his right ring finger, adorned with an Irish devotion ring, against the back of the chair.

"You like the décor," Scott said, noting North's exploratory gaze.

"Gives me an urge to hide under a school desk, frankly," North said.

Scott smirked and rolled his eyes. "Doesn't it? Place was like this when we moved in. God-awful."

North was surprised to hear this, and remiss at having started to form an idea about the two men and their decorating tastes.

"Not our taste, I'll tell you that," Scott said.

"Just as long as we don't trade up to stainless steel and polished granite," Gregory said and affected a shiver.

"Give me Formica and linoleum," North said, running with it, banter a fine way to loosen up interviewees. "Just no baby blue and twinkling stars." The décor here made his wife Loretta's kitchen—for it could not be thought of as anyone else's kitchen, despite who paid for it—of granite counters, terra-cotta flooring, stainless-steel appliances, and gas stove even less urbane, as Loretta had argued, and more bloodless and unoriginal, as North saw it. Well, she had her kitchen, and her living room, parlor, formal dining room, and breakfast nook; and her mother had the mother-in-law apartment; and North had . . . what? The shed in the back corner of the yard, under the pine trees next to a small trout pond fed by a cool clear brook. It was perfectly fine with North. It was all he needed. A place to have a beer, sit back and watch trout dimple the pond's surface as they rose to mayflies; his need to cast to them, to catch them and tear them from their underwater world having long ago abated. He preferred to use the serenity of his modest retreat to crack open a biography of famous and infamous men, and to dwell upon his most pressing cases.

He plucked a pencil from his shirt pocket, tapped it on the tabletop. "So," he said.

"So," Gregory said. He turned a kitchen chair around and sat with his arms folded on the back of it.

"I have to ask these questions," North said.

"Of course," Gregory said.

"Do you know of anyone who hates what you stand for enough to kill a child to send a message?"

"What do we stand for?" Scott said. He blew on his coffee.

"Challengers of the status quo," North said, embarrassed without knowing why exactly. "Champions of civil rights."

"Are you a champion for straightness because you're straight?" Scott said.

Gregory drummed his fingers on the edge of his backward chair. "You know what he means," he said. "We're suing the state after all. We're not just sitting around being our gay selves."

"Plenty of people despised us," Scott said, "before we sued. More people hate us than 'tolerate' us."

"Enough to kill a girl?" North said.

"You think someone killed that girl because of us?" Scott said.

North didn't think anything, not yet. For all he knew, and he knew nothing except that a girl had been killed with a savage blow to the head, there was no link at all to the case. It paid to keep an open mind.

"Maybe they went in there for your attorney's wife," North said. "Found the girl down there and thought that would be good enough to get the point across."

"How'd anyone know Bethany would be home alone?" Scott said.

"I don't know," North said. He didn't. It was a good point.

"You said 'they.'" Scott lit a cigarette with the snap of a gold lighter.

"If it was a kid, he was put up to it, I'd bet," North said. He didn't believe anyone was put up to anything. But he rarely told anyone he interviewed the truth, or what he believed. He told them what he thought would get the most useful reaction out of them. He told them things to take them off guard, set them on edge, or make them think.

"Think," North said. "Is there anyone at all you think might be capable of this?"

"Jed King," Gregory said. Fast. Without thought.

Jed King. Ah yes. He'd been in the paper recently. He and his infamous plow blade. North had arrested him for domestic violence when North had been a trooper. King's wife had dropped charges, of course.

"I don't know. I despise King," Gregory said. "But killing a young girl—"

"He could do it," Scott said. "Easily. I could see that fuck doing it in a heartbeat."

This got North's antennae up. "Why do you say that?"

"Fucking bully. The looks he gives Gregory and me," Scott said. He blew a thread of smoke toward the ceiling. "I've seen that anger, that *fear* in the faces of every asshole whoever teased me or kicked the shit out of me in a locker room or outside a bar. Until I got big enough to give it the fuck back. The man has serious issues."

"His last wife left him for domestic abuse," North said to test the reaction of the couple.

"Surprise, surprise," Gregory said.

"Was she raped? The girl, I mean," Scott said.

The abruptness of the question caught North off guard. "I'm not at liberty to say."

"It's one sick fuck who does something like that," Scott said. "And they think fags are sick."

North flinched at hearing the word *fag* dropped so casually.

"No one thinks pedophiles represent straights any more than they think Leopold and Loeb were typical gays," Gregory said.

"Don't bank on it," Scott said. "And no straights except those into esoteric fucking *art* films even know who the fuck Leopold and Loeb were. Thank fucking God." He took another drag of his cigarette.

North didn't know what the two men were talking about, but he knew he wanted to gag from the cigarette smoke. It had been ages since he'd been forced to breathe in secondhand smoke and his eyes were tearing up, the back of his throat burning.

"King is a first-rate bigoted asshole, but he's no dummy," Scott said. "He's too self-serving to put his own neck on the chopping block. I could see him convincing some poor redneck kid. Get him drunk. Get him worked up into a lather of bigotry."

"Who?" North said. One quick blow. Expert. Not luck. Full

of rage. Yet. Dispassionate. Perfunctory. Or was it luck? *Damn it*, North thought, *I haven't a clue.*

"Victor Jenkins," Gregory said. "Worst kind of bigot: Proud. God on his side. King's the arrogant lout who shouts the *Truth*. Jenkins is scary because he comes from it with some cockamamie religious-based theories—quiet, sneaky, with backward logic and the Old Testament behind him. Some born-again Christian: doesn't know to keep the Old Testament out of it."

"Both dipshits were born in the forties or fifties," Scott added. "But it's harder for the Jed Kings of today to rally the troops than it was back then. If he had put those stupid signs out twenty years ago, he'd have people in town openly clapping him on the back. New laws send the Jed Kings into the dark corners. Unless they make it about religion."

Gregory grinned. "Scott's been rehearsing his stump speech. He says we gays should give the general populous of homophobes the age-old argument they can relate to: We like cock. You like pussy. More pussy for you."

"Except they think we're after their cocks too and you'll never convince the fucks otherwise," Scott said.

"There's the rub," Gregory said. "Pun intended."

"And you two, you were where last night?" North said. He'd waited for a moment when the two men were at ease and unsuspecting to drop the question on them.

Scott laughed and flicked cigarette ash into an empty champagne flute. "You're fucking kidding, right?"

"No."

"Here," Gregory said. "We were both here. I assure you. We were having—" he swept his hands around at the place, "—a bit of a do."

"Others can confirm that?" North said.

"Wouldn't be much of a do with just two, would it, Detective?" Gregory said.

"What time did this do start?" North asked.

Gregory glanced at Scott. "Eight-ish?"

"What were you doing prior to that?" North inquired.

The men were agitated now, body language prickly.

"Getting ready for the do, of course," Gregory said.

"I worked out and went for a run," Scott said.

"Alone?" North asked.

"Yes."

"Time?"

"You're thorough, I'll give you that. Six thirty to seven or so."

"Right," North said.

"What does 'right' mean?" Scott said.

"Nothing. So King's at the top of the list?" North said, shifting gears.

Scott nodded. "Or maybe it's some sicko radical from out of state. You can't rule out someone like that."

"I haven't ruled anything out," North said.

Not even you two, he thought.

Chapter 14

"MOTHER OF GOD," Test said as she pulled her Peugeot off the washboard dirt road onto Jed King's long, private gravel drive. She gaped at the Fisher plow blade situated at the entrance. The blade spray-painted in dripping blood-red letters: GOVERNOR DREW TRADED FARMS FOR FAGS!

Test dialed down the volume of her *Reckoning* CD and drove up the steep dirt drive.

Her Peugeot's muffler had come loose on those damned school speed bumps, and the car blatted and backfired as she downshifted.

Though he had to have heard the racket, Jed King did not look up from where he stood outside his sugar shack chopping firewood as Test pulled up nearby.

Test watched him from her car for a moment. She wanted to ask about the sign left in the Merryfields' lawn. King's sign. Everyone knew. She found it hard to imagine anyone stupid enough to kill Jessica would leave behind what basically amounted to a calling card. But arrogance and pride ran lockstep with hatred and stupidity.

King hefted the axe over his head, the blade gleaming in the sun, then brought it down on a chunk of wood set on a stump. Split the chunk of wood cleanly in two. He set another block of firewood on the stump. He spat in his palms, rubbed them together, clapped them, rubbed them on his Carhartt pants.

Test got out of her car and walked toward King.

The T-shirt King wore was too cold for the day and too tight for his big chest, a chest King probably still thought of as broad, masculine, bullish, but was simply thick with fat. The Indian Motorcycle logo on the T-shirt stretched across the flab.

He continued to ignore Test as she shut her car door, loudly.

He chopped the piece of firewood, split it clean in two, picked up another piece.

"Mr. King," Test said.

King chopped.

"Mr. King."

Test stepped closer to him.

A car pulled in at the bottom of the long dirt drive. A cruiser. Detective North. *Here we go*, Test thought. She knew she was poking a hornets' nest by going to the school independent of the state police earlier. Now, North was tracking her down, likely.

King looked up, past Test, through her, toward the cruiser. He watched North pull the cruiser up and get out, the sun glinting on North's sunglasses. "Afternoon, how are you?" North said.

"Dickie North," King said and placed another log on the stump.

Dickie. Wonderful, Test thought. *Are the two men old drinking buds?*

North nodded curtly at Test. "What are you doing here?" he said.

North's condescension rankled her, but she did not show it. He was surprised to see her, so he clearly wasn't here to give her grief about conducting the student interviews. He wasn't here for her at all.

"Following up on a few things," Test said.

"Such as?" North said.

King rolled his T-shirt sleeves up to bunch them at his shoulders, revealing a Don't Tread On Me tattoo, a nice pairing with the *18:22* tattoo on his forearm.

He raised the axe. "I ain't moving my plow. It's on my property. Legal." The axe hovered above his head. "And I ain't covering up what it says." King brought down the axe; the log split in two. "You're wasting your time, Dickie." Test realized now that King's use of *Dickie* was not one of friendly familiarity but a sarcastic jab of disrespect.

King still had not acknowledged Test's existence.

"It's not about your plow," North said. "It's about the murdered girl."

King set a new log down on the stump. "Don't know the girl."

"Jessica Cumber," Test said, and stepped toward King. "That was her name."

"Still don't know her." King raised the axe. It was a monstrous axe and the morning sunlight glanced off its polished blade again so brilliantly that, for a second, Test was blinded.

"Sir," Test said. "Put the axe down and address us like an adult."

King turned to "Dickie," who took a step closer to stand behind and to the side of Test.

King lifted the axe and buried it into the firewood. He spat. "I said I don't know the girl." His eyes were hard, dark, antagonistic. They dared you to push him so he'd have a reason to strike. Test almost wished he'd go back to ignoring her. Almost.

"Where were you last night?" she asked.

"None of your business."

"It is my business," Test said, her voice flat and calm, even as her heart raced. "It is exactly my business."

"Murder's a state police matter," King said. "Not pissant locals. Ain't that right, Dickie?" He shot a taunting smirk at North, then dug a thumb into his lower lip and flung out a wad of chewing tobacco to the ground at Test's feet. "I said, 'ain't that right?'"

"Officially," North said.

"I'll share what I learn," Test said.

"She shall 'share,'" King bellowed to North. "Ain't that generous of her. Except," he jutted a chin at Test now. "There ain't nothing *to* share. You plan to arrest me? You got a warrant?"

"I can get one," Test said and saw North shake his head in a way barely perceptible. She was bluffing; she had no idea if a judge would grant a bench warrant or not. Likely not. The sign in the Merryfields' yard might be enough to rise to probable cause, with King's open history of hatred toward gays. Then again, likely not.

"So go get you one then," King said.

"We just want to ask," Test began, "I want to ask—"

"Ask all you want. I didn't know the girl and don't know nothing about what happened to her."

"Then you won't mind telling me where you were last night." Test glanced at a sign in the yard: TAKE BACK VERMONT.

"You deaf or just dumb? Is she fucking retarded, Dickie? You hiring retards now, you're so hard up? I *do* mind. Because where I was—" King took a step closer. He was almost in arms' reach. "Is my own business."

"We found one of your signs on the lawn of the house where she was killed," Test said. Her heart was jackhammering now.

"So sue me," King said. "Someone stuck one of my signs in a yard. A lot of people take them from me to get out the word. A lot of people believe in what I believe. More than your type think. You got evidence I planted it in the yard, fine me for trespassing. Even if I did put the sign there, it wouldn't have anything to do with that girl."

That girl. His callous tone enraged Test. What kind of man was so dismissive of a murdered fifteen-year-old girl? A misogynist as well as a bigot. "So what *does* putting the unwelcome signs in yards have to do with then?" Test said.

"Helping the average Joe get his voice heard."

"Getting political are we?" North said. He moved a small step closer to King, nearly side by side with Test.

"Put it however you want," King said.

"How would you put it?" Test said. She wanted to instigate him. Wanted to rile him and get him emotional, if possible. Though not anger him. He was angry enough by nature.

"Doing what you have to do." King took a step closer now. His eyes had a sheen to them, a bright, savage meanness. He was a step away from being in Test's personal space, close enough to reach out his long arms and grab her throat or punch her.

Too close.

Test was trained to order a civilian who got this close to take a step back. But she knew King would not step back. He'd take her order as an invitation to step closer. He'd be all too pleased to show her who was boss here. Her order would escalate the situation. She did not want that. Neither did she want to step back to a safer distance. That would be worse. That would be a surrender of her authority and power.

She stood her ground.

That North was close to her side helped. King may have called him Dickie, but North was still a seasoned cop, an armed cop.

"And what is it you feel you *have* to do? Have to prove?" Test said.

King crowded so close to Test that Test was forced to look up at him. He stood a good ten inches taller than her five feet five inches and likely had 150 pounds on her. Before driving here, Test had switched her sidearm from the chest holster she normally wore to her belt holster. Now she realized too late that she should have unsnapped the strap over her M&P40 before she'd gotten out of her car. There was no way to do it subtly now. And though she wasn't afraid, unstrapping her sidearm holster would show fear, not strength.

"Whatever it takes," King said, staring down at her. His breath stank sour of chewing tobacco.

"And what would that mean?" Test said.

"I'm proud to have the balls to say we don't think fags should get married. They cry about equal rights and—"

"What does 'whatever it takes' mean?"

"Means what it means."

"Stop at nothing?" Test said.

"Dickie," King said. "Let's skip this small-town cat-and-mouse bullshit. It ain't becoming. This little Chihuahua here wants to yap while I got wood to chop. Likes the sound of her own voice. I guess she thinks it sounds sexy." He locked eyes with her and took a step, closed the gap. The reek of his tobacco breath ate up the oxygen between them, his bottom lip stained a cancerous brown with tobacco juice. She heard, thought she heard, North work the snap on his holster. "Well," King said. "It *don't* sound sexy. It sounds like a fucking—"

"Sir, watch what you say," Test said. She squared her shoulders and, instinctively, before she realized what she was doing, unsnapped the strap over her sidearm and set her palm on the butt of it. "I will arrest you."

King laughed. A bark. His eyes on Test's, setting hooks into her.

Test's blood pounded in her ears.

"You want to know if I killed her," King said. "If I want to get a message across to Merryfield, I can say it to the queer-lover's face. And to the two queens he represents. And I *have* said it. Of all the issues that lawyer could be fighting for, he picks this to get attention for himself. Guy's always been a self-promoter. What the fuck's he think is going to happen he dips his dick in that pot?" King inched closer to Test.

"Step back." Test squeezed the butt of her M&P40.

A smile oozed across King's face. He shook his head subtly. His spittle misted Test's face.

"Step back," Test said. "I will not ask again."

King rolled his eyes and took two long, mocking strides backward, his arms out wide. "Happy? Feel better? Feel safe now?"

Test eyed the axe buried in the stump, within arm's reach of

King. Had he moved back to get closer to the axe? "What happened to that girl; she's collateral damage?" Test said.

"Don't put words in my mouth. I know her mother. Good woman. But she can blame Merryfield for what's happened."

"It's Jon Merryfield's fault? The person who actually killed Jessica Cumber isn't responsible?" Test said.

"A man can only be pushed so far."

"And has someone pushed you too far?

"This country's about standing up for what's right."

King wasn't actually answering her questions. He was reciting a list of tired clichés regarding manhood and so-called patriotism.

"You happen to know anyone who would take it that far?" North said. *Another country heard from*, Test thought.

"If I did, I wouldn't tell you, Dickie," King said.

"You'd protect someone like that?" Test said. She'd not thought it possible, but the more King spoke the more she detested him.

"It's not my business to tell the cops anything," King said.

"If you're withholding information, you will be arrested as an accessory after the fact," Test said.

"Is that so?" King said.

"We'll see justice is done."

"Well then, we're after the same thing, sweet cakes."

Abruptly, with no warning, King swung away from her with a swift animal movement and grabbed the axe from the stump and wielded it above his head.

Test had her M&P40 out in an instant. Safety off, finger on her trigger, ready to shoot.

"Wait!" North shouted.

King smiled his nasty smile as he came down with the axe and drove its honed blade into the stump.

He glared at Sonja, her legs spread in a shooting stance, side-arm trained on him.

Her blood sang in her veins, her fingertips pulsed with electric ticks and surges.

"You done?" King said, looking straight at the muzzle as tran-quil as someone watching an ocean sunset.

He'd made a fool out of her. Tricked her into drawing her sidearm. If she'd put a hair more pressure on her trigger, she'd have shot him. Dead. And what would North have testified as the witness? That King had gone for an axe? Or that Test had overreacted?

Test, as calmly as she could, returned her sidearm to its holster as she came out of her shooting stance. "Unless you plan on telling me where you were last night," she said.

"Get a warrant." He leered at her crotch, stained with coffee. "Think she's pissed herself, Dickie." His leer showed his gums were black where they met his stained teeth.

Test breathed through her nose to calm herself, the corner of her left eye twitching.

"Get off my property," King said. "Or I'll have *you* arrested."

North put a hand on Test's shoulder, a gesture Test found more patronizing and inappropriate than anything King had said or done. She shirked free and marched back to her car.

As she opened the door to get into her car, North hurried behind her. "You—"

She spun on him. "You are *not* my superior. You are not my partner. I don't answer to you or—"

"Listen, you—"

"I'll share what I learn."

She got in and slammed the door.

As she wheeled her Peugeot around, she cranked down the window and said to North, "And do not ever put your hand on me again."

It all sounded good. But it didn't make her feel any less mortified.

She pulled out on to Canaan Road, her hands trembling, finally taking her first full breath of the past half hour.

PART II

Chapter 15

BABY JON CRIED softly in Bethany's arms while Bethany waited for Jon at the Willow Inn's registration desk. The lobby smelled of potpourri, and the throw rugs on the pine floors depicted upland scenes of feathery setters and flushing game birds, hunters at the ready with shotguns. Frosted glass sconces cast a tarnished light on the dark woodwork, lending the air of a tobacconist's shop to the space. It was all too much for Bethany, the naturalist romanticism was tired and staid to her mind. Just because the inn had been built in the 1860s, did it mean the décor had to be ancient too? Perhaps the market expected doilies and gun dogs, so that is what it got. How would she know, she wasn't in the bed and breakfast industry. Whatever the case, the place would have to suffice. For now.

Jon burst into the lobby from the blustery day, stamping his wet boots as he pecked Bethany's cheek and put out his pinkie for baby Jon to squeeze. Baby Jon ignored the gesture.

Jon tapped the service bell, too loudly, so the tinny ring seemed to clang in Bethany's skull.

A woman bustled from the back room where a television played *Family Feud*. She fastened her white hair behind her head with bobby pins, then smoothed out the front of her corduroy dress. Even a Marriott or Double Tree would have been better than this, if there was one within fifty miles, Bethany thought.

The woman took a key down from a pegboard shaped like a maple leaf. She gave Jon and Bethany a broad smile that seemed genuine enough but must have gotten tiring after a while.

"We have you in the Ruffed Grouse Room," the woman said. "A crib has been set up." She put the key on the counter. Jon snatched it up.

"We offer a full breakfast in the Ethan Allen Fireplace Lounge," the woman continued. "Right behind you through the French doors. Dial zero if you need anything. Anything at all. Anytime. I'm here all night." She smiled.

"Thanks, Anna," Jon said. How he knew the woman's name, Bethany did not know, or care. He knew everyone's name, it seemed.

Jon put his hand to the small of Bethany's back, picked up the suitcase, and guided Bethany up the stairs.

IN THE RUFFED Grouse Room, Jon and Bethany collapsed on the edge of the canopy bed.

The mattress was too soft and the place smelled musty.

Jon tugged off his boots. The room exuded the requisite colonial charm: the antique armoire, a dry sink, a stone fireplace, crown molding, wainscoting. The bathroom doorway was outlined with stenciled vines. A Homer knock-off print of waterfowlers caught in a gale graced the wall above the fireplace. Doilies lay on the bedside tables. Doilies, doilies. It felt more like a museum than a place to spend a night.

The room was cool and drafty. Around the window, cold air bled in from the outside. The lace curtain rippled. "Can you turn up the thermostat in here?" Bethany asked.

Jon looked around the room helplessly, then went to the fireplace and flipped a switch. From beneath faux ceramic logs, gas lit to weak flames with a whoop and the faint smell of propane. *At least we don't have to build a fire from rubbing two sticks together*, Bethany thought and sagged against the headboard with the baby. She didn't know if Jon could start a fire from scratch. Not without bitching. Anything manual, Jon ended up bitching.

The events of the past day had left her beleaguered and bitchy herself. *Is nothing ever good enough for me?* she wondered. Her mother had often thought not.

Baby Jon whimpered. "Shhh. Baby," Bethany said. "Momma's tired." Her voice was a frayed thread about to break.

Jon touched Bethany's cheek and, unexpectedly, Bethany began to weep, taken aback by her own tears. She was so tired. So scared. Whoever had killed the girl in their house was still out there. What if they had been hoping she and Jon had been home, and killed the babysitter as a consolation? What if they still had sights on Jon and Bethany? And why did she keep thinking it was *they*. Two killers? It was irrational. The cops needed to locate the boy, whoever he was.

"I'm sorry," Jon said and put a hand on her shoulder as she stifled her tears. She despised crying. *Put a good face on it*, her father had said when she was upset as a girl, tilting a martini glass or waggling his practice putter at her for emphasis.

"It will be all right," Jon said.

"No. It won't."

"I promise."

"You can't promise that." She clutched baby Jon.

"You'll see," Jon said.

"I'm not going back there."

"That's why I arranged to come here. We'll rest, give ourselves a break and—"

"I'm never going back."

Jon lifted his hand from her shoulder. "What are you saying?"

"I can't live there."

"It's our *home*," he said. "Your dream home."

"Not anymore. Sell it. Sell everything in it. Sell the clothes and the furniture. The appliances and TV. Everything. I don't want anything from that place. Burn it to the ground for all I care."

"The house didn't *do anything*."

"You're shouting," Bethany said.

"I am *not* shouting."

"You're scaring the baby."

Jon looked up at the ceiling and shook his head, as he always did when she called him out.

He let out a long breath, as he always did. Predictable Jon. "A person did it," he said.

"A sick person. We had a monster in our house. Because of *you*."

Jon cringed. "It was that boy, whoever he is," he said, but his voice held no conviction, and the lost, searching look in his eyes seemed to betray thoughts to the contrary. "And they'll get him.

They will. And we'll move back in just like we were. And that will be that."

Bethany sat up rigid against the headboard. The baby was awake now, struggling to get loose of his swaddle and mewling. Sometimes the kid sounded like an animal instead of a human, Bethany thought. "No. *That won't* be *that*," she said. "That girl will still be dead. That house will still be where she was murdered. I'll still be the one who found her. And I'll still be the one who insisted we go out to dinner. Pushed. To have my way, knowing you'd go if I pushed. *That* is *never* that." Her gaze wandered about the room as if her eyes had come loose in her head.

"Fine," Jon said. "You want me to sell it. I'll sell it. Sell everything. But *you* need to rest. Collect yourself."

He attempted to help her lie down, but she shrugged him off.

"Sell it," she said.

"I said I would."

How did our conversations ever devolve to such a state? Bethany wondered as she closed her eyes and tried in vain to wish it all away.

Chapter 16

IN THE BATHROOM, Jon splashed cold water on his face. He removed his glasses and set them on the sink edge, avoided his reflection. Often, he went weeks—sometimes months—without looking himself square in the eye, never really seeing himself. Just enough to shave. He'd done this for as long as he could remember. Since. Well. Now, he looked. Stared at a tired man pushing forty. In his mind he pictured himself as twenty-five, still in law school, a time when he thought he'd had his future figured out, and his past behind him. A time when the architecture of his master plan to find peace through success was first set in motion.

He glanced in the mirror now to glance at the reflection of Bethany, who was now asleep on the bed behind him through the doorway. Her son was asleep, safe under her arm. What had happened in the house had crushed her. Jon had thought she'd suffer it better. The girl may have seemed nice, but Jon knew better. She'd been screwing in his home, for starters. Jon had known girls like Jessica in high school. He had all right. At the only party he'd ever attended, a bunch of girls who'd seemed shy in the school hallways had, with a few wine coolers in them, writhed in bikinis around a bonfire like genies wriggling from bottles. A girl in a kimono had handed him a bottle of schnapps. He'd taken a drink. And another. And another. His first taste of alcohol. A joint was passed. The girl in the kimono slipped her arm around him. "I'm Suzy," she'd said.

"Sushi," Jon slurred as he swayed.

Underneath Sushi's loose kimono peeked powder-blue terry-cloth shorts and a tube top. She drank. Jon drank. She removed her kimono, took his hand and led him to the beach.

They laid on their backs on the lakeshore, drinking. Stars fell. The night hot. She'd lain on top of him. Her mouth on his. His head pounded. His hands searched. He'd wanted them down her shorts. Inside. He wanted, for once, to feel normal. To do what other teens did. To *be* normal. That night had been his chance.

They'd kissed. She'd moaned. Her eye shadow glittered. She'd pressed against him. Ground against him. He'd rolled over to lie on top of her. Her neck fiery hot. So soft. Such softness. His first feel of female flesh.

His heart had buzzed. He'd chewed her neck. She'd arched her back. The stars fell. She'd bitten his jugular. His head full of stars. He couldn't breathe. He'd inched her top down. "Hey," she'd said. He'd put his mouth on her bare breast. "Hey." His fingers had slipped in her waistband. She'd grabbed his wrist. He'd kissed her. She turned her face away and tried to speak. A racket in his head. All the jocks in school who had girls fawning over them got their way because they were confident. Aggressive. That was the way of things. So easy for them. So damned easy for everyone fucking else.

He'd kissed her harder. A window opened in his mind. A cold breeze blew through. He'd pushed two fingers into her. God. She'd scratched at his back. Clawed. He'd read about this. The throes. Three fingers. The fourth wouldn't go. Just wouldn't. He'd needed time, to keep working her, because something was wrong. He was not ready. He'd curled his fingers into a fist of rage.

He looked down on her. His knees had somehow pinned her arms. Sickened, he pulled his fingers from her and wiped them on his leg as she'd scrambled from underneath him and shrieked, "You fucker. You creep." She rubbed her wrists where he'd held her. "Don't you know anything, you idiot?"

His neck hurt from looking up at her from where he lay in the sand, but he feared that if he tried to stand she'd run away. His skull felt fragile.

"You do this often?" she said. "Get girls drunk and—"

"I've never even—. You got me drunk."

"It doesn't matter. A boy can be drunk, a girl can't. That's how it works."

"You're creeping me out now," he'd said, confused. Always so confused.

"Good. You should be creeped out. You're lucky I didn't scream rape."

The word slammed inside him. Echoed in his head. He'd felt sick and terrified, and angry. So fucking angry and confused. Anything but normal.

He'd reached for her.

She'd slapped his face, hard, and run off.

He'd never gone to another high-school party. Never looked at another girl. He'd feared the humiliation. Ridicule. Condemnation and disgrace. He'd had no way to know if what he had done was aberrant or typical. He had no friends to afford perspective. He'd had only himself and his grandparents, who were so out of touch with any generation that had come after their own.

For years, he'd feared what he was capable of doing and how to cultivate and to maintain an image of normalcy.

He thought of Jessica in the cellar of the creamery.

Everything that had come before had led to that moment.

He was a fly caught in the web of his own lies.

JON LAY IN bed beside Bethany, not quite touching her.

He watched her sleep. Her eyeballs shifted beneath their lids, as if still trying to see.

She was lovely. So lovely.

Each time he watched her sleep, the sweet calm of her face left him overcome with a sense of sorrow, guilt for all the times he'd treated her poorly, argued, turned away.

He wanted to wake her, felt an urge to confess to her things he had never told another soul. He felt compelled to lay himself bare. Let her see him, know him, for who and what he was, whatever the cost. Even if he lost her. If he did not do it now, he never would. He felt the truth in him. It lay burrowed deep, cold and sour, a slow-working poison he needed to bleed out.

He thought about the messages he'd erased from his voice mail.

That voice.

It turned his blood to dust.

He slipped his cell phone from his pocket and brought up the e-mail with the subject line: "You Should Have Helped Me."

The e-mail read:

> *You have a week to confess on your own.*
> *Then, I tell them how sick and evil you are.*

Jon deleted the e-mail, knowing it would do no good. Nothing was ever hidden forever, he'd begun to realize.

He rested a fingertip on his wife's wrist, his hand shaking uncontrollably.

Her wrist was so slender, so warm. His own flesh cold.

He felt a pulse at his fingertip but he did not know if it was her pulse or his own.

Chapter 17

JED KING KNELT at the edge of the cedar swamp, peered under a blown-down tree, straight into the eyes of the red fox caught in a #2 Victory leg-hold trap.

Foxes had been working the swamp edge pretty good of late. King had discovered this while running his beaver and muskrat trap lines, so had run a string of fox setups. There was good money in fur again. Not as good as in the eighties, before all the bleeding hearts fussed and cried. He'd never see those prices again. But current prices made trapping worth the effort.

He stared at the fox. A male. It was early in the season and the fur was not nearly prime. Still, it was worth a good sixty bucks.

King took an old axe handle from his trapper's basket.

He tapped the ax handle in his palm, looked at the fox.

The fox hunkered, bared its teeth.

King stepped closer.

The fox tried to pull free of the trap, but couldn't.

It stared up at King, snapped its jaws, spitting.

King tapped the axe handle in his palm. "Hold still. It's no use."

There were many who believed what King did was cruel; even those who wore fur. They didn't like that the fur came from *cute* animals. Cute. Anyone who'd ever seen a mink or a beaver close up knew how foul they were. Vermin. Their fur stank of algae and glandular musk. They had teeth as yellow as an old woman's toenails. They boiled with parasites. Beaver dams flooded farms and ball fields. The red fox was a handsome animal when it was a kit, King gave them that much. But even then the feral beasts crawled with fleas and ticks. Their ears so full of mites they leaked puss from infection. Their haunches caked with shit.

Activists knew squat about wild animals. No shock when they only left their work desk and computer to sit their lazy asses in front of the TV or maybe go hike on a *nature trail* that had signs posted along the way to identify everything they observed.

What these people did not understand was, for a wild animal, there was no more humane death than the trapper's club or the hunter's bullet. Any natural means of death in the wild was long and slow and torturous and *painful*: gangrene from a cut that never healed; slow starvation and dehydration over foodless months in the winter; drowning; brain tumors and heartworm; cancer with no treatment; slipping on the ice of a frozen pond and being unable to get back up; being dragged down by coyotes by your haunches, then ripped open, intestines fed on while you still kicked and bleated. That was nature. That was the *cute* world of the wild. Just what the fuck did these people think happened out in the wild?

King often asked folks who railed against trapping what death they would prefer, if they had a choice: The slow, anguishing, humiliating death nature offered or a sudden, skilled, painless blow to the skull, a quick bullet to the heart, and then, nothing? He knew which he'd prefer. What ass-backwards hogwash. Jesus, it infuriated him, the hypocrisy: These bleeding hearts who *loved* animals so much but wanted them to die cruel and humiliating deaths were the same damned ones who pushed for legal euthanasia and suicide for humans, railed about death with dignity. Shit.

King took no pleasure in killing.

He offered what the market wanted.

He was professional.

Humane.

He did what a man needed to do.

King tapped the axe handle in his palm.

The fox thrashed wildly in a futile attempt to escape.

King brought the axe handle down on the fox's skull with a single clean, expert blow.

The fox flattened, its back leg jerking, then falling still.

It was over.

Painless.

Just like that.

You should be so lucky.

Chapter 18

JUST PAST A cluster of rusted mailboxes, Richard North pulled his car off Route 12 on the outskirts of the neighboring town of Ivers and down a dirt road whose sign read: BARKER FARM MOBILE HOME PARK.

Inside the park, the road turned to dirt at a T and made a one-way loop through the park. Drivers entered on the right and exited back out on the left. There was no sign but everyone knew that was the way it worked. The trailers sat perpendicular to the road to allow more of them per acre, placed so close together the only real estate between them was a shared dirt driveway; and so close to the road that dust from cars blew into open windows to collect, North imagined, on the tops of big-screen televisions and the arms of beer-stained velour loveseats.

A Rottweiler charged out from under a parked pickup truck. It barked and bared its fangs and black gums, lunged at North's door to be yanked hard onto its back when it hit the end of its rusted chain. It yelped and lunged again, was yanked back again, saliva slinging from its mouth. Dope dealers owned dogs like that.

There were plenty around. Marijuana: cash crop of Vermont. The nascent craft brewing rage had nothing on the dope growers. Not yet, anyway. He had nothing personally against marijuana. Didn't believe it was a gateway drug, and in his day as a patrol officer had always been far more at ease and safe when he dealt with stoners rather than drunks during a call in the middle of the night.

North crept the cruiser along.

A gaggle of barefoot boys dressed in torn jeans and sleeveless flannel shirts played football in the road. They disassembled and shuffled slowly to the roadside, where they gawped at the patrol car. Their faces glistened with sweat as they stood with their hands on their hips, thumbs crooked in the corners of their pockets, or arms folded across their chests. They spat and scuffed their feet and kept their narrowed eyes on North. The boy with the football stood with the ball tucked under his arm. Blood trickled from his nose into his mouth. He licked at it.

Trailer #47, painted a sunny lemon yellow, occupied a piece of ground a good three times larger than any of the other trailers. A recently painted green door and green shutters graced the façade. Tidily shorn shrubs grew along its skirt not quite concealing the cinderblock base, which was also painted yellow. From window flower boxes, dried husks of geraniums faced a long winter before they would see weather warm enough to bloom blood red again.

Jessica's mother, Marigold Cumber, had owned all of this land in the late eighties. It had been what was left of her family's generational dairy spread. Marigold had sold the land to a shyster developer from Montreal in a knee-jerk decision after her brother and husband were killed in, of all things, a marijuana raid gone bad. She'd moved down to Florida to be with her mother. But years later, moved back after her mother passed on. Right back where she started. Except now instead of living proudly in a modest trailer with astounding views of open family land all around her, she paid rent to a crook to live among folks who hooked Rottweilers to chains.

Marigold had returned home with a three-year-old daughter in tow. Rumor had it that the father was some teenage kid named Jessup that Marigold had fallen in with and who'd moved away after Marigold set out for Florida. The math didn't work, but maybe Jessica was his namesake for other reasons.

Now, that daughter, the only child Marigold would ever have, was dead.

Some people lived lives of perpetual hardship. Endured rather than lived.

Good people.

How is that? North wondered.

The driveway sat empty. North pulled the cruiser in and shut down the engine.

He got out.

The sun shone keenly, cruel and cold. In a window of the neighboring trailer, a curtain flicked. North was still bothered by what had happened at Jed King's place. If he hadn't needed to come out here, he'd have gone after Detective Test and spoken his mind freely. Told her just what he'd thought of her actions. But, duty called. He'd make it a point to find her later. It was not something he wanted to say over the phone. It was something better left in person.

A tiny porch enclosed Marigold's front steps.

An American flag hung limp in the cold, dead air.

North walked up the two steps and rang the bell with a sense of dread. He knew patrol officers had come in the night to inform

Ms. Cumber of her daughter's death. But the look on a mother's face, her posture, when the wound was so fresh was almost unbearable. There was nothing that could be said, nothing that could be done, to help those drenched in such profound and piercing grief. They were alone in their suffering, even if they were in conversation with God.

He rapped on the door.

No answer came.

He rang the bell.

No one came.

He rapped on the storm door's Plexiglas window.

The boys who had been playing football now stood on the road out in front of the trailer and stared up the driveway at the porch, hands stuffed deep in their pockets. At least there were no media lurking about the park. Perhaps they'd come and gone. More likely they were more interested in the gay-marriage angle. It was juicier, seamier. It sold papers and got page views. True or not.

North was about to knock again when the main door opened just enough to straighten its chain lock. A sliver of an old woman's face appeared in the crack. Too old to be Marigold Cumber's face. An eye worked over North. The woman pulled the collar of a plaid bathrobe up around her neck. Cigarette smoke drifted through the screen and North held back a cough. The woman did not open the storm door. "No comment," she said. "Hear?"

"I'm not a reporter, ma'am," North said.

"Who're you then?"

"A detective, with the Vermont State Police, ma'am."

"Quit calling me ma'am, we aren't in Alabama."

"I need to speak with Ms. Cumber. Is she in?"

"You expect her to be out shopping? The reporters finally pushed off, now we have to deal with you?"

"May I see her?" North said. He showed her his ID.

The old woman disappeared from the door. Muffled voices found their way to North from inside. The old woman reappeared. She glanced toward the cruiser. "She's too tired."

"I really do need—"

"Not now you don't. She's—"

The woman's eyes drifted to look behind North. He heard a car with a bad exhaust pull in and a car door shut. He turned around. Unbelievable.

Sonja Test was walking toward the trailer. Did she never give up? There was nothing he could do to prevent her from speaking with witnesses or persons of interest, but to come to the mother's home. It took a pair. She was—

The old woman opened the door slightly as Test came to stand beside North on the crowded porch steps.

"She your partner," the old lady said.

"No," Test said.

"You a cop too?" the old woman said.

"A detective."

"A lady cop." The old woman disappeared from the door without any warning.

"Look," North said, facing Test. The two stood closer than King and Test had been to one another earlier. "About earlier, you need—"

The old woman returned, waved her cigarette at Test. "You can come in. He"—she clicked her teeth at North—"can't."

North saw a smile quiver at the corners of Test's lips.

"No," Test said, surprising North.

"How's that?" the old woman said.

"All due respect," Test said, "Detective North is the lead on this investigation and he's here for one thing only: to help find who murdered Ms. Cumber's daughter. So. Please. Don't impede him from—"

"Don't do what?" the old woman said.

"Please, let him in with me," Test said.

The woman shut the door.

North stared at the door, confounded. "Thanks," he managed.

"I only said it because it's true. And all I care about is—"

The door opened. The old woman waved them in as if waving at a mosquito in her sleep.

North opened the door and the two detectives stepped inside.

Chapter 19

A CRAMPED LIVING area lay in near darkness. The scent of vanilla air spray could not cloak the odor of cigarette smoke and fried food. The paneled walls, which undoubtedly had once been a faux wood grain, were painted pink. Across from a sunken couch, almost within arm's reach of it, stood an enormous particleboard entertainment center that ate up most of the room. In the center of it, where a TV would sit, an aquarium more massive than any North had seen in a home, sat on display.

The aquarium teemed with luminous, exotic fish that swam in circles, darted, and finned in place. Some appeared dead, their lips suctioned to the glass. A black light lit pink pebbles littered across the bottom, and illuminated the stripes of fish to a neon glow. North didn't care for fish. He didn't like fishing and he didn't like to eat fish. Found their taste foul and flesh grotesque. Probably because he didn't like water. He'd nearly drowned as a boy, the memory of which he now pushed down as it tried to rise. *Where's my focus gone?* he thought.

On the shelves to either side of the aquarium sat precisely arranged porcelain horse figurines. A red ribbon hung from around the neck of one horse, a rearing black stallion.

On the top shelf sat dozens of framed photos of Jessica.

In one photo, Jessica leaned forward astride a horse, arms wrapped adoringly around its neck. A red show ribbon was attached to the bridle. Jessica's eyes were closed, her face lit with a smile so ecstatic, so simple and joyous, so *youthful*, it broke North's heart for knowing he'd never find such sheer happiness again, and neither would she. The happiness of a child.

"Fourth place at a 4-H show. You'd swear she'd won gold at the Olympics," a woman's voice said.

Marigold Cumber, Jessica's mother, sat in the tiny kitchen at a small white wrought-iron café table with a scalloped edge. Her chair, one of a pair, matched the table, its back fashioned of a single piece of iron bent to approximate the shape of a heart. The sort of table set you might find in a Paris café.

The old woman dragged on a cigarette and looked at the photo of Jessica on the horse. "Girl was so full of sunshine you'd swear one day she was going to burst into flames."

"Will you please go outside with that cigarette, Aunt Jean?" Marigold said.

The old woman rolled her eyes. "Person can't smoke nowheres these days. Not even after traveling across the country to lend a hand."

North's abdomen tightened at the woman's careless words as Test stared coolly at her.

The woman hacked. "I'll leave her with you two then." She was halfway out the door when she said, "That gang a boys is back. You think they'd have more goddamned respect." She stepped out onto the porch, the door snapping shut behind her as she railed: "You boys get the hell onto your own damned business!"

Marigold tugged a window shade near her and let it go so it rolled up with a sharp snap. As she wrapped her hands around a brown bottle on the table, sunlight angled through the window and bathed her in its light. The bottle's label had been peeled off and lay in shreds on the table. Marigold took a long drink from the bottle. "Please, in here," she said, "it's more pleasant."

North crossed to the kitchen. There was scant room for him and Test to join Jessica's mother.

"There's a folding chair there behind you," she said to North. He took the metal chair and unfolded it and squeezed in at the table.

Marigold drank. "Can I get either of you a drink? I'm afraid all I got's water and"— she raised her bottle—"cream soda."

North felt shame course through him for assuming Marigold had been drinking beer.

"No thank you, ma'am," Test said.

North placed his elbows on the table. It teetered. It may have been the style of a table found in Paris, but it was made of cheap plastic. A knockoff found at any chain hardware store.

The kitchen counters were spotless, bare of anything save a compact microwave. On the refrigerator door, magnets held up more photos of Jessica.

Test's gaze roved over a photo of Jessica who had her arm around another girl.

"We're sorry for your loss, Mrs. . . . . is it Mrs. or Ms.?" Test said.
"Marigold."
"Marigold," Test said.
Marigold tightened her mouth and looked at the pile of shred-

ded label. "It hit me last night," she said absently. "Then. Today. Nothing. For a spell. Even if I'm thinking of her or looking right at a photo. Nothing. Then. It comes." She scratched her thumbnail across where the label on the bottle had been, scraping back the glue so it curled under her nail. Her tears dripped on the table, but she made no sound.

"If you need a moment," Test said.

Marigold nodded. "I do."

North set his notepad on the table. The table teetered.

"If you fix the matchbook under the leg on your side," Marigold said.

Richard leaned over, wedged the matchbook he saw under the leg and sat back up, dizzy. He tested the table. It was level.

"That usually does it," Marigold said.

The aquarium's aerator gurgled.

Marigold looked at Test. Her gaze was unwavering, her eyes lucid.

"If we may," Test said.

Marigold nodded.

Test looked at North to ask a question. Instead, he nodded to Test to begin.

"Did your daughter have a boyfriend?" Test said.

"No."

"How sure of that are you?"

"Sure as a mother can be. So. Not very. We all know we don't know everything about our kids, having been kids."

"But as far as you know?"

"Far's I know."

"How about friends who were boys?"

"She talked about them. Pals. I never met any of them."

"None of them?" Test said.

"She only ever brought her around." Marigold pointed at the photo on the refrigerator, the one Test had been studying, the one with Jessica's arm slung over the girl's shoulder.

"Olivia," Test said.

North fixed his eyes on Test. How did she know the friend's name?

"Do you know any of the other kids' names?" Test said.

"If I thought about it, I might. It's hard to focus."

"Of course. Was there anything troubling about her behavior lately?"

"Nothing I noticed."

"Nothing out of the ordinary?"

"No."

"No change in mood or personality?"

"Not really."

"Not really?"

"She was cracking down even more than usual with her studies. Spending a lot of time at the town library at night. She always studies so hard. Better than I ever did. She gets *so* upset by a couple Bs. Imagine? Upset over Bs. I'd a been thrilled to get a B, just once."

Test glanced at North. He gestured for her to continue.

"So the extra studies were her idea?" Test said.

"I was all for it, of course. But I wasn't exactly cracking the whip after her getting three As and two Bs."

"I see," Test said. "Why'd the library? Why didn't she study at home?"

"The Internet. It's lousy and slow here. And. Well. Expensive. I couldn't swing it. Or a laptop." She blushed. "I was saving for one.

For college." She closed her eyes. The tears came again. A river of them. Sudden and silent. They spattered the table. She took a deep breath and squeezed her eyes tightly. Deep wrinkles sprang at their corners. She opened her eyes and offered the most pained smile North had ever seen. He bit the inside of his cheek. He saw Test's own cheek twitch but her face otherwise remained comported, her gaze compassionate.

Test cleared her throat. "Take your time."

Marigold nodded for Test to continue.

"Did she have a cell phone?" Test said.

Marigold shook her head as her fingers worked at remnant glue stuck to the side of the bottle. "I . . ." Her voice broke. "I have one in the cabinet over the fridge. A pay-as-you-go cheapie. Nothing like her friends have. I'm sure. But." She bit her lip. "I was saving it for Christmas. I wanted her to have it." She stopped. "For her safety."

North saw Test's fingers twitch, as if they wanted to reach out and hold this mother's hand.

"Did she study with Olivia or anyone else? Any of Olivia's boy-friends?" Test said.

Marigold sipped her soda. "Never mentioned anyone. Just said she had to use the Internet for papers. She must of met up with Olivia one time or another."

"Would you mind showing us her bedroom?"

Marigold hung her head. "I can't."

"We'd be very—"

"You can look. I can't go in there. Not yet. It's the first room on the right."

"Of course," Test said. "We'll be respectful. There might be something to help us find who—"

"I don't care who," Marigold said.

North felt Test's eyes on him.

"I don't care if you find him or not," Marigold said. "Except to spare someone else."

"We'd like to do that."

"I wish it had been me," Marigold said.

Test put a hand on her hand.

"She was going to be a veterinarian," Marigold said. "She was going to make something of herself."

Chapter 20

TEST OPENED JESSICA'S bedroom door. The window shade was up, the room bright and stifling with trapped sunshine.

She took two pairs of surgical gloves from her jacket pocket and handed a pair to North.

"You carry two pairs?" he said.

"Four."

They put the gloves on, and stepped inside the room.

The paneled walls and a tiny girl's dresser were painted a matching lavender. Posters of horses covered every wall except the one facing the door. This wall was adorned with posters of the Eiffel Tower, l'Arc de Triomphe, the Place de la Bastille, the Louvre, the Royal Palace, and prints of Picasso's *The Doves* and Monet's *Water Lilies.*

Each poster hung perfectly square.

In the right corner, a twin bed sat on a frame with no headboard or footboard. The mattress had no bedspread, but the top sheet was pulled tight and neat and the single pillow was fluffed and placed at the head. On the pillow perched a white teddy bear that clutched a red velvet heart to its chest. To the left was a door-less closet. A half-eaten bag of potato chips and a neat stack of textbooks sat on the floor beside the mattress. There was scarcely enough floor space to take a step in the room.

Test knelt at the textbooks, each wrapped with a dust jacket of paper lunch bags. Test recalled covering her books in high school, writing R.E.M. lyrics on them. She was surprised and touched that kids still used paper lunch bags when most rituals of one generation never made it to the next generation. Jessica's covers were blank.

Test opened each book. On the inside cover of each, in neat print, was the name *Jessica Jean Cumber*. Test removed the dust jackets: *Geometry I, Earth Science, American History: The Colonial Period, Francais II*, and *Biology I.*

As North investigated the closet, Test sat on the edge of the mattress. She lifted each book by the spine and shook it to rid it of loose papers. Only one book produced anything: a quiz on biology: 10 out of 10. *Excellent work, again!*

Jessica, as Test had been told by Gardiner and Jessica's friends and teachers, was not just smart, but studious. Curious. She enjoyed learning. She embraced it. Test remembered the exhilaration she herself had felt when first learning new subjects that had stimulated her young mind. The world was astonishing, bursting with magical possibility. It still was. If you looked. Claude, bless his artistic wiring, reminded her every day of what he called Common Joys. He was sappy and a sentimentalist. But he was right, mostly. She loved that about him. It was one of many reasons why she'd asked him to marry her.

She flipped through the pages. She recalled doodling and writing notes in the margins of her books, but the margins of these books had remained clean. She leafed through book after book. Nothing.

Then, on page 145 of *Biology I*, next to the image of a protozoa, in a miniscule version of the neat hand lettering from the inside cover was written, *I love you know who.*

"Look," Test said.

North leaned over her shoulder.

Test put her fingertip under the declaration.

"Hers?" North asked.

Test flipped from the page to the inside cover and back again.

"Keep looking," North said.

They sifted through the room.

They searched the pockets of Jessica's clothing.

They emptied dresser drawers onto the mattress to file through bras, and through panties blotted with menstrual fluid.

They found an old diary whose last entry was 2007, when Jessica had been twelve.

There was nothing in it that pointed to anyone or anything threatening, or any emotional upheaval. The entries were mostly about plans. Plans to own her own horse. Plans to be a veterinarian.

They found a sheaf of letters, all of them from Olivia. Gossip about other girls, movie stars, unfair teachers and their teacher's pets. It comforted Test to see handwritten notes between friends, charged with emotions, with possibility. Already, though cell service remained atrocious in many pockets, Test saw teenagers texting all the time wherever they got service. She wondered if texting would supplant the secret note passed among the grapevine of friends? It probably already had. She supposed one didn't miss what one never knew. It wasn't as if she missed phonographs.

Not one note from Olivia indicated troubles or a boyfriend.

"How did you know her name?" North asked.

"Whose?"

"Olivia's."

Test arranged Jessica's clothes back into their proper drawers.

North sighed and rummaged through the coats and shirts in the closet.

"About earlier, at King's place," North started, then stopped. "Look," he said.

North handed Test a scrap of paper. It had been folded twice. It contained Jessica's handwriting:

I wish I could tell the world about him. I wish I could tell someone. Anyone. It's not fair. Mom's mom got married when she was like sixteen, to a 27 year old! Married! All I want to do is date him. If I could, I'd hire Mr. Merryfield to sue the state and free me and V to be together. Even if he is such a jerk sometimes.

"V," North said.

Test reread the note, an electric pulse surging along her spine at a possible lead. But, that was all it was. Possible. She would not make assumptions. Would not form a theory. Not until they discovered who V was and how, and if, he fit.

"This is it," North said. His face was set with certainty.

"Maybe," Test said. "I don't want to rush—"

"The note is dated last week."

"I know."

"So, if this V had nothing to do with it, where is he? Why hasn't he come forward if his girlfriend, the girl that loved him so much, just got murdered?"

"He's older. Maybe too old. She's fifteen, by weeks. How do we start to figure out who V is, when none of her classmates so much as mentioned a boy, let alone a boyfriend?"

"That's how you knew Olivia's name," North said. "You *went* to Jessica's school?"

"To interview her friends."

"You can't do that."

"I can."

"But you shouldn't. I had people going there at noon, damn it. We need to coordinate. Not waste resources on redundancies."

"Our budgets are separate."

"I'm not talking about budget. I'm talking about time. Wasting time. Your chief Barrons is not going to be pleased his budget is eaten up by redundant interviews. I can assure you."

Test kept her back to him. "We can trade notes." She said it coolly, but North's mention of Barrons left her uneasy. Would North report her to her Barrons, use budgetary reasons to keep her at bay? The more Test learned of Jessica—serious, quiet, studious, curious, goal oriented—the more Test felt an affinity with her. The more Jessica reminded her of herself. The more she needed to feel a need to act on her behalf, as a detective, and as a woman.

"You need to keep your word. Share information," North said.

"I just *got* it this morning," Test said. "Was I going to talk shop in front of a grieving mother out there? When I go over the recordings and make notes, I'll give them to you."

"You should have told me you were going in the first place. Beforehand. I hope for your sake you'll cooperate and not—"

"I got you into this house," Test said. She could not restrain herself. It was juvenile to bring up, but it was true. She had gained capital for providing North entry into this home, but she had to spend that capital judiciously. Not push. She wanted to be done with this prattling.

"We'd have been glad to include you this afternoon," North said.

She didn't believe him.

"Now you don't have to," she said.

North worked a palm over the back of his neck and squeezed. "OK," he said. "Maybe my men will get something you didn't. Or maybe the kids you spoke to were lying about a boyfriend. Hiding it."

"All of them?"

"Some. Olivia. For example."

"If she knew, there'd be mention in the notes between the girls."

"Maybe."

"No. No maybe. I know. I was a girl."

"Kids lie. They're no different than us."

"Cynic," she said, though she knew he was right.

"Realist."

Test held no naïve delusions about kids being wide-eyed innocents. She'd seen enough from George and Elizabeth to know how manipulative they could be. King and queen. Ugh. She'd never once given thought to her kids' names being linked to royalty. *George* was an old family name on Claude's side, and Test was simply fond of the name Elizabeth, though not Liz or, God forbid, Lizzy. Never Lizzy. But when she'd told friends what she'd named the second of her two children, her friends had yipped: the king and queen! Test had been aghast, and swore she'd never refer to her kids as such; though now she used it when she was peeved at the two children for giving off an air of snootiness and entitlement, especially when they lied to get their way. Sure, kids lied. All kids. God, had Test ever lied to her parents. North was right. Still, there was a balance to be drawn. Kids lied, usually, in *reaction* to something: to get out of something, mainly trouble. Adults lied for the same reason, too, of course. But they also lied premeditatively to *get* something. For personal gain. An end game.

"Jessica never told *anyone* about V," Test said. A theory was forming in her mind. The waters still muddy. "V is a secret for a reason. The tone of the note. The content." She read the note again. "V is older. It's plain."

"How much older?"

"I hate to think."

She tapped the bag that held the note to her lips, thinking. Aligning her thoughts.

How would they track down this V? She'd need to go over her recording of the kids and teachers she'd interviewed. Perhaps there was something there. Perhaps—

A thought tugged at her mind but she could not place it.

"You all right?" North said.

"Ruminating."

North nodded. "Earlier, at Jed King's, you—"

Test didn't want to hear it. Not while she was trying to focus. And she didn't need to be reprimanded by North. "It'll have to keep," she said and left the room.

Chapter 21

Jed King sat in his truck in the parking lot across the street, staring at the queers' house. His idling truck rocked on its springs. Rain dappled the windshield. The windshield wipers swept. The rain dappled. Jed watched.

He powered down his truck window and fished the wad of tobacco out of his lower lip, flicked it off his fingers, spat to the pavement, and packed a new pinch in his lip, resting his arm on the window frame, the rain wetting his shirt sleeve.

He enjoyed the buzz as the nicotine spiked his blood and he stared at the pansies' house.

The truck's radio was set to an AM station, the volume low, as if the talk-show host and his guest were sharing secrets not meant to be overheard by just anyone.

"They *want* you to like them," the host said. "They *want* your *kids* to *like* them, to see them as flawed but good people, just like you and me."

"Amen," said the guest.

"But they're *not* just like you and me. Are they?"

"No," King said.

"They want you to believe their issue is the same as that of blacks in the sixties. A human-rights issue. It is not. Being black is not a choice."

King nodded, pounded a fist on the steering wheel.

"I have with me today Malcolm Johnson, an Afro-American minister who feels it's an insult for homosexuals to relate their cause to that of the civil rights movement of Afro Americans."

King turned up the volume.

The front door to the queens' house opened.

A neighbor's dog barked.

The screen door slammed.

Jed sat up, gripped the steering wheel.

The windshield wipers swept.

Rain dappled.

Jon Merryfield stepped from the house and pulled the collar of his jacket up against the rain then waved back toward someone King could not see.

How could a man defend such people? It made King sick.

Merryfield had always unnerved King in a remote way King couldn't quite nail.

King had known Merryfield since Merryfield was a strange, lonely kid living with his grandparents.

He'd always been off.

Fey.

King wondered.

Merryfield jogged across the lot behind King's truck. The guy was married, but that meant squat. Years ago, King used to spot Merryfield at Sarah's Sawmill when Merryfield had just come back from some fancy-ass southern law school. He'd shoot pool in a polo shirt but try to act like he belonged among working men. He'd curse. Swill cheap draft beer. Dip tobacco. But his pool game betrayed him; it was all geometry. Dry. Calculated. No instinct. Just like a lawyer.

A guy who tried so hard to belong where he never would had a screw loose, if you asked King.

King watched Merryfield climb into his fucking Land Rover and rest his forehead on the steering wheel. Merryfield remained like that so long King thought he'd fallen asleep.

Finally, Merryfield stirred, stared out his windshield in a trance, then drove out of the lot.

King looked back at the entrance of the queers' house, eyes squeezed to the slits.

The ginger-haired queer sauntered out of the house now, a black scarf tucked down the front neck of a buttoned suede coat as he swished down the sidewalk in his hurried fussy gait, as if he'd been born late and ever since had been trying to catch up to the person he was supposed to be. He had that lame old mutt on a leash with him. Not that the damn thing needed a leash. It could barely walk, and could barely squat now as it took a dump on the lawn and the queer scooped it up in one of those yuppie crap sacks. Why they didn't show the damned dog mercy and put it down, King didn't know. Selfish was what.

The queer brought the dog inside and came back out alone.

King grabbed a ball cap from the dash and got out of his truck.

The November wind raked his face. The air was raw and wet. He liked it.

A murder of crows swam overhead on the stiff winds, cawing raucously.

King set the ball cap on his head and squeezed the bill tight.

The queer disappeared around the corner.

King followed.

As the queer ventured into the Riverside Card Shop, King staged himself a couple doors down.

A few minutes later, the queer reappeared carrying a small bag.

King bent as if to tie his work boot as the queer entered Brew Ha Ha coffee shop one door down from King who spat tobacco juice on the sidewalk.

The queer walked back out, an enormous coffee in one hand, the bag in the other, headed toward King.

Here we go, King thought, and he came at the queen full stride, shoulders squared, and caught the queer hard in his shoulder.

Steaming coffee sloshed from the cup all over the queen's suede jacket and hands.

"Fuck!" the queen shouted, dropping his coffee and the bag and gripping his burned hand with his good hand. He looked up at King.

King stared him cold. Into silence. The pussy.

"Careful," King said and ambled back toward his truck, spinning his truck keys around a finger.

Chapter 22

TEST PUSHED THROUGH the double doors of the Canaan Public Library, relieved to have given North the slip, for now. She did not look forward to a scolding about drawing her weapon. She wondered if she should tell Chief Barrons, preempt North. It'd be best for her to inform the chief first. She'd put it in her log, of course. But the chief would never read that. It was a dilemma. If she told the chief out of fear that North might tell him first, then he'd know for sure about her drawing her weapon. And North might not have any plan to do so. Still. If she did not tell Barrons and North got to the chief first, Test would be up against it then. It would look like she was not forthcoming. Which would be true. She'd rather Barrons never discovered her actions at King's. She'd rather no one ever know.

The odor of lemon Pledge that struck her as she entered the library reminded her of her childhood. Her mother's spastic cleanups before company arrived at their Michigan Avenue town house always included tossing toys in the closet, shoving dirty clothes under beds, and squirreling dirty dishes under the sink.

All accompanied by hyperbolic exclamations about the house being a *pigsty* or looking like a *bomb went off*, and all followed with a flurry of dusting with Pledge. As a girl, Test had never known what all the fuss was about just for friends or family. And, unlike her own adult friends now, who confessed they sounded just like their mothers, Test *still* did not know what the fuss was about. If her friends gave a damn about the lived-in state of her home, they never said anything. And if they did secretly care, she couldn't give a shit.

Test ventured past the Vermont History stacks, past tables and chairs and a rack of newspapers fastened in wooden spines that somehow seemed as ancient now as a rotary phone. Behind the circulation desk, under a sign that read, Ask (Quietly) and You Shall Receive, sat Calvin Trout. Behind Trout stood a half dozen computer cubicles. The computers were colossal and clumsy-looking, seemed more ancient than the wooden newspaper spines, if possible. One of them, for God's sake, was a blue Mac G3. As budget-conscious as she and Claude were, Test made a note to send the school a check. Even $50 would be a godsend.

A sign above the computers read, The Milking Parlor. Pull Up a Stool.

A few patrons sat at the computers, hunched over, faces close to the screens, tap-tap-tapping keys like ravenous woodpeckers attacking rotted trees.

Test strode toward Trout.

Calvin Trout was a legend in town, one of the first local characters that lifelong Canaan residents could not wait to tell newcomers about upon the newcomers' arrival.

Trout had been the librarian since card catalogs and microfilm, when the library's vinyl LP of Lenny Bruce's *What I Was Arrested For* had turned into the freedom-of-speech battle of Calvin Trout vs. the People of Canaan for Responsible Citizenship Group. Calvin had won his battle in a town meeting by instigating his chief nemesis, Gloria Marshall, into such a fury of indignation that the old woman had lost it and shouted at Calvin *shut your fucking pie hole*, thus causing a roar of laughter and undermining all her credibility to censor "indecent language."

Test had seen pictures of Calvin back in the day. The local paper had run a profile of him once. In the pictures, he was the definition of flamboyance, with his Afro and his striped bell-bottoms, satin shirts, clogs, and muttonchops.

To this day, his quoting of poetry, the U.S. Constitution, or a rock-n-roll lyric to make a point gave him an iconic stature among the kids.

"Cal," Test said.

Trout looked up from his game of solitaire on his laptop. He ran a hand through his receding hair. His chinos and crew-neck sweater were wrinkled, his penny loafers scuffed. He stood. He was shorter than Test by half a head.

"I wondered how long it would take you to show," Trout said.

He must have noted Test's confusion.

"As a figure from Sir Albert Conan Doyle's work once said, 'Elementary, my dear Watson.'" Cal puffed out his chest and offered the dour profile of Holmes smoking a pipe. "Actually, Holmes never said that. But, you know. Anyway. She, Jessica, was in here all the time. Using the Internet. I was going to call the police. But. Here you are."

"Here I am," Test said. "And it's *Arthur* Conan Doyle, not Albert."

"He knows," an elderly man with a cane said as he creaked past. "It's a game. To see if *we* know."

"Do you have a sign-in log?" Test said.

"We do. But I don't need it. Jessica used one computer, the one in the farthest corner." He wiggled a finger toward the Milking Parlor. "She used it every Tuesday and Thursday, three thirty to five."

"I'd like to get on the one she used and see if I can bring up any history during the times she was here," Test said. "And I'll need the logs."

Cal rubbed his jaw. "I don't know," he said.

"I can get a subpoena."

"I could check the history during her visits myself, give you an idea, see if she was surfing any porn or weirdo dating sites."

"Porn? In a public library," Test said.

"Freedom of Speech."

"We expose kids to that crap in the library?"

"I've mixed emotions about it," Trout said.

"We never had hard copies of *Hustler* in the library growing up. Just because it's electronic doesn't mean kids need access to the adult world at every turn." Her voice was clipped and, unexpectedly, if not unjustifiably, nasty. Kids saw too much shit these days. She minimized George and Elizabeth's screen time to a half hour on Friday night and an hour each weekend day. No screens, no iPad or computer or TV Monday through Thursday. They'd get their fill of staring at screens soon enough. She and Claude had raised their kids thus far in believing that their TV only worked on weekend days, if it rained. Which had proved an issue when they got rain all weekend, and as George wised up from exposure to friends with more lax parents.

Porn in the library. It scalded her. Saddened her. The library was supposed to be a safe haven. "Mixed feelings," she muttered.

"OK," Cal said, "OK."

"Don't OK me."

Cal put his hands up. "I'm guilty. *Freedom of Speech*. What a crock. If that girl was lured by some predator."

"Forget it," Test said. "And forget you looking at her history, if there is one. That's my job. I'll be getting a subpoena for the computer anyway, to take it and have it scoured by professionals." Who those professionals would be, Test had no idea. Normally such work was outsourced and Test would be the one to whom the consultant reported findings. But since it was in connection with Jessica Cumber, it'd be given over to the state police, and be out of her hands. She could allow that, but not until she gave it her own best effort. She'd call Sheila Silvers. Sheila would help. Sheila would not say a word.

"If you'd show me the computer," Test said.

Trout nodded, his face clouding. "She was a pleasant girl," he said. "Serious. I've never seen a young girl set her eyebrows so straight one second, then, just when you were about to forget she was a kid, burst into a giggle. They don't make kids like her anymore. They never have, actually. She was one of a kind. I—" He stopped himself and tugged at the hem of his sweater to straighten it. "We close in five. I'll clear the kids out, then you can have at it."

Test pulled her cell phone from her backpack.

"No reception here," Trout said. "Outside, on the green, you can get a bar or two if you stand near the cannon facing west toward Mount Monadnock. But you can go ahead and use my office phone."

SHEILA SILVERS SAT in the cubical named Johnson Farm.

Test sat beside her like an expectant niece waiting for an aunt to produce a goodie. Sheila was a widow in her late fifties. Her husband had passed ten years prior and left her money enough to never work again. Instead, she'd begun an education, eventually gaining her PhD in computer science, and starting a part-time career. She wore eyeglasses on a chain, though Test had never actually seen her put the glasses on her nose.

Sheila clicked away at keys to reveal the computer's history against the times in the library log Trout had left with them. "There." She pointed at the screen without touching it with her pink fingernail.

Test leaned closer.

"Her history for the last day she was here. Tuesday. She was logged on for one hour and forty-two minutes. She browsed an e-mail account, Veterinarians Society of America, Equine.com, Yahoo, Tufts University. We'll want to get into that e-mail account."

It struck Test that none of the browsing history revealed anything that might be of help to schoolwork Jessica had told her mom she needed to do at the library. Neither were the sites at all suspect from what Test knew of Jessica.

"Can we do that here? With no password?" Test said.

"Child's play," Sheila said. "And if she didn't delete history from the last time she logged on, odds are she didn't delete it any other time. People tend to think they're anonymous on a public computer. Leave their history up when they might not on a work computer for instance. Or a home computer, say if a wife is running up the credit card on Internet shopping or the husband is deep into offshore gambling."

"What if they erase the history?"

"It's there. Desktop History is just a superficial interface to help the user see where she was previously. There's pretty much no way for a layperson to delete anything from a computer. That's the first mistake people make using their PC for illicit means. Everywhere you go on the Internet can be traced by someone who knows what they're doing. Which, I do."

Her fingers worked like a concert pianist's as she typed a complex series of keys.

"Getting a password to get into e-mails and the like, however, *is* hard. You normally need a warrant or subpoena for one."

This was true, but that was in the case of investigating a living suspect, not a dead victim.

In the case of a suspect, subpoenas were acquired so law enforcement could approach the carrier, Yahoo or Hotmail or whoever, and they would then retrieve the password from their server, or even get into an individual's e-mail without a password.

"Getting a password for Jessica, frighteningly, will be much easier than normal, I suspect."

"How?"

Sheila noted Jessica's e-mail provider as seen in the history browser and brought up the log-in page.

"What's her e-mail address?"

Test didn't know.

"Call someone close to her who does. And keep them on the line."

Test went to the cordless phone at the circulation desk, dialed 411 and asked for the telephone number for Olivia. She waited as she was connected. A woman answered and Test asked to speak to Olivia. The woman sounded guarded and suspicious, and asked who was calling. Test told her who she was. The woman's tone altered to one of concern and soon Olivia came to the phone. Test kept it brief and pointed, passed along her condolences again, and asked Olivia to remain on the line. "I may need you for a minute or two but it's important," Test said and returned to Sheila.

Sheila typed in the address, then clicked the link for *forgot password*.

A page came up that asked security questions:

Mother's maiden name:

Test told Sheila, Cumber.

Sheila typed it in.

Name of first pet:

Test asked Olivia.

"What do you want to know that for?" Olivia said.

"I need to know. Please. I can call her mom if you don't know or—"

"Baxter," she said. "An old cat she adopted."

"Baxter," Test relayed to Sheila, who typed in the name.

"And, last one," Sheila said, "dream job?"

"Thank you for your help," Test said to Olivia. "I'm very sorry for—"

"You're going to get them right, whoever did this?"

"Your help got us closer," Test said.

She heard Olivia begin to sob and Olivia's mom got on to say that was enough. Test wished her good night. "Veterinarian," she said to Sheila.

Sheila typed it.

A new screen came up for Sheila to enter a new password in two separate fields.

She did so.

Then she logged in.

"Scary," Test said.

"Not only that, but now we have a password that, if the user herself were alive, would not know in order to get into her *own* e-mail. We could then change all the security questions so the owner of the e-mail could never access their own e-mail again. Pretend we were that person. Read and respond to all new e-mails, and old ones."

Test made note to change all answers to her security questions to ones that made no sense and had no real personal connection to her.

Sheila scrolled down the in-box. She shook her head in disbelief.

"What?" Test said.

"Barely two days of inactivity and she's flooded with spam. I can print out the in-boxes to get a line on incoming e-mail addresses to start, before we go into the body of e-mails."

Test knew she should have included North in this. But if something good came of it perhaps it would be good enough information that he'd overlook her leaving him out. If nothing came of it, she'd tell him she did not want to waste his time on a long shot. "Print the addresses," Test said and took out her notebook and pencil and wrote herself a note.

"Nice," Sheila said, nodding to the notebook and pencil. "There's something about chicken scratch I like. Tactile. Real. It's funny, we store millions of files on these contraptions but then print them out and put them in the same old cluttered filing cabinets anyway. Somehow records and the like just don't seem real till they're in our hands. On paper. I figure that's why people chat so openly with total strangers online, about topics you would never speak of out of the blue, face to face. Doesn't seem real. That's the second mistake people make. Because it is very real."

Sheila printed out the in-box pages, then read each address aloud for Test to tally. "VSA@vet.org: opened; Olivialuv@aol.com: opened; Olivialuv@aol.com: opened; Olivialuv@aol.com: unopened; TheArm@hotmail.com: opened; tothevictor@hotmail: opened; Humane: unopened; JillGirl@yahoo.com: opened . . ."

Finished, she said, "What's the tally, Sonja?"

"Eleven from tothevictor: one unopened. Seven from Olivialuv: only one unopened. Three from the Humane Society: one opened; One from the VSA: opened; two from JillGirl: both opened; one from BenG: opened; one from KitKat85: opened; and one from StarGazer: unopened. That's it. I'm curious about StarGazer and tothevictor. Now what?" Test said.

"Let's read a few."

Sheila and Test huddled at a table, the printouts spread before them as if they were treasure maps. Something had to be here. Test knew if she found a lead or, better, evidence, she'd put herself in a predicament with Detective North, and with her Chief Barrons.

Barrons would side with North. With this being Test's first major case, and only in a supportive role, Barrons, instead of loosening the reigns, would be more anal than usual about procedure. It was a thin line between being applauded for taking initiative and being reprimanded for going rogue. Test needed to take the risk. She hadn't chosen this career to stand on the sidelines.

She planted her elbows on the table, fingers buried in her hair. Sheila stood bent over her shoulder, a finger underscoring each line of each e-mail as she read it aloud with a deliberate cadence, as though tutoring Test with a Dick and Jane reader.

There it is, in black-and-white, Test thought. On paper that one could pick up in one's hands to smell the pulp, crease into a fan to cool yourself, or set afire to keep the dark and cold at bay; printed in black ink that smudged under your thumb and left your fingertips tattooed as if ready for the booking blotter.

Sheila was right.

What seemed unreal on a screen was made real on paper.

Test read an e-mail:

> *Bonjour,*
>
> *I wish we'd never fought. We should never fight again. Don't you think? Please talk to me. I'm sorry I even said anything about it and made you mad. But it's fun to make up! Right? Riiiiight? ;) If you're not at the Family Matters thing, maybe I could sneak over? I have to babysit 2nite, but Mr. M's been sick and they'll be home early. But. Do NOT come over. I'll call from the Ms' after the baby's down and I take care of some chores. You could tell me all the ways you want me to make up to you! I'm really really sorry I made you so mad. I didn't mean to. I hope you get this. Sorry.*
>
> *Love, little lamb*

This is it, Test thought, *a real break*. She needed a list of local Family Matters members. She'd cross-reference those names with any that had a teenage son.

Tomorrow, early, she'd get the autopsy report on the body. See if Jessica had been sexually assaulted, or when she'd last had sexual relations, if she had. Which seemed likely. Test wouldn't have guessed it from Jessica's pictures. Test's own mother had blown a fuse when she'd learned Test had lost her virginity on her sixteenth birthday, in her own backyard in a tent while she was supposed to have been enjoying an outdoor slumber party with her girlfriends who had themselves invited the two boys from school. The act had been clumsy, embarrassing, and, blessedly, brief. Four years had passed before Test had repeated the act.

The info, Test knew, was enough that she needed to call North.

"DAMN IT. YOU should have included me," North said after she'd briefed him on the phone. His tone was barbed, but in his pause afterward she sensed he would not push. After all, he should have thought to come to the library himself. To torch her too much over not including him would put the spotlight on his own failing to make the leap that if Jessica had been coming to the library to use computers there might be valuable information to find on said computer.

"You don't want me calling you and dragging you into every cockamamie hunch I have, do you?" Test tried to strike a contrite and self-deprecating tone. Neither tack was a strength.

North did not answer. She took that as a sign of his biting back unkind words.

"I'm calling you now," she said. "Seconds after the hunch paid. We've just scratched the surface. I'm going to go over to the town hall before they shutter. Family Matters hold their meetings there and groups have to fill out a roll call. If I find anything—"

"Anything *at all*," North stressed.

"You can grab Sheila if you like, or have her send you everything."

"You need a subpoena for access to that computer," he said. "If you got info by ill-gotten means—"

"Trout granted me permission."

"Who?"

"The librarian. It's library property, not Jessica's." She did not know if that permitted her access to e-mails or not. She supposed not. But it did make searching browsing history OK. In fact, anyone could check that. "Besides, her mom is not going to take issue with it. It's on behalf of her daughter. Like searching her bedroom."

North again remained quiet.

"Did you come up with anything after Marigold's?" Test asked and wished she hadn't. Now she was acting as though they were partners, equals; they weren't. North didn't have to share info. It was a one-way street. And if North had come up with any leads, he would not have been as miffed at the start of the call.

"Maybe," North said.

Test could not tell if he was bluffing. "Good," she said, having nothing else to say.

"I'd like to talk to you, in person, about what happened at King's," North said.

In her enthusiasm Test had forgotten about it.

"Tomorrow," North said.

"If you insist."

"I do. Your station. Noon. I'd like to see Barrons while I'm there."

Shit.

Chapter 23

TEST WALKED THE wet sidewalk along Maple Street at a clip. Night had fallen and a sharp November wind knifed through her jacket.

The sidewalk lay empty and dark.

Dark ghostly imprints of maple leaves appeared here and there on the damp sidewalk, where the leaves had fallen earlier in the season and stuck to the wet concrete. The images were detailed to the finest of veins. They reminded Test of grave rubbings. No two alike.

The whole world was damp. The dark trunks of the maple trees glistened with wetness and gave off a pungent earthen scent that mixed with the oily odor of the asphalt street. The trees' black calligraphic branches dripped rainwater.

Test enjoyed the tranquility of this second week of November.

Since moving to Vermont, she'd grown fond of November. Most everyone complained of its gray solemn skies. They faulted November because it was winter's prologue. Stick season.

Test looked forward to the winter to come. She enjoyed sledding with kids, making snowmen and coming in and stomping off snow before setting about making hot chocolate. Most of her friends groused about the dark evenings, but she loved nothing more than to hibernate with Claude, to nuzzle before the fireplace in a flannel robe and shearling slippers. To burrow deep beneath heavy blankets together, to feel their heat trapped in with them, to make love while the snow outside blasted sideways, blown by an arctic wind that shook the corners of the house and cried its lonesome accompaniment in the eaves. She liked knowing that she and Claude were inside, safe.

Except now all of this was tainted.

It should not have surprised her. Nothing should ever surprise a cop.

You just never knew. That was the only truth. You just never knew.

Test traipsed along. The rain had started again and the wind had risen, grown to a bitter and nasty gale. She wished now for the warmth and brightness of her home, the chaotic hilarity of her children, the steadfastness and good charm of her husband. This was not her case. She could go home now and call North and tell him to follow up her lead. In twenty minutes she could be welcomed home by the warm smiles of her children. She could go for a run; a long, demanding, blood-thumping run of hills that would tax her, push her to the edge of her stamina, make her want to quit. A run to flush out the day's toxins. She could indulge in a bath afterward. Shed this horrific day.

All the things Jessica's mother could not do.

All the things Jessica would never be able to do again.

Detective Test put her head down and pushed straight into the storm.

Chapter 24

JED KING SAT at the card table in his sugar shack drinking beer. He studied the map of Canaan, the map peppered with X's of red pencil.

The heat from the woodstove warmed his face. Nothing like the roaring heat of an ash-wood fire. Ash burned hot and clean. Its grain lay true and you could cleave it cleanly with a single blow of the axe. He refused to operate a hydraulic wood splitter. If a man used the correct wood, ash, and dried it right, it was no big yank to split ten cord to make a few bucks off those too lazy or too inept to do it themselves. A man only had problems when he used inferior wood, or he hurried to split the wood while it was still green and not seasoned properly. Doing things the right way, living right, made life easy, because you were always sure in what you were doing.

The woodstove sat in the center of the sugar shack, where the boiler pan used for reducing maple sap into maple syrup had been gutted a decade previous.

Jed had built the new shack up in the middle of his twelve-hundred-tree sugarbush. State-of-the-art equipment, gravity and vacuum fed. Reverse osmosis. All its guts and components American made. Most sugaring operations used crap equipment out of Ontario, or worse: fucking Japan. King paid for the American-made quality. Bet your ass. There were those who resented his treating a romantic tradition with such a business acumen, or spited him for not joining up with the co-op. But running a tight ship didn't lessen his love for the feel of evaporator steam on his face, the faintest sweet taste of sap on the tongue. He boiled near to four hundred gallons of Grade A each spring. Seven hundred gallons of Grade B.

He made the finest maple butter and confections, too. Never use the tired mold shapes of a maple leaf or a mom-and-pop puritan couple other operations used, but crafted his candies in the shape of chainsaws and pickup trucks, bikini-clad girls and sexpot milkmaids. His candies were the best, and his Kingdom Sugarworks operation had been written up in the *Boston Globe*, *New Yorker*, *Yankee* magazine, and *New York Times*.

The urbanites lapped up his old-timer, salty act, bought into his gnarled wit as much as they gobbled up his maple products and shoved fistfuls of money at him. They'd heard about him and each spoke of him to other flatlanders as though they had discovered him themselves. They knew not to expect the usual homage to maple sugaring history at his operation. No old tin sap buckets hung out for posterity. No black-and-white photos of horse-drawn wagons in heavy snows or old awls and taps and maple-sugar canisters lining the window ledges. Just like in this old sugar shack, the new shack's walls were pasted with cheesecake calendars of big-busted women in swimsuits stroking power tools and transmission shifters. Boy, did the flatlanders get a kick out of that stupid ass ploy.

King finished his beer and nodded to nobody.

Time.

It was time, again.

KING EASED HIS pickup behind the recreation park and killed the lights. He fished a pack of Pall Malls from his shirt pocket and punched the lighter into the dash. He'd paid an extra $220 to get that lighter, and had to get the truck out of fucking New Jersey. Never thought he'd see the day a lighter cost extra in a working man's truck. But there it was.

A phosphorescent lamp lit a bank of mist that crawled along the ball field. The cold November air poured into the cab and bit at him. The lighter clicked. King touched it to his cigarette, inhaled deeply and exhaled a thread of smoke out the window. He smoked slowly, savoring it. He stepped out of the truck. Mist curled around his work boots. He grabbed a small plastic grocery bag from the truck bed.

He sneaked across the lot and worked his way down a grassy bank to the baseball field. As he moved away, out of the range of the lamppost, he dissolved into inky blackness.

He stood on the pitcher's mound. He'd never played sports. Never watched them. Neither had his old man. The old man never understood how a working man could sit around on weekend afternoons and *watch* other men *play*. From the age of twelve on, King had spent his weekends operating chainsaws and brush hogs to improve the property. There was always work to be done.

King unzipped his pants and pissed on the pitcher's mound, then headed off through the dark cedar trees.

Not too far off, a dog barked.

Chapter 25

THE SCREAM OF a woman startled Test who looked up from being lost in thought on the sidewalk.

Outside the town hall a crowd of people clamored to speak to television and newspaper reporters stationed on the sidewalk. A woman wailed: "Love the sinner, hate the sin!"

Picket signs read: TAKE BACK VERMONT and TAKE YOUR HATE TO ANOTHER STATE.

To get to the office for the Family Matters roster records, Test needed to push through the throng occupying the public-meeting section of the town hall.

Inside, every seat was taken. People stood with no space between them, from the front stage all the way back into the vestibule and outside onto the steps. As Test elbowed her way, she took note of faces. The body heat from the mob tamed the November cold coming from outside, but that heat compared little to the heat of emotion, hatred, and vitriol as the news-camera lights set throughout the hall turned faces waxen.

At the podium, district representative Jasper Madock, owner

of the local lumberyard empire, tapped the microphone at his podium at the front. A popping noise came from two car speakers wired into the corner of the place.

Test tried to push her way through the crowd, putting to memory faces as she did.

"This issue hits home," Madock said. "But we must act with civility. Everyone has a right to be heard and everyone *will* be heard." His persuasive tone explained some of his business success. That he was strikingly handsome perhaps did not hurt either.

"Each person who chooses to speak will have one minute of the floor. Janey there, my daughter," Jasper nodded to a young girl with bad skin who blushed at her mention, "will come around with the microphone. Let's hear one another out, even if we disagree. My brother down at the Bee Hive is having a special Night Owl Breakfast. Two eggs, bacon, toast, and coffee for ninety-nine cents, *if* we can get this done by six in the A.M."

Laughter erupted.

Jasper cleared his throat, the phlegm in his lungs sounding like an old boat motor failing to start, and wiped sweat from his brow with the sleeve of his Carhartt jacket. He wasn't nervous. The lights caused the sweat. Not the crowd.

Test edged sideways between two women, one of whom smelled of beer.

"All right, raise a hand and I'll call on you in an orderly fashion," Madock said.

Almost every hand shot up.

Test cut along the back wall, some people put out to have to make room for her. She wished she were wearing a uniform.

Madock's daughter handed the microphone to a woman.

"I know that these people," the woman said, "and those supporting them, they believe this is right. That it hurts no one. But what do we tell our kids?"

Test had heard it all before. *Yes*, she thought, *what about our kids? What shall we do if we can't mold them in the image of our bigotry?*

Test was halfway to the door that would lead her to Public Records.

The sharp odor of drugstore perfume and noxious aftershave seared her throat.

"Do we tell our kids it's OK?" the woman said. "They are good people. I pray for them, but I cannot support this."

"Moral rot!" a man shouted.

"That's once." Jasper stared the man down, a man Test could not see in the crush of people.

A young man with muttonchops and a faded army surplus jacket not unlike the kind Test had worn in high school when she'd wanted to come off as ironically anti-establishment, took the microphone. "I'm a law student," the young man said. Three middle-aged men groaned.

The young man continued, "These instances are precisely what the law is for: to assure the rights of the minority are protected. We should be proud."

A man shouted: "Let's not wrap this up in pretty PC BS! Call a spade a spade!"

"That's twice," Madock said. "I must ask that you leave."

"I won't!" the man shouted. He was close to Test. A big man with a roughhewn face. If he got physical, Test would have to intervene. She didn't want to. She was within sight of the door to Public Records.

"We'll have even more gays pouring into our state!" the man shouted.

People clapped, others hissed.

"Enough," Jasper said. "Please, leave. Or you will be escorted out."

Test followed Jasper's eyes to see, to her surprise, officer Larkin in civvies and a camo Red Sox cap. He stood in the back wings, nondescript. Larkin approached the man through the crowd, showed the man his badge. The man scowled and left with Larkin at his side.

A woman shouted, "Take your hate to another state!"

Several other people joined: "Take your hate to another state!"

Jasper pounded the gavel until calm was restored.

Test made it to the door to Public Records.

"We are never going to get that ninety-nine-cent-breakfast deal if we keep this up, people."

The microphone squelched. "The Vermont Superior Court legislated from the bench and whatever comes of this should be considered a bastardization of the process itself," a woman said. "Why is no one up in arms about this? Thank you."

Test slipped into Public Records, and the voices from the main hall dulled as she leaned against the shut door and sighed.

"Exhausting, isn't it?" a voice said.

Test looked up to see the clerk, a tiny woman in her fifties or sixties, smiling at her from behind her desk. She held a spoon in one hand and a yogurt container in the other. She set them down and dabbed with a napkin at yogurt staining the front of her red sweater, which sported a big snowflake on the front. "Detective Test, right?" she said.

Test nodded, embarrassed she did not recall the woman's name. She'd interacted with her numerous times to pay for her dog's license and buy a beach sticker for Maidstone Lake.

"How can I help you?" the woman said. "Or are you just seeking refuge?"

AFTER NEARLY AN hour, Test found the roster she needed. In a small cone of light cast on the clerk's desk by a brass lamp, she worked her finger down the list of names. Many of the signatures required deciphering. She knew most of the names. Some surprised her.

The members were a disparate lot: farmers and store owners, plumbers, teachers, a family physician, a gas-station attendant.

"V. Who was V?"

She looked down the list. Looking for a V.

It took her nearly a half hour to find a name that started with a V.

It smacked her in the face.

Victor Jenkins.

Test had seen him on local TV and in the paper, taking opposition to the gay marriage bill. But he was in his fifties. Test couldn't see any young girl being smitten with him. Was there a Victor junior? No. Jenkins had just the one son, Brad, who was in the paper regularly: The most gifted high-school football player ever to hail from this tiny state, perhaps New England, excluding Flutie, of course.

What did Test know about Victor Jenkins? He coached at the

high school Jessica had attended. He'd been a star athlete in his time, as Test understood it. Test could imagine a scenario where an older man might hold sway over a teenage student because of some leverage, but not a girl actually having affection for that man, as Jessica's e-mails and letters clearly showed; though it did happen. Nothing good ever came of it.

Test set herself up at the lone computer made available to the public in a small cubicle.

She Googled Victor Jenkins, Canaan Vermont.

He had no Facebook page, no social media presence whatsoever.

The articles she found on him mentioned him by way of being father of Brad, star quarterback and pitcher for Lamoille Valley High School. There were plenty of such articles to mine; it seemed Brad was mentioned in every Sunday sports section of the *Lamoille Register* during football and baseball seasons. There were annual profiles on him too. And a profile on Victor, who had apparently made it to Syracuse University, a Division One program, with hopes of a possible NFL career waylaid by injury.

Test looked up.

The time had gotten away from her while searching online. It was nearly 10 P.M.

She pulled the chain on the lamp at the cubicle desk, turning off the light so she sat in the opaque glow from the streetlamp outside the window, thinking for a good long time.

She needed to call North.

But didn't want to.

In the hall, she drank at the water fountain, sloshed water in her mouth and spat. Wet her hands and doused her face.

The outside office was dark. The clerk had gone home, either thinking Test had left or trusting Test to lock up after herself.

Test could hear voices beyond the door. The meeting was still going.

Test locked the door behind her.

Out in the old theater, she worked her way back through the crowd as a woman spoke softly into the microphone. "I represent Family Matters," she said.

Test stepped up on her tiptoes to glimpse the woman who tucked the microphone close to her chin. "There's many here tonight," the woman said, her voice so quiet it was hard to hear even with the microphone. "While we reach out to all God's children and we pray for those living in sin to come right with the Lord, we cannot stand aside while secular laws overrule the law of God. We therefore stand opposed to bill H eight forty-seven. We pray for another solution that protects our children and our most holy of all traditions: holy matrimony. Amen."

A murmur of Amen went up.

A young man beside Test muttered, "I guess she knows what God wants better than the rest of us."

Test pushed her way outside and was glad for the cold fresh air. She felt soiled and sticky from the closeness of bodies in the town hall, and the noxious tenor of the place. She was exhausted and starving. Exhilarated too, by her find in the roster. She hadn't felt this bone-tired and amped up at the same time since her Dartmouth days pulling all-nighters.

She still did not want to call North, especially at this hour. But she needed to bring him in on it. Keep her word.

She brought out her cell phone and called him.

He did not berate her but thanked her for keeping him up to

speed. He sounded tired, and something else, too. Preoccupied. Perhaps she'd wakened him. She asked him to meet her at her office at the station.

As she spoke, she noted that the windshield of a VW Bug was smashed and a message had been written in shaving cream along the hood: **Learn from tonight. Vote for what's right.**

It was impossible to determine which side of the issue the messenger supported.

If Larkin was still inside, she'd tell him about the vandalism. Except, going back in there was the last thing she wanted to do.

She told North about the vandalism and he said he'd send a trooper out to look into it.

She called Claude next. He'd sent her several text messages and she saw now he had left a voice mail shortly after 9:00. Likely to tell her what the texts told her: he was going to bed. He hoped she was all right. Wake him if she wanted when she got into bed.

Chapter 26

NORTH PULLED HIS cruiser into the parking lot of the Canaan Police Station. He felt too overheated and damp. He'd come straight out of a hot shower at home when Test had called and had thrown on warm winter clothes before his body had cooled or he'd even toweled off properly. Then, he'd sweated. He hoped he didn't stink. He had forgotten deodorant.

He didn't see Test's foreign heap, so decided to go for a stroll around the block and enjoy his nightly cigarette. It was a lousy habit that Loretta forbade him since cancer had invaded her mother, but he had a lot on his mind and the cigarette helped calm him.

Even after being back from Boston for years, the nights here still felt ominously quiet.

He had realized he needed to get out of Boston the day fifteen-year-old Luke Johnson had stabbed his father twenty-seven times to keep his father from killing his mother.

The number of stab wounds had brought images of savagery to the public's minds, and the press had asked what was wrong with a child that he would stab his father *so many times*? Twenty-seven times? It was too much. Even in defense of a mother. Stabbing once or twice was enough to stop someone after all, wasn't it? Yes, the public and press had decided.

Any cop or criminologist knew the answer was *no*. A person being stabbed did not die easily, neatly, or quietly. True, there was something wrong with the boy: a childhood of broken bones. Emergency-room visits that included internal hemorrhaging at ages five, seven, and nine.

Two stab wounds did not stop the likes of a father who had stood six feet three inches and weighed 278 pounds. Whose wife stood five feet flat, and whose son came up to his father's chest and weighed one third what the old man did. It took effort and will to stab to death a person with so much physical dominance. But the boy had done it; he'd done what was needed to protect his mother, knowing if he had not killed his father once he started stabbing him, his father would surely kill him and his mother. Of that, there was no doubt.

Young Luke, the state wanting to set an example, had received life in prison.

With that injustice, North had returned to Vermont.

It wasn't just that case that drove him back home, he thought now. As a youth he'd mocked Vermont and its small-town ideals, wanting more; so he'd relished his first several years in the city, and never returned home. After a while though, the grind got to him, and he'd started to flee on Fridays, heading north on 93, all four lanes packed tight as cordwood with vehicles in a weekly migration of SUVs that would rival a migration of wildebeest on a National Geographic special. It slowly dawned on him that living in a place he wanted to escape was not living. It was merely surviving.

So, he'd come back.

And now this.

The people of his town, his state, at war with each other. The murder of a girl.

He was not on his A game with this case, not as he needed to be.

If the murder was a warning to Jon Merryfield and Jon did not back down, North believed it would lead to more murders. But if Jon did back down and leave the case, another attorney would take it up. It was a career maker. And why shouldn't an attorney take it? Even if North personally disagreed with gay marriage, he could stand aside enough to understand the greater societal picture in a way others could not.

The cigarette held no appeal, so he snubbed it out on the heel of his boot and dropped it in his coat pocket, exhaustion washing over him.

His sleeplessness came too from worry over his failing mother-in-law. When Loretta's mother did finally succumb it would deliver the sharpest pain; but there would be relief, too, that the suffering was over. Guilt would accompany Loretta's relief. He was prepared. Hoped he was. Loretta was so strained she'd sobbed when he'd brought her the bouquet of asters, and it was her infirm mother who had taken Loretta into her frail arms to offer her daughter comfort.

Loretta's mother was a good woman. Loretta was a good woman. It was his greatest fortune to have good women in his life.

North turned and walked back to the station, hoping Test would be there. He planned to speak to her about what had happened at King's place, too. Get it out of the way. She'd been dodging him, and enough was enough.

Chapter 27

TEST POINTED TO the printed-out e-mails she'd organized on the table. North caught her eye lingering on his waist; he'd missed a belt loop. A grease stain smeared his shirt pocket, and his face was unshaven. He never left the house without shaving; it made him feel conspicuous, vulnerable.

"We'll need our people to do a deep dive on the library computer," he said and slumped in a chair. He was sweating, and stank of sweat.

"We have about fifty e-mails sent to tothevictor," Test said. "I've arranged them in chronological order, so you can get a feel of the ongoing exchange. Read them and see what you conclude, and I'll fill you in on what I found at the town hall."

She was thorough, he'd give her that. He took his time reading each e-mail, taking notes. Then he read each e-mail again and wrote more notes.

His mind was working now, clearing out the clutter of the personal life and regaining focus.

"Whoever this is," he said, "he was sleeping with her. And

he had the power. Most of it, anyway. Wanted their relationship hidden. Because he's of age and she was fifteen."

"Right," Test said. "The only lead I could glean was Jessica mentioning in the one e-mail about V and Family Matters."

"What did you find?"

Her look was inscrutable. An admirable trait in a detective. He'd not want to be interrogated by her.

"Besides a pack of lunatics from each end of the political spectrum?"

North looked at her quizzically.

"A 'town hall' meeting about the gay marriage legislation," Test said.

"Lovely, those. What did you find?"

"I cross-referenced all the names with any initial for V. I found one. Victor Jenkins—"

"Shit. To the Victor," North said.

"Jenkins was at the previous three Family Matters meetings. But he wasn't at the one held last night, when Jessica was killed."

North walked a slow circle as he pondered. Victor Jenkins. Jenkins and his wife were the vocal, strident evangelical type, strong proponents of the Defense of Marriage Act. North understood their position. Agreed with it. To a point. Though publically, North kept his personal views unknown.

He'd seen Victor and his wife in church, spoke with Victor on occasion in the rectory after mass, over weak coffee and cakey, store-bought donuts. While Jenkins was devout and more than a touch too literal in his biblical interpretations for North, he seemed a good man. It was hard to imagine him killing Jessica. Impossible, really. But, it had once been impossible to imagine a fifteen-year-old boy stabbing his father twenty-seven times, too.

Victor. His name had come up with Gregory and Scott earlier in the day. Had it really been the same day? It felt like weeks ago.

"I just don't see it," North said, finally.

"*Victor?*" Test said. "*To the Victor?* What's not to see?"

"I see the connection between the name and the e-mail. I just can't imagine Victor doing such a thing."

"Sir. Your imagination doesn't figure into the equation. Victor Jenkins is a radical."

"That's an opinion."

"Held by most."

"Some."

"He runs with Jed King. He testified at the state legislature last year about—"

"Political activism does not make a murderer."

"Is there a history between you two?" she said, eyes sharp. "What am I missing?"

No, North decided, *I definitely would not want to be interrogated by Sonja Test.*

"Victor Jenkins works at the same school Jessica attended," Test argued. "That put him in proximity to her."

"I understand all that, what I don't understand is—"

"We need to check this lead," Test said.

"We will. The problem is—"

She fidgeted, tense, ready to put forth more evidence. Prepared to counter.

"Even if I could imagine Jenkins killing the victim," North said, "which I can't—"

"You keep calling her the victim. Why don't you call her by her name?" Test said. Her tone was increasingly combative; a quality that undermined clear judgment, in North's experience.

"You know why," North said. Avoiding names that might create an emotional connection to a victim or a perp, and cloud judgment in a case, was a tactic cops used to remain objective.

"This isn't Boston," Test said. "We don't have an onslaught of murders every other day. We don't have dozens of open homicide files to guard against emotional overload."

"No, it's not Boston," North said. "It's my home."

This seemed to hit a nerve with Test, as she refrained from a retort.

"I think," North said, "the victim being essentially a neighbor to us both, there may be more reason than ever to maintain that distance. Don't you?"

"No," Test argued. "I'll call her Jessica. Because that's who she was. She was *made* a victim and I don't care to give the person who did that the power to take her name away."

In all his years, North had heard dozens of pleas for calling a victim by her name. None convincing. Except this one.

He'd forgotten what they'd been talking about and was trying to pluck the thread of conversation from his mind.

"Why don't you think Victor Jenkins is our guy?" Test asked, as if recognizing his memory lapse.

"I don't put anything past anyone," North said. "Given the right motive or emotional context. And, as you said, whether or not I can imagine a suspect being capable of or not, is moot. For the most part. But what I can't see is a young girl like Jessica being taken with Victor Jenkins. That's my snag. Those e-mails are love letters. To Victor Jenkins? No. No way. The man is in his fifties. It makes no sense. That's what gives me most pause."

"Unless," Test said, "he had something over her."

North considered this angle. "No. If he had something on her—

and what could he possibly have over a fifteen-year-old girl?—and took advantage of that, that's possible. But again, the e-mails express adoration. She certainly isn't going to adore a man like that."

"Right," Test admitted, clearly resenting having to do so. "So how *does* he fit? Because, he *does* fit. Somehow. He has to fit."

"Let's go ask him."

"It's eleven o'clock."

"It's best to take possible suspects off guard. Besides, you got somewhere to be?"

Home, she thought.

"No," she said.

Chapter 28

ON THE DRIVE over, following North's car, Test sent a text to Claude:

> Dartmouth Days Redux. All-nighter. But I think we got our guy.

Claude and the kids were long asleep now. Or so Test hoped.

From outside the raised ranch situated in a 1970s-era cul de sac, Test could see the glow of a TV flickering on the wall. Thin clouds cloaked the full moon, but enough natural moonlight remained for Test to see several Take Back Vermont signs stuck in the lawn. Pinecones lay scattered across the driveway, their massive trees crowding the house. Test kept stepping on the pinecones as she and North approached the home and went up the concrete steps.

North punched the doorbell.

The sounds of a football game, then a sports announcer's voice bled through the door.

North pressed the doorbell again, keeping his thumb on it.

The porch light winked on above them.

The door opened slowly.

Victor Jenkins stood before them in khakis and a T-shirt and bare feet, digging a pinkie into his ear. He was in pretty good shape for a man his age. Test was surprised. He had a slight paunch, but overall his build would put a lot of younger men in their beer-swilling thirties to shame. He was not wiry or ropy, nor bulked up. He had, simply, an athletic build: the kind you thought of when you thought of a classic male physique. Wide shoulders, narrower waist. Good arms. His face, though, carried every bit of his age, and then some. Soft, pouched around the eyes, more than a little jowly. It seemed out of sync with his frame.

From behind him, in the shadow of the back hall, a woman peered at them. She was short and her face was made-up heavily, though she wore a bathrobe. She tightened the belt around the robe.

The voice of the sports announcer putting words to highlights drifted from upstairs. Jenkins blinked at Test and North, as if not sure he was really seeing them.

An uneasy look passed on his face. "Yes?" he said.

"Mr. Jenkins, I'm Detective North with the state police and this is Detective Test from the Canaan Police department."

The woman, Jenkins's wife, Test assumed, put a hand to her lips.

"What is it?" Jenkins said. His voice was phlegmy, as if he'd just woken up. Perhaps he'd fallen asleep watching *SportsCenter*.

"We'd like to speak with you," North said.

"Now?" Jenkins said, befuddled. He glanced back at the

woman, who now had both of her hands cupping her lower face with dread.

"What's this all about?" Jenkins said.

"We'd like to speak to you, if we might come inside. It's cold out."

North stared at Jenkins, his posture square and assured.

"Let them in," the woman said as she stepped toward them, into the light spilling from the porch. She laid a bony hand on her husband's shoulder. Resting it there as if blessing him.

Jenkins seemed to consider his options. Then, realizing he didn't have any options, offered a strained smile and permitted North and Test entrance, closing the door behind them.

He did not lead them into another room, instead he flipped a light switch at his side and a harsh light illuminated the foyer where they stood. It was a small space, and though there was the pleasant scent of pine from the boughs wrapped around the stair rail, the space felt awkward for the four of them to stand there together. But Jenkins made no move to permit them farther into the house, upstairs.

"So?" Jenkins said.

"It's about last night," North said.

A nervous light flitted through Jenkins's eyes.

The wife clutched her hand on her husband's shoulder. It looked like an uncomfortable position to hold, as she was a short woman and Jenkins stood six feet two inches or better and she had to reach her arm up to full extension to do so.

"What about last night?" Jenkins said.

"Where were you?" North said.

"I was at the Family Matters meeting, with my wife." He flicked his eyes to indicate Mrs. Jenkins. What is this about?" His voice was clearing, taking on a more forceful tone.

"You weren't at last night's meeting," Test said.

"What are you—" Jenkins began.

"You weren't, sir," North said.

"He most certainly was," the wife chirped.

"Not according to the roster," Test said. "You were at several other meetings, according to the logs. But, not last night."

"I was. People saw me. Dozens of people. I must have forgotten to sign the roster," Jenkins said with calm confidence. It would be easy enough to check out, Test thought. If people saw him. His wife's word had no value. Spouses lied for one another all the time, for endless reasons. Not the least of them fear. But this wife didn't seem afraid. At least not of her husband. But her face did seem to have the look of fear of another sort blooming in it. One caused by confusion, of the sort when outside facts don't meet one's internal reality.

"You never forgot to sign in the other times," Test said.

"What is this?" Jenkins said. "I demand to know." He brushed his wife's hand from his shoulder with the annoyance of one ridding a fly.

"You are in no position to make demands," North said.

Test thought she heard a noise, coming from the top of the stairs. She peered up but saw nothing. It had sounded like a door creaking open. Or perhaps it was just the baseboard radiators turning on, or some other common house noise. Still, she kept one eye on the head of the stairs.

Jenkins crossed his arms over his chest.

"We will tell you what it's about. If you tell us the truth about your whereabouts last night," North continued.

The wife stuffed both hands in her robe pockets. She looked as though she were trying to chew off her bottom lip.

"You've been checking into who attends these meetings?" she said.

"I told you, that's what they do," Jenkins said, evidently to his wife, though he made no gesture to otherwise address her presence, as if taking for granted she would always be there, behind him. "That's what they do. It's a police state against good people like us. The families who stand for values are watched and monitored and harassed, while the deviants are—"

"We were looking into the Family Matters roster because certain information has come to light concerning last night's murder of Jessica Cumber," North said.

Test felt a flush of satisfaction at hearing North use Jessica's name.

"Please leave," Jenkins said.

North ignored him.

"Since you were not at the Family Matters meeting last night, do you have another alibi?" Test said.

"I was there. I didn't sign the roster."

"Were you there the whole time?" Test said. "What time did you leave?"

"You need to leave," Jenkins said, his voice rising.

"Let's all just, please, calm down," the wife said, touching Jenkins's shoulder tentatively.

"I want them out," Jenkins said, more loudly, nearly shouting now.

"Please," the wife pleaded. "You'll wake Vic."

Test felt her jaw drop. Her mind tripping over itself.

"Who?" she said at the same time North said it.

Test shifted her eyes to look up the stairs.

"Vic. Our son," the wife said.

Test looked at North. He wore the same look Test must have worn, one of confusion, but also of a certainty that the confusion was about to be cleared away by a revelation.

"Your son's name is Brad," North said.

Test heard a noise from upstairs. No denying it this time. The click of a door handle perhaps. A footstep on floorboards. North glanced up the stairs.

"To everyone else he's Brad," the wife said.

Now Jenkins wore the same look as North; but for other reasons, Test assumed.

"We, his father and I, call Brad Vic, at home," the wife was explaining. "He hates it. So we refrain in public out of respect. But it's his given name. Victor. Brad is his middle name, his father—"

"Enough," Jenkins barked.

"Where is he? Your son?" North said, visibly coiling, alert to every sound, as was Test.

"Sleeping," the wife said.

"Wake him," North said.

"No," Jenkins said. "We won't. He needs to rest to have a good game this weekend. We request you leave our home now. Or we will—"

"Is he in trouble?" the wife said. "Is my boy in trouble?"

"No, he's not," Jenkins declared, and squeezed his wife's hand. "Let me deal with this."

A loud banging sound came from upstairs.

Like a fist pounding on a wall.

"Sounds like he's awake now," Test said.

There was a sound of smashing glass.

North pushed past Jenkins and bounded up the stairs.

"You can't do this!" Jenkins shouted, but he made no move. Instead he drew his wife to him and held her; she looked faint.

Test ran outside to the front of the house and heard a clattering above her. A boy dangled from a window—a good fifteen-foot drop to the roof of an adjacent shed.

"Hey!" Test shouted. The kid looked back over his shoulder and lost his grip, falling hard to the steep shed roof and tumbling in a free fall. About to launch over the edge, he grabbed a satellite dish. It slowed him, but his momentum was too great and he plummeted off the roof into a heap, his right forearm taking the brunt as it folded and cracked beneath him. "My arm!" he shrieked, looking up at Test. "You broke my fucking arm, you fucking bitch!"

He leapt up in an athletic move that took Test off guard. He was set to run.

"*Vic!*" a voice cried. His mother's voice. At the sound of it, the boy paused, and Test was on him. She knocked him down and shoved her knee into his lower back and yanked his arms back, cuffed him. His mother shouted as she ran to him in her bare feet. "Stop that! What are you doing!" she screamed, drumming her fists on Test's back. "My boy's done nothing wrong!"

Test spun, knocking the woman back as she drove her knee harder into Brad's back. Brad grunted and the woman tripped backward. "Hit me again," Test said, glowering, "and I'll cuff you too."

"I didn't do it!" Brad shouted.

North rushed out of the house, Jenkins in lockstep, face puffed up with insolence. "Get off my boy," Jenkins roared. "Get off him."

"Not another step," North barked. He grabbed Jenkins by the arm. Jenkins was the bigger of the two. But that did not seem to account for much against the glare North gave him. "Don't make this worse," North said. "Your boy needs you in charge of your God-given reason."

Jenkins nodded and relaxed.

"What are they doing?" Jenkins's wife said.

Test yanked the boy up by his cuffs.

"My fucking arm," Brad said. "I swear, if you fucking broke it . . ."

"Stop that language this instant," his mother scolded.

Brad gave her a look that seemed to wither and age her in an instant.

"You didn't have to do that to him," the mother said to Test, her voice feeble but nose flaring.

"Yes. I did," Test said. She led Brad to North's cruiser.

"We're going to follow you," the mother said. "Don't you say a word to them!" she shouted after Brad.

"Mrs. Jenkins," Test said as she shut the door to the cruiser. "You need to stay here, to answer questions."

"I'm going with my son."

"I'm afraid that's not a choice," North said. "Until you answer the detective's questions."

"I'll follow," Jenkins said. "Are you arresting him?"

"Not yet," North said.

Chapter 29

A TV NEWS van was parked across the street from the Canaan Police Station when North arrived. Word got out fast on the scanners.

The Canaan Police station was nearly an hour closer than the state police barracks, so North had called in ahead to inform them he'd be bringing in a suspect for interrogation. Some detectives believed letting a suspect stew made them nervous, and there was a logic to that. But North was of the mind that the quicker he got the questioning started the less time the suspect had to formulate a story of lies.

North pulled the cruiser around to the back entrance.

Two reporters climbed out of their van and chased after the car on foot. North braked and threw the transmission into park. The cruiser's front end rocked.

"C'mon," he said. He hauled Brad from the backseat, mindful of the boy's head, and led him to the station. The reporters appeared around the far corner of the building at a clip, one clutching a microphone, the other holding a video camera.

"Vampires," North mumbled.

Inside the station, North nodded at the nighttime dispatcher and hustled Brad down the hallway.

In what served as the booking room, North sat Brad down and took out a fingerprint blotter and a card.

He unlocked one of Brad's handcuffs and sat back down across from Brad.

"Let's see the hands," he said.

"Are you *arresting* me?" Brad's eyes were wide with panic.

"We'll see. For now, they're for comparison."

"To what?"

"To those left in the Merryfields' house."

The color left Brad's face. "I haven't done anything."

That's why you just jumped out a window in bare feet, North thought.

"My arm is killing me," Brad said upon finishing with the fingerprints.

The forearm did look nasty: swollen and purpled. But North doubted it was broken. Either way, it'd wait.

"A broken arm is the least of your worries," North said.

Brad said nothing, simmering.

So, North thought, *this was the arm that threw all those touchdowns*. The one that might have been worth a great deal of money. It did not look any different from any other boy's arm.

North gave Brad a paper towel and a handi-wipe to clean his fingers. Then he cuffed him again and led him down to the holding room. A modest rectangular wood table sat in the center of it, two chairs on either side of it.

"Sit," North said. He gave Brad a small shove. "And decide that what you're going say is going to be the truth."

Brad rolled his eyes and slumped into the chair facing the door. "Where's my dad?"

North left the room, shutting and locking the door behind him.

He strode down the hall to see about a cup of coffee. He needed something to keep him awake. He felt like death, his brain quagmired, exhaustion climbing into his bones. The clock on the break room's microwave showed 1:12. Tomorrow—no, make that later today, in about seven hours—Loretta had to take her mother in for a treatment, and North wanted to be there to support her. The treatments made for a grueling ordeal. His mother-in-law was so infirm that even with a visiting nurse helping Loretta and North, it took nearly two hours simply to help her from bed and get her sponge bathed and dressed in the morning. The heightened patience and tenderness needed ate at Loretta's emotions and left her done-in and melancholic. North hoped he would have some energy left after the interrogation to be of use to his wife.

IN THE MEAGER break room he poured the dregs of coffee into a paper cup, heated it in the microwave.

A hollering came from the hallway: "Where's my son!?"

Victor Jenkins thundered past the break room and down the hallway. North slugged down his coffee and jogged after Jenkins, caught him by the arm.

"Where's my son?" Victor said, wheeling on North.

"You can't see him now."

"I can see my son if I damn well want."

"No. You can't. Don't make it worse."

"My son did not kill that girl. He didn't even know her."

"We need questions answered."

"What questions?"

"Why he smashed out a window and slid down the roof, for starters."

"Cops come knocking for me, I might do the same."

"We didn't come knocking for him."

Victor wiped spit from his mouth. "I don't want him saying a word till I get him a lawyer."

"If he's innocent as you say, it won't hurt him to talk, now will it?"

Victor took hold of North's sleeve. "If you think—"

"Let go of me, Victor. I won't ask twice."

Victor let him go.

"Now. Go plant yourself in a seat in the lobby. I'll come back out in a bit, talk to you. I promise. OK. If your son has no link to the girl this will be over quickly and you can be on your way after a routine questioning, and I will formally apologize for the disruption. He has not been charged. We only want to ask him some questions. Like you said, he has nothing to do with it. Fine. He'll be out in no time. But we need his help as a citizen. We'd never have cuffed him if he hadn't tried to flee. Please. Go sit."

"This'll all clear itself up," Victor muttered. "You'll see."

Chapter 30

TEST SAT ON the edge of a La-Z-Boy recliner.

Fran Jenkins sat before Test on a velveteen hassock, her knees pressed against each other, a gin and tonic balanced atop them. She fingered the crucifix hanging from a chain around her neck as she stared at the wall, bare save for a picture of Brad in a football uniform, his arm cocked back for a throw.

"I don't care for sports," Fran whispered. "I'm just not a competitive person." She took a drink of the gin and tonic, smacking her lips. She'd looked through all the kitchen cabinets before finding a dusty bottle of Gordon's in a hall closet. Test gathered she wasn't used to drinking any more than she was used to her son being hauled from home to be questioned for murder.

"Never have cared for sports." Fran drank.

"If you could look at me, ma'am," Test said.

The woman continued to stare at the wall. "Victor said he liked that in me," she mumbled. "Attracted him to me; a girl who didn't care a lick whether he used to be a great football player and no longer was one. That was it. That I didn't care; though I knew it wounded him gravely that he could no longer use his God-given talent. He saw himself as a washed-up failure. *Just a high school coach,* he used to say. Still says, when he's depressed. He was depressed for a long time."

Test could smell the gin. She decided she'd let the woman say what she needed to say before pushing her. Already, Test was formulating a sense of the marriage.

"People talked about Victor having been a bachelor for so long. People can be cruel," Fran said. "I know. I worked in the school cafeteria for years. The lunch lady. No punch line like the lunch lady."

Test nodded.

"People can be good too," Fran said. "Overall, people are good. Decent. My husband is. His father. Now there was a cruel man. If you knew what I knew."

What was it she knew? Test wondered. "Mrs. Jenkins," she said. "I need to ask you a few questions."

Fran Jenkins sipped her drink. The ice had started to melt, the glass sweating. She sat erect to face Test. Her pupils were dilated. "My son did not do it. I don't know why I should sit here and speak to someone who believes he did."

"I don't believe anything. I'm only going on what we have."

"What do you have?"

Test hesitated. She did not want to divulge evidence against Brad to his mother. But, she sensed she'd get nothing from Fran if she did not at least appear forthcoming. The more casual Test's tone, the less Fran would grasp the seriousness of Brad's situation. Test needed Fran to open up, not to go silent.

"We only want to speak to Brad because he knew Jessica. He may have been involved with Jessica. She was underage." If they'd had sex, as the e-mails had indicated, it amounted to statutory rape. "But, you know." Test shrugged, boys will be boys. "Brad's a good-looking, beloved kid, and he's young too. It's just. He's of age. And she wasn't."

"You don't exactly strike me as the type who waited till she was of age," Fran said and cocked her head, judgmental and condescending, her sudden, acidic tone surprising Test. "Somehow, I doubt the boy was as young as you, either. Was he a senior? Or maybe a college boy? You know how many underage girls tempt popular boys like Brad? Throw themselves at him? Test him? Then society blames the boy."

Test had read Fran wrong. She was neither meek nor spacey. She was clever. Calculated. Spiteful. Test regretted the easy tone she'd granted her. It had given Fran license to think less of Test's authority.

"If you think you're insulting me," Test said, "you are mistaken. Far worse things have been said to me. Done to me. But you're not just wasting my time and yours. You're wasting your son's. If you can help him, if you can tell me anything to help me help him, do it now."

Fran twirled a finger in her glass, held Test's gaze.

"I won't say anything you can twist against him to scapegoat some hussy and—"

"I'm not here to get *more* evidence against your son," Test said. "We have more than enough already, frankly. Your son will be charged with murder. There is nothing you can do."

"Then what are you here for? To *help* me? To play good Samaritan?"

"I'm here to do my job. If you have anything to say that can help Brad, now is the time. Can you provide an alibi for him?"

Fran ran a finger round the rim of her glass.

"Were you home last night, between six and seven thirty?" Test said.

"No."

"Where were you?"

"You already know where I was."

"I'd like to hear it from you."

"Attending a meeting."

"What meeting?"

"I don't see how it's important."

"What meeting?"

"Family Matters."

"Which is?"

"Families, parents, who believe marriage is between a man and a woman, that *parents* means a father and a mother who believe in tradition and the right for our kids to go to school free of having to be forced to endure a homosexual agenda. Parents who believe in God."

"And what time did the meeting take place?"

"Five thirty till nine. You know all this." She took a good belt of her drink now.

"Was your husband with you?"

"I told you. Yes."

"And you have witnesses to this?"

"Certainly."

"That he was there, the *entire* time?"

Fran set her drink down on the coffee table.

"Mrs. Jenkins," Test said. "Was your husband with you the entire time?"

Fran fidgeted with her necklace.

"I take it he wasn't."

Fran exhaled. "No." She set her hand on her drink, but did not pick it up.

"When did he leave?" Test said.

"About six."

"Why?"

"I don't see what this has to do with anything. He has witnesses, an alibi, if that is what you are after."

"Who?"

"Jed King."

King again. Test wondered if Brad knew King. And if so, how well. What he might be willing to do for the man.

"Why was he at King's place?" Test asked.

"To spread the word. Distribute signs."

Distribute signs, Test mused. Plant them to antagonize. Test doubted Jon Merryfield had requested one of those ugly signs be put in his yard.

"Was your husband home when you got in?" Test said.

"No."

"And what time did you get in?"

"Nine fifteen or so."

"What time did your husband come in?"

"I was asleep. You'd have to ask him."

"And Brad? Was he home when you got in?"

"Yes."

"You're sure?"

"I would not lie for my son over something like this. You're not a mother, are you?"

Test gave no indication either way. Fran had misread Test and Test would play it to her advantage, if possible.

"So Brad—" Test said.

"What are you, mid-thirties?" Fran said.

"Brad was here?" Test said, ignoring Fran's attempt at diversion.

"Yes."

"Where?"

"Upstairs. In his bedroom."

"Did you speak to him?" Test asked.

"No."

"You saw him?"

"No."

"I see."

"No you don't *see*."

"You never saw him?"

"I heard him."

"You spoke to him?"

"I heard his television," Fran said and stared at her empty glass. She wanted another drink, now that she'd started.

"How do you know he was in there when you didn't speak to him and you didn't see him?"

"I knew."

"I see."

"You don't."

"What about earlier in the day?"

"What about it?"

"Was his behavior normal?"

Fran drew her lips tight. "He ate a big early dinner since I was going to an early meeting. I wanted him to come. I've tried to get him to go. Practically begged. I thought I'd even convinced him to go to this one. It'd be good for him. But he insisted he had to study his playbook for this weekend's game."

"What'd he have for dinner?"

"I don't see how—"

"What'd he have?"

"Chicken potpie, milk and chocolate cake. His favorites." Her lips pursed.

"Did he speak to anyone on the phone before you left?"

"Not that I know of."

"Did he go out?"

"Not before I left."

"When was that?"

"I left to go see how the plumbing was coming in my shop at four thirty."

"Shop?" This information surprised her.

"Petal Pushers."

"The florist?"

"I took it over last month."

"I love that place," Test lied. She knew of it but had never stepped foot in it. She was allergic to the pollen of most flowers, roses in particular. And if she was going to buy them for someone, she picked them up at the grocery store. As much as she supported the local economy, she couldn't justify paying three times as much at the local florist for identical flowers.

"I wanted to own a flower shop when I was a girl." Test lied again, and almost got a smile from Fran. "So you never saw your son after he went to his room following dinner?"

"I heard him."

"You heard his television."

"He did not kill that girl."

"Even if you heard his television. This was at nine o'clock. You can't give him an alibi from six thirty to seven thirty." Test stopped short of saying *the time of the murder.*

"He didn't kill that girl."

"And you went to bed?"

"I was tired."

Test closed her notepad and stood.

Fran stayed seated, her knees pressed together, shoulders caved. She looked like a child. She stared at the photo of her son on the wall. She clutched the neck of her robe tightly. "He did not do it. That's the truth."

Test considered Fran. The corners of her eyes were deeply wrinkled. Her cheeks sagged. Her auburn hair sprouted from gray roots, and though she was tiny, her body still carried the softness of women who never fully rebound from pregnancy.

"Thank you," Test said.

Fran stared into her empty glass, as if she were wondering where the melted ice had mysteriously gone.

Test stepped toward the door, stopped and turned.

"How do you know your son didn't do it?"

"Because he said he didn't."

Chapter 31

TEST ENTERED THE makeshift interrogation room at 2:23 A.M., just as North seemed about to begin his interview with Brad. Apparently, he'd let Brad stew just a bit. It wasn't the approach for which he was known. She'd expected he'd launch in right away.

Test dragged a chair in from the break room and sat beside North.

Brad scowled at her. He sat back in his chair, his chin jutting, cocky. But the hands resting in his lap were cuffed and his thumbs rubbed against one another. His swollen forearm looked painful.

"The little shit," Test whispered to North, only so she could whisper something. She wanted Brad to think she was exchanging vital information about him, at his exclusion.

North played along, nodded seriously. "Yes, I know," he said.

He hit the red RECORD button on the tape recorder sitting on the table.

Test whispered again to North, "You let him stew?"

"I'm having his prints run," he whispered. Then, so Brad could hear: "We've been going around and around. He's playing tough guy."

"I'm not saying a word," Brad said.

North shrugged. "We've got enough evidence for an arrest whether you talk or not."

Brad's thumbs stopped working at each other. "Bull. You'd have arrested me if you did."

A state trooper entered the room. He leaned into North's ear and whispered to him and left.

North leaned toward Brad. "You don't seem to understand. You're here to say whatever it is you can to convince us not to charge you. Just. Give us a good reason."

"I didn't do it. How's that?"

"No crime is perfect," Test said.

Brad's eyes darkened. He twisted a loose thread of his jeans around his finger until it snapped.

"We know you killed her," Test said.

"Wait. You think I *killed* her?" He looked genuinely surprised.

North gave her a savage look. She'd erred. This was not her interrogation. And apparently North had not laid out so plainly to Brad why Brad was here.

"Why else would you be here?" North said, picking up the thread.

"You said you wanted information. I heard you tell my dad in the hall that—"

Brad fell quiet.

Test wondered if Brad had thought they'd wanted to speak with him because he'd been having sex with Jessica, and he was in trouble for that, not the murder.

"We know you killed her," North said. There was no going back now.

"That's crazy. You don't know squat," Brad said.

"Then who killed her?" North said.

"How should I know?" Brad leaned his head back as if working a kink in his neck.

"You were her boyfriend," North said.

"I didn't even know her."

"No?" North leaned in and folded his hands on the table.

"No."

Test laughed. "We know you knew her. And *you* know we know."

North shot her a look, but it was far less grave than the previous look.

"Bull," Brad said.

" 'To the Victor'?" North said. "Ring a bell?"

Brad wiped his mouth with the back of his cuffed hands.

"You're full of shit," North said. "We read all the e-mails between you two." He reached over to a stack of papers on the table. Flipped one over to show Brad. "They're all right here."

Brad set his cuffed hands on the table, fidgeted, then settled into a glower. "So? OK. She had a crush on me, like most girls do. What am I supposed to do about it? I wasn't her boyfriend. Just a friend. So what?"

"So, you lied to us. Meaning we can't believe anything else you say."

"Yes you can. You can believe I didn't do it."

"There must be a reason you lied," Test said.

"Some friend," North muttered. "More like a smug asshole jock taking advantage of an underage girl."

"That's not how it was!" Brad strained forward, veins in his neck rising.

"Awww," North said, mocking Brad. "How was it then? Please, do tell."

Brad sat back, slumped. "I liked her."

"He liked her," North said to Test, maintaining the mocking tone. "You hear that, he liked her?"

"Enough to use her, then get mad when she fell for you and wanted to tell the world about it—" Test said. She wanted to rile him, shake him.

"I *didn't* kill her. Why would I? I got everything going for me."

"Maybe that's why," Test said.

"You had everything to lose," North added. "If she told her friends and adults found out. It's statutory rape. Now I know such small matters as statutory rape certainly may not matter to a first-class NFL recruit playing for Alabama or FSU, but it matters for a high-school recruit from little old Vermont who needs all the help he can get to even get a call from Kent State." He glanced at Test to take a shot. They'd found a chemistry.

"All that matters is you did it and we know it," Test said.

North slid an e-mail printed from Jessica's account across the table to Brad.

Brad's eyes raced down the page. He looked at Test then North.

"Why'd you keep a 'friendship' secret?" North said.

"We didn't keep it a secret."

North laughed this time. "This kid's a riot."

Test stared at Brad. "Detective North gets a kick out of liars," she said. She tapped the page in front of Brad. "It's right there in black and white, as plain as can be. You were angry with her because she wanted to go public with your relationship. If you didn't tell her to keep it a secret, how come no one knew about you? Not even her closest friend, Olivia?"

"It's not like we broadcasted it," Brad said, shifting in his seat.

"I'd say not. Since not one friend or acquaintance of hers knew of you," Test said. "You don't seem too shook up about her being dead."

"I am."

"You don't seem it."

"I'm still in shock. I still don't believe it."

Test took the printed e-mail away from Brad. "She was going to tell someone you were fucking her. And you got mad. Scared she'd ruin your big future."

Brad sat bolt upright, as if stabbed in the back. "That's a lie! You're a fucking liar!"

"Sit," North said.

Brad sat, reluctantly, enraged.

"You better start telling us the fucking truth. Because everything you've said so far is shit," North said. "We know you were screwing her. Using her. We can't do anything about that now. She's dead. If you didn't kill her, it sure looks like you did, so you better start dealing straight with us so we can look for the right person."

"Where were you last night?" Test said. It was two nights ago now, she realized. Time was slipping away fast. But at least they had their doer. Except. Except what? Except his reaction just then when he'd bolted upright and called Test a liar. It was—

"Home," Brad said. "I was at home. I swear."

"All by your lonesome in your room listening to music, I bet," Test said.

Brad looked surprised. "My parents were out."

"Where?" North said.

"Their family shit. Ask them."

"What were you doing at home?" Test said.

"You read the e-mail. I was waiting for her while I studied my playbook."

"For who?" North said.

Test and North had fallen into a natural rhythm of alternating questions, increased the pressure on Brad.

"For Jess," Brad said. "I was waiting for Jess."

"You see how this looks?" Test said.

"Did you make any calls? Send any texts or e-mails? Surf the Internet?" North said.

"When I study my playbook, I *study* my playbook. Being quarterback isn't just taking snaps and stepping back and hurling it, you know."

"Convenient," Test said.

Home alone studying was no alibi.

"Weren't you worried when she didn't show?" North said.

Brad shrugged. "I figured she babysat late and couldn't make it. She knew not to come over or call if it was later and my parents might be home."

"You'd warned her about that, had you?" North said. "Not letting your parents know she existed."

"Because you were sleeping with her," Test said. "Raping her."

"Jesus! I never raped her, or anyone! You can't just say that shit about us!"

"Shut up," North said. He looked fraught and pale. "Shut your mouth. Let me tell you what we have. That trooper who came in a minute ago. He just confirmed. We have your fingerprints all over the Merryfields' house, including on their bedposts. Including on the doorknob to the cellar where Jessica was found."

Brad shook his head vehemently. "I never said I was *never* over there. I was. A lot. But not that night."

"But you can't prove it?" Test said, "because you were all alone at home, right?"

Brad rose from his chair.

"Sit down," Test said.

Brad stared at her.

"Sit your ass down."

Brad's nostrils flared. Test thought he might spit on her. But, he sat.

"You have no alibi," North said. "You had opportunity. You were mad at her. You had motive. One blow with a hammer killed her."

Brad flinched.

"Not just anyone can do that," North continued. "It takes a strong arm. An accurate, powerful arm."

"I couldn't do that."

"He couldn't kill her but he could rape her," Test snorted.

"A real gentleman," North volleyed.

Brad's jaw worked. "You two are sick," he said.

Test wanted it to gnaw at his nerves, the word rape.

"It wasn't rape," Brad said. "Not to us."

"Ah, love. So now you *were* more than a friend?" North said. "Which you know we know since we have all your e-mails."

"I'm not that much older than her," Brad protested.

"Three and a half years," Test said.

"So what? Are you the same exact age as your husband?"

Test wasn't. In fact, Claude was seven years older than her.

"Jessica's grandmother got married at sixteen to a twenty-nine-year-old, or something like that," Brad said, parroting Jessica's line from her e-mail without any conviction.

"Things were different then," Test said.

"Yeah, way less fucked up," Brad said.

He has a point there, Test thought.

"This isn't the nineteen fifties. What do you think a jury will think about the age difference now, in our fucked-up world?" Test said.

"I didn't *know*. OK? I didn't know how old she was, at first," Brad protested, his voice cracking with anger. "She *lied*. She told me she was sixteen. And after. It didn't feel any different, except when she started with the romantic stuff."

"Like the fourteen-year-old she was," Test said.

"She didn't *act fourteen*," Brad insisted. "You're making it out like she was some little innocent creature. You two would never have thought she was that young either. Never. She'd act twenty. And she looked it. She acted older than me, for fuck's sake." He was riled now, agitated. Good. Except. There was something agitating Test again. Something Test didn't like, and for the wrong reasons. A hard pit of doubt was forming in her stomach. It was small for now. But it was nonetheless doubt. Doubt that Brad had killed Jessica. Because he not only seemed vexed, but at ease, too, at least in what he was saying. It felt natural to Test. "She was responsible," Brad said. "Studying all the time. Always in the library. She wore her clothes and hair like she was older. She was . . . mature. But when it came to us, she got ideas."

"So you killed her," North said.

"I slept with her. You got me. But you can't do anything about that. You said so yourself." He stared at North.

A smile seeped across North's face. "I lied. I can lie too, you know. We can press charges against you for raping her."

"You can't," Brad said. "That's not fair."

"Fair?" North said. He looked about ready to reach over the table and grab the kid and smash his face into the table.

"We can do whatever we want," Test said. "Who's going to stop us? You?"

North glanced at Test, then back to Brad.

"Stay put," he said.

He nodded toward the door.

Test followed him out of the room.

In the hallway, North leaned against the wall. "Well?"

"Intellectually. It all adds up."

"Intellectually?"

Test stretched her neck. She was stiff and sore, and if she shut her eyes she'd fall asleep standing upright. "My gut? I don't know. There was something. A moment or two when he was genuinely angry at us and protective of their relationship, I felt a tug of doubt."

"Intuition?"

He hadn't said *woman's intuition*; still, the capital North had built up in his favor during the interrogation vanished with that one word. "Gut," Test said. "Just like yours. It seems he thought we'd hauled him in because he was sleeping with her. Not because he killed her." Her own doubt aggravated Test. She had been all but certain Brad was the doer.

"His fingerprints are all over the house," North said.

"He'd been in the house before. There's genuine fear in him."

"I'd be afraid too."

"True. But. It's more than the fear of losing his future. Or prison. It's more fear from being unable to believe this is happening."

"He better start believing. He's one cold, narcissistic prick. He doesn't care that she's dead, except for how it impacts him. Don't let him fool you."

"He's not fooling me."

"Good. Because it's your work that's led us to this point. And you who got me convinced. It's good work. The library and the checking the roster. Besides." North smiled. It was a goofy, toothy smile, but gracious. "If he didn't do it, who did?"

Yes, Test couldn't help but wonder at what was meant to be a rhetorical question. *Who?*

Chapter 32

IT WAS JUST after 4:00 in the morning when Test got home. She and North had worked on Brad, then gone over their notes. North was a good detective. Thorough. No surprise. And, fortunately, with both of them in the weeds of the minutia of the case, and worn out, North hadn't brought up what had happened at King's place, when Test had drawn her weapon.

In the mudroom, Test shed her coat and let it fall to the floor, then slumped against the wall with exhaustion. She dreaded even the climb up the stairs. She could have fallen asleep if she laid down there on the slate floor.

She kicked her boots toward the neat row of the kids' and Claude's boots. Yawning, she shambled into the kitchen, pressing her balled fists into her sore lower back. Realizing she was as hungry as she was beat, she flipped on the kitchen light and winced at the glare as she opened the refrigerator door to find something to satisfy her empty stomach.

A shuffling came behind her. She turned.

Claude leaned against the doorjamb to the kitchen and stared at her.

"Sorry, didn't mean to wake you," she said.

"You didn't." He looked bushed too and she wondered if the kids had behaved for him. Sometimes he was a softy, and if the kids were in a spirited, mischievous mood, they'd take advantage of that and grind him down.

Test was happy to see Claude, but she needed to eat and get a drink of water before she collapsed.

"Sonja," Claude said.

"Let me grab a bite first," she said and removed her holster and set it down on the counter with a clunk, peered into the refrigerator. She wanted to eat something nutritious. But the long day, the stress, along with the darkness and cold, was triggering a craving for carbs. She stared at a shepherd's pie Claude had made three nights earlier. There were containers of yogurt and cottage cheese and pudding. A chunk of cheddar cheese wrapped in cellophane, sweating. A head of iceberg lettuce rusting at the edges, tomatoes gone soft, a knob of ginger, a cluster of garlic cloves. Nothing appealed, except a piece of chocolate cake Claude had brought home from his showing at the gallery in Cambridge several days before. It had to be pretty dry. Still. The frosting tempted her. She wished Claude had thrown out the cake like she'd asked. If it weren't around, she wouldn't be tempted.

"I'm going to eat the cake, damn it," she said and grabbed it.

"Sonja," Claude said.

She shut the refrigerator door and lifted the cellophane off the plate.

She broke a piece of cake off with her fingers and ate it.

It was dry. But the frosting remained sublime.

Claude was staring at her. His eyes compassionate. But also. Sad.

"Sonja," he said again. The look on his face was more than exhaustion. It was anguish.

Her appetite left her and she set the piece of cake on the counter. "What is it? What's happened?" His face was grim. "Please tell me," she said.

Her heart was skipping. "Is it one of the kids?" she said. And then. She knew. The silence of the house. She'd been so exhausted coming into the house she'd missed it. Charlie had not come to the door to greet her.

"It's Charlie," Claude said.

"Oh," she said and wilted against the counter. "I knew he was slowing down but I—"

"No," Claude said.

"What?" Test straightened, panicked. Claude was scaring her now.

"He ate poison."

Test felt dizzy.

"Poison? What do you mean?" she said. "What did he get into?" Suddenly she was furious, her ire up. How many times had she told Claude to dispense with his paints and thinners responsibly. "I told you to keep your stupid paints sealed up or—"

Claude hung his head. Not with guilt, but with an emotion Test could not quite gauge.

"You don't understand," he said. "Someone poisoned him. I found hamburger outside, near his daytime pen. He—"

This was too much. It was all too much. And it couldn't be. How could it be?

"Where is he?" she said. "Where's Charlie? I want to see him."

"He's in the garage, under a blanket."

"Did the kids—"

"No."

"Why the hell didn't you call me?" she snapped, her ire up, though she regretted instantly her misplaced anger. Her moods were swinging wildly. She was too tired to stem impulsive reactions.

"If I'd called or texted to let you know, it would have only distracted you while you were doing important work," Claude said. "And I knew you would want to come straight home but wouldn't be able to."

He was right. But it grieved her to know Charlie had died and been left all alone on the cold garage floor.

Her heart heaved and she began to sob.

Claude let her. He'd learned not to try to comfort her in such moments, but to grant her the space she needed to collect herself. Then, he could take her in his arms.

She calmed herself and Claude put a hand on her shoulder.

"You're sure he was poisoned?" she said.

"You decide."

TEST KNELT BESIDE her old Charlie, gently pulled back the blanket covering him. He was stiff now, whether it was rigor mortis or from the cold in the old barn, she wasn't sure. Maybe both. It wasn't clear straightaway that he'd been poisoned.

"He was frothing at the mouth," Claude said and cleared his throat. "And. I found this."

He picked up a half pack of hamburger and handed it to her.

"He must have eaten the rest, I found the Styrofoam trays," Claude said.

Test examined the meat. Anger reared up in her again. "Drano?" she said, her voice hoarse. "Fucking Drano?" A sob started to come, but she let her anger rise above her sorrow and crush it. She would need her anger now. Use it to help her focus.

"I'm going for a run," she said and stood.

"Now? No," Claude said. "You need to sleep."

"You think I'll be able to sleep?"

"It's dangerous running in the dark on these roads."

"Not at four A.M."

"What if—"

She knew what he was going to say and cut him off before he could say it.

"Whoever did this is a coward," she said. "They're long gone. We're not in harm's way. The kids aren't. I wouldn't—"

"I stayed up all night," Claude said. He was scared. She'd never seen him scared. "Every little sound. I took out my father's old twenty-two pistol."

"You can't be walking around the house with a handgun, Claude. You don't even know how to shoot. Or *if* it shoots."

"I'm not taking chances. If this is linked to—"

"Trust me," Test said, though she didn't trust her own words. "If it's linked it's only linked by some cruel asshole gay basher who wants to scare off anyone who pursues the case. Not the person who killed Jessica. We have a suspect in custody."

"You have him already?"

"That's where I've been all night."

Claude seemed to relax. It felt odd, Test putting her husband at ease.

"Trust me, no one is out there." She believed whoever had poisoned Charlie was long gone. But she could not know it.

"Go on to bed," she said.

"I must look pretty bad," Claude said, with a dim smile.

"No worse than me." Test smiled too.

Claude relented. He knew when trying to change her mind was futile. He gave her a kiss on the cheek and lumbered off toward the house.

Test remained kneeling at Charlie's body for a long time, stroking his side and talking to him and giving him the love she'd promised she would the other night when she'd shoved him away.

Then she pulled the blanket back over him to keep him warm and went for her run.

Chapter 33

THE NIGHT WAS dark as tar, with only a small cone of light from Test's headlamp.

When she glanced to her side it was as if she was looking into starless deep space. It was unbalancing.

She took the dirt road slow and steady, wanting to work her heart rate up and clear her mind.

The kids would be devastated when they woke in the morning. And Claude would be left to deal with it on his own, because Test would need to be out the door in a couple hours.

She heard a branch snap and slowed her pace, listening.

The sound did not come again, and she relegated it to the noise of a raccoon or some other creature of the night. What else could it be?

She picked up her pace.

A crime committed against a police officer or her family needed to be officially reported and handled, but she would not report the poisoning. She was the detective who would have handled it if it was called in. So. She'd file papers that no one would ever see. She could do that. Right now, the fewer people who knew, the better. If she kept it quiet she'd be able to work this thread herself. Despite what she'd told Claude, she now suspected it was linked in one way or another to Jessica. She just did not know how. She hoped it was a pissed-off local who would not harm the family. Though it seemed extreme and cruel for anyone to do. It occurred to her: What if more than one person had killed Jessica? Brad was in custody. So, he could not have poisoned Charlie. What if he'd had an accomplice? What if it was not Brad at all who had killed Jessica, and Test's gut was right? If it wasn't Brad, the person who killed Jessica remained at large.

SHE TOLD HERSELF again that whoever had killed Charlie was long gone and the kids and Claude were safe at home. But believed it less with every step. Anyone who would kill a dog was a sadist. Why was she not listening to music on her iPod as she always did when running? She told herself it was because she had not thought to bring it. But that wasn't the truth. The truth was she hadn't brought her iPod because she had wanted to remain acutely aware of every sound in the darkness.

She stopped running and listened. It was hard to hear any other sound over the pulse of blood in her ears. But, from the understory of the woods, came a rustling.

It had to be an animal.

No person could possibly keep up with her running on the road by crashing through the woods in the complete darkness.

It was impossible. Even in the daylight, it would be impossible.

Tomorrow she would crack Brad. Break him down and get the confession she knew was coming. Then she would focus on who had killed her dog. Perhaps Brad knew.

She'd break him down for that, too.

She sprinted the rest of the way home.

Chapter 34

BETHANY LAY IN bed, asleep under the quilt.

Except to change and feed little Jon she'd been in bed with her baby every minute since they'd arrived two days earlier. The baby lay asleep in the crib provided by the inn as Jon shaved in the bathroom. He needed to appear ever the respectable, professional man of the law, for the press conference.

He leaned from the bathroom doorway looking at Bethany. She stirred and blinked awake as if feeling his gaze. She yanked back the quilt. The scent of her unwashed body rose up out of the sheets.

"You should get up. Go for a walk, the stroller is downstairs," Jon said.

She shook her head and sniffed. The old pajama top of Jon's she wore was buttoned crookedly. From one pocket she pulled a used tissue. She blew her nose in it, then dropped it to the floor.

"Do you good to get ambulatory," Jon said.

"Don't push."

"I'm not."

"You are. You do."

"Sorry."

She sighed, exasperated. "*Then* you get all *sorry*. It's one or the other with you. Control or grovel. Be something else. Anything else. In between. Be normal. Please."

"OK. All right. Stop. I can't hear this now. You need to get up sometime. Do something. It was awful. But it's over."

"Like you know."

"It is. I promise. I saw on the TV a boy has been brought in for questioning. It won't be long before he's arrested. I promise."

"Promises."

"I lived up to them. The baby and the house . . ."

"I wanted a *home*. And little Jon. I can't believe you."

Jon clenched his fists. Sometimes she pushed him. Pushed and pushed and pushed. Until all he wanted to do was . . . He closed his eyes, breathed. Opened his eyes again. "Right. OK. It's all me."

"Don't put words in my mouth."

"No it is. It's all me. I know." He cracked his knuckles. "But you. You need to get back to the land of the living. Quit wallowing."

"How should I behave? Cold. Like you?"

"I'm not cold."

"You haven't missed a beat."

"I just haven't shown it."

"God forbid you should," she said.

"I need to get done what needs getting done. I won't stop living to grieve for a girl I hardly knew when I have important work to do."

She looked at him, her lips slightly parted. "What's wrong with you?"

"Me? You act as if it was your own kid who was killed instead of a babysitter."

"You're cold."

"This is no time to be a mess."

"You haven't so much as touched me—"

"OK. *All right.* Who's cold? To bring that up."

Jon turned back into the bathroom and slammed the door. The frame shook. Before he could control himself, he punched the mirror. Cracking it.

His knuckles bled.

The baby cried.

Jesus. Why wouldn't that baby shut up?

Trying to collect himself, he rubbed his temples and shut his eyes. He squeezed and unsqueezed his fists, trying to steady his hands, but they would not steady. They trembled uncontrollably. His whole body shook, as if he were standing beside a locomotive as it roared past him.

He slouched against the wall and slid down it until he sat in a heap. He'd not meant to yell. He hated yelling at her. Hated himself for it. She was right. He would crawl back, tail tucked, and say sorry until it sickened them both. Grovel, mouth metallic with the bitterness of a remorse that seemed bottomless.

Ever since the horror in the cage as a boy, he'd calculated every move, exacted it with mechanical precision, however pleasant or unpleasant. It had gotten him through. It had gotten him a wife. It had gotten Bethany her dream house, the baby she'd wanted. She'd had little idea of the legal thorniness and cost related to adopting a white male American baby. How could she? He'd handled the entirety of it, except for their personal interviews. And now all she wanted from him was emotion. Emotion. Life was easier without it. Easier when you saw relationships as they were: a dominant and a submissive. A person was either preyed or preyed upon. He'd learned the importance of control. It was the only way he'd survived.

A knock came on the bathroom door.

"You can't go through with this press conference," Bethany said through the door. "You have to quit the case. I won't stay here with our son if you go out there in public and announce you will push on, like some hero, and jeopardize our safety any further."

Jon opened the door. "I can't quit," he said.

"You *can*," Bethany said. "If you want to."

"It has nothing to do with want. I can't just abandon my clients."

"But you can abandon your family."

"I won't listen to you when you're being dramatic and irrational."

She wagged a finger in his face, nicking the end of his nose with a long fingernail, drawing blood. Her face was distorted with anger. "If you give that press conference, you're inviting more violence upon us."

"No one exacted violence on *us*." He licked his lips. He needed a drink.

Jon turned from her and finished shaving. He washed his face with cold water. He put on the dress shirt hanging from the back of the door. Pulled himself together.

He slipped on his trousers and pushed past Bethany at the door, then lifted the sports coat from where it was slung over the back of a chair and tossed it on.

He put on his best tie and knotted it. "I have to go," he said.

"Go," she said, waving the back of her hand at him. "Go."

"Nothing is going to happen. The kid is locked up and not going anywhere."

Chapter 35

A MORNING MIST rose from the Canaan River and shrouded the town's buildings.

Victor Jenkins hurried along the sidewalk, talking aloud to himself as he rehearsed what he would say to that woman detective and her superior. They'd get an earful. All night he'd waited, and still he'd not seen his son. The cops had told him he would not be able to see Brad until noon today. They told him at eighteen, Brad was an adult. Victor had insisted that either they release Brad or he'd hire a lawyer. One or the other. Not that he had the money for a lawyer. He didn't. The cops had said Brad had to request his own lawyer and so far he had not.

Victor had finally gone home to shower and to be with Fran.

This morning when he'd called the station, nothing had changed. Brad was still being held, and could be held for two more days without being legally charged. God was testing Victor. Testing his faith. Testing his resolve.

At the Church of Brotherly Love, on the corner, Victor slipped inside the side door across from the rectory, and stood inside. The silence was profound and he immediately felt at peace and certain all would work out well. The church smelled of melted wax and burned wicks from the lit votive candles, and of the sweet pine scent of the fir boughs that ringed the altar.

He stepped toward the bank of votive candles off to the side of the altar. Even his soft footsteps echoed in the empty space of the church.

As he did at the start of each weekday morning, he lit a candle and knelt and prayed.

He prayed now for his son. He prayed, as he did daily, for forgiveness of all his own and many sins and transgressions. He asked the Lord with sincerest humility to be forgiven all his trespasses. And he knew he was forgiven; he felt the Lord's forgiveness lighten and buoy him. Why the Lord had chosen to involve his son in this unholy violence, he did not know, and tried not to question. Already, he was ashamed for the way he had behaved in the foyer of his house when the detectives had come to ask questions. He should have listened with respect to their position in the community and with empathy for the heavy responsibility of their profession. He should have acted with grace and tried to understand what was happening as he welcomed them into his home. But. It was not always so easy to behave in a godly manner, to behave as the Lord would have him behave.

And the police. Still, to this day, all these years later, they sparked in him that old fear. He knew he was forgiven. Still. If the Lord worked in mysterious ways, so, too, did the devil.

Yes. He knew what had befallen his son was a trial, a test of all their faith: he and his wife's and his son's. They must all demonstrate unwavering faith now. He knew how faith could transform a person, lift a person out of the muck, if one embraced it.

He prayed for his son to find the faith that had until now been absent in the boy.

He prayed again for forgiveness. Because in the back of his mind a seed had been planted: that what was happening now was linked to his sins of the past.

Forgiven or not.

OUTSIDE, HE FELT calmer and promised the Lord he would act on behalf of his son with forcefulness *and* grace. He'd speak his mind, but speak it without malice or disrespect. With God at his side. On his side.

He picked up his pace on the sidewalk.

Up ahead, a figure walked toward him, an apparition in the mist. It strode with confidence, arrogance, the mist spiraling about it, making way for it.

As the figure approached, Victor saw it was a man, his long black raincoat, worn open, flapping as he strode, the collar pulled up to the side of his face in the way of a vampire.

Victor's eyelashes beaded with condensation.

The man in the black raincoat came upon him. As he passed by Victor, he smiled broadly. "Coach. How are you?"

Victor blinked. He stopped and turned to watch as the man made his way down the street and disappeared around the corner.

Jon Merryfield.

Victor rushed toward the police station.

NORTH MET VICTOR in the hallway. Victor had expected the woman detective. She'd have been easier to persuade, he imagined.

North put his hand out for Victor to shake. Victor willed himself to shake it and give an agreeable smile. "May I see my son?" he said, bringing a tone of respect to his voice.

"Follow me." North led Victor to a door. "You have a half hour."

"My son didn't do it," he blurted, as if someone else had spoken. He was simply unable to control himself.

"A half hour." North opened the door.

Brad sat at the table, hands cuffed on his lap. His face was slack, the skin beneath his eyes swollen. He'd aged ten years in two days and no longer resembled the son in whom Victor had placed all his hope.

Chapter 36

TEST GRABBED A cup of coffee from the pot in the lobby and brought it into her office, shut the door and plopped her weary head on the desk. Claude had been right: she should have gone to bed and not gone for a run. It was harder than ever now to think straight with four hours' sleep in nearly fifty hours. Her obstinacy had gotten the best of her. Even if she'd lain awake obsessing about the case and about Charlie, it would have been better than running at four in the morning.

Her phone rang. She picked it up, stifling a yawn. "Detective Sonja Test."

"They killed Sally."

Test jolted awake now, scrabbled for a pencil and pad. "Who is this?"

"Gregory Sergeant, I'm—"

"What's happened? Have you called nine-one-one?"

"No. I—"

"Call them as soon as you get off with me. Who is Sally?"

"My lab."

"Your what?"

"My dog."

Test stared out the window as her blood drained from her face.

She spoke slowly, in a manner meant to calm herself. "Why do you think someone killed your dog?" She tried to focus on the pencil in her hand but her vision was uncertain, doubling.

"She was frothing blood and I found hamburger she'd eaten and—"

The voice went as muddy as her vision and the pencil dropped from Test's fingers and hit the floor, far, far away.

"He's got to pay for this," the voice said, coming back to her through the clouds.

"Who?" Test said, her voice a whisper.

"Who? That redneck bully who just about knocked me down in the street yesterday. Purposely."

"Who?"

"Didn't you hear who I said? King. Jed King."

"He knocked you down yesterday?"

"I just told you he did. What's the matter with this line?"

"I don't know. I apologize. I've been awake most of the past fifty hours. Why didn't you report him attacking you yesterday?"

"He was careful about how he did it. I can't prove it was on purpose. I scalded my hand with coffee but otherwise I'm OK. I've learned that by not reacting to bullies, it defuses them more often than not."

"Not always."

"No, not always," he said.

"You want me to swing by there?"

"Please."

Chapter 37

TEST KNELT BESIDE Sally the same way she'd knelt beside her own dog just hours prior. Gregory Sergeant knelt on the other side, stroking his dog's head.

Scott Goodale stood with a hand on Gregory's shoulder.

Sally lay in vomit that appeared to consist mostly of raw hamburger.

"She's been poisoned, hasn't she?" Gregory said.

Test nodded. Her assurances to Claude now seemed misplaced. He'd be angry with her, accuse her of patronizing him, and he wouldn't be that far off base. Sally being poisoned in the same way indicated more calculation and premeditation than just an asshole bigot behaving in a knee-jerk fashion.

"Who does such a thing?" Gregory said.

"Homophobic bastard," Scott said. "I'll kill him."

Test shook her head, looked at Gregory. "King knocked you down yesterday?"

"Slammed into me. I scalded myself with hot coffee, coming out of Ha Ha's." Gregory showed Test the back of his left hand, along the thumb. It was red and blistered. "King said, 'Be careful.' The man is a menace."

"A menace?" Scott said. "He's a fucking asshole."

Or a murderer, Test thought.

"I told Greg," Scott said, his face red with anger, "let me pay that fucker a visit and get a hold of him myself and—"

"Do *not* do that," Test said. "Do not antagonize him."

"*Me* antagonize *him*? There's one way, *one way*, to handle a fucking bully."

"I'll speak with him," Test said.

"I hope you do more than that," Scott said.

"I'd like to. But without proof."

"Get proof," Scott said. "You get some goddamned proof. It may be just a dog to you, but Greg's had her since—" his voice trailed off.

"Believe me," Test said. "I know how you feel."

Gregory and Scott eyed her, puzzled.

Test would get proof. And figure out how King fit into this whole mess.

"Get that hand looked at," Test said. "And contact your attorney."

Chapter 38

Victor sat at the table and crossed his arms over his chest and stared at his son. He sat staring for a long time. He needed patience now, to practice his own form of forgiveness.

Brad kept his eyes downcast. "Where's Mom?" he whispered.

"We thought it best to split our time," Victor said. It was a lie, and he silently asked forgiveness. He'd convinced Fran to stay home, wanting to spare her. This was a matter for a father.

Brad rubbed his eyes. The boy looked haggard and scared.

"Please look at me," Victor said.

Brad lifted his head.

Jenkins studied his boy's face. The confident light in his son's eyes was extinguished.

Jenkins got up and paced in front of the room's tiny, wired window. He looked out on the town green. A few rusted leaves clung yet to the uppermost crown branches of the oaks. The Civil War cannon's muzzle was aimed right at him.

He came to the table and looked at Brad. "I need you to be

straight. Dead straight. Understand? Tell the truth as God would have you tell it."

Brad rolled his eyes.

"Do not mock me, or the Lord," Victor said. His son's insolence, his arrogant dismissal of God, would undermine him in the end.

"No lies," Jenkins said. "No matter how hard it is. You are my son. I will get you out of this. With God's help."

Brad refrained from his mockery, though Victor saw it shimmering just below the surface.

"I have to know the truth," Victor said. "Did you hurt that girl?"

"No," Brad said, anguished.

"We've all made mistakes. If you hurt her by accident . . ."

"I didn't *touch* her. Not like that."

Jenkins studied his son's eyes, shot through like bad egg yolks with bloodied veins.

"OK, I'll find a way to make this right." He held his hands out to Brad. "Pray with me."

Brad refused his father.

A thought passed through Victor's mind like the shadow of a bird. A single wingbeat of thought. He tried to capture it, but it flew away, gone.

"Dad?" Brad said, concern creeping into his voice. "What is it?"

"Nothing." The thought was gone. "Why did you refuse a lawyer?"

"I'm innocent. I don't need one."

"Your fingerprints are all over the house."

"I've been to the house before, a ton of times."

"I'm getting you a lawyer. I don't know how we're going to pay for it. I may have to use a public defender."

"I'm innocent. You believe me, right?"

The thought passed through Victor's mind again, a veil of smoke that vanished as he tried to grasp it.

"Dad?"

"You had sex with that girl?"

"So?"

"You tell them you want a lawyer."

"Why, if I'm innocent?"

"Because you're innocent. But you're still *here*."

Jenkins cursed himself. He'd erred. Brad being eighteen or not, Victor should have called a lawyer, straightaway. He was ignorant of the intricacies of law. But as a father, he'd let his son down. If he'd brought in a lawyer, perhaps Brad would not be here now. "The lawyer will figure it out. If you didn't do it—"

"I *didn't*."

"Then we have nothing to fear."

Victor tried to keep his voice firm, yet doubt soured his blood at the thought of the evidence against his son. It seemed overwhelming. Who else would have known the girl was alone in Jon's house? The shadowy thought fluttered through his mind, stirring a memory that dissolved away.

"What?" Brad said. "Why do you keep looking like you've seen a ghost?"

"I don't know," Victor said.

A rap came on the door. North poked his head into the room. "Time's up."

"Pray," Victor said to Brad as he left the room.

He closed the door quietly behind him and stood in the hall-way.

His head pounded. He needed to think.

Something's going on that I don't understand, he thought. *And I need to understand it.*

He walked down the hallway feeling disassociated from his body.

At the dispatcher's desk, he glanced toward the corner of the waiting room. Fran sat there. Victor stopped abruptly.

Fran stood up.

Victor took her by the elbow and guided her to the corner of the lobby.

"I thought we agreed you were to stay home," he said.

"He's my son," Fran said. She'd left the house without makeup. What used to be a sprinkle of youthful freckles across her cheeks had become a blight of age spots. How lovely she'd once been. How he'd thought she was going to be his salvation.

Her eyes were red, her hair in a bun, the way she wore it when she'd not showered. She attempted a smile, but failed. He was a stranger to his wife and she did not know it.

She put her hands on his. He could not recall the last time they had embraced. She squeezed his hands. "He didn't do this," she said. "I'm not just saying it because he's my son."

Jenkins nodded.

"Did you get him a lawyer?" Fran said.

"I'm working on it."

"Get one. Today. Whether he wants one or not." She let go of his hand. "I want to go see my boy."

Chapter 39

Outside, an icy wind blew. A woman reporter rushed at him as he came down the station's steps to the sidewalk. He did not know where she'd come from, the bushes perhaps.

"No comment," Victor said. He quickened his pace.

The reporter quickened her pace.

"Just one question," she said and thrust a small recorder toward him.

"No comment."

Victor walked faster.

The reporter stayed with him.

"I'd like to ask just one question. If . . ."

Vic stopped. The reporter bumped into him. Her recorder clattered to the sidewalk. She snatched a pen and pad from her purse without a blink.

"Just one quest—"

"I'd like to ask you just one question," Victor said. "What word is it you don't understand in 'no comment'? Are you a total idiot, or just too callous to give a shit?"

The woman's face reddened. "I'm just trying to do my job."

"And I'm just trying to live my life. Which do you think I care about more? Your job or my life? Now leave me alone before I shove that pen so far up your ass it comes out that pretty fucking mouth. Do you understand me now?"

He stalked off, blood hot as lit gasoline in his veins.

At the corner, he looked back sharply. The reporter stood there, watching him. What he'd said to her was not how he wished to conduct himself. But he felt better than he had in two days. A man had to speak in earthly terms at times, to stress a point.

He yanked the collar of his denim jacket up tight to his neck. He strode quickly.

The cold settled in on him. It was one of those days when the temperature dropped throughout the afternoon, and as soon as the sun set the air drew close and frigid and you knew autumn was not coming back and winter had you in its cold clutches.

Chapter 40

TEST PARKED HER Peugeot in front of Jed King's house, stepped out and looked around the place. It seemed eerily quiet. From where it hung on the porch, a Don't Tread On Me flag flapped lazily in the wind.

King's truck was nowhere to be seen.

Test stared at the old sugar shack.

She walked up the slate walkway to the porch of the house and knocked. No one came to the door and she heard no sound from within the house.

She shielded her eyes with her hands and peered through the window.

The inside of the place, what she could make out of the living room and kitchen, was immaculate. A stack of magazines sat on a coffee table, each magazine perfectly squared with the others. Three TV remote controls sat aligned beside the magazines. The end tables had not so much as a coaster on them. All four kitchen chairs were tucked up precisely to the kitchen table. Nothing sat on the table. The countertops were bare, except for a toaster. The refrigerator door did not have a single magnet stuck to it. The place was as neat as a drill sergeant's quarters. Though she'd expected the slummy disorder of a two-time, late-middle-aged divorcee, a militant tidiness did not fully surprise her now.

Test stepped off the porch and walked toward the sugar shack. The door to the shack was ajar. Test knocked, then opened it.

Inside, propped in the corner, were dozens of Take Back Vermont signs.

"Find what yer looking for?"

Test spun at the voice behind her, hand going to the butt of her sidearm.

"Going to draw on me again, are we?" King said, smirking, his eyes gleeful, almost childish, with contempt.

"Push me. Find out," Test said.

"I'll file a harassment complaint if you don't have a warrant to be on my property, is what I'll do."

"You'd know about harassment. According to Gregory Sergeant."

"Go running to the cops, did he."

For a moment Test thought he was about to confess to poisoning the dog.

"All because I accidentally bumped into him on the street," King continued. "Figures. Drama queen. Jacked with paranoia and seeing enemies all around."

"You kill his dog?"

"Now why would I do that?"

"You tell me."

"I'm not going to do your job for you, Officer."

Test wondered if he used the word *Officer* as a knowing slight, or didn't appreciate the difference between an officer and a detective.

"Where were you last night?" Test said.

"Right here."

"Doing?"

"Making more signs. They're in high demand."

"Making them alone? You have an alibi?"

"Don't need one."

"But do you have one?"

"I have more than you. You have squat. Just like last time. Just because you don't like that I speak the truth, you hound me without a lick of evidence. If you did have anything on me, we wouldn't be here gabbing about it like silly gossiping school twats, now would we?"

"I'll find something," Test said.

"You know where I am."

In her Peugeot, Test slammed her palm on the steering wheel. The fucker. He'd killed both dogs and was going to get away with it unless she found physical evidence. All she had was her gut, and King's smug response. A man who would do that. It shifted her idea about Brad. King had no alibi for the night Jessica was killed. He'd been on his own, distributing signs. And he had no alibi for last night. Whereas Brad Jenkins had the ultimate alibi for last night.

Test needed to bring North up to speed on the dogs; it might alter his theory on Brad as it had started to alter her own.

King had some balls, too, knocking Sergeant just about on his ass in broad daylight. Threatening him. Then the dogs. Her dog. Charlie. It had to be him. It had to be. He'd killed the dogs and Jessica. She hated the man, she realized. Truly hated him.

She wondered if she was letting her personal emotions cloud her objectivity.

No, part of her hatred of King came knowing what he was capable of doing.

But being capable of something and doing it are not the same, she thought.

"Shut up, shut up," she said and pulled her car onto the road, its bad exhaust backfiring like a rifle shot.

Chapter 41

VICTOR ENTERED THE Beehive Diner.

The usual suspects sat at the counter and in their booths. When they caught his eye, they looked away. *God forgive their turning their backs on me,* he thought as he sat as his stool beside Larry Branch and ordered a late breakfast. Larry nodded but said nothing. The place grew tense as conversations lulled.

When his breakfast came, Victor mashed his fried eggs and hash together but did not eat it. He sipped his black coffee. He needed to get his energy up to speak with the lawyer. That's what he needed. That's what he told himself. With a full stomach, he'd be able to concentrate. He took a bite of his eggs and hash, not tasting it. With no appetite, he dug in to the breakfast to get it over and done.

As he swiped up the last of the hash with a wedge of toast, Gwynne refilled his coffee. "There's been a mix-up, I'm sure," she said. But her voice a whisper, so others would not hear.

"Yes," Victor said. "Boy'd have to lose his mind to throw away the future he's got lined up." There he went, unable to check his pride, even if it came with its price.

The bell above the door jangled.

Victor glanced in the mirror behind the counter to see the reflection of a black raincoat.

Jon Merryfield took the stool on the other side of Victor.

Gwynne swooped in, coffeepot in hand. "You're a sight. Been a dog's age."

"I've been trying to eat well," Jon said.

"Tsk. What can I get you?"

Jon eyed Victor's plate. "Whatever he had. Looks like he licked it clean."

Gwynne glanced at Victor, then whispered to Jon, "I'm awful sorry for what happened in your home."

Jon glanced at Victor. "Coach. How are you?"

Victor stopped drinking his coffee. "How's that?" he said, not meeting Jon's eyes, which felt as though they were boring into him.

"I said, 'How are you, Coach?'"

"How do you think?"

"I suppose as good as ever by the looks of that cleaned plate. Though you do look a bit green about the gills."

"You read the paper?" Larry Branch said to Merryfield.

"Haven't had a second," Merryfield said. "Pretty occupied with my own case."

"His boy's been taken in for questioning for what happened at your place," Branch said.

Jon stared at Victor. "Is that right?"

"You know it's right," Victor said. He wanted to leave, this moment. He felt too hot. The air in the place seemed to shimmer.

"Guess I might have heard something," Jon said.

"You know damn well," Victor said.

"Do I?"

Gwynne stared at the two men, confused, the coffeepot suspended in midair from her hand.

Victor brought his eyes up to glare at Jon. "My boy never did nothing wrong."

"Then I guess he's got nothing to worry about," Jon said. "Yet there he sits. Even with you praying for him nonstop."

Victor stood abruptly, knocking over his coffee mug and spilling coffee on the counter. Gwynne broke from her trance and wiped up the mess as Victor tossed down his money and huffed out of the diner.

Jon watched him go.

"You think he did it, Victor's boy?" Gwynne asked Jon.

"Cops don't arrest someone unless they got them dead to rights. Not for murder," Branch said. He passed his check across the counter to Gwynne, who rang him up.

"They haven't arrested him," Gwynne said. "They're holding him for questioning. There's a difference, isn't there, Jon?"

Jon stirred his coffee, watching as Victor strolled past the window, looking inside the diner as he made to cross the street.

"Remember that guy and the Atlanta Olympics bombing? Everybody had him hanged," Gwynne said.

"I don't doubt for a second the boy did it," Branch said. "Pampered, entitled jock who thinks he can get away with anything. And his old man excusing any behavior. Hypocrite."

"I thought you liked Vic," Gwynne said. "You talk to him every morning."

"A matter a proximity," Branch said.

"Why sit next to him at all then?"

"*He* sits next to *me*. I sit right where I've always sat for thirty years. I like my stool."

"You know what," Jon said. "I'm good, Gwynne. I lost my appetite."

He put a twenty-dollar bill on the counter and walked out, his mind buzzing.

Chapter 42

NORTH SAT SLUMPED at his desk, dozing.

When his phone rang, he fell out of his chair and cracked his elbow on the floor. Coffee spilled from a paper cup all over the front of his shirt. "Son of a bitch," he shouted. He stood and picked up the phone. "Detective North."

"It's Test, I have something I need to fill you in on."

"Shoot."

"In person."

"What's it about?"

"Brad. In a way. Maybe."

"That sounds concrete." North looked around, bewildered. "What time is it?"

"Ten thirty."

"Shit. Meet me at the coroner's in ten. We'll talk then."

"I—"

"It's there or nothing." He hung up and strode out of the office.

NORTH MARCHED DOWN Main Street, past the old Palladium Movie House.

Its marquee had gone unlit for fifteen years, though now with a grant and donations it was under renovation to regain its former prominence as the town centerpiece.

North had seen *The Omen*, *Rosemary's Baby*, *Soylent Green*, and every other horror or sci-fi movie that had passed through town at the Palladium. The old theater was unlike any movie experience in suburbia today, the Cineplexes with their stadium seating and plush chairs and surround sound. The Palladium was grand but intimate, its plaster and tin ceiling ornate, the screen set on a proscenium stage whose smoky velvet curtains lifted at the start of each showing in the tantalizing manner of a burlesque performer slowly hiking up her skirt.

The Palladium boasted a balcony, an adolescent hideout. What better place in the world for a kid to while away a wintry Saturday than in the balcony at a movie house, his girl beside him? The thrill and heartbreak of it: holding hands, that first kiss. Even just being close enough to smell a girl's shampoo, to watch the Junior Mints melt on her fingertips, leaving them stained with chocolate she licked off, utterly oblivious to how her every tiny, casual gesture cleaved a boy's heart in two. North's heart, anyway.

The darkness made a boy brave, too. If you got there early, you got the front row of the balcony. You could prop your feet up on the rail. You could see the screen better than from any other place in the house, and you could see the audience laid out below you. At times, if he'd seen a film more than twice, which he often had, he would spend most of the matinee observing how the audience reacted to certain scenes. Mrs. Marsh, petite and bespectacled, one of the two pharmacists at Whipple Pharmacy, always squished herself up into a tiny ball when a character inflicted a wound on himself, cut a wrist, or held a hand over a candle. Yet, when mass bloodshed took place, she leaned in closer, plucking Jujubes from her box with the frenzy of a squirrel heisting seeds from a bird feeder. Coach Jenkins—Victor Jenkins—North remembered, was unmoved by violence. He sat stone-faced during the most brutal of acts. He stirred only for sex scenes. He would fidget, unable to get comfortable. He seemed to be a movie buff. But around the time of North's freshman year, Coach had stopped going to the movies. He was rarely seen in public. People talked. Then, he'd reappeared. Born again.

Chapter 43

THE BRIGHT, STERILE odors of stainless steel, formaldehyde, and ethyl alcohol did not mask the morgue's underlying stench of death.

North and Lloyd Jorgenson, the coroner, were already standing at the autopsy table when Test arrived.

Lloyd, a widowed grandfather, was a humongous man whose gut slung over a tightly cinched belt. He was chronically short of breath, his brow speckled and the underarms of his scrub top stained with sweat.

North nodded to acknowledge Test, but he did not speak. The mood was intense and, somehow, scared. For Test at least, if not for Lloyd.

Test stood beside North at the table.

Jessica's cadaver was illuminated. The lights radiated an uncomfortable and unnatural heat. The room was preternaturally still. The permanence of death lived in this room. It was bodily. Even the glare of the lights seemed cold and clinical, violating in how savagely it lit Jessica's corpse, allowing Lloyd to work with scalpel and scissors, saw, cutter and spreader. Acid boiled in Test's stomach.

Lloyd wandered away, stripped surgical gloves from his hands as he sat on a stool at the back of the room. The light there was poor and shadowed compared to the table's lights. He sat at a stainless-steel counter that might have been chic in a New York nightclub.

He nodded at Test as he ate a double-decker liverwurst sandwich and washed it down with a liter of orange Crush.

He set the bottle down. Its plastic popped back into shape with a crackle. He put a fist to his mouth, muffled a burp. He set his sandwich down on a piece of waxed paper and wiped mustard from his knuckles onto his cords.

"Junior Detective Test," he wheezed. "I haven't finished her yet. But I do have some revealing results thus far." He picked up a manila folder beside the waxed paper on which his sandwich sat.

He handed it to Test.

"Sorry to be late," Test said.

Neither man indicated they'd heard her nor cared.

Lloyd pinched his brow. "First. She wasn't molested sexually. Forced, that is. That's clear. Thank God for small mercies. Not so much as a superficial bruising or tearing. One tiny nick I determined was from a razor where she'd shaved what little pubic hair she appears to have had. The girls do that these days. At least the ones I've had the misfortune to see on my table. She was killed by massive blunt force trauma to the frontal bone of the cranium. This bone was crushed and the frontal lobe of the brain suffered catastrophic injury. What appears to be a hammer drove through the skull into the brain, which also drove sharp shards of bone deeper into the frontal lobe."

"Detective Test and I were initially under the impression that it was luck more than practice," North said. "But, with the suspect we have, perhaps it was more an athletic precision."

"She did not die instantly," Lloyd said. "But very soon after being struck. However there was no struggle. No scratches on her face or arms, which makes me assume, and this is unofficial, that she was either taken by surprise or knew him. She definitely saw it coming at the last. She was facing whoever it was."

"Brad," North said. "The two were having sex since she was fourteen."

Test held her tongue. Her confidence in Brad as the killer had waned with the dogs being killed. He was still a high probability, but it changed things for her. It would change things for North, too.

Lloyd sniffed. "You never know," he said. "By the sweet picture of her in the paper, you'd peg her for a good girl."

Test wanted to know just what that was supposed to mean.

Lloyd coughed. "That leads into my last, but certainly not least, tidbit. She was approximately three to five weeks pregnant."

"Got him," North said.

For Test, Brad jumped squarely back into the prime-suspect spot.

"You're sure?" she said.

"You insult me," Lloyd teased.

"That locks motive," North said. "What's one thing that makes a kid with a bright future risk messing up that future?"

"Trying to get rid of an even bigger risk of that future being messed up?" Lloyd said.

"You should be a cop," North said.

"I hear he's a hotshot and a hothead," Lloyd said. "Struts around like king cock of the barnyard. Though I had a swagger too when I was starting quarterback in the seventies."

Test felt her jaw drop. She snapped it shut. Her eyes roamed over Lloyd's massive and soft body, as though she were a sculptor trying to see her David in shapeless stone.

"I know," Lloyd said. "You'd never imagine it."

"No, I—" Test said.

"I get it all the time from people I went to high school with, from 'concerned family.' Truth is, I have the same appetite now as I did then. But not the workout routine, never mind the metabolism. I loved football but hated the workouts. Add three pounds a year for thirty years . . ." He took hold of his gut, jiggled it and laughed, "See as much death as I do, you better enjoy life a little. We'll need a DNA cheek swab from the boy," Lloyd said, switching gears, "to confirm a paternal link."

"We'll charge him to make it mandatory," North said.

"Can we? We don't have hard physical evidence," Test said. "His prints are in the house, but their e-mail exchanges confirm he'd been in the house plenty of times."

Lloyd closed the folder.

North grabbed it. "If we let Brad read this, he may cop without a swab."

"Still need a swab," Test said. "Physical evidence to lock it."

"I'm aware," North said.

"OK kiddies," Lloyd said. "Go harass the lad, then give me a jingle."

Chapter 44

BRAD SAT AT the table, his face slack and bloodless as Test and North entered.

Dark green moons rimmed his blank eyes. He had not showered since he'd been held, and Test got a whiff of body odor. His shoulders were slumped. He seemed smaller, his athleticism diminished.

Good, Test thought. *We'll see what he's made of now.* The pregnancy had lit a fire in her and left her theory of King sidelined for the present.

"We ran tests on your dead girlfriend." North slapped the folder on the table. "Any guesses?"

Brad seemed not to hear him. He rubbed his eyes and blinked.

"Wake up." North snapped his fingers in front of Brad's face.

Brad looked with eyes unfocused.

"We know why you did it," North said.

"I didn't do it. Why don't you believe me?"

Test thought of what Fran Jenkins had said when asked how she knew Brad didn't do it: 'Because he said he didn't.' Was it denial? Or did a mother just know? Would Test *know* if George ever did such a terrible thing but told Test he was innocent? Would she feel it? Or could she be fooled by her own son? Could her son look her in the eye and pull off such a soulless lie?

The truth was, she just didn't know.

"You have no alibi," North said. "You were sleeping with her. And it wasn't just that she might tell someone."

Brad rubbed his face.

North slid the folder to him.

"Read it," North said.

Brad slid it back to Richard.

"You don't need to read it?" Test said.

"I don't want to."

"Let me give you the gist," North said. "It's a postmortem test for pregnancy and your dead girlfriend passed."

Brad stared at North. A thought seemed to pass through Brad's eyes. He snatched the folder and opened it. If it was an act, it was a damned good one.

"I didn't know," he said. "I swear to *God*."

"How quickly they come around to God," North said.

"You'd be better off telling us what happened," Test said. "If it was an accident, perhaps, or if she instigated it." The words felt foul and bitter in her mouth, but this approach could make the perp feel understood, make him believe one empathized with his own irrational motives.

Brad blinked rapidly, as if he'd just climbed out from a dark hole into violent sunshine.

"If it was an accident, an argument that went too far," Test pressed again.

"I don't understand how this happened," Brad said. "Where's my dad? He was supposed to get me a lawyer."

Test glanced at North, who grimaced. If Brad came right out and asked for a lawyer, the interview would end now. Technically he had not asked, but they were walking a fine line.

"Just tell us what happened," Test said.

"I can't," he said. His nose was running.

"Yes you can," Test said.

"I don't *know* what happened. I wasn't *there*. I swear."

North stood. "Swear all you want. You have the right to remain silent."

"What?" Brad said.

"Anything you say can and will be—"

"Do something," Brad pleaded with Test.

North finished the Miranda warning. "Get up," he said.

Brad remained fixed in his seat.

North walked around the table, seized Brad's shoulders and pulled. "Get your ass up."

PART III

Chapter 45

TEST CLOSED HER office door then stood by the window looking out at the town green as North sat in the chair before her desk.

"I'd swear you believed that kid," North said. "Kids like him turn it on and off like a faucet. The act."

"I know." Test breathed on the window and a circle of fog grew where her breath touched the cold glass. She ran a finger through it twice, to make an X. "The kid seems genuinely scared, though," Test said.

"He's *caught*."

"He seemed shocked to see the pregnancy report."

"He's shocked to find out we can tell a dead girl was pregnant. Don't fall for it. He knows we have him and he's going to go to jail and there is nothing his old man, his golden arm, or any lawyer can do about it."

"I see all that. I'm not naïve." Test rubbed the fogged window clean with the cuff of her shirt.

"So, what's the problem?"

"No problem. Just keeping an open mind."

"Don't. Not at this juncture. Now, we focus. We concentrate to build the case." He pulled what looked like the remains of a melted candy bar from his jacket pocket and ate it with a bite, licked his fingers. "You said on the phone you had new information that had to do with Brad."

North crumpled the candy bar wrapper and stuffed it in his pocket. Then leaned back in the chair, cupping his hands behind his head. "So. Let's hear it."

"Two dogs died last night," Test said.

"And?" North raised an eyebrow to prompt her to continue.

She didn't appreciate his tone or his manner that suggested she get to the point so he could get on with his investigation. What was she even thinking? The two cases were not linked. The pregnancy provided an even stronger motive than the statutory rape. *If* Brad knew Jessica was pregnant. If it was his baby. That was yet to be determined. Every other thought in her mind contradicted the one before and after it. Which meant what? She wasn't sure about anything.

"The dogs were poisoned," she said.

North perked up and unclasped his hands from behind his head. "You sure?"

"Yes. But I plan to have tests done."

"You have the resources?"

"I want them done."

"It's your budget."

He was losing interest.

"I don't see any connection with Brad," he said. "If this happened last night."

"I'm getting to that. One of the dogs was Gregory Sergeant's."

"OK."

"The other dog was mine."

North frowned and leaned forward. "I'm sorry to hear that. But what's your thinking? I still don't see how it has anything to do with Brad."

"These dogs were targeted."

"Sure. Of course."

"As a threat, or a warning. My kids are crushed their dog is dead. If they knew why, they'd be scared shitless."

"Obviously." North stood, as if preparing to leave. "I understand. And whoever did it should be charged. It's serious. But it certainly wasn't Brad." His hand was on the doorknob.

"That's *exactly* what I'm saying," Test said, her voice rising.

North turned back to her. "*What* are you saying, Detective?"

"It *could* be some asshole getting off from scaring us. But it could be someone else, with a different motive."

"Like?"

"I don't know." She resisted telling him she'd been to see King because she did not want to get into the conversation about her drawing her weapon.

North turned the doorknob.

"I don't know *yet*," Test said. "We don't *know* who did it, but we can't deny it's linked to this case."

"Yes, we can. Brad killed her because she was pregnant and that was going to fuck up his life. The victim happened to be babysitting at Merryfield's house. A teenage boy killed a teenage girl for selfish reasons. Whoever killed the dogs may *think* Jessica's murder is connected to The Case, so poisoned dogs owned by two people associated with it, to pile on. But we know Brad killed Jessica. We know he did it alone. We know he couldn't have poisoned the dogs. End of story. They're not connected in a material way."

"Here me out. Please."

North looked at his watch. "Two minutes."

"There are three possibilities. One: Brad killed Jessica, and the dogs were killed by some hothead who took advantage of The Case to be part of the limelight by stirring the pot. Two: Brad killed Jessica, but had help, or did it for someone for other reasons. And that someone killed the dogs."

"One minute left if you still care to argue point three."

"Three: Brad never killed Jessica. And whoever killed the dogs, *my* dog, killed Jessica."

North gripped the doorknob tighter. "I'm sorry someone killed your dog and it's traumatized you."

"*I'm* not traumatized. My kids, yes. But not me."

North held up his palms in the demeaning "I surrender" gesture males used whenever they believed a woman was becoming "unreasonable."

"You're wrong here, Detective," North said. "If Brad had done it for someone else, he would have copped by now. He's soft."

"Why hasn't he copped his own plea by now, if he's so soft?"

"He will. It's different trying to save your own ass than saving someone else's at the expense of yours. Brad did this. You see that, I hope. Since it's been your legwork that got us here. Everything points to him."

"But there's no real physical evidence."

"The DNA will show he impregnated that girl. We'll get a warrant for his parents' house. Search it. We'll find something. Bloody clothes, other notes. Something he did or searched for online. The damned hammer itself."

"Maybe."

"No. *Not* maybe. He's our doer. And he's going to be transferred to the St. Johnsbury prison now soon as he's formally charged."

"I—"

"Enough. Relax. We're both so tired it's a miracle we haven't gone blind. And you're dealing with this dog thing, too. Neither of us can think straight."

"I'm thinking straight."

"Well I'm sure not. And while I'm here. What you did out at King's place—"

"Not now."

"You need to hear it," North said.

She didn't need to hear a damn thing. But she braced herself because it was coming anyway, whether she liked it or not.

"You did the right thing," North said. "You did everything right."

Test blinked, feeling a rush of embarrassment and . . . what? Pride?

She folded her arms at her waist, as if she had stomach cramps.

"You hear me?" North said.

"I'm waiting for the *but*."

"No but, Detective. You stood your ground. You walked a precarious line between exerting authority and not instigating that asshole or escalating the tension. When you drew your weapon, you were entirely justified. He wielded an axe in a threatening manner. You showed enough restraint *not* to fire."

It hadn't been restraint. She was not sure what it had been, but it wasn't restraint. If she was honest, it was the paralysis of indecision, or perhaps fear.

"Restraint is a trait even a seasoned cop has a hard time putting to practice in such instances. King could have swung that axe and struck you. You had every right to fire. *I* probably would have. And now I'd be on leave awaiting investigation."

"But you didn't even draw your sidearm," Test said.

North smiled. It wasn't the most handsome or charming smile, with his smudge of chocolate from his candy bar stuck to his top front teeth. But it seemed genuine enough. "*I* didn't have time. You had your weapon up before I could blink. And that may have saved your life and King's."

She felt tension she'd been holding inside over this melt away. "I thought—"

"I *know* what you thought. That's why I wanted to tell you earlier, but you deflected and avoided at every turn. But you needed to know. Like you need to know now."

"Know what?"

The tension was returning. A tightness. She was so damned fatigued. All she wanted was sleep. Her body felt like it had molasses running through its veins instead of blood.

"I let you in on this case because you show promise," North said. "But you are off the mark about the dogs. Brad killed Jessica. Trying to draw a connection from the dogs to Brad or, worse, another killer, is a waste of your time. More important, it's a waste of my time."

"But something doesn't add up and—"

"A lot *does* add up. You want to get who killed your dog. Do it. I have a murder case to build for the prosecutor. We do. If you'd like."

Her evidence was thin. With no proof. No real suspect, other than King. She wanted to bring up that King had no alibi for the night of Jessica Cumber's murder or for last night with the dogs, but North was already out the door. Her two minutes were up.

Chapter 46

Victor Jenkins sat in Public Defender James Allard's office. Atop Allard's desk sat family photos. In each was James Jr., with a thicker head of his father's flaming red hair to go with the florid cheeks, British-bad teeth, and eyeglasses as big as the father's glasses. Between Jr. and Sr. stood a woman who might have been pretty if her almond eyes were the same size as each other and one did not seem to float aimlessly, even in a photo.

In the series of staged photos, the Allards smiled as though they had guns aimed at their heads.

"Let me ask. First thing. Up front." Allard paused and nodded to the door. "Close that door for me? This is private."

Victor shut the door.

Allard said, "Do you believe your son did it?"

"No." What kind of question was this to start out?

"I can tell you believe it. But that doesn't make it so. Nor does it matter. It doesn't matter what you or your wife or I or the police or the judge or the media or anyone else believes. You know what matters?"

Vic was frustrated already with this circular talk.

"What matters is what twelve people in a jury box think," Allard said. "That's it. Nothing else. We are planting the seed of reasonable doubt and letting it grow into a big redwood of not guilty."

It mattered to Victor that Brad was innocent. Murder was *not* the same as other sins. Victor would not be able to bear the shame if Brad had killed that girl. His life would be shattered, his name and family ruined. His wife shamed. He would not know how to forgive his son.

He glanced at the dead fern on the bookshelf. He nearly got up and left. But he thought about what a real lawyer cost and remained seated. "This is going to court?" Victor said.

"I will need to speak to Brad, ASAP. He's spoken too much to the police already."

"I don't think he said anything damaging."

"*Everything* he says is damaging. Your son has no alibi?"

"No."

"He was seeing the girl?"

"Yes."

"And that girl was pregnant?"

"What?" Victor felt as if a jolt of electricity had shot through him.

"You didn't know?" Allard said. He waved a hand. "I'm privy, as the PD. It doesn't matter."

"Doesn't matter, of course it—"

"And his fingerprints are all over the house," Allard said.

"He'd *been* there before. And if they had prints on the murder weapon, they'd have arrested him as soon as they got a match. So. That's good."

"Maybe."

"How can it not be?" Victor wondered if this guy was on Brad's side or not.

"If we had the weapon and there were *someone else's* finger-prints, *that* would be good. We need evidence that points to some-one else. Not just less evidence against your son."

"It's all circumstantial."

"Not his prints. While the police can't prove they were left the night of the murder, we have no way to prove they weren't. And. I have to be honest. I'm a straight shooter if nothing else. People are convicted. Every day. On circumstantial evidence. Every day. On much less of it too."

"You think he did it."

"I am your son's attorney. My sole priority is to create reason-able doubt. Or unearth evidence that points elsewhere."

"Can you?"

Allard glanced at the folder. "Honest. Based on what I see here."

"Have you even handled a murder case?"

"They don't come up much in the Kingdom. I've handled plea bargains to manslaughter. I really need to speak to your son ASAP."

"How about now?"

Allard snapped his arm up so his shirt cuff receded to reveal a gold wristwatch. He lowered his arm with a snap, as if performing a magic trick, concealing his wristwatch again.

"Okeydokey."

Chapter 47

BRAD'S EYES WERE beads of fear. A rash bloomed on what had always been the clear skin of his forehead. Fran appeared as if she'd just finished a crying jag. Victor stared at them both as he entered the visitor room at the state prison in St. Johnsbury.

Allard looked Brad in the eye. "You do it?"

Brad did a double take, as did his mother. "What? Why would you—"

"The answer is *no*. And the answer comes fast and it comes with certainty," Allard said. "No hesitation. No answering the question with a question. Understood?"

"Yes."

"Atta boy. I am going to do everything I can. What about your fingerprints in the house?"

"I've been over and over this."

"And you will go over and over it again and again," Allard said. "Stop being defensive."

"Those prints are from the other times I was there," Brad said.

"We'll argue that. I'm on your side. Honest," Allard said to

Victor. "Either your son is lying. Or we are up against a calamity of circumstances and grave misfortune."

"'Calamity?' What do you mean, calamity?" Fran said and put a hand on Brad's shoulder.

"What if it's more than that?" Victor said.

All eyes moved to look at him.

"How's that?" Allard said, squinting as if to decipher a code.

"What if someone deliberately made it look like Brad did it?"

"Like who?" Allard said.

Victor shrugged. He had no idea. He was grasping at straws.

"We can't be wasting a second of energy or focus on preposterous notions," Allard said. He addressed Brad. "You know anyone who would 'set you up?'"

"I don't know anything anymore."

"Chin up," Allard said. "We're not even at halftime. We may be down a couple touchdowns, but that's nothing for you, right?"

"Sure," Brad said with no fight in his voice.

"What are we going to do?" Fran chimed.

"Fight," Allard said. "We argue that while Brad has no alibi, no one can place him at the scene at the time of the crime either. A male was seen by Jon Merryfield. But he can't give a positive ID. We argue that your son's fingerprints are from earlier. We argue that he was at home. We argue that no e-mails of his mention or even allude to the fact that he knew she was pregnant, or even that *she* knew she was. It's quite possible she never even knew. If *she* didn't know, Brad sure didn't. Unless the victim mentions anywhere in her private writings or we find other evidence, a doctor's appointment, purchase of a pregnancy test, anything to indicate for a fact that she knew, we can argue she didn't know. Thus, Brad couldn't have known either. Thus, the strongest motive is taken away. You *didn't* know about her preg-nancy, right?" Allard said.

"No, sir," Brad said.

Victor's spirits were buoyed. He felt hope run through him.

"Atta boy," said Allard. He placed a hand on each of Brad's shoulders but looked at Fran, giving her a reassuring nod. "We argue someone else did it. Someone who wanted to threaten Jon Merryfield. Plenty of whackos out there who hate the man. The prosecutors will argue that this is smoke." He looked Brad straight in the eyes. "They will say you were sleeping with her. She was un-derage and wanted to announce your love to the universe. She was pregnant. You knew. You argued. You wanted to keep her from ruining your future. But we'll tell the jury there's no physical evi-dence. Zero."

"That's *right*," Victor said, feeling the rush of optimism. Of faith. He realized that until now, he had not been sure of Brad's innocence. Now, he was certain. His boy was innocent.

"You speak as if we are going to trial," Fran said to Allard.

"I have to be straight," Allard said. "I'm nothing if not a straight shooter. This is a hard case. If I didn't think your boy was inno-cent, I'd have him plea to manslaughter. Get it done. Say it was an act of passion. He hit her out of fear. Nothing premeditated."

Fran clutched at her throat. "He'd never do that."

"They'll push for first degree. That brings a minimum of twenty-five years in a maximum security. Vermont's prisons are full up. He'd be shipped to Kentucky or Virginia. Manslaughter, he'd get five to ten. Be incarcerated in-state. Maybe out in three."

Victor felt his faith bleeding out of him. "He's not pleading to a thing," he said.

"I didn't say that. Follow me here," Allard said. "I was saying *if*

I thought he was guilty, I would not take this to court, because it's a tough one. But I believe we'll win it because I believe the system works. We do not convict the innocent. And any damned idiot can see Brad's innocent. So. You keep telling me the truth and we stand a good chance."

"A chance?" Fran said.

"A very good chance," Allard said.

"I find out who did this, I'll be the one up on murder charges," Victor said.

"No, you *won't*," Allard snapped. "You will be a model citizen. You. Your family. You will act and speak exactly as I instruct. Otherwise you undermine the entire case."

"You believe your theory?" Victor asked Allard. "That some crazy killed that girl because of Jon representing the homosexual couple?"

"I just don't see why else anybody would have done it."

"Can we talk privately?" Victor asked Allard.

Fran looked at Victor with fearful, distrusting eyes.

"Whatever you have to say, say it in the open," Allard said.

"In private."

"Say it in front of us," Fran said, alarmed.

"You think I did it," Brad said. "Just say it."

"I don't. I just have something to ask him."

"Ask away," Allard said.

Victor sighed. "OK. What are the odds that my boy is found guilty?"

"I don't give odds."

"I need to hear them."

"I don't give odds."

"You're the straight shooter. Shoot straight."

"Fifty-fifty," Allard said.

Fran sobbed.

It was worse than Victor had thought. Even now, he swayed between being certain his son was innocent, and thinking his son had murdered the girl. Brad didn't look like he had it in him to commit such an act. But Victor knew how looks deceived, how even those closest to us can harbor secret sins.

"It's not just the circumstantial evidence. It's people's *emotions*," Allard said. "Say all you want about facts and evidence, in a case like this, emotions often rule. It's the human condition. People judge others based on emotion when there are no hard facts. And the emotions lean toward the girl. Not just because she's dead. But because, one: she was cute. Two: she was young and likeable and naïve and your boy took advantage of that."

"He did not!" Fran said.

"Yes, he did," Allard said. "Three: As you said, people are envious of Brad. They envy his talent and his drive and his looks. A star QB. They find him arrogant and spoiled; they think—"

"Enough!" Fran cried.

"Mrs. Jenkins, your boy committed ongoing statutory rape," Allard said. "If that girl wasn't dead your boy would be charged with a crime if he were found out. Let's not make him out to be a saint. Your husband wants me to shoot straight. Here it is. Here is how the jury is going to see it. Your boy was raping that girl . . ."

"I don't have to listen to this!" Fran shouted.

"Yes you do," Victor said, trying to keep himself from yelling.

Fran quieted.

"Let him talk," Victor said.

"Fifty-fifty," Brad mumbled.

"*Unless*," Allard said, "new evidence arises. And believe you me, if it exists, I'll find it."

"What's the statute of limitations on sexual assault?" Victor blurted, not meaning to speak aloud the shadowy thought that had just flitted through his mind.

"Statutory rape?" Allard asked.

"All kinds."

"In Vermont. If violence is involved, aggravated sexual assault with a weapon, there is no limitation. But if no violence was perpetrated, that is *no weapon involved*, I should clarify, for all acts of rape are violent, then the statute of limitations is six years."

"And beyond six years?" Victor asked.

"Prosecution cannot take place."

"A person can't be arrested or charged?"

"No." Allard looked at Brad. "I'll tell you this once. Lie to me. We're done. You can find someone else. Got it? I need the truth the whole way. Good or bad. The truth."

"I'm fucked," Brad said. "That's the truth."

"Don't use that language," Fran said.

"I need to get out of here." Brad clawed at his handcuffed wrists.

"Let's go over everything together from the very start," Allard said. He placed a micro-recorder on the table. "Leave nothing out. You were seeing Jessica Cumber . . ."

Chapter 48

SOMETHING IS WRONG, Test thought. *No. Not wrong. Unclear. Mis-understood.* She pondered now how certain she had been initially that Victor Jenkins had murdered Jessica when she'd first found his name on the Family Matters roster. She'd been as certain as could be. She'd imagined Victor leading Jessica astray, taking advantage of her with some sort of leverage. The older man with the power. It was absurd now. Yet she had believed her theory as if it were fact.

There was evidence against Brad. Circumstantial, but mounting each day.

Still, the killing of the dogs nagged.

If whoever had killed Jessica was still out there, and Brad was in custody for the killing, why would the real killer call attention to himself by killing dogs? Perhaps he felt invincible. Like King.

King, who had no alibi.

And neither did . . . Who? Who else could not account for their actions in the time frame? Who else was not in the company of anyone during the window of time Jessica had been killed?

King. Victor. Brad. Any number of people who had made threats against the Merryfield family.

She was missing something. She felt it. Knew it. But could she any longer trust what she felt, or what she supposedly *knew*?

Brad seemed like the only suspect who was aware that Jessica had been alone in the house babysitting. Could King have known this? No. Unless he'd been planting the sign and peeked in a window and seen the opportunity. But there was no proof he'd planted the sign. The fingerprints were too smudged to be of use. Besides, the Merryfields' other car, Bethany's Lexus, had been parked in front of the creamery, suggesting that an adult could be present. So. No one else besides Brad knew Jessica was alone babysitting, except Jessica's mother and the Merryfields. Jessica's mother was ruled out. So were the Merryfields.

She wondered if North had gotten his hands on the incoming phone calls through the telephone company's Local Usage Details. Perhaps there was something to be found in the LUD. A recurring number. Test found it odd Jon Merryfield had said he thought there were messages on his voice mail, but the following morning when Test had checked there had not been any. Or any numbers on the caller ID. Had Jon deleted them? What possible reason could he have? An affair. Was he having an affair? Had *he* had an affair with Jessica?

Test recalled information Bethany and Jon had mentioned when interviewed at their home the night of the murder. Bethany had repeated it the next morning when Test had spoken with her. Something that had happened at the restaurant. It was probably nothing. Still. Test wondered if North had checked up on it, just to take it off the table, if not for anything else.

She looked at her watch. It was nearly 3:00 P.M. She had an

hour and a half before she had to leave for home. Claude was in St. J, preparing his exhibit at the Kingdom Gallery. George and Elizabeth would be dropped off from the after-school program by 5:00 P.M. and Test needed time to stop to get pizza.

Before Charlie was poisoned, she wouldn't have had any grave misgivings about leaving her kids to their own devices for a half hour or so. The bus driver made sure to watch until George and Elizabeth entered the house or were greeted by a parent before driving off. In the one or two rare instances when Test or Claude were running a few minutes late, George had locked the door behind him, and knew that he and Elizabeth were allowed to treat themselves to the Sprout Channel. Reduced to zombies by TV, there was no risk of the kids even glancing away from the screen, let alone breaking an arm or knocking out teeth with horseplay.

Test called North to ask if he'd gotten the LUD records of incoming calls.

North let out a breath. "Those were a bitch to sift through and no help. So I hear. I put two others on it. We have numbers and can trace some back. There are a lot. But without voice mail messages we don't know who left what kind of message, who is friend or foe."

"Can we have the Merryfields give a list of 'friendly' numbers?"

"We did that," North said.

"Can we go to the unfriendly people and interview them?"

"Sure." She sensed frustration.

"But?"

"If you left a threatening message, even if you had nothing to do with the murder, would you confess to it now?"

Playing devil's advocate, she said, "If I was proud or loony enough about my stance."

"I don't have the resources or inclination to track calls not germane to our investigation."

"Threatening calls aren't germane?" she snipped.

"Not with our doer charged. And, I had the numbers checked to see if Brad's cell or home number came up. They didn't. That's all that matters." North yawned. Test wished he would at least get angry. Instead, he simply sounded bored.

"Were there any repeats from numbers the Merryfields don't know?"

"Of course," he said, exasperated, like a parent tired of a child saying, *But why? Why?* "But we don't know whose numbers they are. The phone company provides the numbers under subpoena, they don't give names or addresses. We'd have to dig for those on our own. And my team isn't doing that because there's no need."

"Can I have a copy LUD?" Test said.

"Be my guest."

Test looked at her watch. The conversation had gone longer than she'd imagined.

"What's this all about?" North said.

She took a deep breath, cringing as she prepared to say what had struck her earlier.

"Did anyone follow up on Merryfield?" she asked.

"What are you talking about?"

"He was alone an undetermined time in the restaurant bathroom. He claimed he was sick but—"

"*Claimed?* No. No one *checked up.*" His tone one of finality.

"Of course. Would you have someone fax me the LUD report?"

"I'll have it e-mailed."

"I'm in a rush. Fax it. If our spreadsheet programs aren't compatible, the attachments will be all buggy and useless and I'll just have to call back. And I won't have to open all the attachments and print them if you fax hard copies. I'll get them faster. Tell a subordinate. Please. Send them straightaway. I'll owe you."

"You already owe me."

"I'll go stand by now."

Test hung up so she could switch over her line to receive a fax.

Chapter 49

"STEP IT UP," King said and clapped a big hand on the middle of Victor's back so hard it stung Victor's flesh and made him wince as he bent over a pile of tomato stakes, stapling Take Back Vermont signs to them. He handed a pile of signs over to Banks and Graves to load into their cars. The three men had been at it for hours and Victor felt he might pass out on his feet; but it kept his mind occupied, for the most part.

As King marched toward his truck he pounded a fist in the center of Victor's back again, barked: "Stack 'em neater. We need to get 'em out of the vehicles easy and fast."

Victor rubbed his back where King had struck him. Fran had begged Victor not to come here tonight. She understood the cause was just, but insisted their priority was Brad. Victor had argued that he needed to keep to part of his normal routine, so he wouldn't feel overwhelmed with helplessness and distress. Now, he saw, she'd been right. He sighed and closed his eyes.

"That guy," someone whispered.

Victor opened his eyes to see Daryn Banks glancing at King, who was loading his truck.

"What?" Victor said, looking to make certain King remained out of earshot.

"Nothing, sorry." Daryn shrugged. "Judge not." He smiled. His eyes and easy manner made a person feel like you'd known him all his life. A gift, that.

"What is it?" Victor said.

Daryn glanced at King. "He's just crude, for a man of God. And. Punching you like that."

"It's nothing."

"It's not nothing. You shouldn't take it. I wonder sometimes if he uses the Bible, and our faith, not out of love for the word of God, but out of his own mean-spiritedness."

Victor thought about the fist-sized knot of pain where King had just pounded his spine. He thought about Fran's take on the man. Had Victor blindly followed King? He wondered now if King had left the sign in Merryfield's yard. Someone had. And King had been the one out that way the night of the murder; a murder for which Brad was now charged.

"Forgive me. I spoke out of turn," Daryn said. "I hope your son is faring OK. I've been praying."

"Thanks," Victor said. "Some folks we believed were friends have distanced themselves."

Daryn reflected. "They'll come around. I'd bet. We should put together a prayer circle for your boy." He lay a hand on Victor's back, where King had punched it.

"OK, ladies," King snarled as he strode from his truck,

glaring at the two men and punching Victor square in the back, the pain flaring up again. "Back to work. This isn't a circle jerk."

Victor kept an eye on King as the pain throbbed through his back.

Chapter 50

TEST WAITED FOR the faxed call records to arrive. None appeared. She'd checked the machine twice now.

Time was getting away. She had less than an hour before she had to leave to meet the kids. Pizza might be out of the question; but she had nothing else at home and the kids would be starving, which meant they would be ornery and whiney. And if they got there even a few minutes before her, they would go ballistic when they had to turn off the TV. She called the pizza joint and placed an order.

When she hung up, the faxes still had not come. Whoever had possession of the LUD, she realized, might not have hard copies. Which meant *they* would need to print them first, before they faxed them.

She deliberated calling North and having the records e-mailed, as he'd suggested. But she did not want to hear his weariness, or admit her flawed thinking. She was berating her poor decision when she heard a fax spit out from the machine in its herk-a-jerk manner. A faxed page curled and floated to the floor. She picked up the page. It was a list of the friendly numbers, as provided by the Merryfields. This would make her work easier and faster. If she hurried, she'd get home in plenty of time. If she couldn't finish here, she'd take the work home.

She took a highlighter and started poring over the phone records at her desk as the fax machine spat out more pages.

She studied and cross-referenced the numbers with meticulous attention. There were a lot of phone numbers and the task proved tedious. No wonder North didn't want his people on it.

She'd reduced perhaps a hundred individual telephone numbers down to a list of twenty-three. Daunting, but manageable. The duration of each call was included in the log. She excluded from her shortened list those calls that had lasted longer than a minute, assuming the calls had been answered by Jon or Bethany, and were conversations.

She narrowed the list to seventeen phone numbers.

Of them, only three numbers had called more than once.

If the killer was not Brad, but someone who had made threatening calls, Test posited the killer would be more likely to leave several threatening messages before escalating to murder.

Of the three phone numbers that had made more than one call, only one of them had made more than three calls; and that number had made five calls.

She would track these three numbers first. It was a place to start anyway. The pages kept spitting out of the fax machine.

On Switchboard.com she did a quick search. Two of the numbers came up. A Kate Atkinson in Clearbrook, New Hampshire, and a Jon Harvey in South Burlington, Vermont. The third number did not appear. She called the number that had made five calls, the one from New Hampshire.

Test was about to hang up after many rings when the reedy voice of an elderly woman answered, "Yes?"

"Is this Kate Atkinson?" Test inquired.

"Who is this?"

"I'm a police detective, ma'am."

"Is this a joke?" The woman coughed a dry harsh cough that made Test's throat hurt just to hear it.

"No ma'am."

"Why are you calling me? How do I know you're the police?"

"Your phone number came up while we were investigating a crime and—"

"A crime?" her voice sounded like a creaky hinge now.

"Ma'am, do you recall calling a number in Canaan, Vermont, several times over the month of October?"

"I call lots of numbers, I don't know to who or where."

"I don't understand," Test said.

"I make calls for charities and political parties and like that. I can't get out of the house to volunteer anymore, so I help by phone."

Test was about to thank the woman for her time when an idea struck her. "Does anyone live with you?" she asked.

"I'm all alone, dear," she said.

"Thank you very much for your time," Test said and hung up.

Test called the next number. A kid answered, "What's up?"

"To whom am I speaking?" Test said.

"Davy."

"Davy who?"

"Harvey. Who's this?"

"How old are you, Davy?"

"Fifteen, what's it to you?"

"I'm a police officer."

Silence.

"Tell me, Davy. Is this your phone you answered?"

"Why should I believe you're a cop? Is this one of those radio shows, am I being punked?"

Test was pleased that neither of her callers believed she was a cop just because she said she was; it gave her some hope for the savvy of citizens, though the statistics on people scammed over the phone would not bear out this anecdotal evidence.

"No," Test said. "You're not on the radio."

"Ah, damn it. I hoped I would win something. I never win squat."

"I can visit your house and speak to your parents if you'd rather," Test said.

More silence.

"Davy, is this your phone you answered?" Test said.

"Yes, so what?"

"Did you make prank calls to an attorney last month?"

For a moment Test thought the kid had hung up.

"Davy? We have the phone records."

"OK, yeah, me and some friends, so what? The guy's a creep. Or so my mom says. I don't give a crap. But. We make a lot of calls. To all kinds of people. We're not prejudice against who we prank. I told those idiots to press star-six-seven to block the number. Idiots."

"They did use star-six-seven. We have official telephone company records. I'm a real cop."

"Oh. Shit. We were just bored. We—"

"How old are your friends?"

"Same as me fifteen, fourteen."

"Any of you drive yet?"

"I'm the oldest. I get my permit next month, if my grades improve."

"None of you drive then?"

"I wish."

"Thank you, Davy." Test hung up.

So. An elderly housebound woman who makes blanket volunteer calls, and a teenager with no ability to drive anywhere who admits making prank calls.

She struck them off the list.

That left the last number that had turned up nothing on the Internet.

She called Officer Larkin at his desk on the other side of the station and asked him to run a check on the third number and see what he came up with, and get back to her as soon as possible.

A harsh beeping took her out of her work trance. The fax machine. It was out of paper.

"Shit!" Test shouted. She looked at her watch with horror.

Time had melted. Shit. She needed to go if she was going to grab the pizza and meet her kids.

Outside, snow was falling. Hard. Shit. If she left now, she could get pizza and be there just before her kids.

Test snatched her coat from the back of her chair and yanked it on. Just in case, she dialed George's cell phone number. George was just seven, but had a cheapie phone strictly for emergencies. This qualified. She dialed and listened to her son's cell phone ring and ring. Then, her heart sinking, listened to her own voice on the voice mail. She left a message, clear and direct. Mommy would be home very soon, she was on her way. Watch all the TV you want.

Just don't horseplay or use the stove. Don't answer the door for anyone, and *lock it.*

She hung up and sent a text with the same message.

She contemplated calling Claude, but he was an hour farther from home than she was, maybe more with the snow always worse in the mountains he had to travel.

She hurried out of the station thinking she'd pick the kids up some hot wings, too. They loved the hot wings.

THE PIZZA JOINT was packed. A man in line ahead of Test had to dole out exact change. A pack of teens kept changing their orders. Test cursed herself. Checked the time on her cell. *Come on come on come on already,* she thought, tapping a boot. All she could think of was Charlie. Poisoned Charlie. And her kids. She called George's number again. Left a similar message. Again. Texted it. Got no reply.

When she reached the register, the kid behind it shoved her boxed pizza across the counter at her and, wiping his sweaty, pimpled forehead with his forearm, said, "Anything else?"

She thought about the wings. "No." She paid and grabbed the pizza box and hustled out to her car.

Where someone had double-parked a Jeep and blocked her in.

She tossed the pizza onto her car's passenger seat and hurried inside. She brandished her badge over her head: "Whoever double-parked a Jeep better move it right now!" she shouted.

People gaped at the crazy shouting lady, until they saw her badge.

A middle-aged man in a cheap suit looked at her sheepishly as he stood at the counter with his wallet in his hand, about to dole out cash to the kid at the counter. He started to make a gesture to Test to give him just a second to pay. "Right fucking now," Test snarled.

The man scurried out past her, mortified, but also shaking his head incredulously.

"Watch the attitude," Test admonished and tracked him outside.

She kept her eyes locked on him as he moved his Jeep, then hopped in her Peugeot and headed home, car sliding as she shifted into second gear.

She was halfway home, making better time than she had expected and glad for it. She'd be no more than a half hour late. Tops.

She was beginning to calm when a thought struck her and her mind went frantic.

George didn't have a house key to let himself and Elizabeth in the house. The few times Test and Claude had even thought they'd be late, they'd left a key hidden for the kids. She did not think George knew of the key hidden in the carriage barn.

It would be dark before she got home. George and Elizabeth would be sitting on the porch in the snow. Hungry. Cold. The person who poisoned Charlie still around.

Damn it.

She pulled over on the side of the dirt road and texted George.

If u r locked out get key on nail under canoe in carriage barn let urself in & lock door! Pizza coming! Luv mama!

Chapter 51

THE SNOW GREW heavy and impeded progress as paranoia and guilt gnawed at Test.

She finally pulled her Peugeot into the dirt drive so fast she nearly smashed into the back end of Claude's Bronco II.

Relief washed over Test.

But relief was swiftly overridden by unease. She'd not imagined getting home so late that she'd arrive after Claude. She'd hoped to be at the table eating pizza with the kids by the time he came home; the kids coached not to mention her tardiness to Dad. *You know how he is.*

She could only imagine the kids' distressed state, and Claude's reaction to finding his kids stranded on the porch so soon after their dog had been poisoned. George had never called or texted back, so Test had no idea if he'd received her messages. It was unforgivable if her kids had waited in the cold. Claude would say he forgave her, and he'd probably believe it. But there would remain a piece of him that wouldn't. Couldn't. Justifiably. It's how she would feel if Claude did such a thing. Which he never would.

The front door was locked. Which worried her. Claude never locked the door when it was just him and the kids at home. But perhaps he'd locked it because of Charlie. She unlocked the door and entered as she readied herself to plead unpardonable selfishness and throw herself on her family's mercy.

Out of habit she hoisted the pizza box over her head to prepare for Charlie's crazed greeting.

She was greeted by silence.

She set the pizza box down on the mudroom bench, her palms greasy from the underside of it.

No boots or jackets hung in the mudroom.

That couldn't be. They had to be here. She went to the kitchen and looked at the clock. It was 6:12. The kids got their bath at 6:00, and as freewheeling as Claude was with his own time during the day, he was regimented about the kids' schedules. She pieced together the evidence: The kids had waited outside for her in the cold; Claude had swept them into the house and straight up to a warm bath, no time to take off their gear.

Except there should have been water, melted from their snowy boots.

She called up the stairs.

No response came.

She'd expect Claude to give her the silent treatment. But not the kids.

Disquiet fluttered in her chest.

Calm yourself, she said.

She hurried around the kitchen island, kicking Charlie's old feeding bowl and scattering the kibbles across the floor. She went to the back playroom. The kids and Claude were not there.

She took the stairs two at a time, thinking maybe the bathroom door was shut, or the kids had already bathed and were exhausted and in bed, and Claude did not want to yell down to her for fear of waking them.

That was it, she told herself.

It had to be.

The bathroom and the kids' rooms were empty.

Her family was not in the house.

The barn. Of course. They were all out in Claude's studio.

She looked out the upstairs hallway window at the old carriage barn studio, eyes searching. But there was no sign of lights coming from inside the barn.

There'd be no reason Claude would take George and Elizabeth to the barn studio. The kids disliked the studio. The noxious odors of oil paints, thinners and solvents were hard for Test to stomach for even a few seconds with the windows open wide. The fumes gave her a constant worry about Claude's health. Whenever he got a nasty cough, her first thought was lung cancer.

Still, he and the kids had to be out in the barn. There was nowhere else they could be. No reasonable explanation. Unless.

She shoved the thought out of her mind as she reached under her jacket and brought out her M&P40.

She took the stairs back down three at a time and raced out the door and into a heavy wet snow that fell in big wet flakes the size of crabapple blossoms.

As she strode toward the barn, sidearm in her hand, she kept her senses keen, eyes sharp, images of poisoned dogs and Jessica corroding the edges of her panic.

The snow fell fast, watering her vision.

She peered in a window of the carriage barn's door. The inside of the barn was dark. She knocked.

No one came to the door.

She blinked back the fat snowflakes from her lashes. Her face hot and slick with sweat as her body hummed with fear.

Where were they?

She yanked on the carriage barn handle.

As the door slid back in its track, Test took a shooting stance. But no one advanced on her from the darkness. What was going on here?

She looked back across the darkening yard to Claude's Bronco II.

She told herself to calm down. Still, she found it hard to breathe, on the edge of hyperventilating.

She should never have even called North. The case was wrapped up. She'd obstinately followed dead-end theories out of pride or naivety. Left her kids alone, in jeopardy.

If someone had done something to her family because—

She tried to clear her mind of rampant thoughts that did not serve her.

She switched on the barn lights. The ground floor of the barn was empty. Test rushed to the door to the stairway that led to the studio in the barn's old loft. The door was locked.

She looked under the canoe. The key chain hung on its nail. There was no way to lock the door from the other side. Her family could not be upstairs.

Where is my family? her mind screamed.

She looked out into the strengthening snow.

The floodlights had blinked on with her movement and cast a swath of yellow light in which the snow jigged. She heard a grating sound and flinched, tightening her grip on her sidearm.

The weather vane atop the carriage barn, a copper pig, squeaked in the changing wind.

Damn it. Where were they?

Her eyes lit on Claude's Bronco II, parked in the shadows beyond the reach of the floodlight.

It was the only place left for them to be.

Except.

An image of Jessica in the Merryfields' cellar flashed in Test's mind.

And if they are in the Bronco II. They—

She ran to the vehicle as if it were on fire, her family trapped inside.

She got to the driver's door—too dark to see inside the vehicle—and yanked the door open.

The wind blew snow straight into her face.

Her gun was cold in her hand. Her fingers stiff around its grip.

As her vision returned and she stared at the empty vehicle, a shriek rose from behind her. Her heart jumped and she wheeled around, her gun coming up, thumb blindly tripping the safety, finger slipping inside the trigger guard.

She leveled the M&P40, ready to fire this time.

The shriek rose through the snow.

A figure bore down on her.

She gripped the pistol, finger against the trigger.

One step closer and she'd fire.

"Mama!"

Test's breath left her in a heaving rush, as if she'd been struck by a wrecking ball. She collapsed to her knees, staggered with relief and by the horror at what she'd almost done. "Oh God," she said, fingers limp around her handgun as Elizabeth crashed into her. "Oh God."

George smashed into the both of them, knocking Test onto her back on the wet gravel, grinding her cheek against it. She slipped her weapon's safety on and tossed the sidearm under the Bronco II.

"Mama!" her kids wailed as they mobbed her and pinned her to the ground with smooches. Her heart seemed about to burst as their father materialized from the snow.

"Let your poor mom up," Claude said.

"They're all right," Test said and wrapped her arms around her kids and pulled them to her, pressing her face into them so they could not hear her sobs. "They're all right."

After the kids quieted and eased up, she rose.

"What are you doing out here?" Claude said. She tried to gauge his tone, but her mind was free-falling.

"Where were *you*?" she said, trying to mask her shame, an irrational anger smoldering in her.

"Behind the barn."

Her anger flared, tamped down quickly by confusion. "*Why?*"

"The kids wanted to visit Charlie. Put some pictures they drew for him on his resting place."

If she'd thought she could not feel more sorry or pathetic, she'd been mistaken.

"Why didn't you wait for me?" she said.

Claude slung his arm around her shoulders as the kids ran ahead of them into the house. "You were late, so we figured you'd be a while, picking up pizza and fending off the snow."

"When did you get home?"

"A half hour ago."

"The poor kids," she said. "I'm—" He must have sensed her anguish, because he took her face in her hands and kissed her. She felt repulsive. She did not deserve forgiveness.

"The kids were fine," he said.

Fine, how could they have been fine left in the dark and snow alone?

"George got the key just like you told him and they went inside and vegged in front of the tube," Claude said. "He even brought it back out to its hiding spot. Our son is nothing if not diligent."

She swallowed a sob, but felt the tears welling at the rims of her eyes.

"I'll be right in," Test said, slipping from under her husband's arm. "I'll get the barn door."

He stared at her.

"Go on. Get the pizza warmed up for the kids."

Claude shrugged and walked toward the house.

Test shut off the barn light and closed the door.

She went to Claude's Bronco, reached her hand underneath it and dragged her weapon to her. She double-checked the safety, then holstered the gun. She'd almost pulled the trigger. On her own child.

She sagged against the Bronco and let the tears come.

After a spell, soaked by the snow, she managed a deep breath and strode toward the house.

The floodlights had blinked off to leave the yard in full dark.

Chapter 52

VICTOR LAY ON his couch in the dark living room. Last he knew it had been 1:00 A.M. An hour ago. Or maybe two. Or three. Who knew? His mind was rubble; confusing thoughts crashed in his skull after having run into Jon Merryfield. Twice.

He sat up and turned on the end-table lamp, picked up the previous day's newspaper from the table and read the story about Brad, again. He'd read it dozens of times.

But Brad's was not the story that opened old doors in his mind.

It was the photo at the bottom of the front page. The photo of Jon Merryfield.

Mr. Attorney.

Mr. Successful.

Mr. Look at Me.

Mr. Champion of the Weak.

Hard as Victor tried to quell his envy, Merryfield's success made him sick.

Victor stared at the photo of Jon.

The bird's shadow fluttered across his mind now, as it had earlier.

It battered around, flapping its wings, trapped in Victor's brain.

And Victor caught it.

Finally. He snatched it.

He stared at the photo.

Coach. How are you?

Of all the times Jon had passed Victor in town, Jon had never said a word to Victor. Never so much as given any indication that Victor was alive.

Until now.

Coach. How are you?

Why?

To taunt.

But it was more than taunting.

An old icy fear started to crawl around inside Victor again, after all these years.

Chapter 53

PUBLIC DEFENDER ALLARD had demanded Victor and Fran act and say as Allard advised.

But Victor would not do that.

Could not.

He stared at the ceiling. If Fran was still awake upstairs, she made no sound to betray it.

Outside, down the street, a dog barked.

What was Victor to do?

Fifty-fifty odds. What was wrong with the world that his innocent son was being charged, let alone facing even odds at being convicted? A father had to do something. A father had to sacrifice for his family.

But am I prepared to do this? Victor thought.

He was a weak man, he knew. Weak and pathetic.

He made his way sleepily up the stairs and slipped into bed beside his wife, with his clothes still on, too tired to take them off.

Outside, the dog barked again.

Fran shifted. "That dog," she mumbled.

"I wake you?" Victor looked at the clock: 2:47 A.M.

"I was awake. I feel so sick."

Victor said nothing.

"My heart hurts so much," his wife said. "It feels like it will cave in."

She rolled over to face him. She had not lain like this in years. Eye to eye with him. It startled Victor. Early on in their marriage they had faced each other each night before falling asleep. The other's face was the last thing each saw before the light was turned out, as if each were afraid the other might not be there upon waking. And perhaps they had been afraid. Victor had been. He still was. Afraid of what she might learn. If she ever learned the truth, would she leave him?

Victor shifted and lay on his back, stared at the ceiling. He could see his wife's face from the corner of his eye. She pressed her hands together as if about to pray, then tucked them between her cheek and her pillow. "I don't know what I'll do."

"He'll be all right."

"I don't know."

"He will. You have to have faith."

"You sound so certain."

"He didn't do it."

"I don't know if it matters."

"Of course it matters," Victor said, though he was not sure he believed it.

"Where's my faith gone?" she said.

"It's still within you."

"It just looks so bad."

"Looks can be deceiving."

"I don't know what I'll do if he goes away." Her voice splintered.

"He won't. I promise. Not while I'm alive. Would you forgive me anything?"

She sighed. "You frighten me when you fall into your dark mood. I want Brad freed. Don't make it worse."

"Answer me."

She squeezed his hand. "Yes," she said. "I'd forgive you anything." She let go of his hand. "But I don't know if I could stay with you."

Victor made to touch her cheek. She shrank away, as if he might strike her. Then relaxed. He was her husband, after all. He put his arms around her and pulled her to him. Her body felt foreign. The last time he'd felt her against him, she'd probably weighed twenty pounds less.

"Okay," he whispered and cupped her cheeks in his hands.

"You can't blame this on things you did or didn't do right as a father," she said. "You had it hard. With your own father."

Victor felt ill at the mention of his father. *Father*: Other than the biological term, the word was too good for that man. That creature.

"I'm going to get Brad out of there," he said. "I'm going to see Detective North. Tell him some things." *Whatever the sacrifice*, he thought.

She kissed his forehead. "This has changed Brad. Even if he's freed. He's lost something."

"His youth," Victor said. "It only takes a moment, a single act."

He knew then his instincts about what was happening were right.

"What are you going to tell the detective?" Fran asked.

"The truth."

She untucked a hand from under the pillow and placed it on his chest beside where she now rested her head. "You're a good man," she said.

"No," he said. "I'm not."

Chapter 54

TEST WAS SITTING on the living-room floor with Elizabeth and George, unpacking the Lite-Brite from its musty, mildewed box. She divided the Lite-Brite pegs between the kids. Immediately, fastidious George began sorting pegs, one by one, by color, into Dixie cups he'd gotten from the kitchen for just this task.

Elizabeth, red bangs curling in front of her eyes, hurriedly heaped her pegs in one pile, her legs bent backward under her in a way that hurt Test's knees and hips just to look at.

The Lite-Brite was Test's, from her childhood. Many pegs had been lost along the way, sucked up by a vacuum, chewed by dogs, wedged under cushions. Most of the black construction paper patterns had been used up moons ago.

Still addled after what had happened the night before, Test wanted nothing more than to spend the morning with her children. Be Mom. She was pulled in so many directions—mom, cop, wife, runner, but mostly cop. With Claude off to get extra house keys made before he headed to St. J to finish setting up his exhibit, Test luxuriated in the calmness of this morning as Mom. Feeling so tranquil, she hardly had to work at all to quell her thoughts of the case simmering on the back burner of her mind.

"I wanna make a clown," Elizabeth said.

George pushed the construction paper pattern for a clown at her face.

"I wanna make a clown by my own self," Elizabeth stressed.

"You need the pattern," George said and dropped a purple peg into a Dixie cup.

By the time he gets his pegs all sorted it will be noon, Test thought and smiled.

As Elizabeth worked on her freestyle clown, Test wondered idly if Lite-Brite was made anymore. She did not recall seeing it in stores. She thought she recalled some fiasco of Lite-Brite causing house fires and getting banned. Maybe she was thinking of the Easy-Bake oven.

She put a hand on Elizabeth's head, stroked her daughter's hair, pleased to have her thoughts occupied with nothing more than the nostalgia of old toys.

She'd hauled the Lite-Brite down from the attic, where she stored a cache of toys from her childhood. Spirograph and paper dolls. Shrinky Dinks kits. Operation. All of the games and toys were tactile, required fine motor skills and imagination. Whenever she took a toy down from the attic, the kids glommed onto it, their emotions foamed over into a near hysteria, ecstatic to see a toy none of their friends had, as if the toy were from some alternate universe instead of the seventies and eighties. They'd fall into the silent attentive worship of the toy, and forget all about streaming videos and iPads. For an hour, anyway. Soon enough—too soon—their interest would slacken and they'd tease for a keypad and a screen. As much as Test and Claude had done to raise their children in a rural area and get them outside for hikes and explorations, mushroom foraging, sledding in the winter and swimming in the river in the summer, the kids still pleaded for their screen time. What was it that created such a lunatic addiction to *watching*? What primal need did voyeurism feed?

Test could not claim immunity. Nor could Claude. In bed at night, after they spoke about the day, made love, or fiddled with remnants of work, they flipped on the flat screen affixed to the wall opposite their bed and stared at it for a couple hours. Often they dialed for dollars. Most of what Test watched she could not remember two days later. She wondered what people had done with their evening time before all this technology. She could not remember herself. Read, she supposed. Yes. She had read a lot more books before streaming video and their 42-inch HD flat screen had come along. Made love more too, perhaps.

She and Claude had made a "date" for later, after the kids were in bed. Claude would be back from St. J. in time for the four of them to make ice-cream sundaes and watch *Ratatouille*. Then, it was adult date time. Test and Claude wanted three children. An only child had seemed a lonely existence to Claude and Test. Two children felt like a census bureau statistic. Three seemed just right: The Goldilocks trifecta.

"Can you help me sort, Mama?" George asked, looking up at her with her husband's deep brown eyes.

"Of course," Test said and readjusted how she was sitting to rid her hip of a dull pain.

She helped George sort the pegs as Elizabeth, tongue sticking out for utmost concentration, continued crafting with purple and white pegs an image that looked more like a balloon than a clown.

Test's cell phone rang on the arm of the couch near her head.

"Daddy said ignore it," Elizabeth said and twirled her hair in her fingers. She still pronounced her S sounds with a *shh*, from giving up her binky late.

"It might be your daddy," Test said. Claude had told her if she was taking the morning off, to take it off. For real. But she couldn't just ignore her phone if it was about the case, even if she were not expected or required by North or anyone else to participate in it.

"No," George said and picked a purple peg from a Dixie cup and dropped it into another cup. Apparently there were two shades of purple. "Daddy's ringtone is 'Back in Black.' "

Smart kids. Too smart. Test disliked Claude's ringtone. She was perplexed how her artistic, romantic husband liked AC/DC, Guns N' Roses, and System of a Down. Pearl Jam, she understood. While Eddie's lyrics were nearly as inscrutable as R.E.M.'s, Test adored his voice, and his looks, even if his hair was thinning and his face's once refined structure had grown puffy. Test was at least in good company in being unable to escape time's wrath.

She glimpsed her cell phone as it rang. UNKNOWN CALLER. A telemarketer. How did they get cell-phone numbers?

"Lizzy, it's my turn!" George shouted.

Test's phone stopped ringing.

"I don't wanna wreck mine!" Elizabeth shouted.

Test put a consoling hand on Elizabeth's arm. "Let's select a new pattern for your next turn," she said as Georgie plucked pegs from the Lite-Brite.

"No!" Elizabeth wailed and slapped at George.

"Here," Test said, and got to her feet with a groan, her hip making a popping sound. She took her phone from the couch. "We'll take a picture. How'd that be?"

Elizabeth pondered.

"When your brother makes his design, you can destroy it before your next one," Test said.

Elizabeth smiled.

Test's cell phone rang in her hand.

"Don't answer," George said.

UNKNOWN CALLER. Test was tempted. Bur resisted.

She took a photo of the Lite-Brite clown and sat again, placing the iPhone in her lap.

"After, can we watch a video?" George said.

"Not today," Test said.

"Why?"

"Because I said so."

"Why?" Elizabeth said, joining in, keyed on the idea instantly.

"Because," Test said. The image of her drawing her 9mm and pointing it at her own child invaded her mind, made her shudder. "I want us to spend time together."

"We can spend time together watching videos," George protested.

"That's not the same thing." Test smoothed her hand over the rug beside her tucked legs. It was polluted with dog hair. Test couldn't bring herself to vacuum it up. Once it was gone, it was gone.

Her thoughts returned to the eddying backwaters of her mind, mulling Jed King's role in all this.

Her cell phone rang.

Three calls in ten minutes.

UNKNOWN CALLER.

Elizabeth's eyes were on her. So were George's. Test grabbed the phone and started to push herself up off the floor.

"*Mom*," Elizabeth pleaded.

"I need to see who's calling," Test said. Her left foot was asleep and she had to shake the life back into it as she limped onto the couch.

"I'm gonna watch a video then," George snipped.

"No," Test put a finger up in the air. "Give Mom one minute."

Whoever had been calling didn't wish to leave a message.

"You said you wanted to spend time together," Elizabeth protested.

Test's phone stopped ringing. Damn it. She sat there, thinking.

"*Play*," Elizabeth whined.

"I am," Test insisted, though her attention was drifting from her kids, as much as she wished it wasn't. The case was like being swept into a strong river. The only way to avoid being taken away by it was to stand far from its banks. She could have turned her phone off earlier. But she hadn't. She'd stood beside the riverbank. Now, holding the phone in her hand awaiting the next call, she'd slipped into the current and could not get out of it.

PART IV

Chapter 55

Victor awoke later than he had in decades. The clock on the night stand showed 10:30.

Fran lay asleep on her back, mouth agape. Asleep, Victor knew, she felt no pain.

All these years, she'd been asleep to Victor, too.

By evening, she would be awake to it. It would shatter her, but her son, their son, would be free. *It's going to be all right*, he thought. *My boy is going to be all right.*

He would reveal all, even if it meant losing Fran to free their son.

Victor would be free too. He'd found a way to confess his sins and to be free of them. Finally. God, through this trial, had shown Victor the way to relieve his burden and return to the light of the truth.

His chest felt lighter than anytime since his days on the football field. It was as though his heart had been encrusted in a black shell. And last night, when he'd made his decision, whatever repercussions it might lead to, he felt that shell crack. Pieces fell away, as if another man lived inside him, a better, more Godly man, ready to be born.

"Yes," he would say. *Yes,* he would *shout.* "I did it. A sinful act. Do what you will to me. Call me what you will. Judge me as you will. Only one can truly judge me and He is not you. Just let my son go. Release him."

Victor rose from bed and stretched, ambled to the bathroom.

The window Brad had smashed in his attempt to flee was boarded over, but the cold air found its way in enough so Victor could see his breath. Everything he touched was cold. The light switch. The counter. The faucet handles. The linoleum floor was icy on his bare feet. He stood before the medicine-cabinet mirror. He was surprised to see his face bearded.

Despite the beard his face appeared skeletal, his cheekbones pronounced. His eyes looked feral. He looked like one of the hikers on the news who'd lost his way in a vast wilderness he'd thought he could handle, but couldn't; and though he'd found his way out, he looked ravaged, as if he'd gone without nourishment of body or soul for years.

He cranked the faucet and filled his cupped palms with cold water, pressed his face into them. Then he lathered his stubble with shaving cream and heated a razor beneath scalding water, swiped a circle in the fogged mirror and shaved.

He was struck by the face gazing back. He looked almost boyish.

Almost innocent.

He took a hot shower. The heat revived. Melted away at the casing he had lived in for so many years. It was nearly too hot to bear. He put his face to the water and let it pound him. His back was still sore where King had pounded on it.

Showered, he stepped out, braced himself against the cold of the room. Steam eddied. He felt as though he were moving through clouds.

In the bedroom, he selected his best corduroys, the ones whose fraying at the cuffs was least unnoticeable. He put on the whitest of his T-shirts and a flannel check shirt. The shirt was missing its lowest button on the front, but when he tucked it in you could barely notice. He pulled on the new boots he'd bought, wishing now he had not scuffed them in a pathetic attempt to appear more salt-of-the-earth. He was done pretending. He put on his windbreaker then left the house with his wife sleeping, safe from the wakened world.

THIS WAS IT. He would tell Merryfield what he knew first; tell him he was going to the cops and Merryfield's world was about to unravel. It did not matter that Victor's world would unravel too. His boy would go free with what Victor revealed.

He strode down the sidewalk, hurrying toward Merryfield's office building on Main Street when his cell phone rang and he was told the news that stopped him.

He turned and ran back for home.

Confronting Merryfield would have to wait.

Chapter 56

Test flinched when her cell phone buzzed in her hand.

Whoever had last called had just left a voice mail.

She accessed her voice mail and stepped away from her kids.

"You stink, Mom," George said and huffed over to the coffee table where Test's iPad sat.

"Watch your mouth." Test snapped her fingers at her son. "And don't touch that," she said as she listened to an old woman's voice saying, "I thought of something you said and it just doesn't make any sense. I wanted to get hold a you before my son picked me up for the day. It was bothering me. I think you may want to know."

Test dialed the number back.

The phone on the other end rang.

George gave Test a sidelong glance, testing her, and picked up the iPad.

"I'm warning you," Test said to him.

"Mom," Elizabeth said, tugging at Test's sleeve as Test drifted toward the kitchen.

"One *second*," Test said more harshly than intended. Tears welled in Elizabeth's eyes.

"Hello," the old woman said.

"This is Detective Test."

There was a moment of silence.

"Oh, yes. Of course," the old woman said.

"What was your call about?" Test said.

George tried to covertly swipe his finger across the iPad screen. Test snapped her fingers.

"Well," the woman said, "it occurred to me you asked if I made calls to a certain number and I said I made a lot of calls, being a volunteer for that sort of thing."

"And?" *Get to the point*, Test thought.

Elizabeth was tugging at Test's sleeve, trying to crawl up her leg. How come her kids never wanted to crawl on her except when she was on the phone? As soon as she got on the phone, they were all over her—Elizabeth anyway.

"Well. I don't make calls," the old woman said.

"I don't understand." The old woman was a crackpot.

"Plural," the woman said. "I make a lot of calls but I never call a house twice if they don't answer. I just mark the box that reads Contact Did Not Answer."

"Could you have called the same number on behalf of different organizations?"

"No. Besides I checked my phone bill. I usually don't check it, because it's just me and I don't call long distance except for my volunteer work and I just give the organizations a copy to get reimbursed. But. I see a number in Canaan was called a bunch of times."

Test's pulse quickened. "You said you live alone."

"I do."

"Then how could—"

George sat with the iPad in his lap. Face wild as he blatantly played a game, to control his urges, glancing at Test with a challenging look on his face.

Elizabeth was now weeping disingenuously in the corner.

"I have a volunteer who comes several days a week," the woman said. "He does odd chores for me. Laundry and dishes. Runs to the store."

Test knew it. Knew something in the LUD would link back. But how? As North said: so what if there were other threatening calls, Brad was the doer. "You think this person called?"

"I know he did. The times on the billing," the woman said. "They are all times when he's here. And he's the only person ever in my home. Except for my son and his family. They all have cell phones. And use them to text anyway, hardly ever make calls."

"Could this volunteer make calls without you knowing?"

"I go into my room at the end of the hall when he gets to really cleaning. It's too much commotion for my nerves. If he made calls from my kitchen phone I'd never hear him."

Test walked into the kitchen. "What's his name?"

"Mom!" Elizabeth shouted.

Test wrote the name on a pad of paper, then asked the woman the volunteer's age. The old woman guessed mid-thirties. "But he's probably ten years older. Everyone looks like a child when you're my age."

Test asked what he looked like. Average. Medium height. Brown hair. What kind of car he drove. None that she'd seen. He took the bus, she had assumed. What volunteer agency he worked with. Helping Hands. Test thanked the woman and hung up, her heart pounding a staccato arrhythmic beat.

She looked at the name she'd written.

Randy Clark.

It meant absolutely nothing to her.

The old woman's description was of no use. But, with his and the agency's name, all of that information would be easy enough to discover.

Test dialed Officer Larkin and asked him to run a background.

"No problem. What's it about? If you don't mind my asking. Are you onto another case after what that kid did?"

"What kid?" Test asked, confused.

"Brad Jenkins."

Test said nothing.

There was an embarrassed pause. "He tried to kill himself this morning," Larkin said.

"What? How?" It was unbelievable. North had not looped her in on this development.

"He cut his wrists on the metal bedframe in his cell. He's in rough shape. Sorry, I thought you'd have been in the loop."

"I've been offline all morning," she said, "with my kids, not answering the phone. I'm sure I have messages." It was bull, but she'd rather not admit she hadn't made the grade. Yet Larkin *had* been privy. "Who told you?" Test asked.

"I heard it over the radio. Just now."

"Of course."

"So, what case is this background info about?" Larkin asked.

"Just," Test began. Nothing now, she thought. Suicide. Brad might as well have confessed. The woman's call, her information, it didn't amount to anything—just a threatening call with no tie to the murder. If the calls had even been threatening. Of which there was no proof. "Vandalism," Test said. "No hurry. When and if you get a chance. I don't want to waste resources."

Test hung up as Claude came into the kitchen, his hair still slightly damp and tousled from the shower he'd taken just before he'd left for the store. His plaid L.L. Bean shirt was tucked into his jeans, and he was sporting a belt. It was as professional a look as he'd ever muster, and Test loved him for it. But, just now, as he caught Test shutting down her phone, he gave her a put-upon look she did not love so much; even if she deserved it.

"What," she said.

Claude set the extra keys on the counter and glanced into the living room where George was absorbed in the iPad and Elizabeth sobbed in silence, giving her parents the pitiful woebegone look of a Dickens orphan.

"That didn't last long," Claude said.

"I had to make a call," she said, tightening at having to explain herself. Feeling the tug-of-war of guilt and resentfulness. She was dejected that her lead proved to be all smoke and no fire. No wonder North hadn't called her.

Claude worked a finger in his ear.

Test's phone rang.

She wanted to look at the screen, but refrained.

Claude stared at the phone, glanced at George toying with the iPad, Elizabeth simpering.

"Answer it," he said, shrugging.

Test glanced at the screen. UNKNOWN CALLER.

Perhaps the old woman had changed her mind and decided that she'd made the calls after all. Who knew? If so, Test would call Larkin and put the kibosh on the BG of Randy Clark.

"Hello?" Test said as she answered the call.

"I've been trying to call you," North said.

"I'm with my kids. Your calls came in as unknown."

"My home line's unlisted. I'd have left a message but wanted to get you in person to tell you—"

"Larkin told me." So, she was in the loop after all. "Is—"

"He's critical. He better pull through to face the music. The coward. I'm going to call to see when I can interview him. He may be in a mindset that prompts a confession, if he comes to enough. Or ever. If he doesn't, at least it will save the taxpayer."

It's over, Test thought.

She had a brief urge to ask North if he thought Brad had tried to kill himself because he was guilty or just scared. But it was her stubborn side that wanted to ask. The stubborn side that had embarrassed her enough already.

"Well," she said, "If he comes to—"

"I'll call. *And* leave a message."

Test got off the phone, Claude lifting an eyebrow at her.

"Our suspect tried to kill himself," she said.

"You sound disappointed."

She shrugged. She was. For many reasons. Her instincts, and her hard work at putting together pieces, phantom pieces, had proved fallible with this turn. But. At least now she could focus on whoever had poisoned Charlie. "I want the doer to pay for what he did," she said. "Not take the easy way out. I may get called in if Brad wakes. I'd need to get a sitter if that happens."

Claude nodded.

"If he does wake. And I go late. I'll make it up to George and Elizabeth," Test said. She could hear the disappointment in her voice, feel it harden like setting concrete in her gut. The harder she'd try to make up for it, the worse she'd feel, and the more pronounced her own failing as a mother would be to her. There was no making up for lost time. Lost time was just that: lost.

Claude grabbed an apple from the bowl on the counter. Stared at it, contemplating. He set it down and snatched a handful of mini Snickers from the bag left over from Halloween. "Do what you think is best," he said and gave her a kiss on her cheek, his hands slipping along her hip. "I look forward to our date later, if you're here," he said, a wildness in his eyes. This time he kissed her on the mouth.

He leaned into the living-room doorway and said, "See you kids later. Be good for your mama. And George, be fair to your sister."

George didn't glance from the iPad.

Claude headed out for St. Johnsbury.

George glanced at Test. "Go ahead and play on it for a while if you want," Test said and knelt beside Elizabeth, who had stopped her fake sobbing but was pouting. "Will you make Mama a real nice Lite-Brite picture? Then we can all do something special?" Test said.

"What can we do special?" Elizabeth said, a glint in her eye. Already she knew all too well when she held leverage.

"Give it some thought while you do the Lite-Brite. Make it something super duper," Test said.

"Will you stay here and play with us?" Elizabeth pleaded.

Test nodded. "Promise."

Chapter 57

THAT EVENING, TEST, who'd not been called away, enjoyed her family. The pizza she'd brought home the previous night had been left on the counter uneaten and gone bad. So they made custom, individual pizzas, George keeping his toppings simple and organized: three pieces of pepperoni on each slice. Elizabeth added the works: pepperoni, mushrooms, onions, sausage, and left-over mac and cheese. Test was in a mood to let things go, appreciate the chaos, pile the dishes in the sink and leave them for morning. A morning during which she intended to wake up late, make covert love to Claude, and lounge around in her bathrobe.

She skipped the kids' baths and she and Claude helped make a pillow fort on the bed for the kids before they all snuggled in to watch *Ratatouille.*

Elizabeth complained her tummy ached from her pizza, and Test welcomed her snuggling right up to her, so toasty warm.

Test hadn't thought the kids would last for the entire movie, but they had. And it was after 10:00 when they finally shuffled off to bed.

With the kids down, Test rested her head on Claude's chest and ran her hand over his thigh.

The house was so quiet. Too quiet. For eleven years, Charlie had slept on the bed; first Test's bed in her studio apartment, and then her and Claude's bed, in their first shared apartment in Keene, before the kids, and then here. Charlie would moan and groan and nudge and crowd. Whine to go out to pee. After the kids, he had at times been a hassle, one more responsibility for which Test sometimes was just too fried to want to deal with, especially at night. Now, tonight, she missed all of it.

And she wondered: Even if Brad died, even if he'd committed suicide because he was guilty, whoever had killed Charlie was out there still.

Claude played with her hair, rested his chin on the top of her head.

"Want to try?" he said and lifted her chin in his fingers to look at her.

"More than ever."

Chapter 58

At 10:00 A.M. sharp, Detective North visited Brad Jenkins. Or, to be more precise, North stood beside Brad Jenkins's bed and asked questions that went unanswered. Not because Brad was resistant, but because he seemed quite unable to process what North was saying. He'd stare at North with clear eyes that seemed focused and alert. He'd nod as North spoke. But when North finished, he'd squint and tilt his head to the side and not say anything. He did not answer when North asked if he'd like to make a confession, nor when North asked if he'd done what he'd done out of guilt or fear. He simply stared, tilted his head. Like a dumb bird.

Or a smart fox.

The doctor had told North he'd give him fifteen minutes, and if any episode arose, for North to immediately notify a nurse by pressing the red button above the bed. North had expected there to be a network of tubes and monitors and machines hooked up to Brad, but there was no such circus of contraptions, other than an IV to keep Brad hydrated and his vitals monitored.

The sun coming through the south-facing window above

Brad's bed washed out the colors of the room and made it pulse with a heat that made North sweat.

Afterward, North asked if Brad could be faking. The doctor seemed offended.

"Faking what?"

"His lack of processing my questions."

"He's lucky he's alive, let alone conscious. You're lucky I gave you fifteen minutes."

As North was leaving, he encountered Victor Jenkins surging down the hall at him.

By the earnest body language and facial expression on Jenkins, North expected to be accosted by the man, and prepared to rebuff him. Instead, Jenkins smiled. It was a smile with more than a touch of the wearied lunatic in it, but it was a smile nonetheless.

"You see," Jenkins said, his eyes bright with the mania of the sleepless. "You see now he's innocent. He'd never do this if he wasn't so scared," Jenkins said, grabbing North's arm.

North took his arm from the man's grasp and walked away.

"I've got something to share that will prove my boy did not do this!" Jenkins shouted.

The doctor came over and said, "Sir. I understand you're upset, but we can't have you shouting."

"I have proof!" Jenkins shouted at North's back. "Someone else did this. I know the motive! Get ready to release my boy!"

NORTH DEPARTED THE hospital thinking about what the doctor had said. Brad was lucky to be alive. Lucky to be in such good shape, considering. North wondered why a soul like Brad Jenkins should benefit from even a morsel of luck. And, despite the doctor's adamancy, North could not help but feel Brad was playing

North, and the doctor was being duped. Was Brad smart enough to know that if he were mentally incapacitated he'd not stand trial, and would be relegated to a relatively cushy environment compared to that of a maximum-security prison? Could Brad put up such a ruse? Could he fake mental illness so convincingly, even if it meant escape from such an existence? And for how long could he fake it, if he was faking it?

IN TWO DAYS North got his answers, when he was alerted by the doctor, with a certain satisfaction in the doctor's voice, that Brad was "quite lucid now" and could "invite questions and answer them. Provided you go easy."

In that next interview, Brad proved his old self, claiming innocence, insisting his lawyer be present, demanding bail.

When North asked why he'd tried to kill himself if he was innocent, Brad had spat in North's face and said: "Fuck you."

North could not have been more pleased.

Chapter 59

SNOW HAD FALLEN overnight and blanketed the world anew in white, gracing the hills and fields around Test's home with a pastoral calm. The sun sparkled off the snow, dazzling and idyllic. The whole scene put Test and her family in a festive mood. This was the first real, deep fluffy snow, not the heavy wet sticky stuff that had fallen the other night.

Test, Claude, and the kids trudged through the snowy fields to get to the steepest hill on their five acres. It had become a tradition for the family to go sledding together after the first real snowfall.

This year, George was charged for the first time with dragging the toboggan, a beastly but beautiful sled of dark wood and red cushions. He worked arduously, panting, but refused all help. He was especially proud of and enthused about this responsibility.

At the top of the hill, Test and her family stood for a moment and took in their surroundings. This was the life Test had imagined for herself and Claude when they'd bought the property. And here that life was now, being lived. Only a third child would make this moment more perfect. She'd know in a few days if their date night had taken. Making love with the intent to conceive was a different venture from making love on other occasions. It was more meaningful, urgent and intimate, even while it might feel perfunctory. *I'm peaking, let's go.* Whether either of them was in the right space, they dropped everything to capitalize on timing. Then came the period of days when the promise of whether or not "it took" hung over her.

"I'm riding in front!" George exclaimed as he readied the toboggan at the precipice of the steep hill.

"You sit between Mommy and Daddy," Test said to Elizabeth and straightened her daughter's hat to cover her ears. Elizabeth's cheeks were so pink, Test could not help but give them a pinch.

As Test and Claude were about to board the sled, Test's cell phone rang in her pocket. Each member of her family turned to her.

While Test and Claude brought their phones to take pics and videos, ringers were to be kept off during such family excursions. "Sorry," Test said. "Didn't know I had it on." It was the truth, even though is sounded like a lie.

Claude knew she'd been awaiting word of Brad. He was presumably being transported back to prison today, and North believed he had him on the edge of confession.

Test's phone ID showed it was Larkin.

"Let's go!" George said, pushing the palm of his mitten against his runny nose.

"I'll just be a second." Test answered the phone.

"I got the background you wanted," Larkin said.

"Background?" Test said. She had no idea what he was talking about.

"You said it was no rush? The BG on the vandalism," Larkin clarified.

"Right," Test said, "right." The information on Randy Clark, who'd called the Merryfields from the old lady's place.

"Do you still need the information?" Larkin said.

"Go ahead," Test said. She didn't need it, but Larkin had done the work and she did not want him to feel it had been done for nothing. She knew how that felt.

"He lived in Haverhill, New Hampshire. A rental property. Clean record. Single. Never married. No kids. Worked for Help Hand part-time."

"Any other jobs?"

Test's family had boarded the toboggan and were eyeing her expectantly.

"Not that I've come up with," Larkin said.

"He *lived* there? Not anymore?" Test said.

"Till about three months ago. No new address since, that I could find. Doesn't mean much. He could be paying cash to stay somewhere. Or living in a motel. Crashing at a friend's place. Who knows? If you don't own a home, it's harder to track residence. He doesn't work for Helping Hand anymore though."

"Was he fired?" Test asked.

George was starting to shimmy at the front of the toboggan, the curled nose of the giant sled beginning to edge over the lip of the hill.

"He quit," Larkin said. "I spoke to his supervisor. She said he was diligent and caring, punctual and trustworthy."

There was a pause and Test was eager to get to her family, so took advantage of the break. "Well, great, thanks. I appreciate it, I—"

"There is one kicker," Larkin said.

George was now pushing the sled forward with his mittened hands.

The toboggan rocked on the edge of the hill.

"Come on, Mom!" Elizabeth shouted.

Claude widened his eyes: *Hang up.*

"Tell me," Test said, a warmth rising in her chest.

"His hometown is here. Canaan. His family moved away in nineteen eighty-five, when he was eight."

Test felt as if she had the wind knocked out of her. The toboggan rocked at its tipping point.

"Hold up!" Test implored her family, "Wait for me!"

Randy Clark had lived in Canaan? This had to mean something. It had to. But what? Her mind was working now, backfilling all she knew.

"Why did they move?" she said.

"Hurry!" Claude shouted.

"I haven't got that far," Larkin said. "His old man was a professor of some sort. They may have moved for a job. Not certain yet."

"Keep on it."

"I will, Detective. What's this really about anyway?"

Test didn't answer. She got off the phone, mystified. What did this mean? She did not believe in coincidences of this magnitude. Whatever the connection, she felt invigorated; but apprehensive, too. This might open the case in unknown directions, although it was as yet difficult to envision how, let alone understand. She knew one thing: North would never entertain it. She was on her own. If she pursued this and was wrong, her career was over.

The sled was starting to go.

"Wait!" she shouted, "Wait!"

She ran after the sled to try to hop on it.

But she missed it, and her family was carried screaming down the hill away from her.

Chapter 60

At home, while the kids and Claude drank hot chocolate, Test sat at the kitchen table and browsed her notes from the night of the murder to see if anything regarding Haverhill, New Hampshire, or a Randy Clark meant anything.

She found nothing. But the quote from Bethany Merryfield that had given Test pause before she'd learned of Brad's suicide attempt gave Test pause again. Jon had been in the restroom for quite a few minutes. Maybe close to twenty. But there'd been no need to look into it.

On her laptop, Test brought up a Google Earth map of Canaan. Zoomed in. The detail of the satellite images never ceased to astound and disturb her.

She zoomed in closer, looked again at the quote she'd written from Bethany Merryfield.

Looked at the Google Earth map.

"There may be a need now," she said. Even if to eliminate him. Merryfield, technically not having an alibi for an undetermined period of time, had not been officially eliminated. But how did it all fit? Who was this man in Haverhill, New Hampshire, who'd lived in Canaan as a boy? How was he linked? *Was* he linked?

"What'd you say, Mommy?" Elizabeth said as she sat beside Test at the table slurping at her hot chocolate and scooping out mini marshmallows from her mug with her fingers.

"She's talking to herself again," George said.

"How would you guys like a super duper surprise for tonight?" Test said.

Claude eyed her suspiciously.

"What if we went to the real movies at the Village Picture Show, to see *Tangled*?"

Elizabeth beamed, but George scowled. "Where are you going?" he said.

"It won't be for long," Test said, gathering up her notebook and pen.

"Whatever," George said.

"You can't leave," Elizabeth moaned.

"When I get back, we'll go. And, maybe, tomorrow," Test said, feeling manipulative and petty, "we can see about a puppy."

Claude gave her a damning look.

"I don't want a puppy!" Elizabeth said.

Test cringed.

"I'd like a puppy," George said. "I think Charlie would want us to have one."

"I'm sorry," Test said to Claude as she rose. "There's a break in the case."

"What case?" Claude said.

"Jessica Cumber's murder."

"He finally confessed?"

"Not quite." Before Claude could press her, she was out the door.

Chapter 61

VICTOR HAD THOUGHT his son's attempt on his life would make it clear that Brad was innocent; a desperate act of a boy scared he'd be railroaded into serving a sentence among truly violent criminals, subjected to heinous acts Victor dared not entertain. That was why Brad had done what he'd done. But the cops had twisted it to use it against Brad, trying to say that Brad knew he was guilty and had no way out, that's why he tried to kill himself.

Now, Victor feared, the state police detective was going to coerce Brad into a confession. All hope for bail was lost, as Brad was being held under strict suicide watch. Brad's lawyer had begun to hint that Brad consider a plea bargain. Impossible. Yet, despite Victor and Fran's prayers, the noose seemed to be tightening rather than loosening around his son's neck.

Victor had to sacrifice himself to save his son. He thought all this as he set out of his house to walk into town to Merryfield's office; where he'd tell Jon that he knew Jon had killed Jessica and why, and to tell him he'd never get away with it.

It was early morning, too early for Merryfield to be at his office yet. But Victor decided he needed time to think of every angle and to write down notes of what he would, and wouldn't, tell the police.

The streets were damp and desolate in the early-morning gloom. The snow had already begun to melt here in town.

Victor stood across from the Beehive Diner now. From the alcove entrance of the library, his jacket collar pulled up against his face, he watched the usual suspects go in and out of the diner. He could see Larry Branch speaking to Gwynne. She laughed as Larry slid his coffee cup toward her to freshen. The seat beside Larry was empty.

Victor pushed onward and walked around the corner. As he crossed through the back part of the parking lot behind the Lamoille Bank, he saw a pickup truck idling. A plume of exhaust hung in the air around its back bumper, its odor noxious. The side and back windows of the truck were fogged but Victor knew who was inside. The license plate read IMKING.

What was King doing there?

The truck faced toward the home of Merryfield's homosexual clients.

A couple days ago, Victor would have jogged over to see King, nearly desperate to be part of whatever it was King was up to, without a thought. Not today. For the first time it seemed in his adult life, he was thinking straight. He was seeing the world clearly.

He had no urge to speak to, or even look at, King. His back still ached where it had been punched by King. His stomach turned at the thought of what the man might be doing so early in the morning across from the gay couple's house. Whatever he was planning would come back to him in ways he could not imagine. His schemes had left him twice divorced and alone, just as Fran had said. What Victor had seen as strength in King he saw now as arrogance and ignorance. And fear.

King was a frightened man. A frightening man. Who was King to judge others?

Who are you to cast stones, Victor Jenkins? Victor suddenly thought. *After what you did.*

Chapter 62

TEST PARKED HER Peugeot in front of what she thought of as Location A; the Village Fare restaurant. Puddles of slush sloshed beneath her boots on the sidewalk. She knocked on the building's front glass door. The place was closed, but the proprietor was expecting her.

The door opened and Test was greeted by a woman dressed in chef whites, flour dappling the very tip of her sharp, severe nose. Test recognized the woman's face from ads that ran in the local weekly. But the face was somehow off in real life. What, in the ad, seemed a classic face of elegant bone structure was, in reality, bony, with a chin that jutted just enough to be of proportion to the rest of the face, and one eye slightly smaller than the other. And this woman was pushing her mid-sixties. The photo in the ad must have been a good decade old.

"Please," the woman said, beckoning with long fingers graced with the same white powder as was her nose, "come in."

Test stepped inside, blinking back the darkness that temporarily blinded her after being outside. The woman locked the door behind them and walked to a table graced with a fine white linen tablecloth, again gesturing with wriggling fingers for Test to have a seat across from her. The place was impressive, refined. Too refined for Test's taste. Not that she would mind the food. She'd likely love it. Just not the prices or the atmosphere. She preferred a homey, family setting where duct tape served to repair a punctured booth cushion, and crayons and coloring books were brought out first thing, rather than a setting of white linens and candles afloat in scented water where the first thing ushered out to you was a choice between two ten-dollar bottles of sparkling or natural water.

She'd always favored casual restaurants; perhaps because her father had dragged her to Gene and Georgetti's steakhouse since she could walk. A place where she was told to sit up, sit straight, keep her napkin tucked, and forced to breathe cigar and cigarette smoke.

"Can I get you a bottled water? We have sparkling or natural," the woman asked as she picked at some invisible thread on the tablecloth.

"I'm fine," Test said, swallowing a laugh. "I have a few questions."

The woman smoothed her hand over a wrinkle in the white linen tablecloth. "I'll do my best to answer."

"They're easy. One. Are your bathrooms unisex?"

She seemed perplexed. "We have a gents' and a ladies'."

"Do they accommodate more than one person at a time?"

"No." The woman now seemed genuinely amused.

"The CCTV you have, does it cover the back of the restaurant, the hallway to the restrooms?"

"Some. Not much past the back door by the dish room."

The answers the owner gave both muddled and partly clarified the case for Test, as Test began to understand it in a new way. Her blood fizzed with the urgency of culminating facts; she felt like she was George, shimmying and pushing a sled to the edge of a hill. And once she got the momentum and gravity got hold of it, the case would accelerate rapidly, beyond her own ability to stop it, even if she wanted to.

"May I see what we spoke of on the phone?" Test asked.

The woman handed Test a DVD of the CCTV footage taken the night of the murder.

"It's all there, the time span you asked for."

"And the restrooms, in an establishment like this, they must be seen to regularly."

"Oh yes, hourly."

"On the hour?"

"Not quite."

"May I speak to the person who cleans them?"

"Drew. He's not in yet. Give it a half hour."

"May I take a look at the restrooms?" Test asked.

The woman smiled. "Be my guest."

TEST WALKED DOWN the hallway that ran from the bar at the rear right side of the restaurant. She eyed the CCTV camera in one corner of the hallway ceiling as she walked to the men's restroom.

The restroom told her nothing. It was clean and appointed with high-end fixtures, a marble floor. Candles. But it was, after all, just a bathroom.

Standing outside the bathroom she saw the hall went past the dish room to a door that must have opened to the back. She did not know if the door was set to trigger the alarm system so went back out to the front door.

Outside, Test walked around to the back of the place, startled by a crow that burst into flight from the Dumpster.

She stared at the back of the building. It was plain enough. Brick with one door that led to the Dumpster, and a single window farther down.

She looked into the woods behind the place. From the Google Earth imagery she'd studied earlier, it had appeared that if she cut through the woods to the other side, and skirted along the edge of the school park and ball fields, she'd end up on Lincoln Street in minutes.

There was only one way to find out.

THE WOODS WERE not vast by any means, but they were thick with understory and gnarled masses of blowdowns and vines that slowed her progress significantly. One aspect Google Earth did not show well on such a small scale was the few deep and soggy gullies to navigate.

After bushwhacking for several minutes, Test came out at the edge of the school fields and looked at her watch. Five minutes. OK. She edged along the ball fields and the playground and came out toward the end of Lincoln Street. From there, if she were to walk between two houses and cross the street, she'd be at Location B; the Merryfields' house.

Another two minutes. Tops.

It was possible.

Physically.

In the daylight.

But in the dark?

A flashlight would have been risky, and a light in such a dark place did not help you find your way, it only lit up the confusion of branches right in front of you. But without any light, the trek would be impossible in the time span needed.

Perhaps there was a path she'd missed, one the local kids used as a shortcut.

No. On the way back she found no such path.

She'd have to come back in the dark, with a headlamp.

When she did, she would ask the staff a couple questions too.

Even with the lowered odds, her new premise pestered at her. There was something here. If the DVD revealed what she hoped, the rest might be moot.

The sun came out as she stepped from the woods to the back of the building. The crow took flight from the Dumpster, and Test caught a whiff of that sour cabbage-y odor Dumpsters gave off. It made her stomach roil.

She looked at the woods, her eyes scouring for the sign of the most scant trail. There was none.

As she turned to go, something caught her eye. Then it was gone. She stepped closer to the woods, but did not see it again. A glint. A tiny flash.

She walked back a few feet and looked. There it was again. Then gone.

But her eyes were locked on its location now.

She walked up to a tree at the edge. Looked back at the sun in the sky.

She searched the tree, an old cragged maple tree. She almost missed what she was looking for though she was nearly staring right at it from a few feet away. A thumbtack.

Except, she saw, not just a thumbtack. Its surface was coated with a sparkly dust. A reflector. It would be almost impossible to find more of them in the daytime. She decided she would return that night with a flashlight to see if there were more of them, strung together, to make a lighted path someone could see easily at night.

Had Jon Merryfield left out the back way when he'd said he'd been in the bathroom? Was it possible he had sneaked out and slipped through the woods to return to his own house and murder Jessica?

Yes, logistically, if there were reflectors to light the way, it might be possible.

But even if so, the question remained: Why?

Chapter 63

VICTOR WALKED DOWN the alley to come out on River Street. Merryfield's office would not open for a half hour, and Victor needed the coffee he'd normally put down at the Beehive. He stood outside the Brew Ha Ha, a new spot that prided itself on gourmet coffees, organic scones, and tofu omelets. He'd never been inside the place, but it was directly across the street from the building that housed Merryfield's office on its top floor. Beside the entrance, the wall was marked with a slash of red paint at eye level and the words, "Height of 1927 Flood."

Victor went into the Brew Ha Ha and ordered a cup of coffee. The girl behind the counter did not so much as glance his way and none of the few people in the place paid him any mind. This was a new crowd to him, a younger generation raised and schooled elsewhere. Kids who moved here from the likes of Brooklyn and Boston and Boulder. Girls with thick black eyeglasses and goateed boys with retro fedoras cocked precariously atop their heads.

Victor sat by the window where he could keep an eye on Merryfield's building and began to take notes in his pad for his meeting with the police later. He sipped at the black coffee. Sipped again. It was the house coffee. Something called Kenyan Dark. It was pretty good. Really good. He'd never tasted coffee like it.

As he settled in with a second cup, he watched for Merryfield. Where was he?

Daryn Banks ambled past the window and glanced inside the place. Spying Victor, he waved and smiled, entered the café. Victor did not want interruption. He needed to keep an eye out and be able to react as soon as he saw Merryfield.

But, if anyone was going to interrupt him, he supposed Daryn was the most welcome. He'd proved an ally when others had abandoned Victor and his family.

"Victor," Daryn said and eyed the seat opposite. "May I?"

Victor nodded, then eyed the door to Merryfield's office building across the street.

Daryn sat. "What brings you here? This isn't exactly your kind of place, I would gather. Nor mine." He laughed and glanced around, rolled his eyes.

Victor said nothing as he watched Merryfield's office building.

"I won't keep you, I just saw you and thought I'd come in to apologize," Daryn said.

"I don't understand," Victor said.

"I've not put together the prayer circle yet. And with what's happened with your son, I imagine it might have been of use. I *am* reaching out to people though. So, soon, I hope. I can't say how sorry I am for your suffering."

"I have new hope since this morning," Victor said.

"Well, good! It will make a fine starting point for the prayer circle."

Victor tapped his wedding ring on the edge of his mug. "I don't know. I don't know where I might be after today. So much has changed."

Daryn looked taken aback. "I hope in a good way," he said.

"For what's best," Victor said.

"Good. Good. Well. I'll leave you in peace. This place is too rich for my blood anyway," he said with a laugh.

"Sorry. I'm not much company."

"Understandable. I hope you and your family get all you deserve."

"Thank you," Victor said.

"My pleasure. God bless."

Chapter 64

WHEN TEST KNOCKED again on the front door of The Village Fare, a young man with black wavy hair and an olive complexion greeted her in a maître d's classic black suit. He offered a beatific smile and showed her in as if she were a celebrity guest, his hand at the small of her back in a way that managed somehow not to be offensive as he led her to the rear of the restaurant, where he greeted another young man of no more than eighteen in checked pants and a white smock. "Drew," the maître d' said to the boy, "I believe this woman wishes to have a word with you."

The maître d' faced Test and said, "May I get you a bottled water?"

"I'm fine, thank you," Test said.

"I'll leave you two then."

Test and Drew sat at the bar, Drew setting a glass of soda on a leather coaster before him. The soda was poured in a highball glass that looked like genuine crystal. The bar was solid cherry or mahogany or some dark, rich wood. Maybe teak. Claude would know. He'd covet it.

"I have a question for you," Test said. "The owner said you were working the night of the Jessica Cumber murder."

"This about that girl?"

Test nodded. "Were you working?"

Drew nervously sipped soda through a straw. "Yes. I was. I hope you don't thin—"

"I hope you might help. When I spoke to the owner on the phone before coming, she mentioned that something strange happened."

He squinted, sucking the last of the soda with a slurp. He wore an earring, a single stud in his left earlobe. The earlobe was red and irritated, if not infected. He pinched the lobe, gave it a tug. "Strange? No. Nothing strange."

"Did you not have something odd happen when you cleaned the restroom? A man who—"

"Oh. That. The owner had said to wait outside the gents' before I cleaned it, as a prominent patron had just gone back to make use of it. I waited what I thought was more than enough amount of time. Then knocked, afraid he might need help or something. No one answered. When I opened the door, no one was there, but—"

"Yes?"

"I cleaned it and left. Soon after I got out on the floor, I realized I'd left my comb on the sink, having used it. And there was a man heading down the hall at me as if from the gents'. Like he'd just appeared back there. It was strange, but you know, in the scheme of things, on the spectrum of strange, not so much. I figured I must have missed him going back there in the short time I was out on the floor." He shrugged.

"Right," Test said.

"I mean, there's strange and then there's *strange*."

"You remember what time it was?"

"I went back the first time at six forty-five. Waited maybe ten minutes before I knocked. The bathroom took five to clean. Then was on the floor a few more minutes."

"How do you know the time for certain?" Test asked.

"I do the same things at the same times every night. It's my job."

Test thanked him and left, confident that the DVD she held in her jacket pocket would confirm her theory as fact.

Chapter 65

VICTOR SAT ALL morning nursing several coffees until he could drink no more of it. He ordered several sticky buns and ate them slowly, then read through local real estate guides. It was far past lunchtime, when the employees started to give him odd looks.

He'd never laid eyes on Merryfield.

He needed to stretch and move, so left and went a few doors down and bought a *Sports Illustrated* and a *Patriots Weekly* at Whipple's Pharmacy. He sat on a bench outside and read the magazines as he watched for Merryfield. When he'd read the magazines front to back, he worked again on his notes. Laboring to get it just right.

He sat out there reading and growing agitated as the day grew long and Merryfield never showed. Victor knew Merryfield wasn't living at his home, but he had no idea where to find him other than his office.

Cold, he returned to Brew Ha Ha, where fortunately the staff had changed for the late afternoon.

He was on his fourth cup of Kenyan and third blueberry muffin, fingertips abuzz, when he looked up to see Merryfield duck into the office building kitty-corner to the Brew Ha Ha.

It was 4:42.

Victor stood. His legs tingled and he felt dizzy as he pushed past the people entering the shop and stepped out onto the street.

Outside, he leaned against the building, panic gripping him. He put his hands on his knees and tried to catch his breath. Then hurried across the street.

In front of the old building that housed Merryfield's office, he stared up and down the street, as if he were about to rob a bank and wanted to make certain of his escape route.

He went inside.

A duct in the entranceway's ceiling blasted dry hot air down on him, causing sweat to sprout at the back of his neck. He unzipped his coat.

A steep, narrow stairway smelling of the rubber mat beneath his boots rose in front of him. A chandelier, suspended from the ceiling at the top landing, cast a glow of splintered light along the mahogany stairs as Muzak floated down, the sounds of flute and strings.

Closing his eyes, Victor clutched the railing and waited for the dizziness to pass, then he all but vaulted up the stairs.

At the top, he stopped in front of a placard, read it, and turned left to a door marked "Law Office of Jonathon Merryfield, Esquire."

"Esquire," Victor mumbled. *The brat.*

He turned the porcelain doorknob and went inside.

He had expected to find Merryfield sitting behind a desk, alone. Instead he walked into a reception area the size of his home, the area decorated with leather wingback chairs, a coffee table of some dark exotic wood, an antique map of Vermont and sporting prints of waterfowl and fly fishermen on the walls. Behind the table was a marble fireplace, inside of which a fire crackled.

"Can I help you?"

Vic turned from the fire, blinking.

A woman sat behind a reception desk. She looked to be about forty, and wore her hair cropped tight. Like a lesbian.

"I'm here to see Jon," Victor said.

The woman picked up a pair of eyeglasses, put them on and studied Victor. "I don't have anyone penciled in for this morning, Mr.—?"

"Jenkins. Victor Jenkins."

"I see. Can I arrange an appointment for you?" she glanced at a leather-bound appointment book. "Say, Tuesday after next?"

"I'm here now. It won't take long."

"He's very busy. You understand."

"You tell him Victor—" he paused. "You tell him Coach is here to see him."

The woman's eyes roamed over him. "I'm afraid I can't. He's extremely taken with a case. He's taking no appointments at all this week."

"This isn't an appointment. You tell him I'm out here. He'll want to see me. He's been expecting me."

"I'm quite certain if he were expecting you he'd have informed me, sir."

"Not about this. And he may not have expected me this very morning. But he's expected me. And here I am. So you might as well tell him."

"Have a seat," the woman said and stood. "I'll check and see what he has to say."

She pointed at the wingback chairs.

Victor remained standing.

He was afraid if he sat, he might not have the strength to stand again.

The woman watched him as she made for Merryfield's office door and rapped on it.

Victor heard nothing from behind the door, but she opened it and went into the office and shut the door behind her.

At the fireplace, Victor hefted a fire poker from where it leaned against the hearth. He tapped the heavy point of it in his palm. He jabbed it into the burning logs. Sparks exploded up the chimney like a swarm of maddened bees. He jabbed the logs again.

The door opened behind him. He turned, poker in hand.

The woman stared at him, her hand on the doorknob behind her back.

"He says he couldn't possibly have any idea why you would think he wants to see you. I'm afraid you'll have to go."

"I'm afraid he's wrong. You tell him I know what he's done. I *know*. And I know *why*. He'd better talk to me or I'm going to the police. You hear me? You tell him I'm going but I wanted him to know first." His voice was rising, cracking like a piece of shattering ice that had become so cold it could no longer hold itself together.

"He's far too busy for whatever grievance you may have to—"

"This isn't a *fucking grievance*." Victor tapped the fire poker in his palm. It was hot from his jabbing it in the fiery logs.

The woman clutched the doorknob.

Victor stepped toward her. "You either get away from that door on your own power—" He tapped the poker in his hand. The heat of it seared in his palm. "Or I remove you."

The woman looked toward the door that led out to the stairway. The exit. Then looked at the poker in Victor's hand.

She turned the knob behind her and disappeared into Merryfield's office.

Vic came at her waving the poker and threw open the door.

Chapter 66

TEST STARED AT the video footage of the Village Fare restaurant hallway.

Now, here before Test, were the seventeen minutes she'd needed.

She watched it again and again, rewinding and fast-forwarding. Pausing. There. There it was. Again and again.

"The kids are waiting," Claude said behind Test, startling Test and setting her heart skidding. "We're going to be late if we don't leave in five minutes. Elizabeth's whining. She didn't go down for her nap."

"Her throat's dry," Test said absently as she clicked PLAY on the video again. Rewound it. "Did you pick up filters for her humidifier like you said you would?"

"I got busy. You could have done it, while you were out."

"I would have if I'd known you weren't going to, like we discussed."

"We didn't discuss it. You told me."

She bristled. Rarely, only when truly upset and in the right, did Claude wield the truth with such a barbed tongue.

Still, how hard was it to get to the store? Now Elizabeth would be up half the night.

"We'll grab them after the movie," Claude said.

"Good." Test sighed, glued to the CCTV footage.

"I'm dismissed then?" Claude said.

"Don't be dramatic." In her notebook, Test logged the time shown on the bottom right of the footage.

"We said we were going to salvage this evening after you got back."

She spun around to look at her husband. "Please don't make me feel worse."

Claude stared at her. Did he think she enjoyed this, over spending time with her family?

"Go to the movies," she said. "Enjoy the kids. At least one of us can. If I go I'll just be anxious and not present anyway. You know that. Go."

But he didn't go.

"This isn't even your case," he said. "It isn't even *a* case. The kid's all but confessed. There's heaps of evidence. I read the papers. You can put whatever it is aside for two hours."

She wasn't going to give in on guilt.

He saw that.

He turned and left, muttering: "Elizabeth didn't nap because her *dog* is dead and her mom is AWOL, not because her humidifier is off."

Test wanted to go after him, apologize, but what she saw on her screen kept her seated.

Chapter 67

THE SECRETARY COWERED beside the obnoxiously ornate executive's desk, behind which sat Jon Merryfield, his back to an arched leaden window whose panes were warped, so the view of the town green was slightly distorted.

The woman glanced at Merryfield.

"Take the morning off, Cheryl," Merryfield said.

"Do you want me to call anyone?" she said.

"It's fine."

"Are you sure?"

"We close in a half hour anyway. I'll be all right."

The woman nodded at Merryfield and slipped past Victor. At the door, she glanced back quickly, then shut the door, her footsteps hurrying away on the other side.

Victor stepped toward the desk. The scene of the town green behind Merryfield's expansive desk shifted through the vast window with each step. The sun was low, shadows deepening.

Before Victor was halfway across the room, Merryfield said, "Close enough."

Victor thought about going straight for him, but stopped himself. He needed to keep his composure. For Brad's sake.

Merryfield folded his hands behind his head and turned his chair side to side, the arrogant bastard. "Well?" he said. His voice flat. Dead.

"You know why I'm here."

"Do I?"

"I know you did it," Victor said.

"I *did it*? I think it was you who did it."

"I'm not talking about that."

"About what?"

"That."

"*That?*" Jon laughed a cold, heartless laugh.

"I know what you did," Victor said.

Jon spread his arms wide. "Oh, well, guilty then."

"I know."

"Aren't we the detective."

"You killed that girl."

Jon laughed again, dramatically, and shook his head. "Just for the entertainment of it: Why would I want to do that?"

"You know why."

"Refresh my memory."

"You goddamn well know."

"Careful. Taking the Lord's name in vain. I hear he takes issue with that. I think I ought to be told what my motive is, since I surely can't think of it myself."`

"You know."

"Can't say I do."

"For God's sake."

"God's got nothing to do with this. You're regressing, Coach. You sound like a crazy man. Clarify your point."

Coach. Being called *Coach* by *him* scalded Victor. "Goddamn you."

"No. Goddamn you."

"I'm sorry," Victor said.

"Yes. You are." Merryfield flicked his fingers at his tie, as if brushing away crumbs.

"My son doesn't deserve this," Victor said.

"Who of us deserves anything we get?"

"He's got his whole future ahead of him."

"Didn't we all."

"I said, I'm sorry, for what happened."

"It didn't *happen.* It was *done.* By you."

Victor felt the pleading in his voice and was sickened by it. He needed to stay strong. In control. "I think they'll convict Brad if he goes to trial."

"I know they will." Merryfield's eyes flashed with, what? Uncertainty? Fear? Some understanding? There was a change there for sure. Realization.

"I can't let that happen," Victor said. "I'm going to the police. I'm going to tell them your motive. I've learned a thing or two about the law."

"I'm sure they'll arrest me right away. Except, I was with my wife in a restaurant near capacity." He straightened his tie, but that look flashed again. Realization.

Merryfield leaned back in his chair and looked straight at Victor. He smiled. Smug and sinister. "They'll see you for what you are. A sad, sick, desperate father trying to keep his son out of prison by any means. A drowning man grasping for a life jacket that isn't there. Your son *is* going to prison." Jon locked his fingers together and pointed his index fingers at Victor as if the fingers were a pistol. "And *you* can't stop it. Not even your God. You know why? Brad killed that girl. And if he didn't, I know one thing for certain. I didn't kill her." He crossed his arms, a smile of supreme satisfaction oozing across his face. "It will sink in after a while. Just how powerless you are. And, you'll just have to live with it. Being powerless. Like we all do."

Victor stepped toward him; perhaps there was only one way after all to get to him.

"One more step," Merryfield said, "and I'll knock your teeth in and beat the living fuck out of you and throw you out the fucking window. I'll tell them you attacked me. Cheryl will attest to your crazed behavior."

Vic squeezed his hands into fists.

Merryfield stood. Victor was fit for his age. But Merryfield was the younger man by far. A fit, broad man. No boy.

Victor stepped back and opened the door. "We'll see," he said, and left.

FROM THE WINDOW, Jon watched as Victor stood under a street lamp and stared up toward the building. *Let him go to the police,* Jon thought. *Let him pour his guts out. It won't hurt me. He has no proof. I'll deny it. And they will never believe him.*

Victor looked up at the window now. Could he see Jon? Jon had no idea.

Victor had a hand at the inside of his thigh, as if pointing at something as he stared up at the window. He pointed at Jon, then to his own thigh.

And Jon knew Victor had proof. It would hurt him. It would ruin him, if the police believed Victor. Jon could not let Victor get to the police. He needed to stop him.

But Victor was already gone.

Jon poured himself a double of bourbon at his office's wet bar and knocked it back. Poured another.

He sat at his desk and opened his laptop, a headache hammering at his temples as he clicked on the e-mail, the sensation of being watched washing over him.

The e-mail subject line was the same five words as one of the voice mail messages:

You Should Have Helped Me

The e-mail itself read:

Last chance. Meet me. Tonight. Same Place. 7 pm.
Agree to confess.
Or I go to the cops myself.

He had to decide what to do.

Victor was sniffing around and threatening, too.

How could Jon explain it all to the cops without giving up the ugly truth?

Fear lurched in him. He needed to take control, as he'd always done. No emotion had ever helped him, save one: rage. He felt it pushing from inside him, ridding the fear and devouring each cell until he was the incarnation of perfect, crystalline, contained rage. He welcomed it. He would hone it and use it as a spear.

The sender of the e-mail was weak. Soft. He'd chosen to curl up and wither. Chosen to be a victim. Chosen his plight. His destiny. Merryfield would not be dragged into this weakling's world. He would not wallow. He would not allow the coward to get away with this. He would never confess. Or be coerced. He would not be defined by acts over which he had had no control.

There had to be a way out of this.

Then, it struck him. He saw his way out. The only way.

His cell phone rang. Bethany. She'd called five times an hour before Victor had arrived. He'd let the phone ring.

He let it ring now, poured a bourbon and drank it.

He wanted to answer the phone, but he could not bring himself to do it.

Not until he finished what had been started.

His wife seemed more distant to him than ever. She seemed not to exist at all. He did not carry her in his heart. He thought of her, but he did not feel for her. He carried no one in his heart. He never had. He felt for no one. Except for himself. Ever since what had happened to him in the cage.

It had not been until he'd met Bethany his last year of law school that he'd felt any desire for intimacy. Many times when he was an undergrad and as a law student, girls had flirted with him. He'd deflected their advances. They'd mistaken his indifference and fear for shyness, or perhaps quiet confidence, and been even more drawn to him. Asked him out. He'd declined.

Perhaps it had been the enlivening spring weather that day.

He'd been dozing on the steps of the rotunda, soaking up the April sun in a rare moment of leisure he'd granted himself, when a wayward Frisbee sailed into his face from the lawn. He'd sprung awake, discombobulated and ready to strike out at whatever had assailed him, his nose and lips bloodied. Instead he'd seen the most open and cheery face he'd ever encountered, just a nose away from his own face. Her smile swallowed him whole.

Instead of apologizing, the girl had said, "Got yah." And instead of toadying over his bloody nose, she'd snatched up the Frisbee and skipped off down the steps, yelling over her shoulder, "Watch where you doze!"

He'd seen her again a week later in the outdoor amphitheater. Again he'd been dozing, this time to be awakened by something softly tapping his nose. He'd awakened with a start to see her smiling down at him, the sun behind her making a halo around her lustrous hair. She'd been tapping the same Frisbee on the bridge of his nose. "Thought you'd found a safe place to doze, did you?"

A tugging desire overcame him, an urgent force he'd never known. "What's that look?" she'd said, smiling.

"What look?"

"I know that look. Boy oh boy, do I."

They'd strolled back to her studio apartment near the medical center, wending their way past the serpentine brick walls envisioned by Jefferson, the tulip trees exploding with cotton-candy blossoms that perfumed the sweet, sunny air abuzz with the hum of busy honeybees.

In the shadows of a hickory-tree grove, a young disheveled student who'd looked like he'd had a long, rough night had slipped past them on the narrow walk, and upon seeing Jon and the girl, perhaps recognizing the lightness in their carriage, had nodded knowingly.

In another minute, Jon had found himself naked in Bethany's futon bed, surging forward into a new life, sloughing off the old skin to be reborn. The scent of her. The softness of her flesh. The taste. The heat. The hot sunlight pouring in the window above her futon, so their urgency and the strength of the sun left them bathed with a sheen of salty sweat. His new life was beginning. Until it wasn't. Until at the critical moment, he'd thought of the face of the young student who had passed him on the serpentine walk, and he felt himself flag.

He'd collapsed with mortification and lay on his side, his back to her.

She'd laughed. He'd yanked away and grabbed a sheet to hide his flaccidness.

Wanting to end the humiliation, he'd tried to yank on his shorts and fallen over. She'd laughed again, an uproarious, excruciating laugh. "Where do you think you're going?" she'd said.

He'd worked more desperately to worry into his clothes. She'd touched his arm. He'd yanked away. "What's the matter?" she said.

That student, he'd thought. That young man.

"What gives?" she'd said.

"Isn't it obvious?"

"Like I care?"

Of course she cares, he'd thought. She didn't have to debase him more by patronizing him. All he'd wanted was to flee. He'd made a dreadful mistake. Thinking he'd outlived his past misgivings. Instead, it had sunk him under a torrent of vile images.

He tugged his T-shirt on over his head.

"Don't be a dolt," she scolded. She'd stood, naked, splendid in the sunlight playing in the downy hair of her belly. She'd grabbed the Frisbee from the desk and brandished it. "You want another whack?"

He'd tried to pull away, but she had his wrist in her hand, and held fast. She'd looked up into his eyes. "I don't care. Hear me. I don't fucking care. You know how many assholes I've fucked and it meant squat?"

She must have seen the aghast look on his face.

"That's not what I mean." She laughed. "OK. I've had my share. But, believe me. I'm a grad student. In two weeks it's the real world. I don't want just a fuck."

He'd asked what she did want.

"A life. Family. We're all fucked up. I am too, you know. You don't have a corner on the market."

She'd convinced him to stay; and much later managed to coax him through to a finish.

Still. That boy. That student in the shadows. What was it about him?

Later that week, Jon had been eating a burger at the White Spot when the student had strolled in and sat beside him on a stool. This time, he seemed vaguely familiar as he stared at Jon in the mirror behind the counter. "Jon?" he said, and spun his stool to face Jon.

"Yes," Jon had said, perplexed, disoriented. He could not place the student.

"Randy," the young man said.

"Sorry," Jon had said. "Are we in a class together?"

The student had grimaced and gone pale as if Jon had just stuck a knife in his ribs. Except the kid didn't seem like a student at all, Jon noted then. His hair was matted and greasy, not in the practiced manner of kids going grunge, but in a seedy, unwashed way of someone destitute. His teeth were bad; gray as dirty dishwater. And a top tooth was missing. The kid had a spacey look about him, too. A twitchiness.

"We have someone in common," he'd said and laid his dirty hand on Jon's wrist.

Jon stared at the bony hand. He'd wanted to pull away but was afraid he'd instigate the stranger into an outburst, or worse. The short, old black man behind the counter had given Jon a worried look that confirmed Jon's apprehension was not unwarranted.

The stranger was unhinged and gave off an aura of insanity that made all those in his proximity anxious. The stranger slid his hand off of Jon's wrist to sip his water, and the sour stench of the unwashed bloomed up from him, gaseous and repellent.

Jon seized the chance to get off his stool and pay his bill, having hardly touched his burger. He put a ten-spot on the counter and began to stalk away; but the dirty hand clutched his wrist again and squeezed, twisted the skin.

"Don't you want to know who we have in common?" the stranger said.

Jon tried to prize his wrist free without making a scene, but the grip was like a talon.

"You should have helped me," the stranger said. Then he grabbed Jon quickly by the hair and pulled Jon's ear down to his foul mouth and whispered a word and shoved Jon away.

Jon had fallen against the table behind him and staggered outside, where the hothouse humidity of the Virginia spring had nearly knocked him down.

Then he'd run, the word that had been whispered in his ear burning like a corrosive acid.

Jon blinked now as a knock came at his office door.

He stared at the door. Victor? No. Victor would not knock.

The knock came again. Louder.

"Mr. Merryfield. It's Detective Test. I know you are there and I've no intention of leaving."

Chapter 68

TEST TAPPED A fingernail against a glass pane in Jon Merryfield's office as she stood at an expansive window beside his desk.

Merryfield had finally opened the door, looking blurry and distracted, and smelling of booze. He'd claimed to have fallen asleep at his desk; and though Test knew just how possible that scenario was, she did not believe it.

"Why did Victor Jenkins come to you?" Test said, looking out the window. She turned to take in his reaction to her casual drop of Jenkins's name.

"Who?" Jon said.

"Brad's father. I saw him leaving as I parked and hurried to catch him, but was too slow."

"Right," Jon said. He was trying to pour himself a drink of bourbon but having trouble steadying his hand. Finally he set the bottle and glass down.

"So?" Test asked.

"He came to retain me."

"For what?"

"For his son," Jon said, his Adam's apple working.

"Even though the murder his son is charged with took place in your home?" Test said. What Merryfield was saying was preposterous. He had to know that. Of course he knew it. Which meant that the truth was either more preposterous, or damaging.

"He was desperate," Jon said. "He's a desperate, pathetic man. I told him I was too close to the case. It was preposterous."

"Of course it is," Test said.

Merryfield tried again to pour a drink. He managed to just do it, though he splashed booze on the back of his hand.

"How did he handle it?" Test said.

"He was angry. He wanted more than what the public defender could offer. I'm not a defender. I prosecute. Except for my current case. And, honestly, there's no saving his son."

"I guess not," Test said.

He took a drink. "You don't sound so confident for a detective who's been working it."

Test let the comment hang between them.

"Jenkins didn't mention anything about evidence, or proof he had discovered, about his boy?" she said.

"To me?"

"There's no one else here to put the question to, sir," Test said.

"Not to me. He was grasping. To help his boy."

"Except," Test said.

"Except?" He drank, too quickly. The bourbon sloshing. The look he gave Test made her think his mind was sloshing too, with runaway thoughts.

"It's just so odd, him coming to you," Test said.

Jon loosened his tie, trying not to pace, unable to refrain from it. "He doesn't know much about the law. How it really works. Few really do."

"I do," Test said. "I know."

"I suppose," Jon said, tapping his fingers on the rim of his glass, trying to covertly glance at his wristwatch. It was clear he wanted to get away from here; had someplace to go. Test wondered where he needed to be. She'd have thought he'd just want to flee, anywhere. But the glance at his watch made clear he intended to meet someone. Had he conspired all along? Was Brad in on this with him? Was that why Victor was here? Or, was, somehow, King involved? None of it made sense yet.

Jon finished his pacing and sat on the couch, his highball balanced on his knee.

"How's your wife?" Test said.

"Fine. Considering."

"Awful, her finding Jessica."

Jon finished his drink. Sucked on the inside of his cheek. "Some things you never get over."

"I would figure such trying times would make it hard to recover," Test said.

"Recover?"

"You were sick the whole week leading up to her being killed. Isn't that right?"

"Yes. Right. Of course."

"You never went to the doctor for it though."

Jon set the glass down.

"How would you know that?"

"It's my business to know."

"Meeting with doctors is confidential without a subpoena."

"*Not* if the meeting didn't take place. Then all I'd be asking is if you'd had an appointment at all, nothing private about it."

"It was the flu, not cancer." He shrugged.

"I did some digging."

Test produced the CCTV image she'd printed out and set it on Jon's desk, tapped it with her fingers.

Jon did not look at it.

"You know what that is?" Test said.

Jon glimpsed at it. "I haven't the foggiest."

"That's the dishwasher at the Village Fare. Drew Meyers."

Jon rubbed his face and blinked at the photo. "I'll be."

"Specifically," Test said, "that's the dishwasher going into the men's room for his check of the bathrooms as he does hourly each night, to make sure they are clean."

"Good for him."

"That's of no interest to you?" Test said.

"Should it be?" He squared his shoulders.

"I'd think it would be. Since that photo was taken at six forty-five, when you were supposedly sick in the bathroom of the restaurant."

Jon smiled. "That's not possible."

"It is possible. More than that, it's fact. That's the time he checks the restroom every night. And you weren't in there when he went in."

"I was," he said. He risked a nervous peek at his watch.

"We have a photo of you going in at six forty-two. Then. Here. Just before Drew Meyers comes to clean, you leave the bathroom at six forty-three, a minute after going in."

"The CCTV must have the time wrong," Jon said.

"It doesn't."

Jon's Adam's apple stuck halfway through his swallow.

"According to my stopwatch," Test said. "Your home is just a five-minute walk from the Village Fare restaurant where you ate dinner."

"What the hell are you implying?"

"I'm not implying anything. I'm demonstrating a fact through irrefutable video evidence, that you were not in the bathroom when you said you were." Test took another photo out and slapped it on his desk. "This one, seconds after you left the bathroom the first time, shows you heading out the door at the end of the corridor that opens to the Dumpster out back. And here," she slapped another photo down, "is one of you coming in fourteen minutes later. And, as you can see, or as I could see in photos I blew up, you came back in wiping sweat from your forehead, looking shaken and distraught. Perhaps you can tell me where you were," Test said, "when you were supposed to be in the bathroom? And what you were doing, exactly."

Jon stared at her, his eyes going as cold and dead as any she'd ever seen.

She had him.

Then, he smiled, and her stomach dropped.

"I was, if you need to know. Puking. I got sick in the bathroom and desperately needed some cold fresh air. So, I went outside. But I got sick again anyway. Hardly see how it matters where I vomited, do you?"

He poured himself another drink, this time without so much as a tremor in his hand, this time a double.

"I'm sorry you've wasted your time. Perhaps, you can tell me, where you thought I was and what you thought I was doing, exactly." His tone was cordial, but he was mocking her. Making a fool of her by throwing her own words back in her face.

"I think you know," she said.

"Well," he said and finished his drink with a long, smooth, and practiced pull, "I'd kindly ask you to leave. I have a client to meet."

"At this hour?"

"My career knows no civil hours. I'm sure you can relate."

He went to the door and opened it.

"Good evening, Detective. Good luck."

Test passed by him and strode across the front office. She stopped at the door to the stairway and looked back with her hand on the doorknob. "Just one more thing."

"Yes?" he said, impatient. Dying to look at his watch.

"Do you know a Randy Clark?"

Chapter 69

TEST WATCHED THE entrance to Jon Merryfield's office building from her Peugeot parked down the street.

Merryfield had offered a reasonable answer for everything. And every answer he'd told her was possible. Even likely, in normal circumstances. But these were not normal circumstances.

He might have left the bathroom because he needed fresh air. He might have come back inside sweating and looking upset because he'd gotten sick out back. There was CCTV on the back door, but it only showed him coming out of the door and going back inside. Whatever he'd done had been off camera.

Perhaps he did have a client to see tonight. She had not asked who the client was because she knew he'd claim client confidentiality, and the only clients it could be, if true, were Gregory and Scott. He was meeting someone, she was convinced. But not a client. The look he had when he'd last eyed his watch was one of panic that did not come with running late. She wasn't buying the story of why Victor Jenkins visited him either. And then there was her mention of Randy Clark. Upon hearing the name, Jon Merryfield had been unable to stop his jaw from dropping, however briefly, as a look of horror passed over his face like a dark shadow.

Test would wait. When Merryfield came out, she'd follow. If he visited someone other than Gregory Sergeant or Scott Goodale, she'd take him in for questioning. North would go nuclear on her. Until he saw the CCTV footage. Particularly the part she had not shown Merryfield. He was linked to the murder of Jessica Cumber, somehow. He'd either killed her or was an accomplice, or . . . What? Damn it. What could his motive possibly be? There was none, unless he'd had an affair with the girl. But neither his nor Jessica's phone or e-mail or other computer records showed communication between the two. Still, Test knew: If she found the motive, she'd have Jon Merryfield.

She looked up. Merryfield was slipping out of his office building and sneaking across the street to his Land Rover. He started the vehicle and drove off quickly.

Test turned the key in the ignition. Nothing. In her earlier hurry to chase after Victor when she'd spied him coming out, she'd left the lights on.

The battery was dead.

Chapter 70

Jon hurried from his Land Rover into his home, slamming the front door behind him.

He leaned against the door, panting. Thoughts of the dead girl crowded his fevered mind as he rushed into the kitchen to check voice-mail messages.

The same number came up five times. He dialed his voice mail. He could have checked the messages from his office or from his cell phone. But he did not want to leave a number that could be traced back to him. And he needed to delete the caller ID history.

The voice on the first message said: "Like the photo?"

He listened to the others:

"You did this to yourself."

"You should have saved me."

"There's no saving yourself now."

"Killer."

Jon erased all the messages and the caller ID history. Trembling like a china cup in an earthquake, he sat on the kitchen floor trying to catch his breath, trying to think. But his mind was a thorny maze of wild thoughts with no escape route. He told himself to concentrate. He knew what needed to be done.

How had the detective known of Randy?

Jon brought up the e-mail on his phone.

> *Last chance. Meet me. Tonight. Same Place. 7 pm.*
> *Agree to confess.*
> *Or I go to the cops myself.*

The time was 6:50 P.M.

The photo. The photo of Jon slipping out behind the Village Fare, date-stamped just minutes before Jessica had been killed. The photo of him heading into the woods.

There was no way out.

Except one.

The sender had to be shut up, for good.

Jon climbed the stairs to the master bedroom three at a time. The house already smelled of a place where nobody lived: musty, trapped, dead air. Cobwebs clung to a corner of the ceiling of the bedroom. Jon opened his work desk's hidden trick panel. Mouse droppings littered the bottom of the drawer. He took the only weapon he had left to stop the sender of the messages.

Jon brought up his e-mail on his phone.

He typed in one sentence.

> *On my way.*

And hit SEND.

OUTSIDE, THE COLD stung him. Winter had forced itself upon the world yet again, and was here to stay. Snow had settled, hiding the hard, sharp edges of the world under its soft whiteness.

The street was quiet. Jon hurried along the sidewalk.

He met no one.

He wanted to see Bethany, needed to explain himself, tell her everything.

He dialed the inn on his phone as he hurried. Nearly out of breath he asked Anna at the reception desk to put him through.

"She's not there," Anna said.

"Where is she?" He walked into the Village Fare parking lot and headed toward the back of the place.

"Home," Anna said.

"She isn't. I was just there."

"Home to Connecticut."

"Her father's?"

"She just said 'home to Connecticut.' She left a message." Anna paused. "She said she's not coming back."

Jon stood in front of the woods behind the Village Fare. He had five minutes to get through them to the other side.

"You OK?" Anna said. "You sound horrible."

"It's just sort of hit me, all at once."

"You can't keep things at bay forever. Longer you do, worse it is when it catches up to you."

"I gotta go," he said.

"Call her, let her know you're all right."

"I'm not all right, Anna."

"You will be."

"No," he said, "I won't."

He hung up and stared into the dark woods.

Chapter 71

TEST TRIED TO run on the sidewalks, but it was not possible. If Jon Merryfield was truly going to see Gregory and Scott, Test could run to their home in five minutes if she pushed it. But if she called ahead now and told them she was Merryfield's assistant and he was running late, their reaction would tell her if Jon was expected by them or not.

She dialed 411 as she hurried. The number was unlisted.

Beneath the snow, the wet sidewalks were frozen and footing was hazardous. She slipped on the icy sidewalks, her heart heaving.

She was two blocks down from the house, across the street from the Village Fare, when she heard a man speaking loudly.

Jon Merryfield.

He stood just outside the light that lit up the area by the Dumpster, speaking into a cell phone.

He strapped a headlamp on his head, then took something from his jacket pocket. Test could not see what it was. Except that it briefly shone black and metallic before he slipped it back into his pocket.

Test ran across the street, slipping and falling as a truck trundled toward her, its headlights blinding her. She scrambled out of the way and got a purchase again as she rose to her feet and ran as swiftly as she could to the back of the Village Fare.

Jon was nowhere to be seen. All that remained were his footprints in the snow. They led straight into the dark woods; woods that were not navigable without the aid of a light.

Quick research had revealed that the thumbtack Test had found in the Merryfields' yard, and the one stuck to the tree behind the restaurant, were used to mark trails in the woods so hunters could find their way to and from their deer stands in the dark. There were bound to be other tacks in the woods. Jon's headlamp would reflect them, so he could find his way easily in the dark.

Without a light, Test would never catch him. She tried her iPhone light, but it wasn't bright enough. She needed to run all the way back around the woods to the schoolyard, take the long way.

She took off running.

Chapter 72

JON WORKED HIS way in the woods. The going was arduous. It would have been quicker to have gone straight from his house to the destination. But the sender did not want that; and neither did Jon. He could not risk being seen.

The headlamp illuminated the woods a few feet ahead, reflected back to him in tiny fragments by the reflective markers in the trees.

He headed toward a marker, then repeated the search until the next marker glimmered.

He pushed along, branches slapping his face. He shoved his hands into his pockets to try to keep them warm, but the cold steel against his flesh in one pocket only made him colder. Still, he wrapped his hand around it. Its heft was reassuring.

He made his way down a gully and up the opposite bank. It took longer this time than it had the first time. The first time when his heart had raced with such panic for the small window of time he had to do what needed to be done before he would be missed by Bethany in the restaurant.

His heart raced now, but he felt a calm finality spreading through him with each step. It would be over soon. This would cover the ugly truth for good. It had to. He did not care about Jessica. He could not. All he could do was protect and save himself now. Everything was clear.

He saw lights up ahead, sifting through the trees.

He finally came out behind the school, near the back of the parking lot, where this had all begun so many years ago.

The lot was empty. Snow swirled in the pale lamplights.

Then he saw it, off in the shadows. A figure. Him.

Jon turned off his headlamp and walked toward the figure, his legs feeling as if he'd walked a thousand miles. Leaden and sore, yet somehow detached.

His hand wrapped tighter around the cold steel in his coat pocket.

He came to stand a few feet away from the figure, who had now materialized into Randy Clark.

JON CLUTCHED THE cold steel in his jacket pocket.

"Randall," he said.

Randy Clark said nothing. He stared at Jon, and even in the poor light Jon could see the watery weakness in the man's eyes. The boy's eyes. The victim's eyes.

"Randall, it's over. Here. Now. This stops. Your threats stop. I have—"

"You're ready then? To tell the police what you did?"

Jon shook his head. No. Randall looked over toward the parking lot, where so many years earlier, when he was eight, a GMC pickup had been parked. It was a night like this: snowy and cold. Christmas vacation week. The lot empty except for that truck. Jon had been heading home through the same woods he'd just come through, after having left the Town Arcade, where the Village Fare now stood. The woods had not really been woods then. The trees had been small and scrubby, and because kids walked and biked everywhere, there'd been a clear path. Jon had taken the path that evening, and as he'd passed by the truck he'd looked inside.

Jon shivered.

"That's your choice," Randall said.

"They'll never believe it. I'm a prominent man. And you. You're what? Jobless? Homeless?"

Jon recalled the time he'd seen Randall at the White Spot. Jon had truly not recognized him. The last time Jon had seen him before that, Randall had been eight years old. At the White Spot he'd been in his twenties. But Randall had recognized Jon. He remembered the word Randall had whispered in his ear to make Jon suddenly understand who this stranger was.

"You should have helped me," Randall said. He thumped a tight fist against his thigh. His hands were bare. He wore jeans and sneakers and a torn dark denim jacket. "You could have helped me. It was fate I ran into you at that diner in Virginia. A thousand miles from home, ten years later. That was fate. And you spat in its face. You could have—"

"I couldn't." Jon felt the cold steel in his pocket. "And you? You didn't need me. You could have helped yourself, like I did. You could have taken control over your own life. Claimed your life back. Survived. It's the only way. Forget. Separate. Survive. Instead, you played victim."

Randall snarled, spitting his words: "What the fuck do you know? You fucking—" His voice was rising as he pounded a fist against the side of his head.

"No one will believe you," Jon said. "Even with the photo. It's not proof."

He started to ease his hand out of his coat pocket.

Randall licked his cracked lips.

"I'll make this go away," Jon said and started to yank his hand out of his pocket and bring out the only thing that could stop all this.

But Randall, weak as he looked, was fast, and he was on Jon before Jon could finish his move.

Chapter 73

TEST CHARGED TOWARD the two figures grappling in the snowy lot, drew her weapon and shouted: "Stop!"

The smaller of the two men was on top of Merryfield, slapping at him and screaming, crying. "You did this! You did this! You killed her! You killed *me!*"

Test grabbed the man by his hair and hauled him off of Jon. She trained her gun at him.

The man stared up at the muzzle of the gun.

"Do it," he moaned. "Do it. Please. Please. Just end it." He broke down, curling in a ball on his side and sobbing wretchedly.

Jon was getting up, trying to hide something in his jacket pocket. Test brought her weapon around on him. "Drop it," she said.

Jon dropped it.

A black rectangular metallic box.

She kept the gun on Jon as she cuffed the man crying on the ground.

"Hold still," she said to Jon and went to the box. She opened it, unsure what to think. Unsure what was going on here, but knowing it was much more than she'd ever imagined.

Chapter 74

IT HAD BEEN dark by the time Victor strode out of Jon Merry-field's office. He'd stopped by the Canaan Police station to speak with the woman cop, but she had not been in. He'd called and left a message with the state police for Detective North to call him as soon as he could.

Since then, he'd walked about town, too nerved up to go home, trying to get his thoughts straight, and going over his notes to tell the police all of it at one time, collected and calculated. They would press him, and he had to have the story perfect. The memories clear.

Now, as he walked around town, he kept thinking, *It's going to be all right. My boy is going to be all right.* He would reveal all, even if it meant losing Fran and Brad; he'd do it in order to save his son.

He'd confess and when they heard the motive, they'd have someone to investigate, to give reasonable doubt regarding Brad.

The girl had been killed in *Jon's house* after all.

They'd see. They had to.

Victor shivered. The temperature had crashed and the night air felt cold enough to crack glass. The town lay barren.

The frozen sidewalk made the footing treacherous. Victor's feet went out from under him and he fell, cracking an elbow hard on the concrete.

He sat, cradling his elbow. Bewildered.

The ice melted beneath him and the concrete's cold seeped through his jeans. As he reached out for a nearby bench to get support, he heard a scream.

It came violently.

Followed by shouting.

The baying of the wounded.

Victor cocked his head like a dog sensing the distant danger of the enraged master he'd run away from but who now was gaining ground and would find and beat him. But the shouting was not that of a master yelling at his hound. It was that of two men, railing.

And more than that too.

More than heated words, more than anger and threats.

It was wrath. Lunatic. Animal. Incandescent. And it was pain. Feral and unchained.

And it was something else, too, that Victor could taste but could not yet name.

The two voices ruptured the night air with their fury, entangled. They melded into one voice that rose up as if from the earth itself, as if the two voices were two souls trying to rend themselves loose of their purgatory, and only the one whose screams rose above the other could free itself of the hatred that bound it.

The cries were full of blood, and cut into Victor as cleanly as a

scalpel between his ribs. He had lived with such shouting as a boy.
How his father had howled.

Vic scrambled to his feet.

The screams came louder, no longer that of souls or animals,
but humans and their ancient violence.

Victor ran.

He ran as if his father were after him. He ran on the ice with an
athleticism that surprised and elated him, as though a last reserve
of his youth had been stored up to be tapped now, for this purpose, to reach the voices and stop whatever awfulness was about
to unfold.

Fear crowded him with each stride. A pressure so enormous
it seemed he might explode into vapor. Still, he ran toward the
voices.

He came around the corner and saw it.

Saw them.

Across the street.

On the ground, on the village green. In front of the Civil War
cannon. A small crowd circled them, watching. Victor bolted
across the street and pushed through the crowd.

Two men struggled on the ground. A knot of limbs as they beat
each other.

Jed King and Gregory Sergeant.

The icy ground had gone soft beneath them, turned muddy as
a pig sty. The men's fists pounded each other's flesh. A hard fist
smashed an eye socket. Split it. Another fist burst open a mouth.
Blood misted. Teeth broke and bit. A hand grabbed hair to lift
a head and rock it against the ground with the dull thud. Feet
kicked groins, stomped on hands. Clothes ripped. Fingers gouged
and tore. Blood flowed. It flowed as the voices howled.

Victor could not tell one man from the other. There seemed no separation. It was as though the two men were a conjoined creature of mythology, tired and sick and enraged from having to share the same heart, yet separate minds, and each would rather tear the other apart and die than continue as one.

Or perhaps, it was just the opposite.

Perhaps they were two humans tired of resisting the urge to join, to couple, and what appeared as violence was only a sort of ugly, primal lovemaking.

As if in agreement, one of the creatures shouted, "Fuck!"

Then, "You're killing me!"

No one in the crowd blinked. Larry Branch stood smoking a cigarette as if watching friends bowl at Riverside Ten Pins. Another man stood with his arms folded, shaking his head as if disapproving of boys throwing snowballs at a car. Each face watched with the same look. Not afraid. Not repulsed. Not moved. Resigned. As if what was happening was beyond their control, the arrival of a storm they all knew was coming, and now there was nothing to do but look out the window from the safety of their homes and weather it.

King grabbed Sergeant by the hair and pounded Sergeant's skull against the cannon. Blood sprayed. "Fuck you!" King shouted.

"Stop!" Victor roared.

King cracked Gregory's head against the cannon again.

"Stop!" Victor pleaded. "In the name of God!"

King pinned Gregory beneath him and grabbed a rock. His wet hair like a tangle of seaweed, his eyes lunatic. He raised the rock high above his head. Gregory lay motionless.

"You queer fuck!" King roared.

"Stop!" Victor rushed King, lowering his shoulder as he squared himself, as if to put a hit on a wide receiver, to jar that ball loose, one last time.

He struck King with the whole of his upper body.

King tottered backward.

But he held fast the rock.

As he teetered, he swung the rock.

Hard.

Lightning flashed in Victor's mind. He suddenly felt very warm. Hot.

He heard a far-off sound. The thunder that followed the lightning? It must have been. You could not have one without the other.

If you did, the world no longer made sense.

He heard a thud. Saw the darkness. Collapsing on him with the mighty weight of an ocean wave.

A voice said: "You've killed him."

Victor did not know to whom or about what the voice spoke, but it made sense.

You've killed him.

Chapter 75

"Do you want to tell us the truth now?" Test said.

Jon Merryfield sat in the interview room. He'd sat there all night, refusing to speak.

Then, an hour ago, Test had given him the newspaper to read.

She'd read the article for a second time, keeping an eye on Merryfield as he read his copy.

Kingdom Chronicle
Father of Murder Suspect Killed Saving Man

Victor Jenkins, a physical education teacher and coach of Lamoille High for decades, was killed yesterday evening while attempting to break up a fight between two other local men, Jed King and Gregory Sergeant, on the village green.

Mr. Jenkins was killed when Jed King struck his head with a rock. King, a vocal opponent to the proposed gay marriage bill and openly vocal against homosexuality, had, accord-

ing to witnesses, confronted Mr. Sergeant who is one of two plaintiffs in a lawsuit against the State of Vermont.

"He saved my life," Mr. Sergeant said. "Plain and simple." Mr. Sergeant spoke with considerable pain and difficulty from a hospital bed where he is recovering from injuries that include broken ribs, a broken jaw, lacerations to the face, and a concussion.

Witnesses corroborate Mr. Sergeant's statement. "He saved his life," Larry Branch said. "He got right in there. He was the only one of us. He just did what was right. I'm not surprised. He was a good friend."

King was arrested for aggravated assault and second-degree murder and will be arraigned on Tuesday afternoon. He will be charged with a hate crime. A search of his house also revealed evidence that he may have poisoned Mr. Sergeant's dog.

Mr. Jenkins is the father of Brad Jenkins, who is charged with the murder of Jessica Cumber, 15, with whom he'd had a relationship. Jessica Cumber was murdered in the home of Jon Merryfield, the attorney for Gregory Sergeant and his partner.

"He was on his way to tell the police something about our boy," said Mrs. Fran Jenkins, Mr. Jenkins's widow. "He'd learned something. Was going to set Brad free. I don't know what it was," she said, sobbing. "He was a good father. A good teacher and coach."

Detective Sonja Test said that Mr. Jenkins had stopped by the Canaan Police Station while she was out and left a message for Richard North, lead detective with the state police, that he had something to say that would free his boy.

"Whatever his son may be charged with," North said, "Victor Jenkins should be commended for his bravery to protect another citizen from an act of hatred."

Apparently, Victor Jenkins had come into the law office of attorney Jon Merryfield earlier in the day. "He was distraught. Angry," Cheryl Bloom, the assistant to Jon Merryfield, said.

Mr. Jon Merryfield himself has been brought in for questioning regarding the murder of Jessica Cumber. It is unclear why the police are interested in questioning him.

Detective North stated that he believes there is no link between Brad Jenkins' crime and what occurred last evening on the village green. He would not comment on the questioning of Jon Merryfield. "That's a local police department issue. Separate from us." Junior Detective Sonja Test, who brought in Jon Merryfield and another yet to be identified man for questioning, had no comment.

Merryfield set down the paper.

"Ready now?" Test said.

Merryfield wrung his hands, his face grave.

"I—" He took a sip of water.

"Tell me about the money in the metal box."

Merryfield put his fingers to his left eye, swollen and bruised by Randall Clark.

"I was going to pay him. Pay Randall to go away."

"Was he extorting you?"

"Not technically. Not for money." He touched his wounded face. "Obviously he didn't want the money."

"What did he want?"

Jon leaned back so his head was hanging off the back of the chair. He stared at the ceiling and moaned.

"Where did you go when you sneaked out of the restaurant the night of the murder?" *None of the pieces yet fit*, Test thought, *but the pieces were there to be assembled.*

"I—"

Test was sure he was going to ask for a lawyer. He sure could use one.

"I . . . was going to meet him."

"Who?"

"Randall."

"Randy Clark?"

"Yes."

"Do you know he's been going by the name of Daryn Banks?"

Jon shrugged. "What's it matter what name he goes by?"

Test didn't know what it mattered. Or how. But she knew it must. It did matter that Randy, or Daryn, had befriended Victor Jenkins over the past months, through Jed King's inner circle. Become close to him. *Close enough to learn about Brad?* she wondered. Except Brad had told no one about Jessica, least of all his parents. What Randy calling himself Daryn meant, Test did not know yet. But it might come to light when she spoke with Randy, whom she'd left to simmer all night in the room down the hall.

She wanted North in on her interrogation of Randall Clark, but North was also occupied with the Jenkins murder.

"What did you see Clark about?" Test asked.

"Something that happened a long time ago."

"What?"

Merryfield winced, as if he'd bitten rotten meat. "I'd seen something."

"What?" He was going to make Test tease everything out of him. Not out of a game. Or a resistance to cooperate. But out of grief that was as clear on his face as if someone were pressing his hand to hot coals.

"Take your time," she said.

"Can I stand?" he said.

Test nodded.

He wasn't cuffed. He wasn't a threat.

She'd never seen a more defeated man ready to talk.

He paced, swiped the back of his hand across his mouth.

"I saw. I witnessed . . . Victor Jenkins raping Randy Clark."

Test gasped. She stopped most of the gasp, turned it into a sip of air. But she was breathless nonetheless. "You witnessed this? Where? When?"

"In the parking lot where you found us. I was seventeen. He was maybe eight."

"You sure that's what you saw?"

He stopped pacing and looked at her and before he said it she knew there was no doubt about the veracity of what he was telling her. "I'm sure."

"And you knew this how?"

He gave her an eviscerating look. "If you ever witness such a thing, and I hope you don't, you won't have any doubt. I could have told you what I saw, by the look in the boy's eyes alone."

"Is that all you saw? His eyes?"

"I saw more. And heard more. Too much. But I saw his eyes. And he. Saw mine."

Test felt her stomach go greasy, and her neck grow hot.

"And what did you do?" she said.

"Nothing."

His eyes had gone cold. Not with hatred or lack of emotion. But cold for another reason she could not quite pin.

"Nothing," he said again. "I did nothing."

"You must have done something."

"I did nothing."

"Run away, at least."

He shook his head. Laughed. "I walked away. And I put it out of my mind. I shut it out like it never happened. And I went home. And I had dinner with my grandparents. And I slept like a baby. And I never thought of it again. *Forget. Separate. Survive.*"

"What?" Test said.

Another laugh escaped Merryfield. A grunt.

"So, you just walked away and forgot about it?" Test said.

"Right."

"Saw a boy get raped and wiped your hands of it. And how exactly did you do that? How do you expect me to believe that? Because, people can't just block out something like that."

"No?" He fixed her with a look as hot with fury as his previous look had been icy. "How would you know the first thing about it? What a person can and can't block out?" he said. "Have you ever seen a boy get raped to know? Are you some fucking expert on boys getting raped, Detective?"

It was a mistake not to have cuffed him, or at least to have let him stand. He pushed himself off the wall, eyes taunting her. "Just what the fuck would you know about it, Detective?"

"I—" His sudden command of the room sent Test off kilter. She stood and put her hands on the back of her chair. "I would assume that witnessing such a traumatic event would be difficult, if not impossible, to simply forget as if it never happened."

"Not if you've had years of practice with willful repression and compartmentalization."

"What?" Test said.

"Victor Jenkins raped me, too. When I was eight."

TEST PACED OUT in the hall. She needed to find her bearings after what Merryfield had said. If it was a ploy to distract, it was convincing. But all she had was his word.

She called and left a message with North, apprising him of Merryfield's revelation. Then she went to the canteen and drank a glass of water.

When she entered the interview room, Merryfield sat slumped in his chair, looking ghastly. His dominion leeched from him. It was as quick a transformation as any Test had ever seen.

Test sat across the table from him, set her recorder on again. "You want more water?"

Merryfield's head trembled as if he had Parkinson's, and it took Test a moment to realize this was the closest he could muster to shaking his head no.

"Are you hungry?" Test said.

Another tremor.

This was not the same man she'd left in the room minutes earlier.

Test opened her notebook and scratched a meaningless note to gain composure.

"OK," she said. "So, you walked away and forgot about it."

"I was never any good at anything, as a kid. Sports, especially. The last kid chosen and all of that. But I wanted to be. That's all I wanted. To be good at sports. Be good at *anything*."

She could only imagine the astonishment on her face at hearing this confusing non sequitur.

"One day during gym class, I pulled a muscle during floor hockey," he said. He seemed nearly catatonic.

"When was this?" Test said.

"Fourth grade. After class, in the locker room, I remember how much it hurt. God. My groin felt taut as guy-wires about to snap. And on fire. I couldn't bend to untie my shoes or take off my shorts, let alone put on my jeans. So. I'd sat in a toilet stall until the locker room emptied, then slipped into the equipment cage to find a pair of baggy sweatpants to slip on over my sneakers."

Test had the sensation she wasn't present to Merryfield. That he was speaking aloud what he had harbored inside for a long time. Too long. Festering. Corroding him from the inside out. That was the word that struck Test now, the mutation Merryfield had seemed to undergo while she'd been out of the room. It was as if he'd been corroded. And now that he was starting to tell the story, to confess, there would be no stopping it, and his memories would corrode him until there was nothing left of the man who'd entered the room.

"A sign on the cage door said: 'Do not enter cage without coach or coach's permission.'"

"Can you speak up a bit, please," Test said. "For the recorder."

Merrryfield blinked and looked at her with as pained an expression as any Test had ever seen.

"I remember," he said, and made a choking sound. He folded his hands in his lap, in the manner of a boy awaiting a scolding. He seemed to have regressed even more. "The cage stunk of sweat, and socks and jocks and the wet leather of footballs left in the rain." He said the stink made him think of bodily fluids, spit and phlegm. Blood and piss. He sighed. Rubbed his hands together as if they were stained. Beneath the bodily stink, he said, lingered the faint odor of ointment. He was fishing through old gear for the sweats— "when his hand clasped my shoulder."

"Whose hand?" Test said.

"Coach's."

"I need a name, please."

"Victor Jenkins."

"Could you speak up again please," Test said.

"Victor Jenkins. Victor fucking Jenkins. He startled me and asked, 'What are we up to? You shouldn't be here.'" Merryfield sighed. "Right away I was scared."

"Why?"

"Because I wasn't supposed to be in the cage. And I liked Coach. I idolized him. I didn't want him to be *mad*. He was a big-time star. He played football at Syracuse. He might have gone to the NFL if not for an injury."

Even now he spoke of Victor Jenkins with a bizarre sense of misplaced reverence, his voice taking on a soft tone of juvenile adulation.

"I told him about my injury and that I was after some sweats. I could barely breathe." Jon was whispering, lost to memory.

Instead of asking him again to speak up, Test slid her recorder closer to him.

"Coach relaxed his grip and turned me around so I was facing his chest. I remember." Jon's eyes went dead. Not cold. Dead. "There was a sharp bite of aftershave, masking something animal, glandular. And Coach pointed to the sign and said, 'You think the rules don't apply to you?'" Merryfield said with a voice tinged with guilt, complicity.

"He started to rub my shoulders. I tensed up, terrified. But he kept at it. And, involuntarily, after some time, I relaxed. He asked where I'd hurt myself. And I told him inside my leg. My groin. He said, 'Let's get you on the table.' He lifted me up like a doll, and laid me on the table. He was strong. He shut the gymnasium door, locked it. He put a hand on each of my knees and said, 'Which side?'"

Jon peered up at Test, eyes alive now, manic with shame and guilt. And rage. "He told me he was trained. It was physical therapy. That NFL players had it done all the time." Jon closed his eyes. "He told me to close my eyes."

The room seemed to be closing in on Test, she felt claustrophobic and filthy.

"'Close your eyes,' he said. 'Tell me when it hurts.' He said—" Jon laughed, a sad, sickening laugh. "He said, 'It's important to isolate your pain, keep it separate from yourself.' And he had me remove my shorts and started in with the massage. Telling me maybe he could be my personal trainer. How'd I like it if he got me into shape for the baseball team? Got me a spot on the team. How'd that be? I was thrilled. You can imagine. I was a homely, weak, scrawny kid, athletic as spit.

"He must have sensed my nervousness. My innate fear. Because he said he could take me to see Nurse Jill. 'You rather have a woman look at your privates?' I didn't want that, of course. A woman. I was eight."

Jon shook his head.

"He told me to shut my eyes and to think of something I liked. Pain shot down my inner thigh. The muscle was livid, but slowly it loosened, the muscle warmed, and blood flowed. The pain—" He put his face in his hands. "The pain wasn't pain anymore."

He took his hands from his face, his cheeks and forehead florid.

"He asked if it was good. And I nodded. Fuck if I didn't. Fuck if I didn't nod. Fuck if I didn't. Fuck fuck fuck." His voice splintered and pitched with an agony that can only come from wanting to claim back a moment that alters your life for the worse, forever, but cannot be reclaimed. "Fuck if I didn't."

He stood suddenly, kicked his chair back so it slammed against the wall. Test nearly fell back out of her chair at the suddenness of it. Her hand went reflexively for her weapon. Jon wiped at his mouth, his chest heaving. Test relaxed.

"You know what the worst of it is?" he said, pointing at her now, waving his hands around wildly, towering. "I *liked* it. I was eight. Fucking *eight*. It took a long time for me to realize what was done to me. What I'd *allowed* to be done." He looked around behind him, as if he'd heard a sound that startled him. But nothing was there. "In time, living in my own skin sickened me. I've felt unnatural ever since. With myself and with others; suspicious of everyone's intentions, what they really wanted to pry out of me. What they wanted to use me for. Everyone uses everyone else for something. Nothing is free. I was fucking eight. But I was an accomplice to the crime committed against me."

"No you weren't," Test said, spooking herself with her own voice.

"I *was*. I allowed it."

"You were coerced. Manipulated. He was an adult. A mentor. He had the power, he—"

Merryfield slammed his fist against the wall and Test jumped.

"I liked it!" Merryfield shouted. "I fucking liked it!"

This was beyond Test's expertise, this was out of her realm.

This was not a confession of a crime of the murder of Jessica. This was a purging of the soul.

Jon's left eyelid spasmed as his behavior grew more erratic and he stalked about the room shaking his finger and head furiously.

"Please," Test said. "Sit down and take a breath. Please." She got up and picked his chair off the floor. She was aware that this still could be a ruse. She needed to get him back to tonight. To what had transpired between him and Randy Clark.

Merryfield paced, but he finally sat down.

He rested his head in his hands.

"It happened other times," he said, his voice hoarse. "I could have said no to any of them. But I didn't."

Test did not know much about such abuse, but everything she did know indicated that being groomed was not an easy thing to break from, especially if the victims were victimized by someone they admired and trusted. It went far beyond Stockholm syndrome. After everything he'd said, Test remained no more or less certain that Jon had killed Jessica. What was the motive? Had she come on to him, or him to her and he'd been rejected? Was what Test was being told only meant to manipulate her into sympathy?

"Everything that happened during that time, has led to this moment," Jon said. "Led to the murder of Jessica."

"What do you mean?" Test said quickly. Was he confessing?

"Jessica would not be dead if I'd never let that happen to me."

"Tell me why you met Randy Clark the night of Jessica's murder."

"He has nothing on me now," Jon mumbled. "It's all out."

"What do you mean?"

"Two weeks ago, I got a call. It was just eight words. 'It's Randy. Stop what you're doing, or else.'"

"What did that mean?"

"Stop defending Scott and Gregory."

Test was beginning to form a picture. Just a foggy outline of it, like the shoreline of a lake just emerging from the morning fog.

"He was mad about that?" Test said.

"Raving mad. And at me because I never helped him. When I saw him in the truck that night, he saw me too. I was seventeen. And he was the age I was when I was with Coach."

With Coach. The phrase shocked and repulsed Test. It was a euphemism one would use for dating. Test was speaking to a wounded boy.

"I was in high school. A senior. And he was in maybe third grade. And, the look on his face." Jon was silent for a minute, collecting himself. Several times he seemed about to continue, only to hold a hand up: *Give me a second.*

Finally, he said, "The look on his face. What I buried for years, but what won't stay buried now, is not the misery and shame, which were there, but his look of hope. When I appeared outside that truck window and he saw me looking in, a big kid, nearly a man, big enough to take on Coach and stop what was happening, his face of agony lit with hope. He would be saved. Spared. And I walked away and I left him."

Test looked at the clock. It was just after eleven in the morning, but her body had the logy and lethargic torpor of the middle of the night, 2:30 or 3:00 A.M. Her throat was sore, her glands swollen, and it stung to swallow.

"So," she said, "this was the first you'd ever heard from him since then?"

"I ran into him, once. In Charlottesville, Virginia, when I was at law school. He must have been twenty or so. He saw me in passing one day. He seemed vaguely familiar, but I thought he was just someone I'd seen around campus. Then I saw him at a diner. He sat right beside me. I didn't recognize him, but he recognized me. He became unstable when I insisted I didn't know him. He was adamant I knew him. I made to leave and I thought he was going to hurt me. I realized then he wasn't a student. He stank and his teeth were bad, his breath foul, his clothes threadbare. He was destitute, possibly deranged. I pulled away and he said, 'We have someone in common.' And he whispered a word in my ear."

"What did he whisper?" Test asked.

"Coach," Jon said. "And I knew. And I left. Again."

"When he called two weeks ago, what did he want?"

"I told you. To stop representing Scott and Gregory. He thought it was disgusting, me representing them. His mind is confused. He equates their sexuality to the likes of Coach. He can't separate the two. It's clear he never learned to separate, to compartmentalize like I did. I told him when we met the first time at his request a couple weeks ago that he needed to do it to survive. Forget. Separate. Survive. To succumb is to give the predator more power. To be a victim all over again. I made a choice to make a life for myself despite what was done to me. He did not. And now look at him."

"So, you met him the night of the murder in the school parking lot. Why? And why there?"

"He chose that spot to make me feel guilty. To drum up old memories and try to soften me. Like I said, he dwells. He's stuck in that moment. I understand it. I do. It took me years. To escape my memories. And I still trust no one. Not my wife. Not myself. Worse. I don't care to trust. What's the point? So what if someone betrays me. So what if a wife cheats or friend backstabs me. What could possibly be done to me that is worse than what happened to me when I was eight years old?"

It was a rhetorical question, but Test pondered it anyway. There was nothing worse. Nothing at all.

"So, he wanted you to stop, and, what?" Test asked. "Why did you go through the woods? The school is practically across the street from your house."

"It was the direction I'd come from that night, years ago. The restaurant was an arcade back then. It was like he wanted to re-create that night. The ten days prior to our meeting, with his calls coming in and e-mails, I was so scared and confused about what he might want that I couldn't leave home. I pretended to be sick. I didn't want this ever getting out. Ever. It made me sick, too, liter-ally. I lost sleep. I lost my appetite. And he wanted to tell everyone. The press. Everyone. He said he'd go to the police about it if I didn't stop the case, stop representing perverts. I wasn't going to *stop*. No *one* is ever going to make me do anything I don't want to do ever again." Spittle flew as he spat the words. "No one. I cer-tainly wasn't going to let *him* push me the fuck around."

The way Merryfield spoke of Randy Clark felt like he was talk-ing about a brother, a sibling relationship polluted by the bonds of anger and resentment.

"Why didn't you tell anyone what happened to you years ago?" Test said.

"Are you serious?" Merryfield looked at her as if she were an idiot. "Back then? I was eight. He was a legend. It took *years* for me to even understand what happened, that something wrong had been done. And when I finally understood, I blamed myself. Have you seen the media circuses around this shit? These kids get excoriated. I was raised by my grandparents. I was an only child. I was already alone and lonely. And—" A distant look came over him. "I remember after it happened, my grandmother telling people 'He's grown so shy. So . . . *serious.*' Other kids seemed so ridiculous and pathetic and spoiled to me after that. I was no longer a boy, but something else. Not a man. I've never become a man. I was a nameless creature. I lost the few friends I had and I made no new friends. And I *tried* to forget. I willed myself day and night to forget. To be spared a moment without memory."

He took a deep breath.

"Still, when you realized what had happened—" Test began.

"I was going to tell. Once," he said. "I was prepared. When I was fifteen. I had mustered the courage for months. It was the summer that news flooded the region of a teacher in Bakersfield who had had been arrested for 'doing stuff' to junior-high girls. The town buzzed with the words *molestation, pervert, sicko.* For weeks, my grandparents spoke of nothing else. They said things like 'They should cut his balls off. A man like that should never go free. Touching young girls like that. Hang the son of a bitch.' And I realized what had happened to me. I'd been prey. And that felt like the bigger betrayal. That hurt most. Because Coach had told me I was a miracle. And I'd believed it. I'd felt like I was. And I was so stung. I was prepared to tell. Until." He reached across the table and took Test's glass of water and drank from it. "Until I overheard my grandparents and their friend talking. They were entertaining friends in the kitchen below the vent in my room, playing bridge. And I heard my grandmother say, 'You wonder how a man could get away with it so long. I mean for a year, *three* girls, and not *one* of them speaks up? Something's not right with that picture.' Another woman said it made her wonder. And that she'd seen at least one of the girls in town with no bra. Short shorts. She couldn't believe how girls acted those days. How they dressed. So brazen. And it wasn't like he had a gun to their heads or anything. Some of these girls today can seem so innocent but go around asking for it. They like it. They're just plain wicked.'"

Jon peeled at a loose thumb cuticle. "Wicked," he said. "Junior-high girls." He laughed. "Wicked. Like me."

Test missed her husband and her kids so acutely at the moment she had to fight back a sob of emotion. "So. You told Randy you wouldn't stop working the case?"

"I've created an identity. Made a life out of prosecuting scum on behalf of boys like me, but also championing for those who are bullied and oppressed and threatened otherwise." His face was crimson with anger. "No one, especially not Randy, was going to make demands on me and bring this to light and sully me."

"So, you just left it at that?"

"I called his bluff. I didn't believe he'd trot all that garbage out after all these years and subject himself to the ridicule and suspicion. Especially when it was clear I would deny it if he came forward. So, I told him no, I wouldn't quit the case and if he brought it up I'd deny it. He was on his own. And I walked away."

For a third time, Merryfield walked away, Test thought. What had that triggered in Randy Clark? What anger?

"And what did he do?" she asked.

"What do you mean?"

"You left. Did he yell after you? Go after you? Just stand there and let you go?"

"He didn't yell or go after me. I don't know what he did. Or how long he stood there."

"It was your wife's idea to go out to dinner that night."

Test's comment seemed to give Jon a start.

"So?" he said, collecting himself.

"How did you know she would suggest it? That you'd end up going to the restaurant for you to even slip out from there to see Randall? Especially since you'd been sick, if not for the reasons everyone had thought."

"Bethany and I always go to the Village Fare on Wednesday night. I knew she'd ask, even if I was under the weather. She's pushy like that. And if she hadn't asked. I would have gone out for a walk to get some air, or something. Then just walked through the woods."

"And Randall put up the reflector tacks?"

"Yes."

"Why did you do what he asked at all? Why walk through the woods and go through a ritual like that if no one was going to make you do anything you didn't want to do?"

"I had to meet him in person. Assess him in person. And, frankly, slipping out of the restaurant was a good plan, or at least meeting him at night. I didn't want to be seen."

It made sense, to a point, if his sense of shame and life of secrecy were at stake, and if it were all to come out just as he was spearheading the case.

"Was it him you saw, leaving your house?"

Jon looked startled. He was thinking over something he should not need to think about. Either he'd seen Randy Clark or he hadn't. Unless it had not occurred to him before that the person he'd seen might have been Clark.

Merryfield swallowed, agitated. "No. It wasn't. I mean. I couldn't testify to it."

"You couldn't testify to it?"

"It wasn't him. He's troubled. Wounded. And weak. But. Brad. He's your doer, Detective. Whatever sick act played out between Randy Clark and me and Victor, and as much as either one of us, Randy or I, might have had reason to want to hurt Victor, I really don't think he killed her."

"He could have killed Jessica and let Brad take the fall, hurting Victor where it hurt most." *Except*, Test thought, *how would Randy Clark know about Brad and Jessica when no one else did?* Still, she pressed. "Randall Clark had all the motive."

"Sure," Merryfield said. "So did I."

Chapter 76

RANDY CLARK LOOKED dispossessed when Test finally entered the interview room next door. She could hardly see straight after finishing with Merryfield. She'd sucked down a mug of terrible coffee. North called and said, "You handle Merryfield's assault as you see fit. I've got enough shit on my plate with Brad. And the murder of his father."

North was distancing himself.

"Has Brad confessed?" she asked North.

"Not yet," North had said and hung up.

Test made a quick call to Claude, so relieved to hear his calm voice and to know he would wait up for her, however late she came in. "I'll while away my time binge-watching *Breaking Bad* DVDs," he'd quipped. She hung up, never so grateful for her husband and family.

In the room now with Randy Clark, who fidgeted at the edge of his seat, hands cuffed in his lap, Test could smell the stink of fear as well as filth rising off of the man.

"What am I being charged with?" he said as his gaze wandered about the room without focus.

"What do you think?" Test said.

He shrugged, his lips were raw and sore. His nose runny and red. "Assault, I guess."

Test was not going to tell him that Merryfield refused to press charges. Not yet. She wanted him to think he might be held or charged with the murder. She did not want him to know what Merryfield had confessed. Randy could have killed Jessica, she thought. So could have Merryfield. As he'd said, he had motive. And means and opportunity. Perhaps they had done it together and were each playing her, covering. She thought of the sequence of events, of suspects: Victor, Brad, Merryfield, and now Randy Clark. Had she simply needed to work her way through the first three as possible suspects, connect the dots, discover the most plausible motive, to arrive at the correct endpoint? Had she kept an open mind and tracked clues to the final, correct resolution, let the facts form the theory, or had she done just the opposite?

She could not charge Randy Clark for murder.

"So, are you going to charge me?" a voice said.

Test broke from her thoughts and looked at Randy Clark, whose face was one of resignation. "Charge me," he said. "At least I won't have to keep overpaying to stay in a fleabag motel."

"Did you kill Jessica Cumber?" Test asked. She wanted to catch him off guard.

He blinked. "What?"

"Did you kill Jessica Cumber?"

"I— No. Why?"

Why? What kind of a response was that? Why? *Because if you did, you're in big trouble.* Clark stared at her flatly, perhaps bored. Or maybe he was just as fatigued as she was. She imagined he was probably even more so.

"Because evidence points to you," Test said.

"I doubt that."

"But you don't know it for certain."

"I doubt you'd have that kid in jail if you thought I or anyone else did it."

"Sometimes new things come to light."

"It wasn't me. Sorry." He rolled his eyes.

"You had motive."

"I know."

"You know?"

"Of course I fucking know. But he isn't worth it."

"Who? Victor?" Test said.

Randy Clark stared at her.

"I know what happened. In the truck," Test said.

A light came into Clark's eyes and a sense of relief seemed to overcome him. "So. He told you?"

Test nodded.

"Did you believe him?" he said.

"I've no doubt both of you were abused by him."

The flesh nearly slid off Clark's face.

"What?" His mouth hung slack with astonishment as his eyes went bright.

He didn't know. Test realized with a shock. He never knew Merryfield was a victim too. He just knew Merryfield had witnessed his own abuse and walked away from it. He didn't know their vile bond.

"Oh," Clark said. "Oh."

"You didn't know."

"I thought. I thought he wouldn't help me because he didn't want to get involved or . . . be seen as a coward or— I see now. I see."

It was clear that a great deal was dawning on Randy Clark that he had to process.

Merryfield had not reported his witnessing of the abuse because he was afraid his own abuse would be revealed. But Clark never knew it.

"And what is it you wanted from him, the night of the murder?" Test said.

"To drop the case."

"Why?"

"Those people make me sick. Here was someone who saw me, saw me being . . . hurt. And he did nothing. And then I saw him, years later, so far from home in Virginia and it just seemed a sign. Fate. And he ignored me. I knew he recognized me when I mentioned Coach. He couldn't get out of there fast enough. And when I was in New Hampshire and started seeing the news about Jon representing that couple, I couldn't stomach it. I had to try to make him see how hurtful it was. How wrong not to have helped me. To have left me alone as a boy. And now to be helping *those two*."

"And what were you going to do if he didn't do as you said and drop the case?"

He thought about this for a long time. "I threatened to tell all of it, if he didn't come forward with me. What other leverage did I have? But in the end, I couldn't force him. All I wanted was for him to come forward. To help me. To be my witness. I knew if I came forward alone I'd be a laughingstock. Dismissed. But if someone distinguished, like him, spoke for me. I didn't know he'd suffered too. How could I?"

"Why did you attack him tonight?"

"I lost it. All I wanted was for him to *help* me, for others to know, cops to know, that someone else had seen what happened. People would believe Jon. Then, it wouldn't be just my word against Coach's. Instead, Jon tried to *pay me* to go away. I got so mad. I didn't know why he didn't want to help. Still, he should have done it. That's what takes guts. Courage. Coming forward. Not burying the past and forgetting."

"You got chummy with Victor Jenkins. Used a fake name. How could you be close to that man? Why would you do that?"

"When I came here from New Hampshire a few months back, what sickened me most was that Coach did not recognize me. Not that he would. I was eight at the time. I'd come to town to get Jon to change his mind. I didn't even know Victor was still here before I came. I'd never have imagined he'd stick around after what he did. My family, lucky for him, moved away shortly after. They thought my strange behavior afterward was from being up-rooted. They blamed all my poor behavior, outbursts, petty crime and belligerence after that on their moving to try to better my dad's career as a history professor at UVA."

"Why get close to Victor at all?" Test said. "Why run with King and them? You see how it looks, you getting so close to him."

"When I saw he was still in town, I wanted to get close to him to see if he was still at it. I've always had guilt about all the other boys that might have been hurt after me, because I never spoke up. If I even sniffed he was up to that still, I'd investigate it on my own. Report him."

"And do you think Victor was molesting other boys?"

"I don't have proof. And. I think I'd sense it. Smell it. I hope I'm right. But no." A look came into his eyes. "Why do you keep using the past tense for Victor?"

Of course, being cooped up in here, he did not know Victor was dead.

Test told him. She gave him the newspaper article to read.

Afterward, she said: "Jon Merryfield refuses to press charges against you."

Clark looked dumbstruck, then crestfallen.

In the end, there was no hard evidence, no physical evidence to hold Randy Clark in regard to Jessica's murder. No physical link. Except for a few minutes after they'd met in the parking lot, he had Jon for an alibi, and Jon had him.

Test had to let him walk.

Chapter 77

Test was about to leave her office after writing up her reports when her phone rang at 6:37 P.M.

It was Detective North.

"Sit down," he said.

Test stayed standing.

"We found a notepad in Jenkins's pocket," he said. "He'd written some crazy stuff."

"What?" Test sat.

"I'm e-mailing the transcript to you now. Read it. I'll wait."

When the e-mail arrived, Test read it:

What To Tell the Cops

J. Merryfield had a motive, in his sick mind, because of our relationship.

Things they NEED to know:

It just happened and it didn't go on long. A few weeks.

A few minutes each time.

They have to know I never forced him.

I adored him.

The sad little angel raised by grandparents. They must know how his sadness saddened me. And he used that against me. My compassion. How much I felt for him.

Until he changed. And I saw him for what he was.

MAKE IT CLEAR: I ended it. After the last time I knew I was being tested by the devil. I threw up. I called in sick and I lay on my floor for days. I prayed without rest. Asked God for redemption. To give me the strength to resist this devil.

And God spoke. God forgave.

And if God could forgive me, I could forgive me.

But no on else would forgive. The boy would twist it.

When I went back to work, he lingered after the other boys left.

He said, I missed you.

I told him to forget me.

HE threw my words in my face: But, you said I was a miracle.

He tortured me, cried that I hurt him, with a demonic look that said, I'll hurt you. I'll turn this all around and make what we had ugly. I saw then how despicable he really was. Evil.

I need to make them understand, I tried to break it off and he wouldn't let me.

Let them know, I've attended church daily for years, lived a chaste, clean life, never mind my few lapses. They'll see what a monster he was. And is.

If he denies it ever happened I'll prove it. How else would I know of his elegant birthmark at the inside of his thigh?

Then they'll know he killed that girl to ruin my son, to

take from me the one thing I care about most, because he never got over me breaking it off with him. He wants to make me suffer.

Just like he did when he was a boy.

He thought I wouldn't tell what we shared out of shame, but I learned the statute of limitations has run out. I can't be charged by the holier than thou who do not understand how hard it is to resist temptation by the devil.

"Well?" North said.

"As you can imagine, I got a different version from Merryfield."

"Is there anything to this motive? I mean skip the delusion and sickness of Victor. If he did this to Jon, what's that leave us with regarding Merryfield?"

"Motive. But Merryfield didn't deny that it gave him motive. Neither did Randy Clark."

"Clark too?"

"He's likely one of the 'lapses' mentioned. But. There's nothing to make a case against Merryfield or Clark for Jessica. There's seediness. Sadness. Madness. But. From what I can tell, all Clark wanted from Merryfield was for Merryfield to drop the case and help him to out Jenkins. Sad thing is, he doesn't know Jenkins couldn't have been prosecuted because of the statute of limitations. Or maybe he doesn't care, just wanted to stain the man in the public eye."

"So. No hard evidence, no confession that either of these two men trumps Brad Jenkins?"

Test hated to say it. "No. Nothing."

PART V

Chapter 78

EARLY-SPRING SUNSHINE FILTERED through the windows of the Canaan courthouse, causing the wooden pews and flooring to glow.

Fran Jenkins sat in a chair directly behind her son, who sat at the defendant's table. She leaned forward and clutched the rail that separated her from him.

The jurors returned, single file, their gazes landing anywhere but on the gallery of onlookers. They settled in their chairs. Women placed their pocketbooks at their feet or in their laps. The foreman blew his nose. The bailiff appeared from the judge's quarters, hands clasped dutifully behind his back, and asked for all to rise as he announced Judge Arms's court back in session.

Judge Arms entered the courtroom and climbed the few small steps to his bench and sat. He flipped his robe sleeves as if a gospel singer about to clap his hands.

Brad hung his head. His body had grown thin and pale, as if he'd been whittled out of dry bone. Fran placed a hand on his shoulder. Public Defender James Allard whispered in Brad's ear.

Judge Arms took a drink from his bottle of tonic water and cleared his throat.

"Has the jury reached a verdict?"

"We have, Your Honor," the foreman said, his hands folded in front of him.

"Would you please read it?" Judge Arms said.

The foreman nodded. He put on a pair of wire glasses, unfolded the piece of paper.

In the front row nearest the jury, Marigold Cumber sat still as a headstone, her eyes on the foreman, hands folded politely in her lap.

"We the jury. Find Brad Victor Jenkins guilty of murder in the first degree."

"No," Brad said quietly, as if to keep it between himself and God. "I'm not."

Marigold Cumber wept.

Chapter 79

TEST AND CLAUDE lay in bed, each eating from their own pint of ice cream: vanilla for Test, Chubby Hubby for Claude.

Test sighed.

"You need to let things go," Claude said.

"I just wonder," Test said.

"Don't." Claude dug his spoon into his ice cream, pried loose a chunk of chocolate. It popped out onto the bedspread. He plucked it up and slipped it in his mouth. Licked his fingers.

"No wonder our kids have such refined manners," Test said and slipped a spoon of vanilla ice cream into her mouth. She sighed again. "It's just . . ."

"Just what?" Claude said. He offered her a bite of his ice cream. She refused it.

"Brad. He never once broke. Never once has he admitted guilt. It's not normal for a kid his age not to break. He's not some hardened criminal. Usually the guilt of something like that destroys a person and forces them to confess. He was convicted on circumstantial evidence."

Claude scooped out a piece of chocolate and tipped the spoon to her lips.

She waved him off. "And Brad's mother, she seemed so certain he didn't do it."

"That kid threw his life away," Claude said. "That's his fault. People throw their lives away every day. No one can stop them. He got what he deserved. We all do. Plus, she's his mother. She has to believe in him, even when no one else does, against all evidence. The mind can convince itself of anything."

"But the heart," Test said. "A mother knows her child's heart. Doesn't she? Don't I know my children's hearts?"

"Maybe. All the things I kept from my parents. My mother would roll over in her grave." Claude wedged a scoop of ice cream free. Offered it to her. "Almost gone."

She waved him off. He ate it, slipped the spoon around the edge of the bottom of the pint, getting every last bit of ice cream.

"Last bite," he said.

"You eat it."

"It's yours. Open wide."

Test surrendered. She licked the ice cream off the spoon, smiling. "Mmmm. That is good."

"Told you," Claude said. He pulled her close so she rested her head on his shoulder. He rested his hand on her belly. "I'm sorry nothing's taken," he said.

She nodded, though her mind was still on the verdict.

"Would you like to try?" Claude said, his voice tender.

"No," Test said, "I just want to lie here with you."

From her bedroom down the hall, Elizabeth cried out in her sleep. "Mama. Mama!"

Then she quieted.

In the new silence, Test felt the tears come; tears that had nothing to do with the ugliness and meanness in the world, and everything to do with the kindness and hope she had the good fortune to have in her life.

Chapter 80

FORGET.

Separate.

Survive.

He lay awake. The room dark. His breath thin.

His fingers clenched tight, as though holding the handle of a hammer.

He'd lain in bed for hours. Days. Months. Tormented.

The night ate at you. Its darkness brought ill thoughts that rattled in your head like old chains so you could not hear the clear thoughts of daylight when you felt almost rational, almost sane. Almost normal.

In the daylight he tried to busy himself, and thoughts of the girl slid far into the back of his mind as unnoticeably as pocket change slipping between the cushions of a couch.

Forget.

Separate.

Survive.

But at night.

Thinking. Thinking thinking thinking. Imprisoned by thoughts.

It had started with the first time he'd seen the boy's arrogant mug splashed across the front regional sports page. Week after week. After week. He'd seen it. The smiling golden boy with the perfect life. Not a care in the world. Even without his name splashed all over, there was no doubt whose son he was. Quotes from his smug father polluted the articles with boasts and "thank the Lords" for their good blessings. It was unbearable. Something had to be done. The father needed to pay, endure his own living hell.

So he'd come across the river, to get close to the father, who tricked the world so he could live a sick, blessed life, prideful, gloating about his son, to anyone who would listen.

He'd gotten close to the father as his plan began to take root in his mind.

He began to follow the son, who was the way to destroy the father.

That's when he'd seen the two of them together.

The son and the girl. A girl clearly too young for the son.

Another victim of this sick family.

The glorious articles about the boy that never made mention of statutory rape.

He followed the son and the girl. Studied them. Learned their private routine, their secret places and times to meet. Inside and out.

He watched as the boy made out with her in the woods behind the school. Fucked her.

Not a care in the world.

He'd thought of killing the son, taking him from Victor.

But no. At the library, where he'd tracked the girl on many evenings, he'd studied the size and shape of her head from a few computers over; put to memory where her blood pulsed at the temple; at the very front edge where her hair went downy.

He'd studied how beef cattle were slaughtered by the single blow of a skilled slaughterer's sledge. Clean kills were not about force. They were about placement. *Thwack.* The sweet spot. The cattle may kick and drool when they went down.

But they did not get back up.

He'd practiced the blow on pumpkins he'd picked because they were the size of her head, stuck them on a stick about her height of five feet. With a magic marker he'd drawn a circle the size of her temple. He'd kept the hammer at his side, as if a gunslinger. Then yanked it up, snapped it back and cracked it down. Hard. In the temple. *Thwack.* With practice, the marks on the pumpkins caved as the hammer drove into the pulp. He'd not wanted to hit her twice. He'd known he did not have it in him. He'd not wanted her to suffer. He was not cruel. He had not wanted to cause her pain. He'd wanted it over as quickly as possible. In an instant. Humane. Merciful. He had not wanted to scare her. Or to torture her. He had not wanted her to *know*.

But she had known.

The flashlight had blinded her. But she'd moved just enough to see the hammer. See his face. She'd looked into his eyes. She'd known. For an instant he'd almost not done it. Then. Quick. Clean. A trapper finishing off the trapped. *Thwack.*

If there had been any other way.

But there hadn't been.

She'd been the only way.

A sacrifice.

So he'd told himself then.

So he told himself now.

Except now it was not so easy to think of her as that: a sacrifice. Not at night.

She'd been a girl. An innocent. Used, by him. For his own means. Not any different from the way the father had used him. That is what stung most.

In that instant of striking her, he'd felt an unexpected, retching pull from deep inside him. He had thought his soul had been torn from him long ago in a truck parked behind the school; but as the hammer met her skull and she'd stood for an instant looking at him in disbelief, trying to speak but only garble and blood spewing from her mouth, he'd felt as though a grappling hook had been affixed behind his heart, and an invisible rope that led from it, through the center of him, had been given a savage yank and the hook had ripped through him, ripped him open, splayed apart his ribs and pulled everything out of him. Everything.

He'd felt as though God himself had been ripped out of him. And he knew in that instant that he'd had his soul all along. That it had not been taken from him by the father. It may have been buried beneath his pain and isolation, but it had been there if he'd been willing to excavate. And he'd known, as she'd crumpled to the floor, that a soul could never be stolen by acts committed against you, but only lost in acts you committed against others. All along he'd thought vengeance would free him. Would bring him the happiness he had never known.

Instead, vengeance had enslaved him. It could never bring peace or freedom. Only ruin.

Forgiveness of a wrong exacted against you was the only act that brought freedom from those who'd harmed you.

He lay in bed now, feeling as though he were buried deep in the ground, so much weight on his body, his flesh encased in darkness. She'd seen him. And he'd thought he could bear it, and believed he could have if the father were alive to suffer the indignity and humiliation of his star son imprisoned for murder. But the father was dead. He'd been spared. It had been a sacrifice made in vain.

Forget.

Separate.

Survive.

He needed to split himself from his pain.

Forget.

Separate.

Survive.

He was safe from ever being caught. After speaking to the policewoman, an agreement had been struck with the father's other victim: For one man to forget who he might have seen leaving the creamery that night, in exchange for another man never mentioning what had happened to either of them as boys. A willingness between two men to accept a sacrifice now that the other man knew, after they'd fought in the school lot that night, that he'd killed the girl.

The father's bragging had revealed his son was home alone with his beloved playbook, he'd acted spontaneously, knowing the babysitter was alone too, feeling as if the window of time he was given was a gift granted by God.

Forget.

Separate.

Survive.

But he could not forget. Could not separate. He was no longer strong enough. Had never been strong enough.

"Help me," he murmured in the darkness, not knowing to whom he spoke, only knowing that it was not to God.

God was beyond his reach.

"Help me."

He opened his eyes to the dark room.

There was no one there.

He was alone.

As he'd been since that night in the truck.

He thought of the father, who'd died a hero, escaping the torment meant for him.

What kind of God spared such a man?

He could bear the pain he'd made for himself no longer.

He picked up the phone and dialed.

A woman answered. She sounded as if she'd been crying.

"Hello?" she said.

"Detective Test. This is Randall Clark. Do you have a moment?"

Acknowledgments

While I am sure to forget someone and be rightfully taken to task for it, I will try this time to thank all who've encouraged and supported my writing. My lovely wife Meridith, of course. My daughter Samantha, especially for her smiles and hugs. My mother. My sisters: Beth, Judy, and Susan. Jake Tobi. Bryanna Allen-Rickstad. Gary Martineau. Dave Stanilonis. Libby and Herb Levinson. Ben Wilson. Todd and Diane Levinson. Bill and Mary Wilson. Dan Myers, Dan Orseck, Tom Isham, Roger and Susan Bora, Mark Saunders, Lailee Mendelson, Alan DeNiro. Rob O'Donovan. Jeff Racine. Mike and Janice Quartararo. Stephen and Carol Phillips. Eric Weissleder. Chris Champine. Dave and Heidi Bouchard. Jamie Granger. Jim Lepage. Phil Monahan. David Huddle and Tony Magistrale. Jamie and Stephen Foreman. Paul Doiron. Steve Ulfelder. Roger Smith. Hank Phillippi Ryan. Jake Hinkson. Drew Yanno. Tyler McMahon. Howard Mosher. Rona and Bob Long. And, of course, Philip Spitzer and Margaux Weisman.

If you loved

LIE IN WAIT

read Eric Rickstad's *New York Times* bestseller

THE SILENT GIRLS

Another thriller set in Canaan, VT.

Chapter 1

UNDER THE DIM porch light, the child's gruesome mask looked real, as if molten rubber had been poured over the poor thing's skull and melted the flesh, the features hideous and deformed.

The woman caught her breath and shrank back, the bowl of candy nearly slipping from her hand. *What kind of mother lets a young child wear such a grotesquerie,* the woman wondered. *And where are the child's parents?* Sometimes, parents who drove their kids to these better neighborhoods waited in their cars as they sipped beer from cans and prodded kids too young for Halloween to *Go on up and get your goodies. Grab Mommy a big handful.* But the woman didn't see any adults or vehicles at the shadowy curb.

She stooped to better see the child's mask.

"And what are we supposed to be?" she said.

"Dead."

The child's voice was reedy and phlegmy, genderless.

The woman searched the child's mask, unable to tell where the mask ended and the child's face began. There seemed to be no gaps around the unblinking eyes; the irises, as black as the pupils, wet and animal, swam in the oddly large eye whites.

"You're very scary," the woman said.

"You're scary," the child said in its strangled voice.

"Me?" the woman said.

The child nodded. "You're a monster."

"I am, am I?"

"Mmm. Hmmm."

The woman started to laugh, but the laugh died in the back of her throat, gagged on a sharp bone of sudden, inexplicable dread. She looked over the child's shoulder, toward the street, which was quiet and still and dark. *Where were all the children from earlier, so ecstatic with greed?*

"There's no such thing as monsters," the woman said.

"Mmm. Hmm."

"Who says?"

"My mom."

"Oh? And who's your mom?"

"You."

"I see. And who told you I was your mom?"

"My mom."

A greasy sickness bubbled in her stomach. The dread. Irrational. But mounting. Her blood electric. She reached back to grip the doorknob as blood thrummed at her temples.

A child shrieked. The woman flinched and looked up as a pair of kids in black capes floated along the sidewalk and melted back into the darkness.

Wait! Come back! the woman wanted to scream.

She looked down at the child again. It held something in its hand now: something gleaming. A knife. The blade long and slender. Wicked.

The woman held out the bowl of candy.

"Take all you want," she croaked, "and go."

The child's black eyes stared.

The woman's eyes caught the silver glint of the knife blade as the child jabbed it at her belly.

"Jesus!" she cried. "You little shi—" But she could not finish. Pain cleaved her open, turned her inside out. Her hand slipped from the doorknob, and the candy bowl clattered to the porch.

Oh God.

She clutched her belly—too terrified to look—feeling a warm stickiness seep between her fingers.

The child drove the knife blade clean through her hand, and the woman howled with pain. The child plunged the knife again, just above the waistband of the woman's jeans and yanked upward.

Oh God.

She was being . . .

. . . *unzipped.*

She staggered backward, crumpling in the foyer.

The child stepped into the house and shut the door with a soft *click*. Its face hovered above the woman's. The woman reached up, clutched the mask's rubbery skin. Pulled. The mask would not come off. She dug her fingers in. Clawed. The mask stretched. The knife sliced. She tore at the mask, gasping. The child had been right.

Monsters did exist.

Chapter 2

THE BLOOD ON Frank Rath's hands steamed in the cold October air as he slung one end of a rope over the barn's crossbeam, tied the other end to the center of the tomato stake skewered through the gutted carcass's legs, and yanked.

Pain erupted in his lower back as if he'd been struck with an axe. He dropped to his knees, the dead deer sagging back in a puddle of its own sad blood on the frozen dirt.

Rath remained still, breathing slowly through his nose, counting backward from ten. *Erector spinae.* He'd learned the Latin from studying the anatomy model while whiling away his autumn in Doc Rankin's office.

Rath's cell phone vibrated in his shirt pocket. Rachel, he hoped. For seven weeks now, she'd been away for her first semester at Johnson State, and in that time, loneliness had nested in Rath's heart. The house felt lifeless, no hum of Rachel's hair dryer in the morning, no insistent burble of incoming texts when she left her cell phone idle for even a second on the kitchen table.

Rath reached for his cell phone, but the skewering pain insisted he lower himself onto his back, where he performed an inept pelvic tilt. Doc Rankin had sent him to a whack-job physical therapist, who'd prescribed a contortionist's regimen of humiliating stretches that made Rath feel as though he were about to shit himself: stretches better suited to rich housewives who performed them in steamy rooms while listening to didgeridoo music than to a man whose idea of stretching was reaching in the top cupboard for his Lagavulin 16 and chocolate Pop Tarts. Rath gained his feet with a groan.

What worried him wasn't the pain but that the pain seemed to have no source. He'd simply awoken one morning as if someone had punched a hole in his back and ripped the *erector spinae* from his spine.

He looked down at the deer. He had to get it hung. First the deer. Then a beer. Or three.

Rath's cell phone buzzed: Harland Grout.

The lone, lead detective on the anemic Canaan police force, Grout was as green as the back of a wet frog. He was also a dart player in Rath's dart league. Most important, he had a strong young back good for lifting a dead deer.

Rath answered. "Grout. I'm trying to hang a deer here. Maybe you'd like to earn a six-pack and lend your—"

"There's a car. Out on Route fifteen," Grout said.

"That sort of specificity and twenty bucks Canadian will buy you a lap dance at The Dirty Girl over the border in Richelieu."

"Yeah," Grout said, and Rath noted a barb of severity in his voice that made him regret his initial glibness.

"What?" Rath said, and wandered out of the barn to lean against the fender of the '74 International Scout it seemed he'd been restoring since Lincoln was a Whig.

"The car appears abandoned." Grout paused to wait for the static of the weak signal to pass. Up here, near the border, there wasn't one cell tower within five thousand miles. God bless Vermont. Or not. "The car belongs to my wife's cousin's daughter."

"Shit," Rath said, not even trying to untangle that snarl of family-tree branches.

"She's sixteen."

"Shit." Rath slumped against the Scout. "You think something happened?"

Something happened. What euphemistic bullshit for the images—none pretty—that leapt into Rath's mind the instant he heard of a girl gone missing.

"It's hard telling," Grout said. "I just got the call on the car. When I called her mom, she was worried. Hasn't heard from her in days and asked me to look into it."

"Why call me? She's a minor, you can investigate it straightaway as an MP."

"She's emancipated."

"Shit," Rath said again. His repertoire of blue language needed work.

Unless foul play was clearly evident, seventy-two hours had to pass before an official investigation could begin on a missing adult. And, by Vermont law, an emancipated girl, sixteen or not, was an adult. It made no sense. Sixteen was a *child*, and any adult who looked at a girl that young and saw anything *but* a child was deluded or a pervert.

"I'm on my way there now," Grout said. "For all we know, the car's clean, and she's just off banging a boyfriend or crashed at a girlfriend's. Or something. I got Sonja Test headed there, on her own time, giving up her Saturday training to bumper-to-bumper it best she can *in situ*. That itself is against protocol without probable. But Chief Barrons is out three more days fishing the Bahamas, and—"

"That bastard," Rath said. Barrons had been Rath's senior the three years Rath was a state-police detective in the 1990s. Barrons was an exceptional cop and an even better fisherman. Rath wasn't sure for which trait he resented and envied Barrons more.

"So," Grout said, "I'm taking liberties as it is without leaving my entire nutsack hanging out for Barrons to lop off and brine when he gets back. This girl is, technically, family; if it looks like I'm playing favorites or expending resources without due cause, and the girl just strolls in, my ass is in a sling, right when it's looking like the budget might open up, and there's a shot at a promotion. At the same time—"

"Fuck protocol," Rath said. The hard consonants felt good to bite off and spit out. *But, what promotion?* If Grout wanted to excel in law enforcement, he should have taken Rath's advice several years back and gone to the staties. And he shouldn't have been calling Rath for help. Grout needed to take the helm himself, damn the repercussions: Protocol never outweighed doing what was right. Rath knew that if he wanted to help Grout and his career, he should force Grout to see this through on his own and be either tempered or turned to ash by the heat he'd feel from Barrons.

But there was a missing girl. That came before any career.

"I could use your help," Grout said. "Even if it becomes official, it's still just an MP, a low priority unless it becomes something else."

Something else.

The sun glared on the skin of snow that had fallen overnight, melting fast, water dripping from the barn roof to tick on a sheet of rusted tin that had been leaning against the barn since the Pleistocene ice age.

Rath lit a cigarette and drew in the smoke. All he got from it was trembling fingertips and a numb nose. He needed to go back to dipping.

His cell-phone screen glowed with an incoming call: Stan Laroche. Rath let it go.

"Where's the car?" Rath asked Grout.

Grout told him, and Rath tossed his cigarette into a rag of snow, where it settled with a paling hiss. He ended the call and looked back at the dead deer on the barn floor.

"Not today, pal."

He yanked shut the barn door, to keep out the coyotes that skulked around the place at night; he had a draining feeling that he'd be occupied until long after dark.

In his kitchen, an ember of pain glowing in the old *erector spinae,* Rath scrubbed his hands with Lava soap, the water foaming pink with deer blood. He searched the freezer for an ice pack, remembered he'd left it in bed where it was now thawed, and dug out a pack of frozen peas. He snatched a bottle of Vicodin off the counter, slugged back two pills with a half bottle of Molson Golden left in the sink from the night before, then listened to Laroche's message: "Rath. Laroche. Call me."

Laroche. Mr. Department of Corrections; no doubt calling to weasel out of darts so his wife could strut off to some scrapbooking or karaoke night with the gals. Supposedly. Rath suspected there was a man involved. He deleted the message. Let Laroche swing.

In the Scout, Rath tucked the pack of peas behind his back, sighing at the minor temporary relief it brought. He worked the Scout's choke and fired up the old lady. With 350,670 miles on her, she had leaky gaskets and bad springs, but she kept on stubbornly plugging along. Not unlike Rath.

Chapter 3

RATH DROVE NORTH on his dirt road, past the enormous, looming, granite face of Canaan Monadnock, which gave way to flat farmland with the abruptness of the Fundy Escarpment smacking up to the Atlantic's edge; a geologic anomaly in a state of worn, aged mountains that folded into gentle foothills and gradually leveled out into Lake Champlain to the west and the Connecticut River to the east.

As a boy, Rath had been fascinated by this peculiarity and spent nights tucked under his covers, his sister asleep in her bed beside his, enrapt by books on plate tectonics, volcanoes, and the Earth's molten core. In 1862, whalebones had been unearthed by a farmer's plow blade in the surrounding fields; eleven thousand years before the world's most famed carpenter supposedly rose again, the glaciers had retreated, and the Atlantic had rushed in, creating a paratropical ocean that for three thousand years reached north to the Saint Lawrence and west to Ottawa. Hence: whalebones. Those early years, Rath had been obsessed with the violence of nature and how it shaped the physical world. As he'd grown older, his fixation had shifted from the violence of nature to the nature of violence, and how to stop it.

Rath turned north onto Route 15, toward Canada, lighting a cigarette and wondering about this missing girl.

Up ahead, the mountain foliage was set ablaze with the beauty of autumn's death, a supreme loveliness that people traveled across the globe to view from Peter Pan buses.

Regional tourists, those rocketing up I-89 to flee Boston in their Beemers, cruising in Volvo Cross Countrys up I-91 North from Connecticut, and oozing south from Montreal in Jag XJs were lulled by the pastoral idyll, the dairy farms dotted with black-and-white Holsteins; sugar shacks tucked tidily among the sugarbush; general stores painted "barn red" to approximate the original nineteenth-century pigment created from rust.

As soon as the sightseers crossed into the land where billboards were banned for their affront to nature's aesthetics, they settled into their heated leather seats, bathed in a Rockwellian serenity and liberated from the gray grind of urban life. They'd power down their windows to breathe in the crisp mountain air, buoyed and intoxicated by the setting and by a pang of nostalgia for a past they'd never lived but could taste on their tongues nonetheless. Here, the air was sweeter. Here, they were alive. Safe.

Safe. Rath snorted as he adjusted his back against the pack of thawing peas. Nowhere was safe. No one. Violence lurked here as it did the world over, most often exacted by known parties. Intimate, familial, and unspeakable.

He'd always wondered why people in rural areas, when interviewed after appalling violence, said, "This isn't supposed to happen here." As if violence had forgotten to keep itself within some prescribed geographic boundary.

Rath drove along a piece of road that annually made the *New York Times's Top 10 Fall Foliage Drives,* but was known to locals as Murder Road: the stretch where Gabe Hoyt shot his cousin. The two men had been arguing over a woman in Hoyt's truck when Hoyt crashed his rig. As his cousin staggered away, Hoyt shot him in the head with a .45 he kept in his glove box. Panicking, Hoyt ran over his cousin's skull with his truck, believing it would hide the evidence. Good theory, for a pickled redneck. The blood still stained the road here, a dark smear like that left by a deer mauled by a logging truck.

Rath flicked cigarette ash in the Scout's ashtray.

There was last year's home invasion of two married Vermont Law School professors who had been tied up, tortured with a blowtorch, and bludgeoned with the fire poker they'd last used to stoke a Christmas fire. The fifteen-year-old killers recorded the crime on their cell phones. Neither boy had even a whiff of a violent past. They'd simply skipped school on a whim and along the way gotten it in their heads it would be "freaky" to kill someone. So. Knock knock.

How did one explain such acts? What word did you put to them other than evil?

Rath drew in smoke from his cigarette. The tobacco crackled.

Then, of course, there were the Pritchards, slaughtered on Monday, May 3, 1995, a notorious crime, because of the baby.

At 4:30 P.M., Laura Pritchard had returned home from the farmer's market, put the baby to sleep upstairs, and was preparing a birthday dinner for her younger brother, when the doorbell rang. Her brother was supposed to have met her at the farmer's market. But he'd not shown, as usual. With a woman, as usual.

No regard for anyone but himself. So she'd gone to the door, likely expecting it was him.

But it wasn't him. It was the man who had once mown Laura's lawn. A Mr. Fix It who drove a jalopy truck with power tools clanking around in the bed and a sign on the door that boasted FREE ESTIMATES. Ned Preacher. Though that wasn't the name he used then.

Laura must have been surprised to see him. Not just because he wasn't her brother but because, sixteen months earlier, Ned had skipped town, leaving a check due him for $150. Perhaps she'd thought Preacher had finally come to collect.

Rath had been first on the scene, and in the years since then, he'd imagined every possible scenario that might have transpired in that doorway. He'd found the front door open and a lake of blood soaking the carpet, clots and strings of it slopped on the walls like some macabre Pollack painting.

Laura's body had lain at the bottom of the stairs in an undignified pose: her legs pinned abnormally beneath her torso, her lacerated face turned to the side as if in shame. The plush, wall-to-wall carpet, once as white as a fresh snowdrift, now so drenched with her blood it squished underfoot. Her neck had been broken, and she'd been rudely violated with objects other than the male anatomy though that would prove to have been used, too.

Rath shuddered now, his flesh cold and rubbery.

The broken neck had killed Laura, but she'd have bled out in seconds from where the knife had nicked her superior *vena cava*, preventing the flow of deoxygenated blood from her brain to her right atrium.

Daniel Pritchard's body had been draped over his wife's chest as if trying to protect her even in death, a tableau out of some twisted *Romeo and Juliet*, these players done in by another's dark impulses.

Daniel had been stabbed as he'd walked in, Preacher hiding behind the door, the knife plunged between Daniel's third and fourth ribs, slicing the liver's caudate lobe and hepatic artery. He'd suffered four defense wounds in the palms of his right hand, his right thumb dangling by a flap of skin, and two more wounds in the back of the neck, both puncturing his posterior external jugular vein beneath the splenius and trapezius muscles: death by catastrophic blood loss.

Even now, the images cast a shadow over Rath's soul and left a bitter metallic taste on his tongue. Even now, he tried to beg off the misery squeezing his heart in its ugly, unforgiving grip.

Standing there with the two bodies at his feet, it had suddenly struck Rath: the vacuum of ominous horrific soundlessness. Then. Faintly. A nearly inaudible whine, like the sound of a wet finger traced on the rim of a crystal glass, piercing his brain.

The baby.

He'd scrambled over the bodies, slipping in the blood, mindless of physical evidence, as he sprang up the stairs to thunder down the hallway and smashed open the door across from the master bedroom.

He'd rushed to the crib.

There she'd lain, tiny legs and arms pumping spasmodically, as if she'd been set afire, her mouth agape but just that shrill escape of air rising from the back of her throat, air leaking from a balloon's pinched neck.

Rath had clenched the wooden rails of the crib until they'd cracked. Downstairs lay the baby's mother, raped and murdered by a man who'd prove no stranger to rape and murder. Laura Pritchard. Loving wife. Adoring mother. Older sister to a sole sibling whose presence would have prevented the murder if he'd been on time as promised, but, as always, had failed to be, just like their old man. Laura's only sibling, her younger brother.

Frank Rath.

Rath shivered, that day as alive and crawling inside him now as then. Nothing dulled the guilt or the loss. Not even his deep love for the baby girl.

Rachel.

At the moment Rath had picked Rachel up from her crib, he'd felt an abrupt shift within him, a permanent upheaval like one plate of the Earth's lithosphere slipping beneath another; his selfish past life subducting beneath a selfless future life, a deep rift created in him, altering his inner landscape. A niece transformed into a daughter by acts of violent cruelty.

For six months after the murder, Rath had kept Rachel's crib beside his bed and lain sleepless each night as he'd listened to her frayed breathing, her every sigh and whimper. He'd panicked when she'd fallen too quiet, shaken her lightly to make certain she was alive, been flooded with relief when she'd wriggled in her swaddle. He'd picked her up and cradled her to him as she'd broken into the loneliest cry he'd ever heard, her baby heart pattering as he'd promised to keep her safe. Thinking, *If we just get through this phase with its SIDS and spiking fevers and odd diseases, you'll be OK, and I won't ever have to worry like this again.*

But peril pressed in at the edges of a girl's life, and worry planted roots in Rath's heart and bloomed wild and reckless. As Rachel had grown, Rath's worry had grown, and he'd kept vigilant for the lone man who stood with his hands jammed in his trouser pockets behind the playground fence. In public, Rath had gripped Rachel's hand fiercely, his love ferocious and animal.

If anyone *ever* did anything to her.

Chapter 4

THE MISSING GIRL'S metallic brown 1989 Monte Carlo was parked at a strange angle. Its trunk was backed up to the side of a dilapidated hay barn, so close to the road that the nose of the Monte Carlo jutted out into the soft shoulder.

Rath stood at the road's edge with Grout to study the scene.

A logging truck howled past with a load of cedar logs, its horn wailing as it kicked up a wind that ruffled Rath's thatch of black hair.

Rath spit road grit from his mouth and pulled the collar of his Johnson wool coat up around his neck.

Grout blew his nose into a red bandana. "The car is registered to Mandy Wilks, the girl," he said.

Rath knew Grout hadn't wanted to ask for help. They were friends, and they threw darts together, and Grout respected Rath. Still, no young man wanted to ask for help. Especially involving career.

"Her mother reported her missing this morning, after she got a call about the car." Grout peeked at a sheet of paper in his hand. "Sixteen," he said. "Last seen Thursday night at about eleven."

"Where?" Rath said.

"Where she washed dishes. The Lost Mountain Inn."

"Odd."

"What?"

"Washing dishes. Odd for a girl," Rath said. "I was a dishwasher as a kid. The girls always worked out front."

"Things change," Grout said.

"Some don't. Like missing girls."

"She could have taken off of her own free will with a friend," Grout said, but his voice carried no conviction. It was a loathsome fact about the human condition: Wherever there were girls, some would go missing, plucked like errant threads from the fabric of everyday life and cast into a lurid nightmare of someone else's making. Movies created suspense out of a "forty-eight-hour window" cops had to find a girl alive, as if kidnapped girls had a "kill-by" date. The colder reality remained: A girl gone missing against her will, nine times out of ten, was dead within three hours. Usually after being raped.

"Nobody's touched anything?" Rath said.

"Not me," Grout said.

Rath rubbed his jaw, his fingers still stained pink with deer blood. "Why's it parked like that?" he muttered.

The snow had melted. Rath surveyed the ground and stepped toward the car with the mindful, deliberate motion of a soldier navigating a minefield.

"No sign of another car," Grout said. "No tire tracks. Snow is gone, but the cold snap froze the ground pretty solid last few nights."

"The other car stayed on the road," Rath said.

"If there was another car."

"There was." Rath gazed at the long, deserted stretch of road that ran north into Canada in just under a mile, then looked south to a length of road equally long and deserted. "Unless we think Mandy got out and walked because she was struck with an urge to stroll a country road in the middle of the night with a windchill of ten degrees. Not much chance of getting a boot print."

He inched closer to the car, analyzing the ground. The search was like being hungry but not knowing what you wanted to eat. You had to open the fridge and peer inside until something made your mouth water: a piece of chocolate cake, a stick of pepperoni. When you saw it, you knew it was just the thing you'd been looking for, but you had to look to *know*. His mother used to tell him when he stood with the refrigerator door open: *If you can't decide what you want, you must not be hungry. Shut the door.* But she'd only been concerned with the electric bill.

"What are you looking for?" Grout said.

"Chocolate cake. A stick of pepperoni."

Grout shook his head.

Rath craned his neck to peer inside the car as a late nineties white Peugeot, scabbed with rust at the rear fenders, rumbled up roadside, its hazards flashing.

Out stepped Canaan Police Department's forensics team-of-one and lone part-time junior detective, Sonja Test. Dartmouth graduate, *summa cum laude,* crazed marathon runner with the lean, taut physique to match; wife of Claude Test, wildlife oil-paint artist of limited regional renown; mother of Elizabeth and George, ages six and three.

"Gentlemen," Sonja said as she hefted her kit from the Peugeot's front seat and nodded.

She caught her short red hair in her hand, pulled it back taut to wrap a rubber band around it and make a stunted ponytail. She tugged a white shower cap over it, then peeled surgical gloves on over her long, slender fingers.

As she set to work on the Monte Carlo, Rath turned to Grout. "What else is in that folder of yours?"

The two men sat in Rath's Scout, the folder open between them on the bench seat.

"Sixteen," Rath said. A year younger than Rachel. His stomach felt as if he'd swallowed crystal Drano.

"Hard age," Grout said.

"What age isn't? Emancipated. Nice family you got."

"Extended."

"And you personally spoke to the mother?" Rath said.

"Briefly. This morning, after the car was found, and she got worried."

"Who discovered the car?"

"Lee Storrow. He was spreading salt with the town rig before dawn. Called the dispatcher, pissed off that a car was *parked in the fucking road.*"

Rath pushed the lighter into the dash. If for no other reason, he'd kept the Scout because it had a lighter and a solid metal ashtray.

"So," Grout said, "we can discount any connection between the person who discovered the car and the disappearance of the girl driving it."

"If it was her driving it," Rath said.

"Naturally," Grout said, though Rath could see that possibility had not occurred to Grout.

Rath lit his cigarette, drew the smoke deep. It tasted like dryer lint, but he'd suck it to the filter anyway. That's why they called it addiction. At least his lips weren't suctioned to a bottle of Beam. Lung cancer instead of cirrhosis. Here's to you.

"What's so funny?" Grout said, catching the shine in Rath's eyes.

"Me. I'm an idiot."

"And that's funny to you?"

"I rest my case."

"Can you roll down your window? Your cigarette smoke—"

"My window hasn't rolled down since Letterman wore sneakers," Rath said.

Grout rolled down his window and coughed.

"Now that the drama's out of the way," Rath said. He swept cigarette ash from the report. "I wonder—"

A rap came at Rath's window, startling him. He dropped his cigarette in his lap, snatched it and stuck it back in his mouth.

Sonja stood at his window, a grin pasted to her face. It was a pretty face.

Rath opened the truck door.

"I'm done with cursory," Sonja said.

"You shouldn't sneak up on people," Rath said.

"*I* saw her from ten feet away," Grout said.

Rath made to get out of the Scout, and the nerves in his back exploded. He clutched the door, sweat flooding his brow.

"Bad back?" Sonja said, squinting at him.

"You could say that."

"Heat's good for it."

"My doc says ice."

"He's the doctor, I guess."

Rath flicked his cigarette to the road and stood erect with a wince.

"What's the short version?" Grout asked Sonja.

"Tons of prints. It's like an iPad screen in there. Some hair. Long, red. Probably hers. No blood, to the naked eye. I'll know better once I put the Luminol to it."

"You won't find anything," Rath said. "The car's clean."

"That'll have to wait till Barrons is back anyway," Grout said.

"It shouldn't. We should move on this," Sonja said. "No sign of a struggle either. Which means if she was taken, it was someone she knew and trusted, or—"

"—someone who tricked her," Grout finished.

"Right," Sonja said, not one to be interrupted apparently, even by her pseudosuperior. "Nothing in the trunk but a tire iron, a spare, jumper cables."

She led them to the Monte Carlo, her pert runner's backside pushing snugly against her faded jeans. Rath looked off toward plowed-under cornfields.

Sonja pointed at the ignition. The keys were in it. "There's cash on the floor," she said. "Three fives and twenty-eight ones."

"Forty-three dollars," Grout said.

"Math whiz here," Sonja said.

"Her share of tips," Rath said.

"This isn't going to end the way the mother hopes, is it?" Grout said.